The Secrets of
Paradise Bay

The Secrets of
Paradise Bay

Devon Vaughn Archer

www.urbanbooks.net

Urban Books, LLC
97 N. 18TH Street
Wyandanch, NY 11798

ISBN 13: 978-1-60162-701-8
ISBN 10: 1-60162-701-7

First Mass Market Printing November 2014
First Trade Paperback Printing July 2010
Printed in the United States of America

10 9 8 7 6 5 4 3 2 1

Distributed by Kensington Publishing Corp.
Submit Wholesale Orders to:
Kensington Publishing Corp.
C/O Penguin Group (USA) Inc.
Attention: Order Processing
405 Murray Hill Parkway
East Rutherford, NJ 07073-2316
Phone: 1-800-526-0275
Fax: 1-800-227-9604

The Secrets of Paradise Bay

by

Devon Vaughn Archer

Prologue

Willie Munroe sat at a booth in the coffee shop eating scrambled eggs and ham. Neither was especially tasty, and the coffee wasn't much better. But after being unemployed for more than a year now and doing what he needed to do to survive, he couldn't complain much, as it was something to fill his stomach. No one would listen, even if he did voice a complaint or two. They would only bitch about their own problems.

Fact was, few employers were interested in hiring someone who could only see out of one eye, and not so good at that. Willie had been half blinded nearly a decade ago, during a fight in which his life had been spared, albeit barely. Few people could tell that his right eye was there only for effect. It might as well have been a patch or piece of glass for its use to him.

It left Willie bitter to this day that a man had taken the best part of his life away, leaving him a shell of what he once was. Been down on his rotten luck ever since.

There had been a few dead-end jobs, but nothing that did much to pay the bills, let alone allow him to indulge comfortably in other interests. He'd even gotten a woman to marry him a few years back. But because they were so high on meth, neither knew what the hell they were doing 'til it was too late. She'd had his baby before moving across the country, taking the kid with her. Willie could have tracked them down, but felt he was better off without that burden.

Now he simply lived from day to day, sometimes hour to hour, getting high and looking for a reason to get up. He hadn't found it yet, but would keep looking.

Willie stared up at the TV monitor over the counter when a familiar name caught his ear. He listened to a newscaster while gazing at the insert of a man Willie knew of all too well.

"Businessman and civic leader Trey Lancaster has pledged to donate five hundred thousand dollars to hurricane victims. Closer to home, the multimillionaire owner of numerous luxury-car dealerships and movie theaters continues to acquire assets for his empire, while generously giving to those less fortunate. . . ."

Willie frowned, turning away from the screen, feeling sick to his stomach. After a moment, he managed to shake it off. The last thing he needed was to let the likes of Trey Lancaster ruin his meal. The bastard would get his someday. And his brother, too.

"Can I get you some more coffee, sir?"

Willie favored the tight-assed waitress with purplish-raven extensions tied in knots. His scowl faded and a sideways grin took its place.

"Yeah, why not?"

She flashed a toothy smile and he could tell that the lady was into him. *Not bad-looking*, he decided. Even were that not the case, at this point Willie wasn't too picky who he took to bed. After all, he didn't exactly have much to offer anyone he got involved with. So why should he expect that the best women around would be knocking down his door?

He trained his one working eye on the waitress and pondered just what he might get for his trouble. Maybe some free meals and money. Even a place to hang his hat from time to time. This made it worth his while to be nice to her and see where it got him.

"I don't suppose a good-looking lady like you would be up for a night out on the town? I just hate havin' fun alone." Willie offered his best smile and put his well-practiced charms to work.

Chapter One

"Are you crazy?" Ivana Kendall-Lancaster glared at her husband with bloodshot green-brown eyes. She sipped on a chocolate raspberry martini while standing in the gourmet kitchen of their three-million-dollar house.

Trey Lancaster didn't expect this to be easy, but it had to be said. Hopefully she would be reasonable when all was said and done. He wasn't counting on that.

"Not crazy," he responded calmly.

She regarded him petulantly and slurred, "Well, you're sure talking like you are."

Trey wondered if this was her third, fourth, or fifth drink. Seemed like his wife had become an alcoholic, even if neither of them would face up to it. He took the blame for this, wishing to hell he could do things over. Or better yet, not do them at all. He'd messed up by having an affair six months ago. Ivana had a miscarriage shortly after he came clean about it, and had been on a downslide ever since. She'd never forgiven him for, as she put it, "destroying my faith in you."

Trey hadn't exactly forgiven himself for the loss of their child and trust of his wife. The doctor had assured him that, medically speaking, the miscarriage could not have resulted from emotional trauma, and Ivana understood this too. But this did little to make either of them not feel that had he stayed true to the marriage or kept his mouth shut, just maybe things would have turned out differently.

Right now he wanted desperately to try to put the past behind them and rebuild their lives. Hadn't he been punished enough for his sins? He feared that they were close to reaching a point of no return.

Even with those thoughts, Trey knew that what he was proposing would likely drive a bigger wedge between them. But it was something he felt strongly about, if for no other reason than family loyalty. And maybe guilt that he hadn't always been there for his kid brother, possibly contributing to his stint behind bars.

Trey gazed at the beautiful, flawless face that reminded him of a young Tyra Banks. Like her, Ivana had been a top international model before he swept her off her feet and fell in love. She had given up the profession to become the wife of a multimillionaire owner of a string of car dealerships in the Pacific Northwest, including two in Paradise Bay, Oregon, where they lived. Since then, they had added more dealerships and a few movie theaters to their net worth, along with the usual stocks, bonds, CDs, and real estate investments.

But none of that seemed to matter at the moment. What did was the decision he'd made, and Trey saw no turning back, all things considered.

"Clyde's my brother," he spoke in a firm voice.

Ivana's small nostrils flared. "He's a *violent* criminal, Trey, and I don't want him in this house!"

"That's all behind him now," Trey insisted. "Or soon will be."

Ivana rolled her eyes. "I don't think so. People like your brother never change. They only end up repeating history. Well, let him do it somewhere else."

Trey was hard-pressed for words as he watched her storm out of the kitchen, martini in hand. He resisted the temptation to fix himself a drink, preferring to have a clear mind as they dealt with what was obviously a sensitive subject all the way around.

Ivana felt the coldness on her bare feet as she moved across the Brazilian eucalyptus hardwood floor in the great room. It had all the trappings of success, including European custom-made furniture, a home theater, commissioned oil paintings, and a huge picture window with breathtaking views of the bay and Cascade Mountains. She looked back, certain Trey would be hot on her heels. He had uncharacteristically chosen to remain in the kitchen for whatever reason.

Ivana didn't expect it to end there, knowing Trey could be just as stubborn as she was. She supposed that was one of the things that attracted her to him in the beginning—his strong will. But she didn't want to give in easily to the notion of allowing a convicted felon to live under her roof, coming and going as he pleased. Even if it was her husband's own flesh and blood.

Ivana had never met Trey's brother, Clyde, as he'd been in the state penitentiary for a violent assault against a man before she ever came into the picture. Trey had never talked much about him, as if a dark family secret should remain that way. Now that Clyde was about to be released from prison, suddenly Trey wanted his brother to stay with them for who knew how long. How would Trey feel if the violence in Clyde was directed against his own wife? Did he really want to put her in that position?

Ivana could only wonder just what her husband was thinking with this cockamamy idea. She heard movement and turned to see Trey walking toward her. Sucking in a deep breath, she flopped onto a white custom-made Scandinavian sofa and braced herself for what she suspected would be another plea to take in his brother like a stray dog, even if rabid.

Trey knew Ivana was pissed at him. Resisting the effort to put his brother up was a way to express this. He was also aware that Clyde had nowhere else to go and no one to help him get back on his feet after spending nine long years in prison. It still angered Trey to no end to know that Clyde had damned near beat a man to death. And for what: an argument or something to that effect? Clyde had never been exactly clear on the specifics. Only that he and the person he'd fought, Willie Munroe, had been best friends 'til that night when they came to blows. Trey blamed it largely on Clyde, and for good reason. He had talked to Clyde time and time again about his temper and hanging out with the wrong crowd. But Clyde, two years younger, had rejected his wisdom as holier than thou or too straight and narrow for his taste, and went about his business on the wrong path in life.

That had not only cost him his freedom, but made him unable to attend their mother's funeral five years ago. Her sudden death had stunned Trey, leaving him without his biggest supporter and the one person who had always given him and Clyde unconditional love. It was even harder knowing that she had not lived long enough to see Clyde turn his life around.

Maybe he never would.

Trey wondered if it was possible that the two of them could even get along, much less live under the same roof. Ever since they were kids, he and his brother had never truly been on the same page. Or even the same book. Was there any reason to believe it would be different this time—even if Clyde was starved for freedom and a comfortable bed? Probably not. Trey was willing to put forth the real effort nevertheless. But he wanted his wife onboard to present a united front.

Can she get past feeling sorry for herself and hating me to think about someone else for once in her life?

"Give him a chance, that's all I ask," Trey said, standing behind her. He grabbed hold of some of Ivana's lovable long, cappuccino Senegalese twisted hair. "Clyde's done his time, or nearly, and deserves to be given an opportunity to get his life back in order."

"And what if he doesn't?" Ivana whipped her hair away from him. "If your brother goes back to a life of crime and violence and maybe brings it into *this* house, are *you* prepared to deal with the consequences?"

Trey contemplated the question. Frankly, he had no idea how this would work, or if Clyde had been in prison too long to know what to do in the free world. Wasn't the rate of recidivism high among violent ex-cons? What if that damned temper of Clyde's was still like dynamite, capable of going off at any given moment? Could he actually hurt someone again—even Ivana?

It was a chance Trey was willing to take, wanting to give his brother the benefit of the doubt. If he turned his back on Clyde now, there might never be another opportunity to try to make things right between them.

"Yeah, I'm prepared for whatever happens," he said, sounding as sincere as possible. "I'd rather look at the glass half-full and take the man at his word when he told me in the letter that he doesn't want to cause either of us or himself any trouble. I'm sure once you get to know him, you'll see that Clyde has changed for the better."

"If you say so."

"We're good with this, then?" Trey asked.

Ivana paused. "Since it looks liked you've already decided for us, let him come and we'll see how it goes."

Trey took that as her indication that she would at least try to make this work. He kissed the top of her head. "You won't regret it."

She offered no response.

Ivana wanted to protest more, but was sure it would only fall on deaf ears. Trey was determined to disrupt their peaceful and relatively uncomplicated household regardless of what she had to say. And why? For a brother he'd never gone to see in prison a single time since she had known Trey. Was that supposed to be tough love, or what?

Seemed to Ivana that Trey was in denial about his brother and the risk he was taking by inviting him into their home. She wouldn't be surprised if Clyde robbed them blind and took off for who-knows-where. Not if she could help it. Trey had already caused her enough pain all on his own. He had also taken away her sex drive, which was once strong enough to keep her man happy all the time. She had little desire to have multiple orgasms with someone who saw fit to give them to another woman, as if he were not getting enough at home—wanting his cake and eating it too. Like most men, Trey chose to think with his penis rather than head, heart, and soul.

Ivana would be damned if she allowed what she had left in their marriage—this big, beautiful home and at least half of a considerable fortune—to be taken away from her by Clyde Lancaster or anyone else.

She finished off her martini and began to strategize how best to deal with this unwanted guest.

Half an hour later, Trey stood outside Ivana's bedroom door. They had slept in separate rooms for the last six months. It was Ivana's choice and, though he hated it, he agreed to give her the space she needed.

But Trey was still a man and had needs that went beyond simply having mechanical sex every now and then at his initiation with a wife who could clearly take or leave it—mostly the latter. He wanted things to be like they were before, when they were passionate about each other and made love with mutual zest and unbridled desire. He couldn't and wouldn't force the issue, though. It took two to make it work, yet only one seemed ready and willing to move things in the right direction.

Trey knocked gently on the door. "Are you asleep, Ivana?" He could hear her HDTV and assumed the martinis had knocked his wife out.

"What do you want?" she asked coldly.

You. And only you, baby. He twisted the brass knob 'til the door opened.

Ivana was sitting up on her four-poster bed in a silk teddy, her long legs straight with feet touching. An open magazine sat on her lap like a prop.

"I don't recall inviting you in." She fluttered curly lashes at him with annoyance across the long, rectangular split-level room.

Trey ignored this and approached her. She looked sexy as hell and he wanted nothing more than to take Ivana in his arms and make passionate love to her for hours on end. Instead he showed the type of restraint he'd grown accustomed to since she turned her back on their love life.

"I thought you might want some company."

"I'm not really in the mood for sex, if that's what you're getting at." Ivana flipped the magazine pages dismissively.

His brows knitted. "When are you *ever* in the mood these days?"

She shot him a hard look. "Never, okay? And ask yourself why!"

Trey ran a hand through his closely cropped ebony hair, feeling frustrated. "I made a mistake and I owned up to it like a man. Don't you think you've punished me enough?"

Ivana slammed the magazine shut. "This isn't about punishing you."

"Then what the hell is it about?"

"It's about reaching a point where I feel I can trust you again," she responded frankly. "I'm just not there yet."

Trey wanted to reach out and touch her soft skin, but he held back. "We can't go on like this, Ivana. I need you to want me as your husband and not simply as a damned housemate in a very big house where we can avoid each other whenever possible."

Ivana narrowed her eyes. "So now I'm to blame for something you did?"

"No one's blaming you for anything. I take full responsibility for that. But you can't keep holding this thing over me. It's not fair to either of us."

"You want to talk about fair? Is it fair that I gave up my life for you, Trey? I didn't deserve to be so hurt and humiliated."

"You're right, you didn't," he conceded sadly. "If I could take it back, I would, a thousand times over."

"But you can't, can you? What's done is done and nothing can change it."

Trey drew a deep breath. "So what is it you want—a divorce?" The mere thought of losing what they had built together to a piece of legal paper unnerved him, knowing it would be costly to them both in more ways than one.

Ivana's eyes watered. "I just want to be happy again."

"So do I," he insisted. "No reason why we can't both still be happy with each other if you'll only meet me halfway."

She wiped her eyes. "I married you out of love, Trey. I still want it to work between us. Just give me more time. . . ."

Trey touched her warm thigh and felt aroused. "I need you, baby."

Ivana flinched. "If you want to have sex, regardless of my feelings, just say so." She opened her legs as though preparing to accommodate him.

Why does she have to make this so damned hard? "It's not just about sex."

He could feel her stiffening beneath his touch, and he pulled away.

"It's *always* about sex!" she said tartly. "That's why you ended up in another woman's bed. You can't deny that. So let's just get it over with."

Trey gritted his teeth. "I'm not a damned pimp, and you're not a whore!"

Ivana sneered. "I'm the wife of a man who wants to be inside me whether I'm into it or not. What's the difference?"

Trey's anger threatened to boil over. He managed to control it, realizing he'd been his own worst enemy and was now paying the price in a big way. He had to take Ivana at her word and believe that with time she would come around and they could be a loving couple again in every sense of the word. To think otherwise would tear him apart.

Right now, he just needed to keep his head together and at least try to pretend things were fine in his personal life. With Clyde coming tomorrow, the last thing his brother needed was to enter a household beset with stress and strain, while trying to start life over without feeling he was walking on eggshells.

Trey shot Ivana a hard look. "I've never forced you into doing anything you didn't want to, and I'm not about to start now. I'll leave you to your magazine, or whatever." He didn't bother to wait and see if Ivana had second thoughts, wanting only to get the hell out of there before either ended up saying something they truly regretted.

It was only after he was out in the hall that Trey began to seriously wonder if they could ever get past the one mistake he'd made. Or was this marriage doomed no matter what?

Ivana watched as Trey left the room without looking back. She had thought he would try a bit harder to spend the night in her bed, but was grateful he apparently got the message.

Damn you, Trey, for being so cool under a fire of your own making.

Ivana threw the magazine on the floor, putting her hands to her face to have a good cry. She didn't want to live like this any more than Trey did. But she couldn't simply turn off how she felt just because he wanted her to.

Why did you betray my trust? How can I make myself not hate you more than I love you right now?

Ivana ran thin fingers across her high cheeks to remove the tears. Now was not the time to pity herself. Trey's brother was coming, and whether she liked it or not, she was determined to at least keep up appearances. After all, this was only a temporary thing. Or so Trey promised. The sooner they pacified Clyde with the welcome mat after his years behind bars, the sooner he would get tired of it and they could send him on his merry way.

Ivana grabbed the remote and cut the TV off. She got out of bed and sauntered into the hall, looking in both directions for any sign of movement.

After determining that Trey was in his shower, Ivana went downstairs and fixed herself a drink. Thank goodness the hired help was not around to snoop and report back to her husband. She downed the martini in one easy swallow and made another for good measure.

Chapter Two

"Last night for you," Raymond Gunfrey *tsked* from the top bunk bed. "Bet you won't be able to sleep a wink."

"I'll sleep just fine," Clyde Lancaster told his cell mate. *Yeah, right.* How could he even think about sleeping when he was mere hours away from freedom at long last? After spending the better part of nine years incarcerated, the last thing Clyde wanted was to waste one moment unconscious.

He looked up through the darkness at the underside of the bed above, weighed down by Raymond's hefty frame. It was something Clyde had gotten used to for five years now and was glad it was almost over—taking nothing away from Raymond. After a rough start, he'd become good friends with the man who was probably the one person on the inside who kept Clyde sane.

"When you're out, be sure to tell the ladies I said hello," Raymond said.

"You'll be able to tell them yourself soon enough. Three months and you're out of here too."

"It's seventy-eight days, to be exact. And, believe me, they can't come soon enough."

Clyde scratched the stubble on his chin. "Tell me about it."

Raymond was serving time for armed robbery. Clyde had seen a big change in the man over the years. Still had a hard edge to him, but it was no longer channeled in the wrong direction. This was something Clyde could relate to. He wasn't looking for more trouble, only a chance to make something useful out of his life while he still had one to live.

"Hey, you awake, Raymond?" Clyde asked an hour later.

"Am now." He stirred groggily. "What's up?"

"Just do me a favor, man."

"All you got to do is ask," Raymond said.

"Promise me you won't do something crazy like kick your new cell mate's ass when I'm out of here—meaning you extend your stay as the State's guest for no good reason."

Raymond laughed humorlessly. "You got my word on that. I won't do nothin' to jeopardize my release. Besides, I've got something to look forward to once I get outta here. Or was that just prison talk about you and me going into business together?"

"Not just talk," Clyde replied thoughtfully. "When you're out, look me up and we'll see what we can do to put some honest cash in both our pockets."

"Count on it. After surviving this hellish jungle, we can probably do whatever we set our minds to out there."

"Yeah."

Clyde turned on his side and wondered about that. Was there really an opportunity to better his life in the real world? Or would it be even harder to get past the barriers separating the haves and have-nots? Had people like his rich brother gobbled up all the roads leading to the good life, leaving nothing but leftovers for those on the outside looking in who only wanted a fair chance to make it?

Clyde thought about his brother. Trey Lancaster was one of the most successful African American men in Paradise Bay, if not the entire country. He'd read more than his share of articles in the business and community sections of the newspaper about Trey. Even caught him on TV once or twice. Seemed like his brother had the Midas touch when it came to making loads of money and leading a life of comfort and envy.

Trey was a ladies man, too. Or at least one lady. His older brother had gotten married a while back, Clyde mused, having seen a photo of Trey's bride. From all indications, it was a good marriage and Trey was damned lucky to have the eye-catching former model as his bride. Or was it the other way around?

He and Trey had exchanged a few letters recently, which Clyde found uplifting, even if they never really said much to each other as if to risk ruining a good thing. When Trey had offered to put him up 'til he got back on his feet, the pride in Clyde wanted nothing to do with his brother's charity and pity. But the wiser part of him realized it would have been foolish to let pride stand in the way of common sense. Why not live in the lap of luxury for a taste of how the other side existed? As soon as he could, Clyde planned to be out of there and into a place of his own.

Closing his eyes as though he could shut off troubling thoughts, Clyde lay on his back again. His one major regret in being behind bars was missing his mother's funeral. He'd wanted to pay his respects to the only person who ever truly cared about him no matter his faults, but the prison turned down this request, not giving a damn as to how much it meant to him.

Sorry, Mama. I know I let you down. Wish I could've been more like Trey instead of the black sheep of the family. But I've changed after being stuck in this hellhole. Hopefully for the better. I'd like to still make you proud someday.

Clyde found his mind wandering to a secret he'd taken with him to prison and probably would to his own grave. It pertained to the very reason he was sent up the river and robbed of nine precious years of his life.

Hanging out with Willie Munroe back in the day had proven to be the worst mistake of Clyde's life, causing him nothing but trouble. All they did was get high and steal from other thieves and petty hoodlums. Then the moment that changed Clyde's life forever came when Willie decided to up the ante. He planned to go solo, breaking into Trey's place, figuring he could come away with enough to finance his drug habit and a whole lot more.

Though Clyde felt it just might teach Trey the lesson that he could be brought down to earth in a hurry like anybody else, the man was still his brother. He tried to stop Willie from targeting Trey, or at least persuade him that Trey was off limits.

But Willie begged to differ, rejecting any change to his plans. The two of them came to blows. And more blows. While Clyde ended up with cracked ribs and a broken nose, Willie suffered far more. He'd gotten a concussion, lost an eye, a few teeth, and very nearly his life. But he had lived, and so instead of facing a charge of second-degree murder, Clyde had escaped with aggravated assault and a shot at freedom while still young enough to appreciate it.

Trey had publicly lambasted him, distancing himself from Clyde like he was poison and no longer his brother. Clyde had been just as stubborn, never telling Trey that he fought the bigger, stronger Willie to try to protect him and what might have happened had Trey and Willie come to blows that fateful night. He'd figured maybe it was best that Trey continued to believe he was nothing but a lost cause. Thay way they could go on hating each other as always, which somehow seemed as though it were meant to be.

Clyde realized now that he had gone about it all the wrong way. He'd had enough time behind bars to understand that. But he couldn't undo history.

Maybe if I'd been honest with Trey from the start, we could've gotten past this and been brothers again instead of virtual strangers all these years.

Clyde decided it was all water under the bridge now. Did no good to rehash a very stupid thing he did, even if at the time Clyde actually thought he was doing something right for a change in having Trey's back, whether his brother deserved it or not.

He opened his eyes. The clock on a metal table told Clyde that freedom was only an hour away. He could almost taste it, even if bittersweet.

One day at a time to reestablish his life and keep from falling back between the cracks. Clyde took solace in the thought.

Trey waited outside the gates of the Oregon State Penitentiary. Admittedly, he was more nervous than anticipated in awaiting Clyde's exit from the place he'd called home for the past nine years. What the hell did one say to a brother he barely knew anymore?

Just try and let bygones be bygones. We've both grown over the years and can use that as a measure for moving forward.

Ivana had not offered to accompany him and Trey hadn't asked her to. She would see Clyde soon enough. For now, it was best that the two brothers reconcile their differences as best as possible by themselves.

Trey watched as the man he recognized as his brother emerged from the prison and began walking toward him. He waited as if glued to the spot, then at the last moment decided to take a few steps in Clyde's direction.

"What's up, man?" Clyde's voice was deeper than Trey remembered, perhaps the voice of a man too long without freedom.

"I'm good," Trey told him, smiling crookedly.

The two now stood toe to toe, awkwardly, as if sizing each other up for a prizefight. Finally, Clyde stuck out a hand and Trey reached for it. It was a firm handshake, and neither pulled away before Trey felt compelled to hug his brother. He could feel Clyde's hands slapping at his back in return.

"Good to see you, Clyde."

"Yeah, same here, Trey."

Trey stepped back and studied his younger brother. At thirty, Clyde was maybe two inches taller at six foot three, bald, and looked to be in terrific shape, which impressed Trey, considering where he'd been for nearly the last decade. Though he could see the soft lines of aging etched on his brother's forehead, Trey saw this as a sign of maturity, which he hoped would carry Clyde from this point toward a life of responsibility and wise choices.

"Looks like you've been working out," Trey voiced.

Clyde kept a straight face. "Yeah, well, there's not much else to do behind bars but lift weights, do push-ups, and jog."

"I suppose." Trey tried to imagine a life of forced confinement and realized it was something unimaginable.

"Haven't changed a bit," Clyde told him. "Still lean and mean with no gray strands in that hair."

Trey smiled. "There's a few if you look hard enough. As for the weight, I've put on maybe six or seven pounds. I hide it pretty well."

"No reason to do that. You look great."

"You too." Trey met his eyes and felt a little tingle. "My car's over there."

Clyde shifted his gaze long enough to peer at the gray two-toned Mercedes. He grinned. "You always did know how to drive in style, big brother."

Trey grinned self-consciously. "Helps when you own the dealership."

"Yeah, guess it does."

They began to walk toward the car.

The drive was quiet to start, each man preferring to wrestle with his own thoughts.

For Clyde's part, he was simply trying to adjust to the fact that he was actually out of prison and part of the free world again. He had some ideas of what he wanted to do with his life. Making them work was a whole different thing. But hey, after what he'd been through, things could only get better. Or so he hoped.

He looked at the profile of Trey, who seemed deep in contemplation. Clyde wondered if his brother was still the control freak with a his-way-or-no-way attitude. Or had he mellowed over the years? Was he was having second thoughts about putting him up for a while? Maybe the wife was not onboard. Trey hadn't spoken much about her, and Clyde figured he had his reasons. *It's probably none of my business.* Unless it had something to do with his arrival.

"So tell me about your wife," Clyde tossed out for better or worse.

Trey never looked at him while saying, "What do you want to know?"

"Well, how'd you meet?"

"At a charity function in New York City."

"So she took pity on you, huh, bro, and donated to your cause?"

Trey chuckled. "Not exactly. We dated for a bit before things got serious. Then marriage came. It's seven years later . . . and we're still together."

Clyde raised his brow, hearing nothing about love, as if this was something he knew a lot about. He'd been too busy getting into trouble back in the day to get serious with anyone. But that was then, and this is now. "So everything's cool at home?"

Trey sighed. "Not exactly."

"Oh. . . ."

"I might as well be upfront about it," Trey spoke unevenly. "I had an affair six months ago."

"Is that so?" Clyde's eyes grew with surprise.

Trey gulped. "Don't ask me why, because I love my wife and always will."

"Then I won't ask."

"Thanks. Anyway, Ivana ended up having a miscarriage shortly thereafter and things have been strained ever since."

"Sorry to hear that." Clyde was more shocked to find out that his can-do-no-wrong big brother had apparently done some serious wrong. *Guess he's human after all.* "Especially about losing the baby."

"I won't lie, it's been hard, but we're trying to work through it."

Clyde looked at him, ill at ease. "So, I guess my hanging around isn't helping your situation any?"

"It has nothing to do with you," Trey said, stealing a glance at him.

Clyde's thick brows touched. "You're sure?"

"I'm sure. Our problems are just that. Ivana is okay with your spending time with us. She knows you've had a tough go of it and wants to see you get back on your feet. Just like I do."

"I appreciate what you're both doing for me." Clyde planned to tell the Missus in person, but wanted Trey to know right now.

Trey gave a half smile. "I know you do."

"And I plan to get my own place as soon as I can."

"Take your time. We've got plenty of room and a staff who are looking for someone else to cater to besides me and Ivana."

Clyde nodded. He'd already had enough of people catering to his needs, whether he wanted them to or not, and wanted to do for himself. But he realized that this was the life his rich brother was accustomed to and there was no reason to make any noise when Trey was merely showing his hospitality. He was making it hard to resent him, though such feelings still festered inside Clyde like steam in an engine waiting to pour out. Some things couldn't just go away overnight, if ever.

"It's good to be out," Clyde said, even though he knew there would be a period of adjustment. But freedom spoke for itself.

"I'm happy for you," Trey told him. "Whatever I can do to help make thing easier, you just ask."

"Thanks, man."

"Hey, we're brothers, first and foremost. Never forget that."

"I won't," Clyde said. He wondered if that was a good or bad thing, considering how much brotherly love or lack of had cost him. But that was over and done with. He'd paid his debt to society and had no desire to bring up something that would only stir up thoughts better left alone.

"Good." Trey gave him a gentle pat on the shoulder.

He turned onto a meandering upscale residential boulevard lined with alternating pine and oak trees. The evening sun was beginning to set and the sky was a mixture of orange, red, and yellow.

Clyde readied himself for the next big step in his journey to a life post-incarceration. He needed to keep a low profile and not make things any worse between Trey and his wife, even if he wasn't responsible for their issues. Though trouble always seemed to follow him around, Clyde wanted this to be a new day. He saw no reason why that wouldn't be the case as far as he was concerned.

Chapter Three

"So this is it," Trey announced as they entered a gated property and pulled into the circular driveway behind a ginger-colored Jaguar.

Clyde got a look at the Victorian mansion his brother called home, with its Corinthian columns and stained-glass windows. It was a far cry from the cramped cell space he'd grown accustomed to. It also showed just how far Clyde was from Trey's gifted life. One that had caused Clyde to spend the last nine years of his life in hell.

"It's beautiful, man," he marveled.

"Wait 'til you see the inside," Trey bragged. "Didn't start off as much more than a turn-of-the-last-century relic. But with a lot of patience and very expensive renovations, it's turned out to be a pretty good place to hang out."

Now I get to find out for myself. Clyde promised to keep an open mind as he stepped into the life of extravagance and all it entailed.

He followed his brother through the arched French double doors and Clyde immediately felt as though he'd truly entered another world. One that far exceeded even the last place Trey called home. Clyde wouldn't allow himself to get too comfortable. He never wanted to be someone he wasn't, no matter the temptation.

Trey introduced Clyde to his cook, Francine Naughton, and housekeeper, Emily Sengula. They were in their fifties and seemed right at home.

"This is my brother, Clyde."

"I can see the resemblance," Francine said, smiling.

Clyde had never thought there was much physical similarity between him and Trey. Perhaps others saw differently. He shook both women's hands.

"Where's Ivana?" Trey asked, looking from one woman to the other.

Emily touched thinning, gray hair "She's on her way down. You know Ivana . . . always wants to look and dress her best."

"Well, go up and tell her we've got company. Clyde is family, so she doesn't have to try and impress him."

"That's right," Clyde felt obliged to agree. "All she has to do is be herself."

"I'll go get her," Emily said and walked away.

"You must be hungry." Francine looked up at Clyde behind amber-colored glasses.

He nodded. "Yeah. Haven't had a good meal in some time."

"Don't you worry about that. I'll make sure you have plenty of them as long as you're in this house."

"Thanks, Francine," he said with anticipation.

She rested her hand on an ample hip. "Don't thank me 'til you've tasted my cooking."

Clyde chuckled. "Fair enough."

Just as Francine headed toward the kitchen, Clyde and Trey spotted Ivana coming down the spiral staircase. For whatever reason, Clyde felt nervous at the prospect of finally meeting his brother's wife. At the same time, he was very much looking forward to meeting Trey's other half. Even if things were not as they should be between husband and wife.

Ivana had not expected Trey's brother to be so damned good looking. Clyde was taller than Trey, more muscular, and, well, sexier. He was also bald, something she'd always found attractive in men. But Trey would never hear of shaving his head, as if by doing so he would lose his hair permanently—or maybe the distinguished image he'd been so careful to cultivate.

"Nice to meet you too," she said to Clyde, knowing it was what Trey wanted her to say. The truth was, the man had just gotten out of prison, handsome and sexy or not. Ivana couldn't lose sight of the fact that trouble could still be in his system and she wanted as little to do with him as possible.

When Clyde gave her a hug rather than a handshake, Ivana found herself unexpectedly enjoying the feel of his hard body pressed against hers, no matter how brief. Her nipples got a tingling sensation during the experience, causing her to blush. She hoped neither Clyde nor Trey noticed.

"Thanks for letting me chill here for a while," Clyde told her in a deep, masculine voice.

"Don't worry about it," she said with a sweep of her hand. "You're family. Whatever happened in the past stays there, as far as I'm concerned."

"I feel the same way," Trey added. "Make yourself at home, little brother."

With a straight face, Clyde kept his eyes on Ivana as he said, "I'll try my best and hope I don't wear out my welcome."

Ivana gave him a tiny smile. She supposed they would get along just fine so long as he remembered he was a temporary guest and not a permanent resident, even if Trey might have had other ideas.

Clyde found himself unable to break away from staring at the gorgeous woman his brother had married, making him even more envious of Trey. The photo Trey had sent him in prison hardly did her justice. She was tall and naturally slender, with nice breasts that practically clung to the fabric of the designer jersey dress she wore. He loved the long braids that almost seemed to float across her narrow shoulders. She smelled good, too. It had been too long since he'd breathed in the sweet scent of a woman.

Clyde had to check himself to control his unbidden desire to have Ivana right there on the spot. He wasn't sure if it was his attraction to Trey's wife in particular, or a sexual draw to any halfway decent-looking woman after going nine years without any action to satisfy his strong libido. He didn't want to find out.

"Well, think I could use a nice shower before supper," he said, forcing his eyes to turn to Trey.

"I'm sure you could." Trey put a hand on his shoulder. "Why don't I show you your room. It's got its own bathroom, so you can take it from there."

"Sounds good." Clyde gave Ivana a half grin. "Catch you later."

"I'll try not to fall down before then," she said with a twinkle in her multi-colored eyes.

In the shower, Clyde was still thinking about the last words to come from his sister-in-law's full lips. He liked that she had a sense of humor. Or was she serious? He imagined he would catch her in a heartbeat every time. Could Trey say the same about his wife? Or was Trey still pining for the women he'd been shacking?

Clyde allowed the soap to stream down his face along with hot water. He could have stayed in there all day, sort of cleansing the filth of incarceration from his body. Clyde doubted that the past nine years could ever go away entirely. Not when every time he saw his brother it reminded him of everything he'd missed out on in life. Including being with a woman of his own whom he could love and would love him back just as much, whatever his shortcomings. The fact that he had sacrificed his own freedom to stop Willie Munroe from raiding Trey's property, and possibly going after his brother for the hell of it, also irked Clyde. Trey would never know just how much he'd respected him—loved his brother—to do what he did. Clyde wasn't certain he even realized this at the time. Somehow it came natural to defend Trey's turf, even when they had always seemed to be at each other's throat. Might have been the same had the shoe been on the other foot.

Clyde struggled to push those thoughts to the back of his mind. The bottom line was that he had been given a second chance to do things the right way and intended to take advantage of it. He owed himself that much. And Trey and his lovely wife, too, who had been kind enough to take him in even with the baggage he carried like deadweight. He suspected Ivana wasn't entirely sold on the idea of his presence, and more or less went along with it just to keep the peace.

The least he could do was make it as easy for her as possible. Or was easy what she really wanted from him?

Chapter Four

Willie played with the big breasts of the waitress named Roselyn Pesquera as she galloped atop him like a stallion. Her ass smacked against his thighs time and time again, and she began to moan loudly.

"I think I'm about to cum," she murmured, flipping the knotted extensions from her face. "Tell me you are too."

Her vagina, tugging hard on his erection, had gotten Willie excited to the point that an orgasm was moments away.

"Yeah, baby," he hummed. "Let yourself go."

With the strength that had come from lifting weights and doing sit-ups to pass the time, Willie easily rolled them over to the missionary position while still wedged deep inside Roselyn. He propped her splayed legs high on his hips and drove further into Roselyn 'til his climax—and hers—was complete.

Drenched in perspiration, he rolled off her and onto the water bed Willie had gotten a deal on from his last employer. That was before the bastard fired Willie's ass because of a misunderstanding.

"That was fun," Roselyn said, licking what ruby gloss was left on her lips. "Nice to be with a man who knows what he's doing in bed for a change."

Willie took the compliment in stride. Pleasing women in bed was the one thing he had mastered over the years. It was always that much more pleasurable for him while high as a kite, as he was at the moment.

"You had it going, too," he said simply, his mind already wondering what else she could do for him.

Roselyn giggled, then put a serious look on her face. "Can I ask you a question?"

Willie turned from her breasts. "Yeah, go ahead."

She hesitated. "What happened to your eye?"

He suddenly felt self-conscious. It wasn't like he was trying to hide the fact that the eye wasn't worth a damn. Particularly since it seemed to have a mind of its own, not always in sync with the good eye. But that didn't mean he was looking for pity either. Only revenge someday.

Willie blinked. "Hurt it in a fight years back."

"Sorry to hear that."

"Don't be. You should've seen what happened to the other dude." Not nearly enough as far as he was concerned, even if Clyde Lancaster was doing time for the crime. Willie could only hope someone in the pen had given him some of what he deserved.

Roselyn winced. "It's probably better that I didn't."

"Yeah, probably."

"Well, wish I could stay longer, but I have to get back to work."

Ain't you the lucky one? "No problem."

She flashed him a look of disappointment, as if he was supposed to beg her to stay at his apartment for the rest of the day. If not all night long. Not going to happen.

Roselyn climbed out of bed, and Willie watched her rounded ass wiggle. "You want to get together again sometime?" she asked diffidently.

"Yeah, that's cool." Willie eyed her, not particularly turned on, but not exactly in a position to be too choosy either. "Only next time let's make it your place."

"That's fine by me. Just say when."

"How about tomorrow night?"

She frowned, slipping into clothes. "Can't. I work the night shift. Anytime in the afternoon or the next night would be good, though."

Willie didn't want to appear too desperate to get laid. Or to see if he could con the bitch out of some money.

"I'll call you," he said, and got to his feet, making sure he had her number.

Roselyn tossed him a tentative smile. "You'd better, honey."

"Count on it." Now was the time for Willie to act or watch the golden opportunity walk right out the door. "Say, I'm runnin' a little low on funds. You think I could hit you up for a few bills 'til my paycheck comes in?"

Roselyn hesitated, but quickly relented. "No problem." She grabbed her purse, pulled out an amount adding up to twenty dollars, and put it in Willie's hand. "Don't worry about paying it back. We're cool."

Willie grinned. He had a feeling there was much more where that came from and intended to get what he could.

"Thanks, baby." He sucked on her lips 'til he could feel them swell.

After Roselyn left, Willie waited a few minutes before heading out himself. He lived in a low-income housing complex that was barely adequate.

Some day he hoped to change his misfortunes. Right now, he could only deal with things as they were 'til something better came along.

Willie walked around the block and saw the man he was looking for standing on a corner, doing business.

Lenny Johnson dealt drugs on a small scale in the neighborhood. Willie approached the thirty-something, tall, and rail-thin man with slicked-back dark hair, as Lenny backed his head out the window of a pink Cadillac, which sped off.

"Hey, Lenny."

Lenny flashed Willie a half smile. "What's up, man?"

"Just hangin' out."

"Yeah, what else is there to do around here?"

Willie wasn't looking to chat. He pulled the wad of bills Roselyn had given him from his pocket and handed it to Lenny.

"You got some stuff for me?" Willie asked.

Lenny grinned, counting the money. "Yeah, as a matter of fact, I can help you out there." He removed from his jacket a small plastic bag with marijuana. "Here you go."

Willie took the bag like his life depended on it. "Thanks."

Lenny shrugged. "That's what I'm here for. If you need something to really give you a buzz, you know where to find me."

"Sure do," Willie muttered, and planned to call on him again when he needed some meth. He preferred it over crack and heroin, which he'd also done from time to time. "See you later."

"Yeah, later."

Willie had taken a few steps back toward his place when he heard Lenny say, "Guess you heard the news?"

He turned to face the drug dealer, his mind a blank. "What news is that?"

"Your old homeboy, Clyde Lancaster, was released from prison yesterday."

"What?"

Lenny scratched his forehead. "So you hadn't heard. He's back in town and staying with his bro in that big, fancy house Trey Lancaster likes to rub in our faces."

"That ain't got nothin' to do with me," Willie claimed, maintaining a look of composure, even as he felt his blood pressure rising.

"Whatever you say, man," Lenny said. "Just thought you should know. I'm sure Clyde is a reformed man now that he's done his time."

"Yeah, right."

Like hell he is, Willie mused. The bastard should've stayed locked away for the rest of his pathetic life, and away the hell from him. He held Clyde responsible for taking away half his sight and interfering in something that was none of his damned business, brother or not.

There was a price to pay for that. Willie fully intended to exact his revenge. If Clyde thought that bygones could be bygones, he was dead wrong. What was that about an eye for an eye? Even better was an eye for a life. Maybe two lives.

Willie went home and got high, while having a whole new reason to live.

Chapter Five

"How does a Belgian waffle sound?" Francine asked, while filling Clyde's plate.

"Sounds pretty tasty to me," he said. His stomach was growling, in spite of chowing down last night on fried chicken, mashed sweet potatoes, and apple pie. Add to that, he'd probably had a little too much of the bottle of sauvignon blanc Trey had broken out. If so, he hadn't been the only one. Seemed like Ivana had more than held her own in drinking the wine, though she didn't seem the worse for wear this morning.

"Looks like your brother and I will get along just fine, Trey." Francine smiled at the two men.

"Never expected otherwise," Trey said, sitting at the head of the square glass table in the breakfast room. "Clyde always did have a big appetite."

Ivana was seated at the opposite end, and Clyde in the middle. He couldn't help but think that it all somehow seemed a little too formal for his comfort. But he wouldn't complain. Not after having been forced for so long to eat in a cramped space with a bunch of loud, foulmouthed cons.

"With Francine here to feed you whatever your heart's desire, I'm surprised it doesn't show," commented Clyde, glancing at Trey and Ivana. "Or maybe because this house is so damned big, I've lost some perspective."

Trey laughed. "I think your perspective is fine, little brother. The reality is that Ivana can eat almost anything and not gain an ounce. Me, well, I have a pretty good metabolism as do you, but still need a little help every now and then. Having a membership to a good health club does wonders in allowing me to keep the physique under control. Now I just need to find more time to go there."

Clyde stuck his fork into another slice of waffle. "Maybe I can get a guest pass or something to the club and check it out."

"I'm sure that can be arranged," Trey said, sipping on freshly squeezed orange juice.

Clyde eyed Ivana, who had been checking him out but was short on conversation. He wondered if she was simply the beautiful, silent type or if it was just him. Maybe it was the ex-con thing that freaked her out, like she had to be wary of him. He wanted to put her at ease. If this was going to work, Clyde didn't want to have the Missus as an enemy.

"So I hear you were a model, Ivana . . ." he said coolly.

Ivana stopped short of biting into a piece of bacon. "Yes, I did model once upon a time," she said as if it had been ages ago .

"Cool. Runway or print?"

"Both."

He smiled admiringly. "I can see that."

"Ivana worked in all the top international fashion spots," Trey noted. "Paris, London, Sydney, New York, LA, you name it."

"Wow." Clyde wiped syrup from the corner of his lips, gazing at Ivana. "And you gave all that up for my brother?"

Ivana turned to Trey. "It wasn't really that difficult. Modeling can be a hard life. Giving it up for love was a choice I made willingly."

"Yeah, we all make choices in our lives and have to live with them," Clyde muttered, suddenly feeling sorry for himself. He quickly recovered, determined to put his best foot forward from this point on.

"Maybe so," Trey allowed. "But it doesn't mean we have to cling to the past as our lifeline. Mistakes happen and we have to be willing to get past them, if given half a chance."

Clyde sensed that he'd hit a sore spot beyond self-pity. Seemed as though Ivana wasn't quite ready to forgive his brother for the mistake of fooling around with another woman. His eyes wandered to Trey, Ivana, and back again. They had pretty much what he wanted, and shouldn't let one bad thing ruin it, serious as it was. But that wasn't his call. He had his own issues to deal with.

"Look, I know things haven't been as good as they once were between you two lately," he said anyway. "Doesn't always have to be that way."

"Thanks for the advice," Trey said, wiping his mouth hastily with a cloth napkin. "I'm sure we'll be fine, Clyde. And so will you."

"He's right," said Ivana, in what seemed to Clyde more like she was trying to convince herself. "What's important for all of us is where we go from this point forward."

"Yeah." Clyde met her eyes and tried to read into them. "I'm down with that."

Francine entered the room, seemingly on cue. "Does anyone want more waffles? Coffee?"

Clyde waved her off, stuffed. "Now I know what I've been missing all these years, Francine."

"Flattery will get you everywhere," she joked.

He wasn't so sure about that, knowing it would take a hell of a lot more than sweet talk to get his feet solidly back on the ground. But every road had to begin somewhere. His was here and now and whatever came with the territory. Or who.

That afternoon, Trey called Clyde into his study for a little private conversation, feeling the need to brother-to-brother.

"I hope you're starting to settle in."

"Yeah, man, I am," Clyde said, glancing about at walls of built-in bookshelves, walnut furniture, and a wet bar. "You've got one nice place here, if I haven't already told you that enough."

Trey grinned slightly. "Thanks. I worked hard to get it."

"Too bad Mama never lived to see this."

"I know. To tell you the truth, I think she was much more interested in what went on inside of us than our possessions."

Clyde looked at him defensively. "I know I messed up. Let her down, you, the whole world. Wish I could do it all over."

"No one's pointing fingers, Clyde—not anymore." Trey hoped to put them both at ease.

"Sorry. Guess it's hard to let go sometimes."

Trey met his eyes. "It's all right. You've been through some rough times."

"Yeah, guess I have," Clyde said, pinching his nose.

Trey grabbed a couple of beers from the mini-refrigerator and tossed one to Clyde, who caught it without blinking an eye. *Might as well get to the nitty-gritty*, Trey thought.

"So, thought about what you want to do with your life now?"

Clyde opened the beer and took a swig contemplatively. "Yeah, I have. It's practically all I've thought about for the past few months."

"And what have you come up with?" Trey asked curiously.

"Oh, just some ideas about going into business for myself."

"That so? What type of business?"

Clyde hesitated. "The people business. I'm still working on the specifics in my head."

"That's cool." The last thing Trey wanted to do was put any pressure on him to get a job. It could have a detrimental effect. "Take your time sorting it out."

"Thanks." Clyde sipped more beer. "Just so you know, I don't intend to freeload."

"Never thought you would." Trey narrowed his eyes. "What I don't want you to do is fall back in with the wrong crowd."

Clyde's jaw set. "Is that what you think I plan to do?"

"I sure as hell hope not. It's what got you into hot water in the first place. The Willie Munroes of the world are still out there, looking for nothing but trouble. If you let them, they'll pull you down into the gutter again."

"Seems like some things never change," Clyde said, an edge to his voice. "You preachin' to me about how not to ruin my life."

"You're missing the point," insisted Trey. "I care about you, Clyde, and just want to make sure you have a fair shot at getting a life that doesn't include violence and property crime. Is that really so wrong? Or should I just keep my mouth shut like a good brother and not tell you what I think?"

Clyde breathed out his nose. "It's not wrong. I know you're just trying to help. Believe me, I have no desire to get back with the 'wrong crowd,' as you put it. I had a lot of time to think in the pen. I know I don't have many chances left to do it right and I don't plan to blow it this time around. There's definitely something out there with my name on it that doesn't include turning back to a life of crime."

Trey nodded, pleased. "Well that's good to hear." Maybe he was finally beginning to reach him after all these years.

"I mean it," Clyde reiterated, his features softening.

"It's still there, isn't it?" Trey asked intuitively.

"What's that?"

"That infamous Clyde Lancaster temper."

Clyde cracked a half grin. "I suppose so. But I'm different now. I know how to control it, channel in a positive direction."

Trey hoped that were true for his sake "Then you have changed."

"I think we both have."

"You're probably right about that." Trey decided this was as good a time as any to spring his next surprise on Clyde. "I've got something for you."

"Oh, yeah?" Clyde met his gaze curiously.

"Yeah. Follow me . . ."

Trey led them through the twists and turns of the house to the front door, opening it. Both men stepped outside.

Clyde spied the shiny, sapphire-metallic BMW. "What's this?"

"It's yours," Trey said, pulling the keys from his pocket and putting them in Clyde's hand. "I had someone from the dealership drop it off this morning. It's a 650i Coupe that's got just a few miles on it."

Clyde shook his head. "You don't have to do this, man."

"I want to," stressed Trey. "You need some wheels to get around, and I can afford to supply you with them. Seems like the perfect marriage to me."

Clyde was speechless. "Not sure what to say."

"Don't say anything other than you'll take good care of it."

Clyde showed his teeth. "Yeah, I'll definitely do that."

Trey chuckled. "And while you're at it, you'll probably be needing this, too." He took an iPhone out of his pocket. "It's got all the fancy stuff you've been missing. The instruction booklet is in the car if you need help figuring things out. The cell phone has our home phone, my office, and my own cell numbers." He handed it to Clyde. "Now you should be all set to get back on your feet."

Clyde made a face. "You know, though we've had our issues, it's getting really hard not to like you, big brother."

"I think it's time we started liking each other, little brother," Trey countered, and meant every word. Both were in their thirties now and needed to respect the other for their differences, even if it might still be challenging at times. "Now why don't you give the car a spin?"

"Good idea."

"Got a full tank of gas, so break her in like a thoroughbred."

"I'll give it my best shot," Clyde promised.

Clyde was about to hop inside the car when he looked up and saw Ivana peering from a bedroom window. From the start, he'd sensed there was some sort of connection between them. Or was it more his imagination? Or wishful thinking? Their eyes met for a long moment before she disappeared behind vertical blinds.

It happened so quickly, Clyde doubted Trey was aware of the moment. Probably better that way. No need to stir up any trouble by suggesting there was something going on with him and his brother's wife. Not after all Trey had done for him while asking for little in return. He'd ignore the Ivana vibes, hard as it may have been. Even so, Clyde couldn't help but wonder when it would come time to pay the piper. And if he would be able to step up to the plate.

He got in the car and took a few seconds to familiarize himself before starting it and heading out into the real world again, not quite sure what lay around every corner. Or whom.

Willie Munroe entered his head. Clyde wondered what the man was up to these days. Was he even still in town? Clyde regretted that things between them had ended violently after what had once been a good friendship, if not an unhealthy one. But Willie had brought this upon himself by stepping over the line. Had he changed his bad ways—or was he same old Willie?

Somehow Clyde doubted the man had become a model citizen. Willie was the type of person who never seemed to know when enough was enough. Not while he was still able to walk on his own two feet. If he were smart, Clyde would steer as far away from Willie as possible. This one was a no-brainer. He was happy being out of prison and into a slick BMW. No reason he could think of to make things tough for himself on the road ahead.

Chapter Six

"Don't you think you're overdoing it just a bit?" With a drink in hand, Ivana confronted her husband the moment he entered the house.

Trey gave her a dumbfounded look. "I have no idea what you're talking about."

"Like hell, you don't. You've already given your brother the key to our home. And now you're giving him a damned *car*?"

"It's not like we don't have enough of them. Loaning Clyde one to get around in hardly seems like overdoing it." Trey headed toward the stairs with Ivana matching him step for step. "And I don't recall giving him a key to the house—yet."

Ivana fumed, though not quite sure why. She hadn't expected any less of Trey than to lay out the red carpet to try and impress his ex-con brother. Or win him over through expensive toys. Whatever. Didn't mean she would roll over and pretend to go along with every move he made like a China doll. Even if that was what he obviously wanted.

"You can't buy his love, no matter how much you throw at him," she said brusquely.

Trey rounded on her as they reached the second floor. "Is that what you really think: that this is about—*buying* love?"

"You tell me," Ivana shot back, while sipping her martini.

"All I'm trying to do is help Clyde while he tries to sort out his life. If that's simply too much for you to understand, then I'm sorry."

Ivana followed Trey to his bedroom, stepping into the room he'd claimed as his own for the first time in months. Ever since deciding she no longer wanted to share a bed with him, Ivana had welcomed Trey being on the opposite end of the hall. Only once had they made love in that room, which he'd hired a decorator to turn into his mini-palace. She succumbed to his advances while inebriated, hoping it would be enough to keep him at bay. It had worked for a while, but now he was showing signs of wanting more from her sexually. At this moment, that was something she definitely was not interested in. Not with him, anyway.

"You're not sorry one bit," she voiced sharply. "The reality is that you make the rules and just expect me to abide by them, such as inviting your brother into our home whether I gave a damn or not."

Trey sniffed. "You've been drinking."

Ivana saw no reason to deny it. "So I had a drink. I'm entitled."

"Maybe more like two or three." Trey gave her a look of disgust. "Can't you try and lay off the alcohol—at least while Clyde is here?"

Ivana sneered. "And just how long will that be, Trey? A week? Month? Year?"

"However long it takes for him to get his life in order."

"Well, you know what?—that's not good enough," Ivana declared theatrically. "I'm not interested in babysitting your brother 'til he decides to be a man and get his own place and life."

"No one's asking you to," Trey insisted. "Clyde can take care of himself. If it makes you feel better, I'll ask him to try to avoid you at all costs."

"I'm not sure he could even if he wanted to," she snorted and thought about their eye contact at the window. It was as though he had a sixth sense in looking directly up at her as she'd watched him and Trey carry on as though suddenly the best of friends. "Men who've been holed up like he has for so long always find a way to make their presence felt."

"What is your problem?" Trey asked pointedly. "The man hasn't been here a day yet, and you're acting as though he's the scum of the earth. Clyde's not here to cause you trouble. I'm asking you not to cause him any. Just give my brother a damn chance."

"Like you gave our marriage a chance when you decided to sleep with that whore?"

Trey sucked in a ragged breath. "I'm not going to talk to you about this right now."

"Why not?" Ivana challenged him. "Or is it easier for you to talk about the long-lost brother you now suddenly want in our lives?"

"There's not much more I can say about something I regret deeply that hasn't already been said. Trying to somehow equate that with wanting to help Clyde make a smooth transition to the outside world is grossly unfair."

"To whom—you? Or your brother?"

"Take it whichever way you like. In the meantime, don't drink anything else today before you end up making a fool out of yourself."

"And what the hell does that make you?" Ivana tossed at him. "Who's the bigger fool in this house?"

"I'm not going to argue with you right now, as it's obvious that you don't know when to leave well enough alone." Trey grabbed his wallet from the dresser. "I'll be at the office if you need me for anything urgent."

"Don't hold your breath," Ivana said icily, deciding not to take it any further for the time being. Besides, it hurt too much to dwell on the past that had all but destroyed the love and lust between them. It was somehow easier to focus on Trey's brother, an allegedly reformed bad boy. Ivana wasn't sure she bought into that. Or how much it truly mattered either way.

Trey left the room, expecting Ivana to continue to make a scene after she had been on her best behavior in Clyde's presence, which Trey appreciated. But she did not follow him. He took that as a respite to be resumed at a later time when Ivana was in the mood again to be argumentative.

Now that she had decided to grace his bedroom with her presence for the first time in ages, Trey considered that maybe Ivana might want to do so more often—as a wife wanting to be with her husband in the biblical sense, rather than bitching at him. Whether that was the case remained to be seen. But he wouldn't stop trying to win his wife back in heart, soul, and body, even if she was making it difficult and seemed in no hurry to put the past behind them.

Trey found Emily downstairs, dusting the custom hand-carved stone fireplace mantel in the living room. He knew she had heard everything. How could she not?

Emily stopped cleaning when she saw him. "Is Ivana out of control again?" Her voice was filled with worry.

The last thing Trey wanted was to involve the staff in their personal squabbles. Fact was, Emily had been there with them from the start and had proven to be a valued and trusted employee. She knew he'd screwed up big-time and didn't pass judgment. He respected her even more for that.

"Ivana's just going through some things right now," he said as an understatement. "She'll be fine."

Do I really believe that? Or am I deluding myself in thinking that things can ever get back to something close to normal between us?

Emily's eyes narrowed. "I'm probably over-stepping my bounds, but I hope having your brother here won't make matters worse between you and Ivana."

Trey appreciated her candor, while choosing to sidestep the issue. "I doubt that. Ivana is good at putting up a front, even if struggling within. She'll deal with Clyde for as long as she has to. With any luck, that won't be for too long."

"I think it's good for you to have Clyde around," Emily said, "even if for only a short time. Family is always important, no matter the baggage."

"I feel the same way." Trey gave a tiny smile and glanced at his gold watch. "Have to run. You know where to reach me if anything comes up."

Emily nodded. "Drive carefully."

"I will." Maybe that sentiment would be better directed to Clyde, Trey thought. After all, the man hadn't driven a car in nine years and just might be a bit overzealous on the streets of Paradise Bay. The last thing he wanted was to see Clyde wrap that car around a tree. Or was he selling his younger brother short?

Ivana watched from her bedroom window as Trey left the house and got into his car, just as she had when Clyde left a few minutes earlier. He had caught her spying on him. Strangely, it turned her on even if she turned it off just as swiftly. She sipped on a martini and pondered what it was about her husband's brother that fascinated her so. Maybe it was the sexy shaved head. The rock-hard body. Or the bad-boy thing, even if he seemed to be legitimately trying to turn over a new leaf. But zebras never changed their stripes. Once bad, always bad.

Bad could be dangerous, she told herself. Especially as a lover who hadn't known the touch or feel of a woman's body in nearly a decade. She could only imagine the pent up desire in him, having little doubt that Clyde Lancaster could wrap just about any woman around his little finger.

But then so could Trey. Only he'd chosen to direct that hot-blooded passion toward another woman, leaving his own woman hurt and confused.

Now Trey had decided to give his brother the royal treatment, as if to make up for past friction between the two. And Clyde seemed to have swallowed his pride and was eating up everything Trey threw at him like candy. Or maybe as someone who desperately wanted to make up for lost time and with opportunity staring him in the face.

Ivana wondered if Trey was ready to give his wife away too, just to make his brother feel perfectly at home. Would Clyde swallow that bait also?

And just how would Trey feel if betrayal were on the other foot? Would he be so easily able to sweep the stinging humiliation and disloyalty under the rug?

Ivana tried to turn off such thoughts, knowing they did her no good. Just the opposite. Yet, it was hard to ignore that there was a very sexy, good-looking man sharing their house, who happened to be her brother-in-law. But a man, nonetheless, with needs as great as hers, if not greater. It gave Ivana a tingle between her legs. Something she hadn't felt in so long that Ivana savored the experience.

She sipped her drink, allowing her suddenly vivid imagination to run wild.

Clyde stood at the gravesite of his mother. She had long ago paid for the spot, which was right next to his father's grave. Clyde never knew him, as he was only two when his father died in a car accident. Now he was without both parents and had no elders to lean on during tough times. At least there was Trey to share the bloodline. They might never see eye to eye on everything, but at least Clyde believed they had a decent chance to become real brothers. Something that their mother had wanted 'til the day she died.

Sorry, Mama, it took me so long to get here. I know I let you down, in more ways than one. Unlike Trey, who I'm sure walked on water in your eyes. I can't undo what's been done, but I'm here to say that I promise you I'll make something out of my life yet.

Clyde felt a warm tear creep down his cheek. He put flowers on his mother's headstone, wondering how many times Trey had done the same thing. He stepped over to his father's grave marker. It was barely visible within overgrown grass.

Hey, Pops. Guess you know who I am. Wish I could say the same. Just take care of Mama up there and we'll be cool.

With that, Clyde walked away, content that he'd made his peace and was ready to see what else life had to offer him as a free man.

Across the street from the cemetery, Willie sat in his old Chevy Blazer observing as Clyde sauntered toward his car, a fancy BMW. Willie had followed him after spotting Clyde leaving the big house his brother lived in.

I should run his ass down right here and now and be done with it.

But somehow Willie considered that too easy for his onetime best friend-turned-nemesis. No, he wanted Clyde to suffer the way he had all these years. If that meant waiting until the time was right, then so be it.

I know where to find him and when.

Willie started the engine and drove away. He put on a rap CD and tried to focus on the words, but couldn't get his mind off Clyde Lancaster. The man had taken something very valuable away from him, and he intended to make Clyde pay big-time.

Enjoy your freedom while you can, punk, because it won't last long. Not in the way you expect.

Willie believed that his streak of bad luck was just about to change. Clyde Lancaster had seen to that the moment he walked out of prison.

"Trey's gone to work," Emily informed Clyde when he stepped in the door.

"Oh, yeah?" He had to remember that Trey was a big man in Paradise Bay and had more on his plate than merely watching over him. But what about the Missus? "Is Ivana around?"

"She's here. In the pool. But I wouldn't cross paths with her right now if I were you."

"Why is that?" Clyde asked curiously.

Emily seemed to consider her words carefully. "Let's just say that Ivana has not been herself lately, so you never know what you're going to get."

Clyde thought about the friction between Ivana and his brother. Or was there something more?

"Sounds to me like the typical woman, present company excluded," he suggested. "I'll keep that in mind, though."

"Good. Francine left you some lunch on the stove."

"I appreciate that. I'm starving!"

In the kitchen, Clyde found some macaroni and cheese and wheat bread. He helped himself, downing it with soda and using the alone time to take stock of his life. *What do I do now?* Realistically, he didn't expect that many people would be willing to hire an ex-con, except maybe jobs on the lower end of the scale or hard labor. He wasn't much cut out for either. Working for Trey was always an option, should an offer come. But Clyde wasn't eager to have his brother looking over his shoulder every step of the way.

What Clyde saw in his future was being his own boss. That would make his life easier, and he wouldn't be subject to overbearing authority that had proven to be difficult in previous jobs. It would take money to go into business, something he had far too little of these days. Maybe he could get a loan from Trey, so long as it was understood that he would pay him back every penny. Trey had done enough for him. Now it was time he did for himself.

Emily stepped into the kitchen. "There's a collect call for you. Says his name is Raymond."

Clyde grinned. He had given his cell mate Trey's number. *I'll pay for the call.* "Think I'll take that in my room."

Upstairs Clyde flopped on the king-sized bed that seemed to fit him perfectly and flipped on the cordless handset. "So you miss me already, huh?"

"Not really," muttered Raymond. "All right, maybe just a little, but don't tell anyone. Thought I'd call and see how life's treatin' you on the outside?"

"So far, so good. I'm just chilling out in my brother's mansion, trying to figure out what's next."

"Thought you had a plan?"

"I do," Clyde said unevenly. "But getting it going might take some doing."

"I'm sure you can handle it. Fact is, I'm countin' on it. Partners, remember?"

"Yeah, I remember."

"Good." Raymond let out a big sneeze. "So is your brother's wife as hot in person as in the picture?"

"Hotter," Clyde admitted. "She could probably burn you with just a touch."

Raymond laughed lasciviously. "Now ain't it just too bad she's spoken for? Maybe she's got a twin sister she can hook you up with?"

"I don't think so." Clyde couldn't imagine there being more than one Ivana out there. "I'm sure I'll be able to find someone all by myself."

"Yeah, like for about twenty bucks on a street corner."

Clyde chuckled. "Hey, I'm not that desperate."

"Whatever you say." Raymond paused. "Well, I'll let you go back to enjoying the good life."

"Your day is right around the corner."

"Don't think I don't know that it. It's what keeps me going."

Clyde could relate, seeing that that was the same position he was in very recently. Now he was in the lap of luxury with a fine car and a path to chart his own future.

After getting off the phone, Clyde got up and peeked out the window. Down below, he saw Ivana lying by an Olympic-sized pool, looking hot, wet, and sexy in a bikini. *The lady is all that and more*, he thought, feeling his libido raise a couple of notches. He wondered if Trey was taking good care of his woman in bed. Or had his cheating ways robbed him of that gorgeous body that seemed made for blazing sexual passion and pleasure?

I think I've been too damned long without the real thing. Maybe Ivana had been that way too. Made for a potentially dangerous situation were they to ever hook up and forget about the boundaries no one was supposed to cross where it concerned kin and sexual vibes.

Clyde chewed on that thought, knowing where to draw the line when it came to his brother's wife. But that didn't mean he couldn't enjoy the view, albeit from a safe distance.

***

Ivana sipped on the martini before diving back into the pool. She'd been aware that Clyde had been watching her— first from his room, and then the deck. There had been no conversation between them, but sometimes words need not be spoken to express yourself. Clyde liked what he saw and Ivana found that it felt good to attract a man other than her husband. Or in spite of him.

She had certainly had her fair share of suitors before Trey swept her off her feet. Seemed that most men fell easily for a tall, beautiful African American model as she strutted her stuff before an international audience. While she had not entered into the marriage as a virgin, Ivana had remained faithful to Trey, though she could just as easily have strayed as he had.

Why do men think they're entitled, but not their women? Even if it causes the woman to lose whatever respect she had for him in the process?

Ivana swam all the way to the end of the pool and back, enjoying the cool feel of the water on her body and the workout that was invigorating. She wondered if Clyde was as good a swimmer as Trey. She could only imagine those powerful biceps and calves at work, moving seamlessly through the water, looking like a perfectly sculpted African warrior.

Maybe I'll get to find out, since it appears he'll be around for a while, like it or not—which I'm still trying to decide.

When Ivana came up for air she almost expected Clyde to be waiting there with her towel, offering to dry from head to toe. Or take a dip himself. Instead, as she climbed out of the pool, Ivana saw no sign of their houseguest. She hid her disappointment while realizing it was probably for the best.

She would do well to keep that in mind.

Chapter Seven

Trey decided to invite his brother and wife out to dinner at a nice restaurant. It seemed like a good idea to get out of the house and loosen up a bit. He was surprised Ivana didn't put up a fuss or accuse him of showboating. Instead, she seemed totally on board, as did Clyde, having doubled his wardrobe in an hour. Allowing Clyde to stay with them for a while just might work out after all, Trey thought, keeping his fingers crossed.

The Ribs Castle was crowded this evening, but Trey had no problem reserving a table, since the owner was a personal friend and customer.

"I'm glad Trey brought you by, Clyde," Kalunga Malkaka said in his thick Zairean accent.

"Me too," Clyde said, and tugged uncomfortably on his sport coat. "So I hear you've got the best ribs in town?"

Kalunga cast a wide smile. "You won't get any argument from me there." He winked at Ivana.

"Be sure to let me know if you need anything."
He left menus.

"So what do you think, Clyde?" asked Trey
a couple of minutes later. "The pineapple baby
backs sounds pretty good to me."

Clyde nodded. "Yeah, me too." He turned to
Ivana. "See something you like?"

Ivana looked up from the menu. "Maybe the
flame-grilled sirloin."

"Then we're all set," Trey said, seeing the
waitress coming their way.

When the woman took the orders, Clyde made
a late switch and ordered the flame-grilled sirloin.
"That sounds even better," he suggested.

Trey was mildly surprised that his brother had
followed Ivana's lead instead of his. Perhaps this
was Clyde's way of trying to get on Ivana's good
side. Given that his wife could be pretty damned
stubborn when she wanted to be, Trey fully sup-
ported anything that could keep her and Clyde
on the same page instead of mortal enemies.

By the time the food arrived, the three had
broken into a bottle of cabernet franc. Trey
thought that the evening had gone well. Ivana
hadn't overdone it with the wine, and the conversation had not stepped on anyone's toes. He
wanted only to do right by his wife and brother,
without sacrificing his own principles in the
process.

"You come here often?" Clyde got Trey's attention.

"We used to." Trey gazed at Ivana, realizing that their eating out had gone to hell in recent memory. His fault. Perhaps this could jump start that part of their lives.

"It's a great place to eat," said Clyde. "But after where I've been, I guess any place would be a treat."

Trey glanced at Ivana. "I'm sure you're right."

Ivana peered at Clyde. "So what was it like being in prison?"

"This isn't the time, Ivana—" Trey said, as if any time would be.

"No, it's cool," Clyde cut in. "Let her ask. It's pretty much what you'd expect. The cells are cramped, the food lousy, the staff indifferent. Inmates keep to themselves for the most part, when not fighting over something usually stupid."

"Do people really smuggle in drugs and stuff?" she asked over her wineglass.

"There's always a way to get something, if the price is right," he answered truthfully, slicing into the tender sirloin.

Ivana paused and leaned forward. "Is homosexuality *really* a big problem in prison?"

"Ivana!" Trey glared. "Don't go there." He thought it might be going too far to delve into that sordid part of the prison culture. Especially if it was something that Clyde didn't feel comfortable talking about. Trey understood that one had to survive behind bars any way necessary.

"I don't mind responding." Clyde smiled crookedly. "Yeah, it's a big problem. But not for me. I don't play that game and made it clear right from the start. No one messed with me after that."

"I'm glad to hear." Ivana sipped her drink thoughtfully.

"Maybe I could ask you a couple of questions?" Clyde put forth.

"Go ahead," she said evenly. "It's only fair."

Clyde tasted the wine, eyeing Trey for tacit approval.

Trey nodded, figuring Clyde was probably just as curious about his wife as she was about him . He hoped the questions wouldn't make Ivana too uncomfortable. Or him, for that matter.

"Where are you from?" Clyde asked her. "I think Trey said you met in New York."

"I grew up in San Antonio."

"You still got family there?"

Ivana wiped the corner of her mouth with a napkin. "My mother and stepfather."

"A friend of mine is from San Antonio," Clyde pointed out. "I told him I'll have to check it out sometime."

"Be my guest. Just be prepared for the awful, dry summer heat. Not to mention those pesky insects."

"Thanks for the warning."

"I like it there," Trey said, though Ivana clearly could take it or leave it. "In fact, I'm thinking about possibility expanding my business interests to the southwest."

"Oh, yeah?" Clyde looked at him.

"Though times are tough, people still need to get where they're going, and the vehicle is still the most affordable, safest transportation around."

"I say go for it," Clyde voiced. "If anyone can get folks there into the car-buying mood, I'm sure it's you."

"Won't be for a couple of years though," Trey downplayed it. He could almost see relief in Ivana's face. As it were, he would never make such a business move that involved committing his time and resources without consulting her first. While he had found much of his success before they got married, Trey believed that marriage was a true partnership, even outside the household. All he wanted was for Ivana to be happy, whatever it took.

By the time things began to wind down, Trey had made a snap decision that he felt made perfect sense. Over the rim of his wineglass, he said in earnest, "Clyde, until you figure out what you want to do with your life, I'd like you to work for me."

Clyde cocked a brow. "Doing what—selling cars? Or maybe you see me filling bags with popcorn at one of your theaters?"

Trey chuckled without humor. "Neither, exactly."

"Then exactly what?"

"I'd like you to start off as my right-hand man—assistant, or whatever you want to call it. You'll report directly to me in—"

"Thanks but no thanks," Clyde said flatly. "Not interested in being your errand boy."

"Neither am I," Trey assured him, not entirely surprised at the reaction, knowing his brother and the pride thing. "I'll teach you the ropes of the car business and you can go as far as you want."

"That's not really my thing."

"So maybe it can be," Trey insisted, glancing at Ivana. "At least think about it, Clyde. You're the only brother I have, and I could use someone close to work with me. We'd be helping each other. And if after a while you decide to go in a different direction, that's fine." *It would be a big disappointment if I brought you in only to quit on me, but I'd get over it. Have to at least try to reach out.*

Clyde ran a hand across his mouth. His features softened. "What the hell? Okay, I'll give it a try and we'll see how things work out."

"Great!" Trey smiled, knowing this was best for everyone, including Ivana, who would not have to worry about Clyde being around the house as much, if that still concerned her. "Why don't we toast to working together just like Mama always envisioned?"

"All right," Clyde agreed.

Trey lifted up the wineglass. He clicked it against Clyde's glass and Ivana's. Though he fully expected to get an earful from her later, Trey welcomed the moment when they all seemed to come together and maybe were setting the stage for future unity and prosperity.

That night, Trey rapped softly on Ivana's door. He really wanted her tonight and hoped that maybe she might want him after what he had for her.

When there was no answer, he went in. Ivana was sitting on the bed, wearing a black teddy and looking incredibly sexy.

"What are you up to?" Trey asked tentatively.

"Just looking at her," she said.

"Who?"

As he got closer, Trey saw that she was holding the picture of their child created on the ultrasound machine. He remembered how joyous they had both been when first seeing images of the girl who was supposed to complete them. She was given the name Catherine, after Ivana's paternal grandmother.

Trey sat beside her. "She would've been beautiful," he said quietly.

"I know." Ivana faced him. "Do you think she would have looked more like you or me?"

"Definitely you. I can imagine her with your high cheeks and brown-green eyes."

Ivana smiled dreamily. "Maybe. Did you want something?"

Trey wondered if the mood had been killed, but decided to go for anyway. "I have a little item I picked up for you from Tiffany's," he said. He pulled a diamond bracelet out of his pocket. "I thought this would look great on you. It has onyx and rock crystal, set in eighteen-karat white gold."

Ivana looked overwhelmed. "Must have cost a fortune."

"It did," Trey admitted. "I'd spend it again. You're my wife and I would do anything for you."

She met his eyes. "Do you want to put it on my wrist?"

He grinned. "I would love to."

Trey watched as Ivana admired the bracelet that was a perfect fit.

"Thanks."

He felt that the moment was perfect to kiss her. Tilting his head, Trey brushed his lips against Ivana's. When he didn't get a reaction, he assumed she wasn't interested in going further and didn't want to push it. Not with the miscarriage fresh on her mind to throw back at him.

"Well, I guess I'll leave you alone."

Before Trey could get up, Ivana grabbed his hand. "Stay.

He held her gaze. "Are you sure?"

"Yes."

Trey kissed her again. This time Ivana opened up to him. He put a hand on her breast, loving its soft fullness. They fell down onto the bed and Trey put his tongue in her mouth, tasting the remnants of a martini. A surge of desire coursed through him, having longed for this moment when they would be together as husband and wife.

In spite of an overwhelming desire to be deep inside Ivana, Trey wanted to pleasure her first. Lowering his head, he spread her legs and put his face between. He used his lips to push aside the silk of her French G-string. He began to lick her clitoris 'til she got wet.

Ivana moaned, putting her hands on his head. It turned Trey on and he continued to kiss her, tasting the deliciousness of her womanhood.

When her quivering body told him Ivana's orgasm had come, Trey moved back up her and pulled out one breast, sucking on its taut nipple like a strawberry while removing his erection. He slid deep inside his wife and they made love.

Leveling his body with hers, Trey grabbed Ivana's buttocks and went deeper as the orgasm drove out of him and inside her vagina. He groaned with passionate release and fell onto Ivana, keeping their bodies close for the waning moments of satisfaction.

When it was over, Trey half expected Ivana to dismiss him from her room. But she said nothing, seemingly content at the moment to be held by him. He wouldn't push for more too soon, happy to take one step at a time in working their way back.

Ivana pretended to be asleep with her back to Trey. She could hear a faint snore coming from him. She had been surprised by the diamond bracelet. He had given her many gifts over the years, but not so many in recent memories that made her take notice. When she let him make love to her, Ivana was not merely showing her gratitude, she was hoping to feel something again inside for the man she married.

Instead, she found herself unable to feel much of anything insofar as strong desire. Until she began to fantasize that it was Clyde who was orally gratifying, then making demanding love to her. It was the first time in a long while Ivana could remember climaxing and relishing the experience. It had been so intense that she felt like screaming—'til it was over and she had to face the reality that her lover was her husband. The same one who had forsaken his marital vows and turned his attentions to another woman. Ivana simply couldn't get past that. At least not to the point where she was ready to invite him to move back into their bedroom. *Am I wrong to feel this way? Should I simply forgive and forget what he did?* Ivana didn't know if that was even possible. There was no putting the genie back in the bottle. Trey had seen to that. What he did couldn't be undone with the stroke of a magic wand. Now they would both have to deal with the consequences, whatever they might be.

Ivana's thoughts turned to Clyde Lancaster, her fantasy lover. The man had come into their lives and turned things upside down in many respects without even knowing it. Or maybe he knew exactly what he was doing to her, even if Trey wasn't the wiser.

Ivana felt embarrassed that Clyde had been the one to awaken the real woman in her, at least in her vivid imagination. It was his touch, not Trey's, that made her feel alive and want to have him wedged as deep inside her as possible, while his fullness gave her orgasm after orgasm.

What would Clyde think if he knew he had that power over me? Would he want to exploit it for his own, no doubt, burning needs? Or would he stay away from me out of respect for Trey?

It was a perilous path Ivana didn't want to go down when looking at things squarely. Clyde was an ex-con who she wanted no part of outside of capitulating to Trey's wishes that they give his brother room and board. But was that possible after tonight? Could she ever see him again without fantasizing about—if not wanting—Clyde as her lover?

Chapter Eight

Trey sat across the booth at the Paradise Bay Restaurant from Helene DeCroch, his former lover and the wife of one of his best customers, millionaire hotel owner Grant DeCroch. At thirty, Helene was as beautiful as she was graceful, and could be a look alike to the sleek actress Audra McDonald. The two had met at the grand opening of her husband's newest hotel seven months ago, and sexual sparks flew, culminating in a brief but intense affair. It was one Trey deeply greatly regretted for the trouble it had caused him. Neither ever had any intentions of walking away from their marriage—only succumbing to mutual attraction and needs for the moment.

Even after the affair ended, the two had remained friends and confidants. Trey had become dependent upon Helene's platonic friendship, filling the void for what was missing emotionally at home.

"Thanks for coming," Trey told her.

"I was happy to," Helene stressed, tossing back stylishly short hazel hair. "That's what friends are for, Trey."

He smiled, wondering for an instant how his life might have been had he met Helene first, assuming she had been single and available. The thought dissipated as Trey realized that Ivana would always be his soul mate and he couldn't imagine life without her.

"You truly are a good friend, Helene."

She blushed and then trained bold café au lait eyes on him. "So tell me what's wrong, Trey."

"Where do I start? Last night I made love to my wife for the first time in months."

"Is that a bad thing?"

"Not at all," Trey stressed. "Just the opposite."

"So what's the problem?"

"The problem is, this morning, Ivana let me know in no uncertain terms that she wasn't ready to resume an intimate relationship with me and I shouldn't expect what happened between us to happen again anytime soon. Apparently last night was just a damned aberration and not a real step forward in our marriage."

"It was a step forward," Helene said. "Maybe a baby step. Just be patient with her."

"I've been nothing but patient for the past six months. I love my wife and really want to give her all the time she needs. But then I say to myself, 'Are we simply going in circles forever with this to forgive and not to forgive? Or am I being the typical male who just doesn't get it?'"

"She's hurting, Trey. I would be too if it was my man who turned to another woman. No matter how much I wanted to accept his apologies and promises that it would never happen again. In the back of my mind, I'd always wonder if he could meet someone else to start sleeping with behind my back."

Trey grunted. Grant was twenty years Helene's senior and treasured his wife, as far as Trey knew. But that didn't mean the man walked on water and wasn't vulnerable to the right temptation if it came along.

"Grant isn't that crazy," he told her anyhow, knowing what a good catch she was for someone else.

"And you are?" Helene eyed him with her face tilted.

Trey shifted uneasily. "Maybe I was a little crazy at the time."

"We probably both were. But for all the right reasons."

Trey wasn't so sure about that. Was there ever any reason to stray from someone you loved?

He enjoyed the intimate time spent with Helene more than he cared to admit, while filling a void in both their lives. He still wished he could take it all back, though. It wasn't worth the aftermath.

"I gave Ivana a diamond bracelet as a small token of my love," Trey said thoughtfully over his cocktail. "I probably haven't done enough of that lately, yet somehow it never seems to be enough."

"Oh, honey, don't beat yourself up. I promise you she loved the bracelet and still loves you. Women are very good at feeling sorry for themselves. We take it out on our men, even when we know that they're as human as we are and can make mistakes—sometimes nearly unforgivable ones." She put a warm hand on his. "Trust me when I tell you that no matter how wishy-washy Ivana has been, she wants this marriage to work. I know firsthand just how tender and passionate you are as a lover; as well as your gentle nature as a man. So does she, deep down. Ivana will come all the way around. Let her do so her own way. She knows what a good heart you have."

"And I know what a good one you have," Trey said, realizing just how much he hoped Grant did 'til the day he died.

Helene colored. "I'm sure Grant appreciates me, even if he doesn't always show it." She removed her hand. "So when do I get to meet this brother of yours—or do I?"

Trey didn't want to add fuel to the fire by suggesting to Clyde that he was still seeing Helene. On the other hand, she was a good friend and there was no real harm in introducing Clyde to her.

"Of course you do. I'd be happy for you to meet Clyde. I'll arrange it."

Helene gave Trey an understanding look. "Has it been rough for him trying to adjust to being on the outside?"

"So far, so good, knock on wood. Clyde seems to have mellowed out a bit. Maybe through years of soul-searching, he's ready to finally get his act together. I've given him a job in hopes that he might want to someday partner up with me. Or at least stick around long enough to get some stability in his occupational life."

"That's wonderful, Trey. I'm sure your brother can use his big brother's support right now. Working together is a nice way to build bridges."

Trey agreed. "There's been too much water under the bridge, so to speak. I hope we can put our differences behind us and just go from here."

"I don't see why not," Helene said, lifting her drink. "Family is supposed to stick together, through thick and thin. Just like true friends . . ."

"I'll drink to that," Trey said, and hoisted his wineglass. "Here's to family unity and unbreakable friendships."

Their glasses clicked and Trey felt better for it. Now for the hard part—trying to figure out precisely what it would take to win Ivana over on every level while remaining true to himself.

"This is our showroom," Trey told Clyde, displaying an array of shiny new cars on multiple levels.

"It's cool," Clyde said, trying hard not to feel resentment toward his brother for making success seem so easy, while his own life had been so damned hard with every step he took. Maybe things were finally about to change for the better.

I won't get too excited in that respect 'til I see it with my own eyes.

"Edwin, get over here," ordered Trey.

Clyde watched the thirtysomething, stocky man in a tight-fitting navy suit approach.

"Clyde, this is Edwin Turner, my top salesman."

Edwin stuck his hand out. "So you're the little brother Trey can't seem to stop talking about?"

"Not so little." Clyde grinned crookedly while looking down on him. "And don't believe everything you've heard."

"Only the good things, right?" joked Edwin.

"Yeah." *What bad things has Trey said about me? Does every one of his employees know I've just gotten out of prison?*

"Well, if you need any pointers on sales technique that Trey can't answer, come to me."

"Yeah, I'll do that."

Trey indicated that a customer had come in, and Edwin excused himself.

"Looks like you run a tight ship here, bro," Clyde said, unsure whether to be impressed or concerned that he might not fit in.

Trey made no apologies. "Wouldn't be where I am today if I didn't."

"I suppose not." *And maybe I'd be somewhere different at this time in my life if I didn't always have to stand in your shadow.*

"Let me show you the rest of the place."

Clyde followed him as they entered Trey's office, which included various framed awards and photographs with local civic leaders and celebrities.

"Nice," Clyde said, as though compelled to.

"Just comes with the territory," Trey downplayed.

In the next office over, a woman was talking snappily on the phone. "Those cars were due yesterday, Fred. I don't want to hear your lame excuses. Just get it done!"

She cut the conversation short when noticing Trey and Clyde.

"Stella, this is my brother, Clyde," Trey introduced. "Stella Rockwell is my assistant manager. She's been with us from the very beginning."

Stella got out from behind her desk. "Nice to meet you, Clyde."

"Same here." While shaking hands, he briefly studied the forty-something, medium-sized woman sporting a dark-kinky twist, and silver glasses.

"Clyde's going to be working with us," Trey said.

"Oh?" Stella was clearly surprised.

"Yes. He'll take Larry's office."

"Uh, all right," she muttered. Her phone rang. "I have to get that."

"Don't let us stop you," Trey said.

Stella gave him a dirty look and said to Clyde, "I'll talk to you later."

"Sure." In the corridor Clyde said uneasily, "That seemed to go over well."

Trey half smiled. "Don't worry about it. Stella's just having one of her moods. Sometimes I think she takes this job way too seriously."

"Yeah, sounds like someone else I know," cracked Clyde.

Trey pulled his nose wryly. "You think?"

"It's probably infectious around here. So who's this Larry anyway?"

Trey led them into a corner office. "He used to work here as our sales manager—'til I had to let him go for spending too much work time on the Internet in porn sites."

Clyde couldn't help but chuckle. "Guess he found something there he wasn't getting else-where."

"Maybe," conceded Trey. "No substitute for the real thing, as far as I'm concerned."

"True," Clyde said, wondering when that might come his way.

"Anyway, that's his problem, and this is your office."

Clyde looked around, feeling not too surpris-ingly out of place. He kept it to himself. "I'll try not to let you down."

"You won't," Trey said confidently. "More importantly, Clyde, try not to let yourself down. This is a chance for you to step up to the plate and make it count."

That's what I'm afraid of, thought Clyde, *striking out and ending up back where I started.* Not if he could help it. He only wanted his piece of the pie. Maybe a little more.

He just wasn't sure he'd find it there.

Ivana went shopping at a fashionable boutique for some new clothes, simply because she could. Ever since her modeling days, she'd appreciated wearing the top designer clothing. She used to wear either to impress or because they made her feel beautiful and sexy. Now it was all about buying what her husband could afford and replacing those clothes that had become too large or hopelessly outdated.

She noticed an attractive African American woman around her age with a baby stroller. The little girl inside had to be around six months old. She was pretty, with loads of dark hair. It made Ivana think about how nice it would have been had Catherine been born a healthy child with a bright future ahead.

The thought was depressing, making Ivana long for a martini to soothe her nerves and make her forget. At least for a short while.

She stopped at a nearby lounge for a few drinks—three or four, she'd lost count. That didn't prevent her from wanting another before heading home. Only the bartendar seemed to have a problem with that.

"Sorry, ma'am, but I think you've reached your limit."

"I think I haven't," Ivana retorted. "Give me another martini now!"

"No can do," the man insisted. "You need to go home now.

Better yet, maybe I can call you a cab?"

"Either you give me a drink or I'll get it myself," Ivana slurred the words.

"I don't think so. We could lose our license in serving someone who has definitely already had too much. Sorry."

Ivana glared. "Screw you—and your damned lounge." She got up and stumbled before sitting back down. Her head spun a little and Ivana wondered if she could even make it to her car, much less drive home.

"Is there someone you can call to come and get you?" the bartender asked.

The first person that came to mind was not her husband, but his brother. Ivana had a feeling that unlike Trey, Clyde was not one to pass judgment.

Clyde was admittedly surprised as hell when he received a call from Ivana, of all people. Not that he had anything against talking with his damned good-looking sister-in-law. Quite the contrary, he enjoyed hearing her voice and being around Ivana—maybe too much.

The last thing he expected to hear her say was that she needed a ride home from a bar. Other than when she requested he not mention a word about it to Trey.

Clyde left work early, saying only that he had a few things he needed to take care of. Trey accepted this, giving him plenty of leeway in adjusting to being on the outside and working for him. Clyde appreciated this, even if it meant not being straight with Trey where it concerned his own wife. But Ivana obviously had her reasons for not wanting him to know that she'd apparently had too much to drink.

Clyde entered the lounge and saw Ivana sitting all by her lonesome at the table, looking lost in her own world.

"Ivana," he said, getting her attention.

She looked up through bloodshot eyes. "Thanks for coming."

"Not a problem. You want to get out of here?"

"Yes." Ivana stood on wobbly legs.

Clyde grabbed her slender waist, sensing she'd never be able to do it alone. He ignored the nice feel of her body leaning against his, knowing this wasn't the time or place—if there ever would be such.

Outside, Clyde led Ivana to his car. He spotted her ride and planned to come back and get it later.

Clyde helped Ivana get her seatbelt on before driving out of the lot. He was curious as to why she decided to get wasted. Or was this a regular occurrence in her life?

"Are you all right?" he asked her.

"I'm fine. Just had a little too much to drink, that's all."

"It happens," Clyde conceded. But not to Mrs. Trey Lancaster. At least he didn't imagine his big brother would approve, knowing how Trey operated in his perfect world that obviously had a few imperfections. He looked at Ivana. Her head was pressed against the headrest. "So what's going on with you?"

"You really want to know?" she asked.

"Yeah, I do."

"All right. I saw a woman at the store with her baby. Guess it just touched a nerve. I needed something to take the edge off."

Clyde couldn't well say he understood what she was going through, having never fathered a child or been involved in the loss of one. "And you don't think Trey would've understood?"

Ivana rounded on him. "Trey only understands himself. If I'd called him, he would have had a conniption, insisting I've got a problem. I didn't want to deal with that—not today."

"Do you have a problem?" Clyde dared to ask, while changing lanes. "It's nothing to be ashamed of."

"No!" she insisted. "Haven't you ever gotten drunk? Or am I reading you wrong?"

Clyde regarded her sideways. "You're not." He was in no position to counsel his brother's wife, even if she seemed to need help of some kind in dealing with her loss. "Guess I should be minding my own business." Never mind that she'd made it his business by calling him instead of her husband.

"I'm sorry for jumping on you," Ivana's words slurred.

"Hey, no big deal. I know you and Trey are going through some things right now, and I don't want to make matters worse."

"You're not." Her words was slow as she spoke. "Our issues have nothing to do with you."

Clyde believed that. His own issues with Trey ran much deeper and over a longer period of time. But obviously his brother, for all his success in life, needed to work more on his home life. Or else risk losing a fine woman like Ivana, whose sexual appeal was hard to ignore, apart from anything else.

"I'm sure you'll work it out," he told her.

"Never be too sure about anything," Ivana said tersely. "Not in this life."

Clyde raised a brow. "You thinking about leaving Trey?"

"I didn't say that."

"So what are you saying?"

Ivana hesitated. "Only that maybe some things happen for a reason. You just have to figure out what that is and do whatever you need to do in dealing with it."

"Sounds deep." Or was it the alcohol talking?

"I get that way some times."

"Cool ," Clyde said.

"Glad we see eye-to-eye there. Honestly, sometimes I think Trey just sees me as this tall, beautiful bimbo trophy wife who doesn't have much in the way of intellect."

Clyde wrinkled his nose. "I doubt that. For all his faults, my brother would not have married you if he didn't think you were someone smart enough to keep up with him."

Ivana eyed him. "Now who's being deep?"

Clyde flashed a little smile. "Guess we're more alike than I thought."

"Should I be worried about that?"

He laughed unevenly. "No, I don't think so. Just gives us a little more in common as in-laws." And just maybe something to build on, down the line.

Chapter Nine

That evening, Clyde was hesitant as he approached the Westside Tavern on Thirty-ninth Street. It was once his hangout when not elsewhere causing trouble. It was also where his old homie, Willie Munroe, hung out. Maybe Willie had found new stomping grounds.

Hope so, as I'm not looking to tangle with him again and possibly end up back in prison. Or worse.

But Clyde did want to see if the bartender still worked there. Albert Lake was probably the closest thing to a father figure that he had, though only ten years older. Clyde regretted not following his advice back in the day. Not too many people could tell him much then. At least not so he listened.

Oh well. Live and learn.

He stepped inside the tavern, knowing he was going against Trey's wishes that Clyde refrain from visiting old haunts that could lead to old habits. But Clyde was his own man and had to use his own judgment.

There were only a few people present; most sitting at wooden tables drinking beer. The mellow sound of blues filtered through the air at a low volume.

Clyde made his way to the bar, which was empty. He took a seat on a stool and waited for someone to come.

A thickly built man with receding gray hair in a short ponytail came from the back and said routinely, "What can I get for you?"

"I hear the malt liquor is pretty good here, old man," Clyde said with a smile, recognizing him as Albert Lake.

Albert looked up. It took a moment before his face lit with familiarity. "Well, I'll be damned twice over. Clyde?"

"Yup, it's me, man."

Albert came from around the bar and the two men embraced warmly. "It's so good to see you."

"You too," Clyde expressed.

Albert pulled away. "You're looking good."

"I can't take too much credit for that. Guess it's in the genes."

"Genes always need a little help," Albert said with a chuckle. "How long you been out?"

"Couple of weeks."

Albert's brow furrowed. "And you're just coming to say hello?"

Clyde ran a hand across his head. "You know how it is. Been trying to readjust to society and all that."

"Sure, I understand."

Clyde smiled. "So how about that drink?"

"Yeah, coming right up." Albert went to other side of bar and got out two cold bottles of malt liquor, sliding one to Clyde, who sat down. "Where you stayin'?"

"My brother's place right now." Clyde almost felt guilty in saying that. He didn't expect it to be forever.

Albert raised his chin. "Trey's a good man and doing good things for this town."

"So I've heard and seen." Clyde gulped down the drink and thought about Ivana, whom he'd rescued earlier and helped settle in without Trey being the wiser.

"Be proud of him, even if that's not in your nature. The man has earned everything he's got in life."

"Yeah, I know." Same old Albert, free with the advice, Clyde mused. Most of it good.

"Heard about your mother," Albert said mournfully. "I'm sorry, man."

"So am I. Mama just ran out of steam."

"Happens that way."

Clyde tasted more malt liquor. "I'm surprised to see you still here after all these years."

"Where else am I gonna go? Steady jobs are hard to come by in this town for forty-somethings with no formal education. Besides, I'm now the manager of this place and only bartending part-time."

"Guess things have changed around here." Clyde glanced about.

"Everything changes over time," Albert said. "It's what makes the world go round."

"I suppose."

The two men gazed at each other thoughtfully before Albert asked, "You seen Willie?"

"No," Clyde said, reacting to the name.

"Probably best that you don't. The man is still up to no good most of the time."

"Kind of figured that." Some things clearly never changed.

"But you've paid your dues and moved on with your life. That's a good thing."

"Yeah." Clyde put the bottle to his lips. Can one ever truly escape the past, no matter the desire?

"Well, look who the dust blew in?"

Clyde turned around at the sound of the recognizable voice and saw Willie Munroe standing there, glaring at him.

Clyde regarded the man he once would have done almost anything for—short of stab his own brother in the back. Willie Munroe was not quite the physical specimen Clyde remembered, but imposing nevertheless. Six feet four, muscular, with black dreadlocks, and a goatee. His eyes were rust-gray with thick bags beneath them. The one eye was unblinking and a bit red, reminding Clyde of what had happened between them.

"What's up, Willie?" he said for lack of any other words to come from his mouth.

"What's up?" Willie's nostrils flared. "That all you got to say to me?"

Albert peered at him. "Do yourself a favor, Willie, and get the hell outta here."

Willie's mouth hung open. "All of a sudden I'm not good enough for this place now that the prison bird is out?"

"That's not it. I just don't want any trouble. And you shouldn't, either."

Willie gave a derisive chuckle. "If I was lookin' for trouble, I'd have come in here with my three-fifty-seven Magnum and put the man out of his misery. You see any weapons on me?"

Clyde appreciated Albert sticking his neck out for him, but didn't want or need his protection. "I can take care of myself, Albert."

"Yeah, that's what I'm afraid of," he scoffed. "You did that once before and look where it got you. I don't want to see you go down that road again—not in here."

"Maybe we can carry on this little conversation outside," Willie suggested. "Or did being in prison make you yellow inside your black skin?"

Clyde felt his ire rise. The man was baiting him and hoping he would swallow. *I can't let him get to me. Nothing good could come out of it. But something bad sure as hell could.*

"I'm not afraid of you, Willie. I should think you would know that by now."

Willie took an involuntary step backward under the weight of Clyde's fierce gaze. "You took half my sight away from me, man."

Clyde stood his ground. "No, you took it away yourself by not leaving well enough alone when you had the chance."

"You could have walked away and everything would've been fine."

Clyde sighed. "Keep telling yourself that, Willie. We both knew the day was coming when we'd square off. It just happened then. So why don't we just give it a rest and move on with our lives."

Willie snorted. "You think I can just forget? Would you, if the shoe were on the other foot?"

It was a question that Clyde did not have the answer to. How could he? "Look, we both know what went down and why. I served my time and you didn't, but should have. I'm satisfied that my debt is paid in full. If you really think fighting me will make you feel better, then go for it. Otherwise get out of my face and go back to wherever you've been holed up."

Willie shot him a hard look. "See you another time."

Clyde watched Willie leave the tavern and then sucked in a deep breath in relief.

"Sorry he had to spoil things," Albert said, frowning.

"He didn't, as far as I'm concerned," Clyde said bravely, putting the malt liquor bottle to his lips.

"The man's holding a grudge. I wouldn't put anything past him. And neither should you."

"Willie doesn't want to mess with me—not again." If only Clyde could believe that. On the contrary, he knew how vengeful Willie could be when crossed.

But I can't let him get to me, or have me afraid of my own shadow, let alone his.

"All the same, I'd watch my back if I were you," warned Albert. "I don't want to see your return to Paradise Bay turn into a nightmare."

"Believe me, neither do I." Clyde finished the rest of his beer. Prison had toughened him against guys like Willie and worse. It had also made him smarter in not jumping the gun, putting himself in a position not in his best interests.

I'm not going back to prison for Willie or anyone else. I did that once for Trey and it did nothing to help my cause. This time around I'll fight my battles another way and hope I don't get burned in the process.

Willie rang the doorbell of the house on Birchdale Lane where Roselyn Pesquera was living. He was feeling frustrated and needed some release. Being inside her would have to do 'til someone better came along.

The door opened and Roselyn's roommate, Gail McCord, stood there. She was shorter and thinner than Roselyn with a dark, curly bob.

"Hey," Willie said in a soft voice. "Roselyn around?"

"No, she isn't," Gail answered with a hard edge to her voice.

Willie stiffened. *I should have called first.* "Is she at work?"

"No."

So where the hell is she? "Well, maybe I'll just wait 'til she comes home."

Gail's sable eyes grew wide. "Not in here, you won't!"

He gritted his teeth. "What's up with you?" *Obviously the bitch doesn't think I'm good enough for her roomie.*

"Nothing's up. I just don't want men in my house when Roselyn's not here. Especially men I don't know—or trust."

Willie grinned wickedly. "So what, you think I'm some bad-ass dude out to harm Roselyn? Or is it that you want me for yourself?" *Or is she a lesbian?*

Gail slapped a hand on her hip. "First thing, you're not my type—okay? As for Roselyn, I don't know what your agenda is. I just don't want to see my friend get hurt by someone who's maybe looking for a sugar mommy."

Willie glared. She read him only too well. "I like Roselyn, all right? End of story. Maybe you should let her decide if she wants to be with me." *I think she already has.*

"I'll tell her you came by," Gail said tersely.

"Yeah, you do that." Willie held back his tongue, not wanting to make matters worse or measure up to her image of him. He walked away just as he had with Clyde, feeling it was better that way. Next time could be different on both counts.

Willie got out his cell phone and called one of his boys. The night was still young. Might as well try to make the most of it.

Chapter Ten

Trey bounced a basketball, eyeing Clyde, before making a move around him toward the basket. Just when it looked as if Trey had a step on him and was about to go in for an uncontested dunk, Clyde seemed to come from nowhere and practically glided through the air, swatting the ball away.

"Get that stuff out of here!" Clyde said, rising to the challenge.

"Foul!" Trey declared, having been knocked on his ass in the exchange.

"I don't see any referees around here," Clyde countered. "Hope you're not getting soft on me, big brother?"

"Not a chance!" Trey picked himself back up, feeling the adrenaline rush of a good workout and some not-so-friendly sibling competition.

Clyde bounced the ball this way and that, sizing up his opponent before he whizzed by Trey and headed toward the basket. Determined not to let him score, Trey slammed into him as the ball went flying out of bounds.

"Sorry, little brother, no can do!" Trey felt a sense of satisfaction.

The two went back and forth with the physical play, making the other work for each and every basket, without backing down an inch in the desire to come away with a victory . During one hard foul they nearly came to blows.

"Hey, what's your problem, man?" Clyde touched a tender spot on his perspiring bald head, which had just been hit with the ball.

Trey did not flinch from the taller, stronger Clyde. "So what happened to the no-referees-around bit? Or does that only work one way?"

Clyde stepped back, forcing a grin. "No harm, no foul, right?" he said, tracking down the ball. "Let's get it on. . . ."

"Yeah, let's."

Trey realized he may have been laying it on a bit thick. Yes, he felt a need to be the leader, not the follower, in their brotherly rivalry, but not to the point where it only ended up putting more distance between them. The point was, to win fair and square, while educating in the art of sportsmanship.

Easier said than done sometimes.

Ivana watched from the angled window in the master bedroom as Trey and Clyde played basketball in the backyard, resisting the urge to go out on the balcony. Both men were bare-chested, wearing shorts, and well, yes, looking sexy. She particularly honed in on Clyde. His body glistened with perspiration, and was well-developed with a six-pack that Trey could only dream of. She could imagine her hands all over him, foolish as it sounded, and his hands on her. Exploring her inch by inch.

The mere thought got Ivana all hot and bothered. She sought to cool it off by tasting the chocolate martini in her hand. It did little to help, so she forced her mind turn to something less tempting.

Ivana refocused on the one-on-one basketball. She could tell that it was more than just a game to Trey and Clyde. Both seemed to want to prove himself to the other. She suspected this had always driven their relationship from childhood. Obviously, for the most part Clyde had gotten the short end of the stick, while Trey had come out the winner far more often in the battle of the brothers. Not including physique, in which Clyde was the clear victor. She wondered if this was what it was like for most siblings throughout their lives. She wouldn't know, given that her parents had stopped with just her and showed little inclination to give her a brother or sister.

Judging by the obvious undercurrent of animosity between Trey and Clyde even during good times, Ivana thought it may have been a good thing that she had gone it alone. That didn't mean she wanted no family of her own. She'd always hoped to have at least two children, to be there for one another. But then she had the miscarriage and well, so far things had not been right between her and Trey to think about trying to have another child. Much less two.

Though Trey seemed genuinely saddened in losing their baby girl, Ivana wasn't so sure that things had not gone according to plan for him. *Maybe he never really wanted a child and got his wish.*

Ivana had gotten so absorbed in her thoughts that she failed to notice someone had entered the room and come up behind her.

"Now just what's so damned interesting out there anyway?" the voice said, giving Ivana a start.

Ivana swiveled her head and saw the smiling, beautiful walnut face of one of her best friends from her modeling days, Naki Aboule.

Ivana felt the long, thin arms wrap around her even as she returned the favor. She had met Naki in Paris during a fashion show. She and the six feet one Nigerian beauty had hit it off right away.

Naki had tried to talk Ivana out of giving up her burgeoning career for a man, but failed to do so, as Ivana was convinced that love was much more important than all the glamour, fashion shows, and money in the world.

Was I that naïve? Ivana wondered, stepping away from her friend, who had gone on to even more international success since then.

"What are you doing here?" she asked in disbelief.

Naki tussled her thick, short dark hair. "I came to see you, darling. Don't you think it's long overdue?"

"Yes, I do," Ivana admitted, feeling bad that she hadn't exactly gone out of her way to visit Naki or others she knew in the modeling business. Ivana had convinced herself that once she'd broken ranks, they had no use for her as a married, retired model.

"Well, I wanted to surprise you—and apparently I did!"

"Scared me to death was more like it," Ivana said, "but in a good way."

"You know me—totally unpredictable."

"And beautiful as ever." Ivana admired her tall, sleek figure in a print tunic and twill gauchos.

"Look who's talking, girl," Naki said. Her big brown eyes peered at Ivana's bracelet. "Are those diamonds?"

"Yes," Ivana admitted. "Trey gave it to me."

Naki gave an envious smile. "Obviously your man is taking real good care of you."

I wish. Ivana had not spoken of Trey's infidelity with many people, preferring to keep it private, so long as they were still together. Maybe had she been still in the loop, it would have been easier to talk to Naki about it.

"Guess you knew what you were doing all along when you gave up the hard life of a model for domesticity."

Ivana pasted a smile on her lips and diverted the subject for now. "So how long are you going to be in town?"

"Oh, just a couple of days. I have a gig in San Francisco coming up. Thought I'd divert to the Pacific Northwest for a little R and R, if you'll put me up?"

"Don't be silly," Ivana said with a wave of her hand. "Of course you can stay here. Stay as long as you like. I could certainly use the company."

"Looks like you already have company," Naki hummed, and moved to the window. "Who is that absolutely gorgeous creature playing ball with your husband?"

"It's Clyde. Trey's brother."

"Well, no wonder you were caught gaping. The good looks obviously run deep in the Lancaster family." Naki faced Ivana. "Tell me that Clyde is single and looking."

Ivana felt a twinge of jealousy that Naki was already throwing herself at Clyde before they ever met formally. And, as he was definitely available, Clyde just might fall under her spell.

"He is single but I don't really know if he's looking."

Naki beamed. "Well, that's close enough. All of a sudden it looks like the trip could be much more interesting than merely catching up on our lives."

Maybe more interesting than I care for it to be, Ivana told herself. *I'm not in the mood to play matchmaker, though it doesn't look like Naki will need my help any in that department.*

"So where have you been all my life?" Naki queried flirtatiously to Clyde as they sat in the living room with Trey and Ivana.

Clyde grinned and might have asked the same thing of the attractive lady, had he not sensed that Ivana was staring him down as though Naki was invading her territory. He hoped Trey didn't get the wrong idea. Though, at this point, Clyde wasn't sure what the right idea was where it concerned him and Ivana.

She's my brother's wife. But that's certainly not the case with her friend.

"Oh, I've been around," he responded, albeit not somewhere she'd want to be. "Though I've yet to get to some of the places you and Ivana have been."

"All overrated, trust me," Naki said.

"If you say so."

"Would I lie?" she giggled, and sipped red wine.

"Are you still living in New York?" Trey looked at Naki.

She returned his gaze. "London, actually. Been there for three years now. Much more charming in a retro and artistic way than Manhattan."

"We'll have to go there and visit her sometime, Ivana," he said.

"I'd like that," Ivana said, tasting her drink. "London's a great city."

"Then consider it an invitation," stated Naki. "You're all more than welcome to visit any time I'm there." She rested her eyes on Clyde. "Especially your good-looking brother-in-law."

Clyde blushed, ignoring the resentment he felt from Ivana at the notion. As far as he was concerned, he had to keep all options on the table at this point. At least the ones clearly available, ready, and more than willing.

"Sounds like a plan," he told Naki.

***

"How long will Naki be staying?" Trey asked Ivana when they were finally able to get a moment alone.

She looked at him suspiciously. "Why do you ask?"

He paused, not wanting to add more tension to their lives, but also feeling it necessary to try and keep her from backpedaling to the substance abusing, partying, and promiscuous lifestyle he was able to pry her away from. As far as Trey knew, Ivana had never been into the hard drugs of the modeling world, but he suspected Naki had been and probably still was.

"I think Naki's a bad influence on you," Trey came right out with it. "The last thing either of us needs is her hanging around here getting high when talking about the good old days."

Ivana's chin jutted. "First of all, Naki is not a bad influence on me. Just the opposite. She's a good friend and always has my best interests at heart, which is more than I can say for you. Secondly, Naki does not use drugs. She has too much respect for her body to go down that road. As for the 'good old days,' why shouldn't we talk about them? It was part of my history and I won't let you take that away from me too."

"I don't recall taking you away from anywhere you wanted to be," he said, feeling the sting of her words.

"You wouldn't, after getting what you went after."

"This isn't about us. I simply want to keep you from getting caught up in two worlds and not being sure which one you belong to."

"I don't need you to protect me from my friends," Ivana insisted. "Least of all Naki. I chose your world and have to live with it, just as you do for choices you've made. Now if you don't mind, I have my own welcome visitor to make feel right at home."

Trey cursed under his breath as Ivana walked away. With Clyde taking up an extended residence, he didn't have much of a leg to stand on where it concerned Naki. Maybe Ivana had matured enough so that Naki would come and go without putting the wrong thoughts in her head.

One could only hope.

When Naki boldly kissed Clyde smack-dab on the mouth the next day by the pool, he had hoped that sparks might fly. Or the earth would shake. But the truth was, in spite of her beauty and obvious sex appeal, he felt nothing. Not that he had an issue with bedding someone for the practice, if nothing else, after a long dry spell.

He didn't want to give Naki a false impression that this could go somewhere—even from long distance. She wasn't really his type, though Clyde had yet to figure out who was. The women in his past did not fit into any particular image, and he liked it better that way.

Naki also wasn't Ivana, who made his blood run hot whenever Clyde allowed it to. Taking her friend to bed would only make him wish it were Ivana, and perhaps make things that much more strained when around her.

Clyde still felt the kiss on his lips as he pulled back from Naki, dressed in a V-front bathing suit, "Look, I think you're hot, but—"

"But you're into someone else?" Naki frowned.

Clyde nodded and glanced at Ivana, who was approaching them from the house. "Something like that."

Naki ran a hand through wet hair. "I feel like such an idiot!"

"No reason to," he insisted. "You're anything but an idiot. If I'm ever in London, I'll definitely look you up."

Naki forced a smile. "That would be nice."

Ivana joined them with a glass of wine in hand. "Did I miss anything exciting?"

"Think I'll leave you ladies alone," Clyde said solemnly. "Have to get to work before the boss man docks my pay."

He eyed Ivana, thinking how fine she looked in another dazzling swimsuit that accentuated toned arms and legs, and gave a brief grin before heading off.

Ivana watched Clyde walking away for a moment—or more specifically, his tight ass moving sexily through trousers—then turned to Naki. "So what was that all about?"

"I've just been rejected, for like, maybe the first time in my life." Naki took Ivana's drink and tasted a generous amount.

Ivana was surprised, but couldn't say she wasn't pleased. "Don't take it personally. Clyde is a complex man who's been through a lot. I'm sure he's just not ready to go down that road at the moment." Maybe he was waiting for the right woman to offer herself to him.

Naki crinkled her nose. "Now you tell me. Just my rotten luck!"

"You're anything but unlucky, girlfriend."

"Funny, I don't feel that way at the moment."

Ivana decided this was as good a time as any to talk to her friend about her own troubles. Maybe that was why Trey wanted to get rid of Naki, so she wouldn't see him knocked off his pedestal .

"Trey cheated on me," she said glumly.

"What?" Naki cast bold eyes at her in shock.

"He decided one woman wasn't enough, so he took another."

"That bloody bastard."

"That's one good name for him." Ivana could think of plenty of others.

"When did it happen?"

"Six months ago."

Naki blinked. "Isn't that around the time you had the miscarriage?"

"Yes," Ivana said emotionally.

"Oh, you poor baby." Naki hugged her. "Why didn't you tell me what Trey had been up to?"

"Guess I didn't want to hear, 'I told you so.'"

"You know me better than that. We all make mistakes."

But some were more unforgivable than others. Ivana took the wine back and sipped. "I've been trying to deal with it ever since—not very well, I'm afraid."

"So why haven't you left him?" Naki asked bluntly.

Ivana couldn't figure that one out herself. She'd thought about asking for a divorce on more than one occasion. But what then? Collect alimony and become an old maid? She had no interest in going back into modeling, though she believed there was still a place out there for older models. She certainly would not return home to San Antonio, only to be once again at her mother's beck and call.

In many respects, Ivana considered herself stuck in a bad situation, but tried to put on a brave front. "He's apologized like a thousand times and swears it will never happen again. Maybe Trey means it."

"So too did men who have cheated on me, I'm sure," Naki said. "But I wasn't married to them. You don't have to put up with this crap, Ivana. You can come to London and we can room together. It would be fun and maybe you can get back into the business."

Ivana was flattered more than she could say, but didn't think that was the answer. At least not right now. "I think that part of me still loves Trey and wants to forgive him." Even if another part felt hatred and found what he did totally unforgivable. And certainly unforgettable.

"I understand that you have mixed emotions, are confused, and probably even afraid to walk away from this marriage," Naki said. "That's perfectly normal. But it doesn't change the reality of your situation."

"Doesn't it?" questioned Ivana.

"How can you stay with a man if you can't trust him?" Naki fixed her with a straight gaze. "In my experience, men who cheat once can never be trusted again. I'm afraid that the same is likely true with Trey, no matter how many expensive gifts he gives you to try and buy his way out of a jam. Who's to say that he won't jump at the next woman who flashes her boobs in his face? Or, for that matter, isn't still involved with this homewrecker bitch?"

"You really think Trey could be . . . or is—" Ivana's voice shook.

"I wouldn't put it past him. Once a dog, always a dog. You deserve so much better, Ivana. What if he is fooling around or decides to again next week or two months from now? Where will that leave you?"

Where will that leave me? Ivana wondered uneasily. *Is it possible that Trey hasn't ridden himself of the cheating bug? Maybe he's using our current situation as an excuse to get some on the side with Helene DeCroch. Or spend time in another woman's bed.*

The thought infuriated Ivana, even if Naki may have been way off base. Maybe she should hire a private investigator to spy on her husband. Or maybe this marriage wasn't even worth holding onto—any more than being faithful to a man who hadn't shown her the respect she was entitled to.

Ivana finished off the drink.

Chapter Eleven

The charity ball to raise money to fight sickle-cell anemia was held at the DeCroch Hotel in downtown Paradise Bay. As one of the sponsors of this year's fundraising event, Trey was obligated to come. Though no one in his family had sickle cell, fighting the disease was important to him, not only because it primarily affected people of African ancestry, but a good friend of Trey's had died recently from complications associated with the hereditary disorder.

Grant and Helene DeCroch were also involved with the event, right down to providing the spacious diamond ballroom in the hotel they owned. Though grateful for their generosity, Trey felt a little uncomfortable being there. Grant DeCroch never knew about Trey's affair with his wife, possibly saving Helene's marriage and a friendship and business acquaintance that meant a lot to Trey.

The jury was still out on Helene and Grant's future. And what about his own fragile marriage? Trey questioned the wisdom of his honesty about the affair. *I should have kept my mouth shut and just let it disappear with the wind. If so, maybe I wouldn't feel so damned guilty having my wife and ex-lover in the same room at the same time.*

Trey observed both women in their designer gowns, looking beautiful and seemingly content for the moment. He could only hope the two wouldn't come to blows. Or worse, let everyone in the ballroom know what was going on.

Trey felt thankful he'd talked Clyde into attending to act as interference, if necessary. While initially reluctant to do so, fearing he would feel out of place, Clyde had a sudden change of heart and was on board.

It had been an even bigger coup to get Ivana to attend this year's fundraiser. Trey had managed to impress upon her the importance of the cause not only for their people, but for business interests. It also happened to be a great occasion for networking and promoting car sales.

"Looks like we got a decent turnout," Trey told Clyde.

"Yeah, I'd say so."

"And that can only mean good news in raising money to fight sickle cell."

"I'll drink to that," Clyde said, lifting his champagne flute.

Trey put the glass to his mouth. He looked at Ivana, who also had champagne in hand. He feared that she would get plastered, embarrassing them both, in spite of promising him she would hold the line at one drink. But not bringing her to the most important social event of the year was not an option in Trey's mind. As his wife, Ivana's presence was important not only to show them as a couple, but to prove to her that his affair with Helene was history and he had nothing to hide.

Ivana pretended not to notice Trey watching her carefully, wondering if she would make a scene with his mistress whore. *Well, let him wonder.* Even if she were to give Helene De-Croch a piece of her mind, it would be something she deserved and damned long overdue.

For her part, Ivana would have preferred to be anywhere other than there, but succumbed to Trey's desire to at least keep up appearances for the sake of his business contacts—or potential thereof—if nothing else.

Is there anything real anymore about our relationship? Or are we to only pretend to be happy with each other for the rest of our lives?

She watched as Trey used a break in the lineup of guest speakers to disappear. Strangely enough, Ivana no longer saw Helene DeCroch. Coincidence? Or would Trey dare carry on with her here under the guise of a charitable cause?

"Are you all right?" Ivana heard the whisper in her ear. She turned and saw Clyde standing there. He was dashing in the ebony tuxedo, his head freshly shaved. She even liked the way he smelled—an enticing, woodsy cologne.

"I'm fine," she replied, feeling goose bumps in the nearness to her husband's brother and thankful for the distraction.

"I guess this really isn't your thing any more than mine?" Clyde said observantly.

Ivana smiled faintly. "Is it that obvious?"

"No, not really."

"Liar." She smiled again. "It's all right. I guess I felt more at home walking down the runway than being somewhere with a bunch of rich folks, all with their own agenda."

"Is that what this is all about?" Clyde made a face.

"More or less."

"Then I guess we must be talking about Trey too?"

"If the shoe fits," Ivana voiced unapologetically, then drank more champagne.

***

"You're looking as handsome as ever," Helene told Trey.

He blushed as they found a moment alone to speak. "Flattery will get you anywhere, except for—"

She laughed naturally. "Such a pity." Before Trey could respond, Helene said, "I'm only teasing."

Trey feigned a sigh of relief, though under other circumstances he might have been all too ready and willing to pick up where they left off six months ago. Only now he had no interest in messing up a nice friendship or betraying Ivana's trust again. Even if Helene was still drop-dead gorgeous in a form-fitting black halter gown.

"Good to hear." He nervously looked around, expecting Ivana to come upon them at anytime in attack mode. If not Grant.

"Relax, Trey," Helene told him. "We're at a fundraiser, remember. It's not like we're doing anything wrong as cosponsors of the event by talking."

"You're right, of course." Trey felt he was being a bit paranoid without just cause.

"This appears to have gone off without a hitch," she said. "I'm told that at least five-million has already been pledged."

"Oh, really?" Trey liked hearing that.

"Yes, and the night's still young."

"Can't wait to see what the final tally is."

"Neither can I." Helene grabbed a glass of champagne from a passing waiter. "So I'm still waiting to be formally introduced to your brother. Or are you trying to hide him from me?"

Trey cocked a half grin. "Not at all." He looked up and, to his surprise, saw Clyde approaching. Along with Grant De-Croch. "Looks like we've got company, including the man you're looking for."

"There you are, sweetheart," Grant said, and gave Helene a kiss on the lips. "Should've known you would be cavorting with Trey here. Don't let the man sell you another car. I think five are enough for now, don't you?"

Grant laughed at his own ostentatious humor and shook Trey's hand with a solid grip. "We did it. Everyone's going home happy tonight. I know I am."

Trey doubted the same could be said for him as he regarded the shorter, heavier man with a salt-and-pepper horseshoe hairline. "As well you should be, Grant." He glanced at Helene uneasily, and then at Clyde.

"I ran into your brother." Grant gazed at Trey. "Seems like an interesting young man."

"He is." Trey took a breath. "Helene, I don't believe I've introduced you to my kid brother, Clyde."

"Nice to finally meet you, Clyde," she said with a broad smile. "Trey's been bragging about bringing you into the family business."

"I think he's just afraid I'll end up with the competition," quipped Clyde.

Helene chuckled. "Who knows?"

"Over my dead body," voiced Trey with little humor.

"Don't think it'll have to come to that," Grant said. "He's far more valuable to you if you're alive, Trey."

Everyone laughed, then Grant abruptly grabbed his wife's arm and excused them to catch up with some other guests.

"Where's Ivana?" Trey asked Clyde, as her unofficial chaperone.

"She went to the ladies' room."

Good, then she probably won't bump into Helene, especially as long as Grant keeps her on a leash, thought Trey. "I see."

"So that's her, isn't it?" Clyde asked intuitively.

Trey lifted a brow. "Who?"

"The lady you got involved with?"

Trey wondered how he came to that conclusion. Could Grant have figured it out too?

"Yes, that's her," he admitted preferring Clyde heard it from him than someone else .

"I can see how you could have fallen for her," Clyde said. "She definitely has it going on."

"Yes, she does," Trey said, feeling regretful nonetheless. "Only Ivana has more going on."

Clyde gazed at him. "You're sure about that?"

Trey met his eyes. "What's that supposed to mean?"

"Well, you went after someone else. Ivana had to come in second at the time."

Trey wondered where the hell this was coming from. "That had nothing to do with my feelings for Ivana. Or the fact that I find her the most beautiful woman in the world."

"Sorry, man," Clyde said. "I'm not trying to cause anything. I think I know a little something about acting irresponsibly. I might've gone after Helene myself had the opportunity been there. The important thing is you owned up to it and are now back with your wife."

"Yeah, I am." Trey calmed down, realizing Clyde meant no harm and had been irresponsible far more in his life. Now they had both been given an opportunity to start over. "Speaking of my wife, I'd better go find Ivana."

"Probably a good idea," Clyde said in a friendly tone.

Clyde tasted the champagne, thinking about how Trey got testy when trying to defend his affair, as if he were allowed to make mistakes unlike others, which should then be pushed under the rug. Maybe Ivana would never let him forget the best thing in his life could slip right through his fingers. Clyde envisioned her in a red strapless gown that contoured perfectly to her slender body and nice-sized high breasts, turning him on. She would look even better with no clothing on at all. He tried to fight the obvious mutual attraction sexually, but found it getting more difficult by the day. He really did want to see things work out between Trey and his good-looking wife if this was possible. But was it?

Clyde sensed they still had a long way to go before getting it right again. In the meantime, he believed that Ivana's sexual energy was probably wound up about as tightly as his, ready to explode at any time. If not with Trey, then somebody else.

He watched his brother move briskly through the gathering, and pondered whether or not the marriage would or even should survive between the infidelity, miscarriage, and barriers the two had formed. Or had it already ended without either Trey or Ivana realizing it?

***

Ivana was at the mirror in the ladies' room applying lip gloss and feeling sorry for herself, when she saw the reflection of Helene DeCroch enter. Helene looked just as surprised when recognizing Ivana.

"Hello, Ivana."

"Helene."

These were the first words spoken between them this evening. Ivana had deliberately avoided any conversation for fear of speaking her mind. As she gathered herself, anger began to build up within like hot vapor. Ivana recalled first meeting Helene while she and Trey were at a restaurant. Even then, by Helene's body language and lack of eye contact, Ivana sensed that something might have been up between Helene and Trey, but tried to dismiss it as women's insecurity or paranoia.

Turned out that her fears were far from unfounded. Trey would later admit that the affair had been going on even then, right under Ivana's nose. And might be continuing to this day for all she knew.

"Are you still sleeping with my husband?" Ivana asked her point-blank.

Helene stopped brushing her hair and met Ivana's hard stare. "No, I am not. What happened between Trey and me happened a long time ago."

"Six months is *not* a long time!"

"Long enough for you to get over it. Can't you see that the man loves *you*?"

"Am I supposed to feel grateful for that when he chose to show that love by putting his penis inside you?" Ivana snapped.

Helene colored. "It was a mistake, all right? For both of us. Why don't we just leave it at that?"

Ivana got up in her face. "Why don't you go straight to hell!"

Helene backed away. "I'm not going to fight with you, Ivana, though I'm sure that would make you feel better about yourself. I can give you some advice, though. If you don't start treating Trey like a man you want to hold onto, you'll lose him for good."

Ivana closed the distance. "And what—he'll end up back in your bed?"

"I didn't say that."

"You didn't have to. Maybe I'll throw myself at your husband like a slut, too, and see if you still want to sleep with him every night afterward."

Helene looked almost to the point of tears. "Do what you have to do. Just remember what I said."

She grabbed her purse and went out the door.

Ivana had a good cry and then made herself presentable before leaving. Trey was waiting in the hall by the bathroom. She suspected he had talked to his former lover and was there to either comfort or lambaste her. She wasn't sure either mattered at this point.

"Ivana—" Trey said.

"Take me home now, please!" she demanded. "Or I'll get Clyde to do it so you can stay here with your precious charity ball and your slut."

Trey eyed her sadly, placing his arm around Ivana's shoulders. "We'll go home together."

Chapter Twelve

Willie sat at a table in the bar with his homie, Luther Raleigh. The two had hung out for a few years and had each other's backs. It was a bond Willie once had with Clyde Lancaster, 'til the stupid bastard turned on him in favor of a brother who never really gave a damn about him.

"This dude musta sucker-punched you to take out that eye," Luther said over his mug of beer.

Willie gazed at the tall, lanky man with a short, curly Afro. "Yeah, that's exactly what happened." He saw no reason to admit that Clyde had simply kicked his ass, even if Willie was positive the man was more lucky than skilled.

"So what you plan to do about it now that he's out?"

Willie drank beer, allowing it to go down slowly. "Still trying to figure that out. He's definitely gonna pay the price for what he did to me." And the friendship Clyde kissed goodbye.

"Why don't you just wait outside that huge house he's staying in and blow the dude's head off when he comes out?"

"Don't think I haven't thought about that," muttered Willie. "But I'm not crazy. I ain't going down for murder—not even for Clyde Lancaster."

Luther wiped his mouth. "So who says you got to make it easy for the police to come knocking at your door? Or don't you want him dead?"

"Yeah, I want him dead all right," Willie said bluntly. He pretended to point at Clyde and unload his three-fifty-seven Magnum, using Luther as a substitute. He flinched, as if really being shot. Willie grinned. "Be cool, man. Just practicing."

Luther's forehead furrowed. "Well, practice in a different direction."

Willie chuckled, then got real again. "I don't want Clyde dead just yet. Not 'til he's suffered some, so he knows what it feels like to lose somethin' important to him."

"You mean like his car? Or you want an eye . . . maybe both eyes?"

"I was thinkin' more like his old lady—if he had one. Or maybe his rich-ass brother, who feels he's better than us."

Luther got excited. "Yeah, offing his girl or brother would be payback."

"Big-time." Willie nodded, pondering the notion. "I'd save Clyde for last, then make him beg for his life, before ending it."

"Sounds good. When do you plan to make this happen?"

"When the time is right and he least expects it."

"You want me to take out his brother?" Luther asked.

Willie contemplated that. It would be a good way to get revenge while having someone else take the rap. But it would still leave him feeling incomplete. Unsatisfied. He needed a hands-on experience for justice to be served.

"Thanks, but I don't need you for this one. I'll handle it."

Luther flashed a look of disappointment. "If that's the way you want it."

"Yeah, it is." Willie finished off his beer. "Let's get outta here."

The two men walked from the bar, smoked a joint in Willie's car, and cruised the neighborhood.

Willie thought about spending the night with Roselyn. Using his considerable skills in the bedroom, he could make her willing to do anything to get off. He'd give her a call later and invite her over. Maybe she could even bring that stuck-up roommate along for a threesome. Or for Luther to have some fun with.

"Look over there," Luther got his attention.

Willie gazed across the street at a vendor selling hot dogs. Only one person was buying, an elderly man wearing a cheap suit. "So what about him?"

"You think he's got any money?"

Willie considered this. "Maybe. Or could be the dude's as broke as we are."

"What do you say we find out?" Luther took another drag of the joint.

Willie needed only a moment to agree. He wasn't much into taking reckless chances. But the man seemed harmless enough. And Willie expected to take two-thirds of whatever they got. "Let's do it."

They waited 'til the man paid for his hot dog and walked away from the vendor. Willie followed slowly. He couldn't let the man see his license plate and report to the cops. So he parked, deciding they would do this on foot and double around for the car later.

Willie took the three-fifty-seven out of his glove compartment, just in case, tucking it inside his pants. "Sure you wanna do this?" he asked Luther.

Luther hesitated, then grinned. "Yeah, might as well."

"All right then. Let's keep it short and simple."

They got out of the car and followed the man for a bit, before moving upon him swiftly.

"We want your money, man," Willie spat, his eye narrowed.

"What?" The elderly man looked dazed.

"You heard him," Luther followed. "Give it up—your wallet."

"I don't have much." He held onto the half-eaten hot dog haphazardly. "Why don't you go after someone else?"

"Because we chose you, asshole!" Willie glared. He removed the gun and stuck it in the man's stomach. "Just hand over the wallet and you live. Give us any trouble and you die. Which is it gonna be?"

The man seemed to nearly lose his balance, fear written all over his face. He took the wallet from his back pocket and handed it to Willie.

A wicked grin parted Willie's lips. "Smart move, old man. You got anything else in those pockets?"

The man swallowed nervously. "Nothing of value."

"I'll be the judge of that." Willie eyed Luther. "Check him."

Luther obeyed, removing a dirty handkerchief and a lottery ticket. "What's this?"

"Looks to me like the man's hoping to get a lucky payout," said Willie. "Only now he's giving us the chance to get rich. Ain't that right?"

The man remained mute.

Willie pushed the barrel of gun against his a rib cage, causing the man to wince. "I didn't hear you."

"Yes!" he sputtered.

Willie smiled. "That's more like it." He watched Luther put the lottery ticket in his pocket, as if his to collect. Willie planned to take possession of it later. He regarded the old man. "Walk away, and don't look back."

The man glowered, but wisely said nothing as he started walking.

Willie kept an eye on him for a few moments; then nudged Luther and the two ran in the other direction.

Luther laughed when they slowed down. "I thought that old fart's eyes were gonna pop out, he was so scared."

Willie chuckled, tucking the gun in his pants. "Good thing for him he didn't do anything stupid."

"Guess he liked living more than being in a coffin."

Willie was glad that had been the case. He doubted seriously he would have shot the man had it come down to that. Killing someone over a few bills was not in the cards. Wasn't worth doing hard time for. But killing someone out of hatred just might be.

Inside his car, Willie saw that the robbery had netted him $157 and a credit card, worth perhaps thousands more. All in a day's work, he thought gleefully. Now it was time to enjoy the night. Roselyn would provide the entertainment, and he would give her his undivided attention. Before turning it back to his nemesis, Clyde Lancaster.

Chapter Thirteen

Clyde sat in a chair opposite Stella Rockwell in Trey's office as Trey ran sales figures off like they were nothing or everything, interspersed with talking about inventory, incentives, disgruntled customers, and expansion. While trying hard to be interested, Clyde knew he'd rather be elsewhere, doing something that made him want to get up in the morning or night.

I don't want to let Trey down, but I don't want to continue to pretend that I'm made out to be a car dealership semi-executive.

"We have to keep our costs down, while maximizing profits," Trey was saying from behind his desk—or more lecturing in Clyde's mind. "Car sales have softened lately, but it doesn't mean we have to soften with them. I want us to look for any means to increase exposure and get the people in."

Stella pushed up her glasses. "I have some ideas I'd like to run by you."

Trey sat up. "I'm listening."

Ten minutes later, Clyde found all the attention on him. "What?"

"I'd like to know what you think about Stella's proposals."

"And don't hold back," she said. "I can take constructive criticism."

Clyde felt put on the spot. He couldn't really say for sure what he agreed on and what seemed unworkable. And that was what was so damned frustrating. He was out of his league here and knew it.

"This isn't working," he said flatly.

"What's that?" Trey said, peering at him.

"Me working for you."

Trey exchanged glances with Stella. "Can you excuse us for a minute?" he asked her.

"No problem." She looked at Clyde and stood. "I'll be in my office."

Trey saw her out, closing the door. "So what's up, Clyde?"

Might as well tell it like I see it. "What am I doing here?"

Trey raised a brow. "What do you mean?"

Clyde ran a hand across his mouth. "Who are we kidding— I don't belong here."

"Sure you do," Trey insisted, gazing at him.

"I'm sure I don't." Clyde's eyes steeled. "This is your dream, not mine. I'm just not cut out for the competitive, high-pressure world of car sales."

Trey sighed. "It doesn't happen overnight, Clyde. You've been here, what, a month? It's taken me more than ten years to learn the ropes, and I'm still learning."

"Maybe you're smarter than I am." Clyde wasn't sure he believed that—at least where it concerned common sense—but it seemed to fit where it involved the car sales business.

"Don't sell yourself short," Trey said. "You're my brother, Clyde, and I need you here."

Clyde looked at him with misgiving. "Why? So you can show all the folks here how you're doing the right thing by taking up your ex-con brother's lost cause?"

Trey scowled. "Now, where did that come from?"

Maybe I was a bit over the top there, thought Clyde. Or maybe right on the money.

"You don't need me, Trey, you never have. It's obvious that your businesses have prospered without any help from me. I'm happy for you and happy that Mama got to see all of this before she died—but I've got to do my own thing."

"And just what the hell is your thing?" Trey blasted. "Or are you still trying to figure that out?"

Clyde paused. "Yeah, that's exactly what I'm trying to do."

"So until you do, continue to work here, get your feet wet. You can walk out that front door anytime you like and I can't stop you. But don't do it 'til you have a viable alternative for making a living."

Clyde wanted to reject Trey's logic that sounded more like a bossy warning. Why did Trey always have to be so sensible—when it came to the business world at least? Whereas Clyde had far too often acted on impulse, and too often paid dearly for it.

"Yeah, all right," he gave in. "I'll stick around for a while."

"Good." Trey gave him a brotherly pat on the shoulder and smiled. "Now get out of here and let me make a few phone calls."

"Yes, sir, boss." Clyde gave him a mock salute and was out the door, while seriously wondering if this could ever work out. Or were they both deluding themselves in more ways than one?

Ivana spent the day getting pampered with a manicure, pedicure, and hair styling—deciding she was worth it, even if there was no one at home she wanted to look gorgeous for. Except maybe Clyde. She was sure he appreciated her appearance and probably fantasized about her as she did about him. But was that where he drew the line? What about her? And was it a line either dared cross?

She seriously doubted that Trey paid much attention these days—or cared—to how she looked. Especially if he still had his wandering eyes elsewhere.

Ever since her falling out with Trey a week ago at the charity ball, Ivana felt more and more distant from her husband, who seemed to enjoy having her and Helene DeCroch at his beck and call. Ivana wasn't sure she could compete with the beautiful wife of a hotel magnate, if Trey chose to be with her. Or that she should even try.

I still have my dignity, and won't simply allow him to walk all over me if this marriage has no solid future.

"Are you sleeping on me?" asked Ivana's hairdresser, Jacinta Bordeau. She was currently restyling Ivana's Senegalese twists to a corkscrew braid interlock.

"No, I'm wide awake," Ivana said, breaking out of her reverie.

"Could've fooled me," Jacinta said in a boisterous voice that matched her large girth. "I was asking if you and your man plan to do anything special for your anniversary this year?"

"Hadn't really thought about it," she admitted, sure that Trey hadn't either.

"Is the sex that lousy?"

"Excuse me?" Ivana tried to turn her head but Jacinta kept a firm grip.

"There's usually only two reasons married folks don't talk about that romantic anniversary getaway. One is they're too broke to do it. The other is that it's just not happenin' in the bedroom. Since I know that you and yours are rolling in the dough, can't be that, so must be the lousy sex. Am I right?"

Ivana was too shocked to be embarrassed. She was used to this sort of conversation with Jacinta, but rarely did they get into specifics, and Ivana liked it better that way.

On the other hand, why pretend she and Trey were Paradise Bay's golden couple as was often portrayed? When Trey had tarnished it much like fine silver?

"How about no sex?" Ivana admitted. Or as little as possible from her end.

"You're kidding me?" Jacinta leaned her face so Ivana could look at her disbelief.

"I wish I were."

"Is he seeing someone else?"

"Only he knows the answer to that." Ivana could only speculate and go by his track record, both of which had her cause for alarm.

"Are you seeing someone else?" Jacinta tossed at her bluntly. "I have to ask."

"No, I'm not sleeping with anyone." Not yet.

"So what's the problem? He can't get it up?"

"Trey's not a candidate for Viagra, if that's what you're getting at." Ivana felt she could read what was coming next. "And I'm not frigid." Or was she? Maybe Trey had made her frigid.

Then Ivana thought of Clyde and his feeling sexually aroused when he looked at her. Or vice versa. She couldn't help but believe they would be all over each other while between the sheets. *I'm definitely not a frigid woman.*

"I give up," voiced Jacinta in a huff. "Maybe you'd care to enlighten your nosy hairdresser?"

Ivana didn't want to spread her dirty laundry around town like a sexually transmitted disease. "It's complicated," she would only say.

"I already gathered that much."

I'll bet you have. Ivana wondered what she could say to satisfy Jacinta's curiosity. Then it came to her.

Even then, Ivana hesitated. "I'm attracted to my brother-in-law."

"Your husband's brother?" Jacinta asked, her eyes bulging.

Do I really want to admit to it? "Yes, as a matter of fact. He's staying with us for a while."

"Hmm . . . that is very interesting." Jacinta grabbed a row of Ivana's hair. "I don't wanna ask how far things have gone there, but I will anyway."

"I've haven't slept with him," Ivana made clear. "But he is hot and very sexy." And probably horny as hell.

"And your man's *brother*. Hope you know what you're doing, girl."

"I'm not doing anything," Ivana said. *Nothing that my man hasn't already done.* "Just talk, that's all. Don't pay me any mind."

Unfortunately, Ivana realized it was too late for that. She had already let the cat out of the bag—but had no idea if it would or should go any further than that.

Chapter Fourteen

"How are you getting along in the free world?" Raymond asked Clyde over the phone.

Clyde was walking though his brother's enormous home, still trying to figure out one way from the next.

"It's good, man," he answered, even if far from perfect thus far.

"What exactly does *good* mean?"

"Means it sure the hell beats being where you're at," Clyde gave a simple answer.

Raymond took a breath. "Yeah, I heard that."

Clyde passed by Trey and Ivana in the living room, which, by the look of them, almost seemed as if they had heard it too. He waited 'til getting out of ear range before saying in an undertone, "You only have, what, six weeks before you get to taste freedom yourself? It'll be here before you know it."

"I keep telling myself that. Helps the time go by faster."

"Yeah, been there, done that." Clyde stepped outside and let the afternoon sun bear down on his face.

"Still working for your brother?"

"Yeah," Clyde said reluctantly.

"Don't sound like you're where you want to be."

"I'm not," he admitted. Not by a long shot. "Just biding my time 'til something better comes along."

"You mean like us going into business together?" Raymond posed.

"Yeah, something like that."

"Cool. I think if we put our minds together, we can do something that'll bring in some bucks and keep us far away from this place."

"Sounds good." Clyde wanted nothing more than to go into business with or without Raymond. He was still short on capital, but long on ideas. At this point, all he could do was keep dreaming, and maybe something good would come out of it.

"Are you banging anyone yet?" Raymond asked straightforwardly.

"No, can't say that I am," Clyde replied honestly. Not that the thought hadn't entered his head. Or the opportunity hadn't presented itself.

"You can't be serious? All those fine, sex-starved broads out there and you still haven't scored?"

Clyde chuckled. "There's definitely some hot babes out here—but my mind's been on other things."

"Like what?"

"Like just trying to adjust. There's plenty of time to get a woman. When I do, I want it to be someone who means something to me other than an hour or two in the sack."

"Helluva lot more willpower than I do. I'll take an hour—make that all damned night long—with a woman as soon as I can get one, and worry about the *means something* bit later."

Clyde laughed. He used to think that way too. Still did to some degree. He thought about Ivana. He'd love to take her to bed, sure she would warm up the sheets in a hurry, if not set them on fire. Especially if she wasn't putting out for Trey. But where would that leave him once the dust settled? There could be no future for them. Trey would never part with her, if he read his brother correctly, even if things continued to be strained between him and Ivana to the point of no return. Not that Clyde would necessarily want that. Better to fantasize about Ivana than to act upon dangerous temptation.

"Just take it nice and slow, Raymond," Clyde advised him. "I'm sure she'll appreciate it even if you don't."

"I'll make sure she does," he said with a snicker. "Been waiting for that moment a long time now. When it comes, I'll definitely cherish every second."

So will I. Clyde wondered when that time would come and if it would mean as much afterwards.

Trey could tell by the gist of Clyde's phone conversation he was talking to one of his prison buddies. Big mistake. Cavorting with bad elements—even those still locked away—was not in Clyde's best interests. If he was too caught up in nostalgia to see that, it was up to Trey to set him straight, without seeming like he was meddling.

I see it as plain old common sense, from someone who doesn't want to see his brother end up back where he started. If not deeper in a hole.

Trey shared his feelings with Ivana, as they were spending what had been a relatively quiet time together before Clyde stepped in.

"Your brother's a grown man," she said sharply. "Maybe it's time you let him run his own life."

Trey begged to differ. "If someone had stepped in sooner when Clyde was heading down the wrong path, it might have made a difference," he reasoned. Not that he hadn't tried to offer his two cents before. Only Clyde wouldn't listen. Would it be any different now? If not, what would come next—reuniting with his old crony-turned-enemy Willie Munroe?

"Or it may have made no difference at all," Ivana retorted . "People have to make their own mistakes in life."

"Says who?" Trey looked at her over the kitchen counter-top. "Why make blunders now only to regret later, if you can change things?"

Ivana regarded him with asperity. "Will you listen to yourself? You aren't your brother's keeper, even if you'd like to think so. Maybe you need to put your *own* house in order, before you try to micromanage someone else's."

"It's not about micromanaging Clyde's life," Trey insisted, ignoring the jab at him. "All I'm trying to do is keep him from making the same poor choices that he made before."

"That's not up to you to decide."

Trey took a deep breath, deciding this was one debate he probably couldn't win. Since when had she taken it upon herself to stick up for Clyde? As if his brother couldn't fend for himself.

"Am I intruding on something?" Clyde asked, walking into the kitchen.

Trey's eyes turned to him. How much had he heard?

Should I interrogate him about who he was talking to and why he shouldn't be socializing with cons? Or would that only create more conflict and make me out to be the bad guy once again?

"You weren't intruding on anything," Trey told Clyde. "We were just having a little husband-and-wife disagreement. Everything's cool."

Clyde stood mute, shifting his eyes from one to the other, making Trey more than a little curious as to what was going on in that head of his. Maybe Clyde would fill him in.

"Well, I'm going to go take a shower," Clyde said, meeting Trey's gaze. "See you in a bit."

"We'll be here." Trey watched him walk away, and couldn't help but wonder what the future held for his kid brother. Not to mention for him and Ivana. Though they still had their good and bad days, Trey wanted to believe that all the negative stuff he and Ivana had gone through lately would pass. With their anniversary fast approaching, maybe they could do something special to celebrate the occasion and reignite their passions.

The Violet Supper Club was on Paradise Bay's posh east end and featured a piano player every night. Trey, Ivana, and Clyde sat at a table, enjoying the prize-winning cuisine and instrumental standards. The owner, a customer and friend of Trey's, had invited them. Trey was glad that for once he, his wife, and brother were all on the same page, wanting to have a good time without the drama.

"How's everyone doing this evening?" asked Blake Lewis, the owner of the club.

"Terrific," Trey responded, looking up at the sixty-something, tall, thin man, impeccably dressed as always in a double-breasted dark suit. He was aware that Blake was closing down his business at the end of year and heading to Florida for retirement.

Clyde and Ivana voiced the same sentiments and Blake smiled. "Now that's the way to go out, with nothing but satisfied clientele."

"It's not too late to change your mind," Trey said. "This town won't be the same without you."

Blake shrugged. "I doubt that. Fact is, I'm getting too damned old for this business. And supper clubs just ain't packing them in the way they used to. Probably because the hip-hop generation is taking over the music scene, if not great eateries. Besides, my wife's been bugging me to smell the roses before they end up on my grave. It's time I started listening to her."

"Can't argue with that philosophy," Trey said, glancing at Ivana and conceding that he had not listened to her as much as he should. He wondered if it was too late to open his ears and mind to what she had to say. "Well, I'm definitely going to miss you, Blake."

"Don't count me out yet. I'll still be around for a few more months. 'Til then, you and your family are welcome here anytime."

"Thanks, Blake." Trey felt the genuineness of the man and would truly be sorry to see him leave. His place was a landmark in Paradise Bay and would be hard to replace.

"In laying out the welcome mat so sweetly, Blake, we'll definitely take you up on that," Ivana said, smiling at him as he walked away. She sipped Pinot Noir, admittedly feeling a bit tipsy. She was sitting between Trey and Clyde and found herself tilted slightly toward Clyde, picking up the scent of Obsession he wore. Ivana wondered if he realized just how turned on she was by his powerful, manly presence. Or had she allowed just enough distance to keep him—and Trey—totally in the dark?

When Clyde looked her way, Ivana averted her eyes and pretended to be focused on the piano player. Only when she sensed that Clyde had turned his attention elsewhere did she once again admire him. Maybe if she had met Trey's brother first, her life might have turned out differently. Or would he too have betrayed her and fallen into the arms of another woman?

Let's not even go there. Trey and Clyde are brothers, but it doesn't mean they're both guided by the part of their anatomy below the waist over and beyond everything else.

Certainly Clyde had not shown himself to be a man who couldn't control his sexual impulses. Perhaps prison life had trained him to show restraint in going after what he wanted. Ivana pictured him as a patient lover who was as thorough as utterly demanding.

Ivana felt herself get aroused, and suppressed it while regarding Trey. He seemed heavy in thought. Perhaps he was thinking about his businesses and ways to make more money, which seemed to occupy much of his waking hours. Or was he remembering his time spent in bed with Helene DeCroch and wishing she were with him tonight instead of his wife?

The mere thought rankled Ivana. She finished off her wine and turned to Clyde. "Would you mind ordering me another drink?"

He glanced at Trey. "If you like."

She chuckled. "Yes, I like." *I like you as the bad-boy brother, who exudes sexuality.*

"Maybe you've had enough," Trey said, giving her a stern look.

"I'm not drunk, if that's what you're trying to say," she lied. "Just trying to enjoy the evening as you promised."

"Let's not make a scene, Ivana."

"I won't if you don't," she retorted. "I'm a grown woman, and capable of deciding for myself when I've had enough."

Trey frowned at her, "I don't think you are—not tonight."

Ivana eyed Clyde, sensing he was not eager to go against his brother in this instance, though she had little doubt that the more muscular Clyde could kick Trey's ass anytime he wanted. After all, wasn't that how he wound up behind bars?

She sneered at Trey, backing down. "Just forget it."

"It's forgotten," he said, seemingly pleased with himself.

"Think I'll go to the ladies' room, if it's all right with you?"

Ivana got up, half expecting him to follow her as she sat on the toilet. Her eyes met Clyde's, and Ivana imagined him joining her in the stall for some dirty sex. It turned her on.

Inside the bathroom, Ivana removed the flask of liquor from her handbag and downed a generous amount, feeling it drain down her throat.

She felt a sense of triumph in that moment, as well as sadness.

Clyde tasted his drink, feeling the friction between Ivana and Trey, even when they tried to sweep it under the rug. He regarded his brother as they sat alone. "Is she going to be all right?"

"She'll be fine," Trey answered tersely. "Ivana's never been able to hold her liquor very well, causing her to act bitchy at times. I admit it's gotten worse since the miscarriage."

Clyde thought about picking her up while inebriated. "What do you plan to do about it?"

"I guess bringing her to an establishment that serves alcohol probably wasn't the brightest idea," Trey said glumly.

"Practically every place serves alcohol. If you think she needs professional help, maybe you should suggest it."

"Maybe I will. And hope she's in a mood to listen."

Clyde watched Trey retreat to his own inner demons, then turned his thoughts to Ivana. Whatever issues she and Trey were going through, there was no denying the strong sexual vibes between him and his sister-in-law. Even right under Trey's nose. Clyde believed Ivana's libido was in overdrive, just like his. She was obviously not getting what she needed in bed from Trey. He wondered if his brother was still hung up on Helene DeCroch, though Trey insisted otherwise.

Better start satisfying your woman, bro, otherwise you just might lose her for good.

As much as Clyde tried to tell himself it was in his best interest to stay on the sidelines and let them work it out, he was beginning to believe otherwise. By living with his brother and sister-in-law, they had made him a part of their world, whether he liked it or not. Part of him admittedly got some sort of perverse thrill in knowing that Trey's ideal life had some serious potholes in it. The other side of Clyde, perhaps the dominant one, had no interest in coming between them, and only wanted Trey and Ivana to work out their differences and be happy.

Clyde hoped such happiness would come his way someday in a special woman who could give him everything he needed, and take whatever she wanted from him. In the meantime, he felt the heat emanating from Ivana working its magic on him, slowly but surely.

Fortunately, he was distracted by something else that played with his psyche. He found himself remarkably at home in the club. It wasn't exactly jumping, and the piano music was a bit bland, but he could imagine much more from a place like this. If it were his, Clyde was certain he could make it into something special.

Maybe this is just what I've been looking for. My own club, that I could run my way and bring something new to the table in Paradise Bay.

Clyde tasted the wine and came back down to earth. It was a pipe dream that he was sure wouldn't fly. For one, he didn't have even a fraction of the money it would take to buy the place, and likely wouldn't even a few months from now when the club was slated to shut down.

I can't ask Trey to help me out, even if the man is drowning in dough. Clyde's pride wouldn't let him go down that road. Besides, he could envision Trey dismissing the idea as foolish, especially given his desire that Clyde continue to work—or slave—for him.

Damn him for thinking he knows what's best for my life. Even who my damned friends should be. Clyde sucked in a deep breath.

That was the control freak in Trey, wanting to be the man running the show. Much like with his wife, only he didn't always play by the rules where it concerned doing right by her.

"How're you doing over there, little brother?" Trey asked, as if sensing his unease.

Clyde immediately buried his resentment, offering a lackadaisical smile. "I'm cool, man."

"You sure about that?"

Clyde glanced up and saw Ivana. She smiled sexily at him and seemed to have gotten herself back together. "Yeah, I'm sure."

Chapter Fifteen

Willie put his face between Roselyn's thighs and tickled her clitoris with his tongue. She giggled and moaned while spreading her legs further, urging him on.

"Ohh . . . that feels so good," cooed Roselyn.

"I know it does, baby." He continued to pleasure her.

Roselyn quavered. "Willie, I'm not sure I can stand much more."

He felt the same, his erection throbbing like crazy. "You're ready for me then?" As if he had any doubt.

"You know I am. I want you inside me. Now!"

"If that's what you want, I'm here to give it to you," he said hungrily.

He lifted up and barely took a moment to suck some air in his lungs before climbing atop her body and pushing himself inside her. She bent her knees and squeezed his hips.

"Go deeper," she practically screamed.

"Yeah, no problem," he yelled, and slammed into her again, and again, and again.

"I'm 'bout to cum." Roselyn clawed at his back.

Willie winced in pain and pleasure. "Go ahead and do your thing. We can cum together."

The bed shook as the powerful explosion reverberated through them as their mouths locked together in a succulent kiss.

A few moments later, it was over. Willie flopped down on top of her, catching his breath.

"Take all the time you need," she hummed, wrapping her arms around him. "I want you to keep your energy up for the next round."

Willie groaned. *This bitch could go all night, if she were able and willing*. Maybe after he smoked a joint, the feeling would hit him again and he could satisfy her and himself.

He lifted up. "Let's get high."

Roselyn licked her mouth eagerly. "Yeah, let's."

Willie grinned. Once they both got a good buzz, there might be no stopping them in the sack.

Two hours later, Willie had backed up his words, having lost count of the times they had given each other orgasms.

"You got any money?" he asked after buttering her up.

"Some."

"Then some will have to do."

Roselyn rolled her eyes. "What for?"

He glared at her. "Just some business, baby, that's all."

"Okay," she uttered without protest.

Willie kissed one of her breasts and watched the nipple rise. She'd earned that pleasure. He was glad to see that she hadn't let that bitch she roomed with poison her mind against him. A woman was supposed to help her man out when he needed it—in and out of bed. And he had no problem exploiting that. So long as they were both getting what they wanted out of this relationship, everything was cool. Once that was no longer the case, it would be time to move on and see what else was out there for him.

Willie drove around the block several times with Luther, casing the car dealership on the corner of Gleason and Twenty-fourth Street that was owned by Trey Lancaster. Willie had heard that it got more business than any other car dealership in Paradise Bay. Meaning it might be a good place to keep plenty of dough and other valuables—along with the cars themselves.

It struck Willie that this was a way to pay back Clyde for starters—by hitting his big brother—and ultimately him—where it hurt most.

I'm gonna enjoy this, Willie thought, feeling an adrenaline rush. He circled the place one more time.

"You sure you're up for it?" he asked Luther.

"Yeah, man, let's do it."

"All right."

The dealership was closed for the day, and traffic in the business area was sparse. Willie parked in the back. He popped the trunk, and they took out black ski masks, gloves, and bats.

After donning the ski mask and gloves, Willie looked to his partner in crime, who had done the same. "You know what to do."

Luther nodded.

Willie led the way, crossing over a small chain-link fence. In the lot, there were lots of brand new, shiny, expensive vehicles. He made his way to a car and slammed the bat into the hood, denting it; then smashed the bat against the front window, cracking it. Another hit and glass went flying. He did more damage to the car's sides.

Willie grinned with satisfaction. He glanced over his shoulder and saw that Luther was doing much of the same in defacing cars.

Let's see how many people will want to spend big bucks on these now!

After taking the bat to a dozen other cars, Willie made his way to the showroom windows, where Luther was waiting.

"There's probably a silent alarm," Luther noted warily. "And security cameras too."

"Yeah, I'm sure. But that means we got to be quick about it," Willie said. He rammed his bat into the front window, causing pieces to fly in different directions. Luther joined in on the vandalism.

The two men entered the dealership through the opening they created and spread out, damaging what they could along the way and grabbing anything small of value.

Willie found his way to the offices and stopped at one that had the nameplate CLYDE LANCASTER. *So he sold out after all once his rich brother dangled a carrot or two in front of him. Bastard!*

This angered Willie even more. He went into the office, tossing things off the desk and smashing them, imagining each item was Clyde, who bore the brunt of his hatred and envy.

Luther ran into the office. "C'mon, man, we gotta get outta here. The cops are coming."

Willie muttered an expletive, wishing they had more time to leave a calling card. "Yeah, all right, let's go."

The two ran out the broken front window and across the lot, waiting 'til they were off the premises before removing the ski masks. Willie glanced across the street and made eye contact with a woman before she ran inside a building. He dismissed it as no big deal and continued to the car, where they put the masks, gloves, and bats back in the trunk.

Willie sped away from the scene, feeling a sense of accomplishment, even as he contemplated more to come before his revenge against Clyde was complete.

Trey was awakened by a phone call. He looked up through sleepy eyes and saw that it was almost four in the morning. *What the hell?* He reached onto the nightstand and grabbed his cell phone. The caller ID revealed that it was Stella on the other end.

"Hey, Stella—"

"Sorry to wake you, Trey," she said. "Someone just broke into the dealership on Gleason."

"What?" He became alert.

"Probably some kids. Apparently they damaged some cars and did a real number in the showroom. The police are there now."

"Damn!" Trey cursed. "I'm on my way."

"You and me both," Stella said tersely. "I'll see you there."

Trey hung up, furious that one of his dealerships had been targeted. He knew that there had been a rise in juvenile vandalism in the area lately, but didn't expect it to hit him. After all, he had been actively involved in reaching out to young people through grants, appearances, and even internships.

Now they do this to him?

What had he done to deserve it?

Trey got dressed quickly. He left his room and stopped briefly in front of Ivana's room, where he thought about waking her up with the news. Trey nixed the idea, deciding he could tell her just as easily when he got back. No need in disrupting her beauty sleep and give her something else to bitch about.

"What's up?" Clyde asked, coming out of his room in pajama bottoms.

Trey's brow bridged. "Someone went after the dealership— did some damage."

"Sorry to hear that."

"Yeah, me too."

"Hang on for a moment," Clyde said. "I'm coming with you."

"You don't have to."

"I want to. Besides, if I'm really part of your business, I need to be able to deal with the ugly side too."

Trey could not argue the point. He wanted Clyde to be there with him through thick and thin, as brothers. "You're right. Let's do this together."

The damage done was worse than Trey thought. The vandals had destroyed virtually everything in sight. He hated to think what this would do to his insurance premiums. Not to mention scaring the hell out of his employees.

Trey reviewed the surveillance tapes along with Stella, Clyde, and the police. There were two vandals—both wearing ski masks and gloves, while using bats to do their damage.

"We probably won't come up with much to identify the perpetrators from the videos," muttered Detective Harold Zabrinski. "They were at least smart enough not to show their faces and to avoid leaving fingerprints."

"I call it just plain stupid to do something like this," Stella said sourly.

"Yeah, tell me about it," seconded Trey.

"Do either of the perps look familiar to you?" the detective asked. "Maybe you recognize them by their height or build? Sometimes these people like to case the place before they hit it."

Trey studied the video images. He wished he could say that either man was familiar to him, but couldn't. That made it all the more frustrating. "I'm sorry, Detective. We get hundreds, if not thousands of people in here each month. It could've been any of them, or none of them."

Zabrinski pinched his long nose and eyed Clyde. "How about you? Recognize either of these men?"

Trey studied his brother, noting that Clyde seemed to be off in his own little world. Was he even paying attention to what was going on? Or was there something more to his rumination?

Clyde felt the intensity of the detective's stare, as though sensing he'd spent time in prison and believed he may have been in on this crime committed against his own brother. The mere notion insulted Clyde, particularly after the sacrifice he'd made years ago trying to protect Trey at the expense of his own freedom.

He focused on the tape of the vandals. Looked just like any other assholes up to no good. *I suppose if I let my imagination run away with me, one of the men does have a similar build to Willie Munroe.* But it didn't mean it was him. Did it? Surely the man, with his one good eye, wasn't stupid enough to try something like this? Not that intelligence was one of Willie's stronger points.

Clyde considered the number that had been done on his own office as though it were personal. Was it?

He realized that with nothing more to go on other than a vague possibility, it would be foolish to bring it up. That would mean answering questions about his history with Willie.

That could somehow end up making me a suspect in the detective's mind, if not Trey's.

"I wish I did recognize them," Clyde said evenly. "But without seeing their faces, who knows?"

"You can be sure *someone* knows," Zabrinski said disappointedly. "We'll stay on top of it and hope we get a break somewhere down the line. In the meantime, if I were you, Mr. Lancaster, I'd beef up my security measures to prevent this from happening again."

Trey's jaw clenched. "Oh, I can guarantee that, Detective. I'm not about to let common hoods destroy everything I've worked for—beyond what they already did."

Clyde met his gaze, wondering what Trey was thinking beyond the words. He decided to give him the benefit of the doubt that Trey was not accusing him of anything. Perhaps he was thinking it would be one hell of a cleanup today. And they all had to do their part, Clyde included. He wasn't afraid to get his hands dirty.

Could Trey say the same?

A half hour later, Zabrinski reported to Trey and Clyde that they had a witness.

Trey perked up at the thought that someone had seen the crime taking place. They just might catch the sons of bitches after all who used his car dealership for batting practice. "I'm listening," he said with anticipation.

"I wouldn't get too excited," the detective warned. "A cleaning woman who works across the street reported seeing two men in the alley behind the dealership around the time of the crime. She said she only got a brief look at them and couldn't be sure what she saw—only that neither man was wearing a ski mask. Not much, but it's a start. We're having a sketch artist come out and see if he can coax more out of the woman."

Trey got the feeling they were basically back where they started. "Was she able to describe either man?"

"She claims she only honed in on one of them," Zabrinski said. "African American, thirties, tall, muscular with dreadlocks. Either of you know anyone like that?"

The detective locked eyes with Clyde. "Doesn't ring a bell," he said.

"Same here," Trey added.

Zabrinski frowned. "Well, ask around. You never know if any of your employees might recognize the description and be able to put a name to a person."

"Are you saying you think it could've been an inside job?" Trey glared in disbelief.

"Can't rule anything—or anyone—out," he responded tartly.

Trey understood it was just standard procedure, but he wasn't buying that an employee would be involved in such a cowardly, despicable thing. For what purpose?

"You're definitely barking up the wrong tree, Detective, if you think for one minute that someone employed here would orchestrate this act of vandalism—especially since it appears that property damage was the primary motivation."

Trey noted that a few items had been stolen—some gold pens, expensive knickknacks, and personal items. But did this constitute a cause and effect?

"I'm sure you're right," Zabrinski said. "Just trying to cover all the bases. Have you fired anyone lately?"

Trey thought about Larry Kellogg, whom he'd canned a couple of months ago. It was not an amicable parting. Could Larry have stooped this low? Why now?

"There was someone recently . . ."

Clyde watched the detective write down information on this Larry Kellogg. For Clyde's part, he didn't know the man. Or if he was capable of committing such a crime. What Clyde did know was the description of the suspect, general as it was in the African American community, sounded a lot like the Willie Munroe he had run into at the tavern a few weeks back.

The man was definitely capable of committing the crime, having been there, done that other times. And much worse.

Willie still harbored a grudge against him. And Trey by association. Clyde wouldn't put it past him to have orchestrated this.

Think I'll have to pay the man a visit, he told himself. Before he made an accusation and involved Trey or the police, it was best to handle this himself. If Willie had gone after Trey, Clyde wanted to make him pay, one way or another; though mindful that this was where he got into trouble before, and had no desire for history to repeat itself. Unless the situation got out of his control.

Chapter Sixteen

Ivana sipped on a cup of coffee in the living room. She had a hangover from the night before with one dry martini too many. She was sure Trey's two snoops, Francine and Emily, had reported her every move or misstep back to him. Damn them. She didn't appreciate being spied on. So what if she drank a bit too much at times to cope with things? Or was bitchy. It was none of their damned business.

Ivana pulled the silk and cashmere robe over her bare shoulder and tasted more coffee. Her thoughts turned to where Trey and Clyde might have gone so early this morning. Since they never bothered to tell her, she could only guess. Perhaps it was to get to the dealership first thing, in Trey's obsession to make over Clyde into the man he wanted him to be. She could even imagine them going to a brothel to fulfill the needs that neither seemed to be getting elsewhere these days. Trey had already shown himself to be

untrustworthy when it came to sex. So why not
corrupt his brother too? Or would she beat him
to the punch on that one?

Ivana allowed her mind to indulge the possibility, and the type of demanding lover Clyde
might be, when the front door opened, bringing
her back to reality. She assumed it was the cook
or housekeeper, ready to do their duties while
keeping an eye on her.

Instead, it was Trey who walked into the room.
He looked disheveled, disturbed.

"What happened?" she asked, expecting to see
Clyde over his shoulder, but did not.

"Someone vandalized the dealership," said
Trey.

"My goodness." Ivana's eyes widened in shock.
"Did the police get whoever did it?"

Trey sighed. "I wish. They've got some leads
they're following, but I'm not holding my breath
for any immediate results."

Ivana wasn't sure whether to comfort him in
her arms. Or remain at arm's length. She wished
their relationship hadn't deteriorated to the
point where they were pretty much like intimate
strangers. And whose fault was that?

"Where's Clyde?" she wondered.

Trey scratched his head. "Damned if I know.
We left and came back together, then Clyde got
in his car and said there was something he had
to do."

"Such as?" *Perhaps I shouldn't pry as if I have a right to. Clyde's a big boy and is capable of having a life of his own without Trey looking over his shoulder.*

"You'll have to ask him. I'm going to take a shower."

"Maybe I'll do just that," Ivana said, curious about what his brother was up to when not at work or home. Could he have a lover? Did she really want to know? Obviously Trey had more important things on his mind. This, no doubt, worked to Clyde's advantage. Might it work to hers as well?

"I'm looking for Willie Munroe." Clyde stood at the door of the last known address he had for Willie. It was a saltbox house in the seedier part of town.

"He don't live here no more," a woman said.

She was in her late twenties and pregnant. Clyde considered if Willie might be the father, but decided it wasn't his concern. "Do you know where I can find him?"

"Who's askin'?"

"Clyde. We go back a ways."

She regarded him suspiciously. "You're probably better off not looking him up for old times' sake. The man is no good."

Tell me about it. Clyde wondered what hell he had put her through, if not getting her pregnant. "Sometimes people change."

She snickered. "What planet you from? Willie Munroe ain't never gonna change. He married my sister, then made her life so miserable that she left his ass, taking their son with her."

So Willie had a son. Probably did him a favor by being as far away from Willie's bad influence as possible.

"Sorry to hear about that."

"Yeah, well, Katie has a real man now, so it worked out for the best."

Clyde was inclined to agree. "I still need to see Willie. Can you help me out?"

She touched her belly as if to feel the child kick. "I heard he's staying at the Strawberry Ridge apartments off Tulane Road. Don't ask me which one."

"Thanks." Clyde looked at her and hoped she wouldn't be bringing up that child alone, only to put the kid at a disadvantage right from the start as too many children were these days.

It took less than ten minutes for Clyde to find the place. He didn't even have to look further, for there was Willie, along with another man. They were standing in front of an apartment talking. Clyde speculated that the man could have been one of the men he saw in the surveillance video, fitting the physical characteristics, with Willie being the other.

Or maybe I'm way off base. Something told Clyde otherwise. He watched as the other man left, got in a car, and drove away. *Now it's time to find out if Willie was behind the vandalism. If so, he had to be held accountable for it.*

Willie inhaled meth into his nose through a rolled-up dollar bill. He winced from slight discomfort before smiling at the anticipation of the drug taking effect. Already, he felt good this morning, knowing that he had put a serious hurt on Clyde and his brother. Maybe that would teach them a lesson on messing with Willie Munroe. With more to come.

Willie closed his eyes and experienced the high while thinking about Roselyn going down on him. He'd make that come true today and give as much in return, enjoying watching her get off.

The knock on the door startled Willie, caught in his buzz and slightly disoriented. He got up from the couch and lumbered toward the door. Probably Luther wanting to get in on the meth, he thought. Better yet, maybe Roselyn decided to take the day off and spend it with him.

Willie grinned at the latter notion as he opened the door. The smile left his face when he saw Clyde Lancaster standing there, scowling at him.

"What the hell do you want?" Willie tried not to show the trepidation he felt.

Clyde's nostrils flared. "I want to know if it was you and your buddy who used bats to vandalize my brother's car dealership."

Willie's first thought was to admit to it and dare him to do anything about it. But that didn't seem like his smartest move under the circumstances. "Don't know what you're talkin' about."

"Like hell you don't!" Clyde barked. "I can tell when you're lying through your meth-stained teeth."

Sensing that he would not take no for an answer, Willie panicked and tried to shut the door in his face. Clyde blocked it with his arm, forcing it open and propelling them both inside.

Looking around the untidy, cluttered living room with an unpleasant odor permeating the air, Clyde first honed in on remnants of the methamphetamine crystals on the coffee table. Next to that, he spotted two gold pens and a plaque from the dealership—unmistakable evidence that the son of a bitch had been there and taken what was not his.

"You bastard!" Clyde glared at him, lower lip hanging.

Willie growled. "If you want a piece of me, man, take your best shot!"

This show of guts made Clyde hesitate for a moment. He thought back to their last confrontation, and the fact that he nearly killed Willie and ended up going to prison. Did he really want to go down that road again?

Before Clyde could answer the question, Willie charged at him like a bull. Bracing himself, Clyde took the hit, but still went tumbling down from the force. Willie climbed atop him and landed a solid blow to Clyde's left cheek, momentarily dazing him.

"It's time I finished what you started years ago," Willie spat.

But in that moment, Clyde had recovered, partially blocked the next blow intended for his face, and landed one of his own. Then another, hitting Willie squarely between the eyes.

Willie grabbed his face, moaning, and Clyde hit him again in the soft part of his stomach before flipping them both to the side and gaining the upper hand by getting on top of Willie.

He managed to land a wild punch that hit the side of Clyde's nose, drawing blood. Clyde bit back the pain and smashed a fist in Willie's face, and two more, bloodying it. Raising his fist for another punch, this time to Willie's bad eye, he watched as Willie cowered, trying to cover his face.

"Don't—" he said, whimpering. "Don't hit me no more."

Clyde shot him a hard look, wanting more than anything to punch his lights out—this time for good. The same way Willie had battered the cars at the dealership. Clyde felt the rage he had nearly a decade ago when he and Willie came to blows. And for the same reason—trying to do right by Trey.

This time, Clyde held up from acting further on impulses. He had no desire to kill Willie or cause serious injury. Or even turn him over to the police. It would only end up leading back to him. Clyde imagined that even Trey would probably place the blame on him, and things between them would go back to where they were before.

Not this time.

He opened up his fist and grabbed Willie by the collar. "You're not worth killing, asshole. If you think you owe me for what went down in the past, the debt has been settled in full by what you and your boy did to my brother's dealership. The cops will never know, and you won't get to see what it's like to spend time in prison for breaking and entering, destruction of property, and more. It's over, Willie, and I never want to see your face again!"

Willie sniffled, but otherwise remained mute. Clyde curled a lip and read into the silence. "I think we understand one another." He got up off Willie and backed away, keeping an eye on him 'til he was out the door.

By the time Clyde had driven away from the complex, he had second thoughts on coming in the first place. He also felt a sense of accomplishment. He had discovered who was behind the vandalism and dealt with it in his own way. And hopefully, had settled the ongoing feud with Willie Munroe once and for all.

Willie was still in pain when he finally got to his feet, blood spurting out of his nose and mouth. Once again, he had been humiliated by Clyde, who had taken it on his shoulders to protect his big brother's interests. Willie felt lucky to be alive, knowing that with Clyde's temper rivaling his own, the bastard could easily have killed him.

He flopped down on the couch and considered his next move. *If you think this is over, think again. It ain't over 'til I make you wish you'd finished me off while you had the chance.*

Willie felt his strength returning on that thought. He reached down and finished off the meth to ease the discomfort and lift his spirits, if only temporarily.

Chapter Seventeen

"What the hell happened to you?" Trey watched as his brother practically staggered into the house. Clyde had a bloody nose and a nice-sized welt on his cheek.

"Nothing," Clyde mumbled. "Just had a little incident, no big deal."

Trey's brows stitched. "Don't tell me it's no big deal. Who did this?"

Clyde hesitated, looking away, then back at him. "I went to see Willie Munroe—"

"What?" Trey hit him with a look of incredulity that he would actually have gone within a hundred feet of the man he went to prison for. "Tell me you're not serious?" It was obvious to him by the expression on Clyde's bruised face that he was quite serious. "Now why would you do something stupid like that?"

Clyde winced, while offering no response, as Ivana approached them.

"You're hurt," she said maternally, touching his cheek.

"I'm fine," he insisted, pushing her hand away.

"I don't think so. I'll go get something to wipe the blood from your nose, since your brother hasn't offered to do anything." She glared at Trey and headed for the bathroom.

Clyde sniffed and faced Trey. "I thought Willie might have been responsible for the vandalism at the dealership."

"And so you went after him yourself like the damned Lone Ranger?" Trey said angrily. "What on earth were you thinking, Clyde . . . that you were better equipped to go after him than the police? Do you want to end up back in prison?"

"No, I just wanted to talk to him, that's all. But things got a little out of hand."

"Yeah, I can see that."

"It looks worse than it is," Clyde said with a shrug.

Trey wanted to feel sympathetic, and maybe he did in a way. But the better part of him was annoyed that Clyde could be so reckless. *Why am I not surprised? Isn't that the way he's been all his life? Why should things change now that he's supposed to be more mature and getting his life in order?*

Ivana returned with a wet facecloth and some napkins. "Hold still," she told Clyde, applying pressure to a nostril to stop the bleeding.

"When did you become a nurse?" Clyde asked, frowning.

"Since you seemed like you needed one." She wiped his face.

"What he needs is a damned shrink!" Trey blared. "You could have gotten yourself killed. Was it worth dying for in going after this man?"

"No," Clyde conceded. "It was a dumb thing to do."

"Well, I'll do something smart for both of us." Trey took his cell phone from his pocket.

"What are you doing?" Clyde's mouth flew open.

"Calling the police. If you've found out who was responsible for the vandalism, we need to notify the authorities."

"It wasn't him," Clyde said quickly.

Trey fixed his eyes. "You're saying Willie wasn't involved in this at all?"

"He didn't do it, man," his brother insisted. "I checked out Willie's place and his car and didn't see anything that was stolen from the dealership."

"So why the hell did you get into a fight with him?" Trey asked suspiciously, though he had a pretty good idea.

"What difference does it make?" Ivana asked snappily. "He's home safe now. That's all that matters."

Trey was taken aback by his wife's acting in defense and being protective of Clyde. Where did this come from? Yes, he knew that things had become more conciliatory between the two lately. Still, Trey had assumed that deep down Ivana still saw his brother as little more than an untrustworthy ex-con taking up space in their precious house. Obviously Clyde's presence, for better or worse, was having a positive effect on her. But at that moment, Trey saw Ivana as interfering in something that was between him and his brother.

"That isn't all that matters," Trey begged to differ, casting a sharp eye on his brother. "Confronting this man like you did was not only reckless but could've put us all in danger. Is that what you want, Clyde?"

"No, man, it's not what I want." Clyde's expression turned rigid. "It wasn't my intention to put anyone in danger. I thought Willie matched the witness's description of one of the vandals. I figured if I brought it up, that detective would start asking me all kinds of questions, and didn't want to deal with that. So I tracked Willie down and . . . well, he wasn't exactly happy to see me, so we got it on. I'm sorry. Won't happen again."

"You sure as hell better make sure of that," Trey said in a tough tone, feeling it was best in this situation than going too soft on him. "Let the police do their job from now on, and you concentrate on your own."

"Yes, masser," Clyde responded sardonically.

"Don't go there." Trey gave him an uneven look. "I'm not trying to boss you around."

"Could've fooled me."

"I just don't want that hot head of yours to cause you to lose your good judgment," Trey said firmly. *Or make me look bad in my own judgment in attempting to steer you in the right direction.*

"I think you made your point loud and clear," Ivana said.

"Yeah," muttered Clyde.

Trey could only hope that was the case. The last thing he wanted was to see Clyde get mixed up with the likes of Willie Munroe again—only to wind up back in the slammer, badly injured, or dead.

"Why don't you go clean yourself up?" Trey told him.

"I'll do that. " Clyde turned to Ivana. "Appreciate your help."

"It was nothing," she said, giving him a gentle smile.

After Clyde disappeared, Trey faced his wife. "It's commendable that you think it's okay for my brother to kick someone's ass whenever he damned well pleases, but that's not how it works in a law-abiding society."

"Don't patronize me," Ivana replied. "Clyde thought he was helping you. Maybe you should give a little credit where credit's due instead of riding him hard all the time."

Trey could barely believe his ears, considering how she had been treating him more often than not. "Clyde is not a kid anymore. He's got a felony record. Beating up someone is a parole violation that could get him thrown back in the slammer. If I can impress upon him that provoking violence is not worth losing his freedom, then I sure as hell will do it every time!"

"All right, I get it. Excuse me for caring."

"You really do care about him, don't you?" Trey studied her face.

Ivana paused. "I thought that was what you wanted when asking me to let him stay with us?"

"That is what I wanted," he conceded, remembering how difficult it was to get her on board with the idea that they would be housing Clyde once out of prison.

"Are you sure? Otherwise I'll be happy to make his life miserable again."

Trey laughed. "No, don't do that, please." He put his arms around her, pulling her to his chest. It felt good to be so close. "Just keep doing what you're doing. Clyde can use a friend. And so can I."

Trey wished they could remain like that for the rest of the day. Ivana seemed to need it as much as him. Unfortunately, his business had been hit, and it was up to him to hold things together and keep up employee morale while the case was being investigated.

Chapter Eighteen

Trey checked in at the front desk of the Las Vegas hotel where he was staying overnight for a meeting with some potential investors. He was always interested in listening to people who wanted in on one of his businesses and were prepared to pay the price. Trey had chosen not to bring Clyde along, deciding it was better that he stay behind and learn to work with Stella, independent of him.

Trey called Ivana from his suite, and got her voice mail when he would have preferred the real person. "It's me. Just wanted to let you know I made it safe and sound. I'll call you this evening. Love you. Bye."

Trey thought of how many times he had told Ivana he loved her, something he never considered routine. Yet the words had rarely been bounced back his way in recent memory. Did Ivana still love him? Or had it become more of a marriage of convenience for her?

His cell phone rang, and Trey lit up for a moment, thinking it might be Ivana. Instead, it was Stella.

"I wanted to catch you before the meeting," she explained.

"Is something wrong?"

"No, other than the fact that it looks like a major storm is headed our way."

Trey rubbed his nose. "Sounds nasty. Let's hope its come and gone by the time I get back in the morning."

"Wouldn't count on that," Stella cautioned. "It's supposed to stick around for at least a couple of days. Anyway, those incentives have helped sales go through the roof last month."

"Really?"

"Yes. I was just looking at the numbers."

"Well, that's certainly something good to know to entice the investors." Especially after the troubles they had two weeks ago with the vandalism, and the culprits still at large.

"Hey, every little bit counts, like I was telling your brother."

"I hope he was listening," Trey said.

"Oh, I think so. Give him time and I know he'll make you proud."

"He already has." Trey truly meant this, even if he probably didn't express it as much as he should, and in spite of some ill-advised actions on Clyde's part. His brother did really seem to be trying, and that was more than half the battle.

After tidying himself up a bit, Trey was out the door, thinking of how nice it would be for him and Ivana to vacation in Vegas. Maybe for their anniversary. It was a pleasant dream, anyway.

Clyde was glad to escape the rain as he entered the tavern. Mindful of his last visit there, he hoped to hell he didn't run into Willie again, though he suspected the man wanted no part of him anymore.

Sitting at the bar, Clyde ordered a malt liquor from the female bartender. She was attractive and in her mid twenties.

"Sure thing," she said. "Nasty out there, isn't it?"

"Yeah, nasty." Clyde shook his head like a dog with fleas, releasing water to the floor.

"I'm pretty much used to this stuff where I come from," she said coolly.

He studied her. She was slender, on the tall side, with long, dark-brown crinkled locks, and bold hazel eyes. "I take it you're not from around here?"

"You're right." She gave him no further information, instead sliding the beer toward him and taking his money.

"Albert wouldn't happen to be around, would he?"

She smiled, displaying straight white teeth. "Yes, he would happen to be."

"Think I could have a word with him?"

"That would be up to him," she said. "What's your name?"

"Clyde."

She met his gaze. "I'll check, Clyde." After taking a couple of steps, she faced him again, and said, "By the way, my name's Stefani."

Clyde watched as she sashayed away with a perfect strut. *Nice form to go with the good looks. A surefire way to keep the drinks coming.*

A moment later, Albert came from the back. "Wondered if you'd ever show your face here again," he said. "Though I wouldn't have blamed you much had you kept your distance after Willie nearly ruined everything."

"Not a chance." Clyde grinned dismissively. "Couldn't keep me away."

"Good to know." Albert gave him a hug across the bar. "I see you met my niece."

"Niece?" Clyde couldn't hide his surprise. "Stefani?"

"I've only got one," answered Albert with a nod. "She's in town for a few days."

"Yeah, she suggested as much. Keep it all in the family, huh?"

"Not really. She's just subbing for a few hours 'til the regular bartender comes in. I taught her a few tricks of the trade."

"I see." Clyde tasted his drink thoughtfully.

"Stefani's from Seattle. She comes down here every now and then to visit friends and of course, her ornery uncle—her words, not mine."

Clyde laughed. "Maybe she knows you better than you know yourself."

"Maybe." Albert scratched stubble on his chin.

Wonder if her friends are all female. Or is there a male included who's maybe more than a friend? Clyde chewed on that thought . He wouldn't mind getting to know Stefani better. Too bad she won't be around long.

Albert cast him a look of unease. "Heard you had another run-in with Willie Munroe."

Clyde swallowed. "Yeah, just one of those things."

"One of what things?" Albert's lips pressed together.

"An unavoidable one." *That I now regret.*

"It can always be avoided, Clyde. You just have to want to stay out of harm's way."

"That's what I want to do from this point on," Clyde insisted.

"So you got it out of your system?"

"Yeah, man. We duked it out a bit after a misunderstanding, and now everything's cool." *At least I keep telling myself that. But is he listening?*

"Glad to hear that, Clyde. People like Willie Munroe will always pull you down, but only if you let them."

"I hear you, Albert." *Should have listened before, but let my hot head get the better of me. Can't let it happen again. Otherwise, no telling how it might end next time.*

"So tell me what else has been happening in your life since the last visit."

Clyde tasted the malt liquor and wondered where to begin.

"I'm leaving now," Francine yelled up to Ivana. *Don't let the door hit you on the way out.* "See you tomorrow," Ivana said unenthusiastically.

She listened as the door slammed shut. Emily had left a half hour earlier, having finished her chores and not having Trey or Clyde around to gab with. That suited Ivana just fine, as she preferred her own company to others of late.

Well, maybe it wouldn't have been bad had Clyde been there to spend time with, independent of Trey. Seemed as though she got on well with the bad boy in Trey's brother—even if they both tried hard to keep some distance, as if to cross that imaginary line might spell the type of danger neither could resist. But Clyde had obviously chosen to do his own thing this rainy evening with Trey out of town.

Well, that's his business. I won't spend time worrying about it. Or wishing for something I can't have.

Ivana walked barefoot into the study, wearing only her robe and chemise. She put on some classical jazz and made herself a martini, settling on the wicker sofa. She thought about Trey's alleged business trip to Las Vegas. Was he really there to conduct business? Or was it just a front for another one of his trysts? For all she knew, he had arranged to meet Helene DeCroch out of town to pick up where they left off, assuming it had ever ended.

Ivana tried not to think about that, for it only caused her pain. Instead she focused on the music, that along with the alcohol, put her in a dreamy state. She found herself mentally wandering through time and space to a period of her life when Ivana challenged herself much more, with satisfying results.

What happened to those days, when she took the modeling world by storm and could write her own ticket in life? Is this what she signed up for—being with a man she wasn't sure she could ever be able to trust again? Or love to the depths of her heart?

Ivana tasted the martini, feeling it coursing down her throat. She had a sexual thought, and wasn't quite sure if it involved Trey or Clyde. Maybe even both. She dismissed it, if for no other reason than that there was no one there to bring it to life. Not that such thoughts had a life of their own these days. Or did they?

"Hope I'm not disturbing your reverie. . . ."

Ivana looked up and saw Clyde hovering over her, his eyes pinned on her with unmistakable interest.

Clyde stared down at Ivana lustfully, realizing just how powerful the sexual attraction was, seeing her sitting there with long legs crossed invitingly and revealing cleavage through the opening of her robe. He had come in the room after seeing the light on and hearing music. Now he wondered if that was such a good idea.

"Didn't hear you come in." Ivana sat up while putting her empty glass on the antique table.

"Probably because of the rain." *Or whatever had you so absorbed. Maybe the alcohol.*

She raised her chin. "I suppose."

"So where is everyone?"

"If you mean the hired help, they've gone home for today. And, of course, your brother is in Vegas doing business."

"Maybe you should have gone there with him, take Trey's mind off of business," Clyde suggested. *And take my mind off you.*

"I'm afraid I'm not much company these days when it comes to his growing empire."

"You don't really believe that?"

"Not sure what I believe anymore these days," she said.

Clyde shared those sentiments, wishing he didn't. Another common thing between them. He thought briefly about Albert's niece, whom he was attracted to, but came back to the woman before him and how hot she was this night. Too damned hot to take his eyes off of.

"Well, I think I'd better—"

"Would you like a martini?" Ivana cut in, standing. "I'm about to make myself another and I just hate drinking alone."

Since when? mused Clyde, having gotten the impression that it was just the opposite. He tried not to read too much into the invitation, but welcomed the opportunity to stay.

"Sure, I'll have a drink with you."

Ivana smiled, and Clyde followed her to the wet bar. She looked like a pro in making the martini. Obviously, it came with lots of practice, considering her drinking habit. And maybe with good reason, not that he was in a position to judge anyone.

"So what have you been up to this evening?" she asked, handing him the martini and meeting his gaze squarely.

"I dropped by a tavern a friend runs and had a drink," Clyde said.

"Just one?"

He grinned. "Yeah. Maybe I wanted to hold off on that second drink 'til I got back here."

"Good answer." Ivana wet her lips with alcohol.

"What about you?" asked Clyde. "Sure you haven't had one drink too many?"

"I'm not drunk, if that's what you're asking."

"I'm not." He wasn't sure if it would matter one way or the other at this point. "Must get pretty lonesome at times in this big house, especially when Trey's not around."

"You get used to it," she told him tonelessly.

"I guess."

"Of course, it's not so bad when Trey's little brother is around to keep me company."

"It's good for me, too," he admitted, finding it hard to back away from her innocent flirting. Or was it anything but innocent?

"Then we do see eye to eye on at least one thing," she said. "And probably a few others."

"Yeah, I think so." Clyde swallowed his drink, trying to hold it together when he wanted her so badly. And she clearly wanted him. Trey had it all, something that Clyde always resented. Now his brother's woman was practically throwing herself at him, giving him the chance to have someone Trey loved—if you could call cheating on her love.

Having a few drinks had softened Clyde's resistance to his stunning sister-in-law, causing him to toss aside any barriers that shouldn't be crossed.

We have to deal with the here and now. To hell with everything else.

"I'm going to bed," Ivana cooed seductively, inviting him to join her with unspoken words.

"No, you're not," Clyde heard himself say.

Ivana widened her eyes. "Excuse me?"

"You heard me."

Ivana locked eyes with him. "So what exactly did you have in mind?"

"You tell me. Or am I reading you wrong?"

She sat her glass down. "I think you're reading me very well."

Ivana backed that up by grabbing Clyde's collar and pulling him to her. He took that as his cue, giving her a hard kiss on the mouth. She pulled away and slapped him. As Clyde took a moment to digest that, Ivana came forward again and pressed her open mouth onto his, kissing with utter abandon. Clyde gave her every bit as much in return, wanting her maybe more than he ever had anyone before. She was his brother's wife, and for the moment he didn't give a damn.

Trey phoned Ivana. Once again, she wasn't picking up. He imagined her in a drunken stupor, lying in a ditch somewhere on the side of the road. The thought scared the hell out of him, as he wasn't around to help her. More likely, she simply didn't care to answer. It was easier for her to wait 'til he was home to bitch and moan.

Maybe I should be happy that I can't speak to my wife only to be given an earful. But I'm not.

He missed being with her, even if she was not all that thrilled these days for the most part to be with him. As she hadn't left him, Trey considered that a good thing. He would try his damnedest and do more to make their relationship work when he got back.

He tried Clyde, figuring he was probably raiding the fridge at about this time, or catching up on some of the TV programs he'd missed over the last nine years.

Clyde also wasn't answering, leaving it to his voice mail.

"It's just me," Trey spoke into the phone disappointedly. "Tried Ivana but . . . you know my wife—well, maybe not in so many words—still trying to get on her good side to stay. Guess that's harder when I'm a few hundred miles away. Keep an eye out on her for me, will you? See you tomorrow."

Trey held the phone for a moment, staring out the window at the glittering lights of the city that never slept. When all else failed, he knew there was someone he could always talk to when feeling the need. And he was ever thankful for that, given the situation of having no one else available.

Should he or shouldn't he? Was it a good idea to ring Helene as a wife substitute and friend when Ivana wasn't interested in speaking to him? Or was he supposed to forever suffer from his wife's detachment and seeming indifference?

Trey punched the redial and sucked in a deep breath. He thought about hanging up again, not wanting to intrude on Helene's life that, for the most part, seemed happy. Or was he simply reading into it what he wanted to?

The phone was answered. "Trey . . ."

"Hey, Helene. Was wondering if you had time to talk?"

"I can make time," she said, "for a friend. . . ."

Trey smiled, appreciating the invaluable gift of camaraderie.

Chapter Nineteen

Clyde carried Ivana up the stairs, their mouths never parting. Bypassing her room, he went to his, setting her on the bed.

"Take your clothes off," she demanded breathlessly.

"Not yet," he said, unable to wait a moment longer to enjoy the wares of a woman. *This woman.*

Ravenously, Clyde parted the silk of Ivana's chemise covering her crotch. Without preamble he spread her legs and put his mouth between. His tongue whipped at her clitoris, and Clyde drank in Ivana's intoxicating scent. Creamy wetness quickly covered his mouth. He had forgotten the thrill in tasting a woman's sex and having her want him to just as badly.

Ivana moaned and shuddered violently in having her orgasm. Clyde felt her holding his head in place between her thighs as he continued to orally gratify. It turned him on to no end, and he couldn't wait to make love to her.

She raised his head up. "It's my turn to give you something special," she murmured.

Clyde had no problem with that, needing the release before they got down to the real business. He allowed her to take control, laying him on his back before unzipping pants and pulling out his erection. She took him full into her mouth, bathing in her warm saliva. It felt so damned good that he was almost frozen with anticipation. She had brought to life his pent-up yearnings, and he was ready to experience the payoff.

But just before reaching the point of no return, Clyde decided he didn't want that first time climaxing since becoming a free man to be in her mouth. He lifted Ivana up and into the air, bringing her gently down onto his erection.

"Make love to me," he ordered, loving the tight, tingly feel of her around him.

Ivana gasped with desire. "Yes, I will."

She galloped wildly atop him, seemingly adjusting to his size with no problem. Ripping his shirt off, she dug long fingernails into his chest, causing him to wince, but otherwise turning him on like the lady herself. He brought her face down to his and kissed every part of it, ending with Ivana's luscious lips, which eagerly attacked his. Feeling his orgasm approaching, Clyde turned them over and pounded into her with elemental need.

Ivana wrapped her legs up high across his back and bit into Clyde's shoulder. He groaned in pain and passion as the orgasm came with a shudder. Ivana cried out loudly and Clyde felt her contractions around his penis as she climaxed a second time.

The intensity of their perspiring bodies entangled in sex waned after a final burst of deep breaths, and Clyde rolled off Ivana. Immediately, he regretted what had happened, in spite of feeling a sense of carnal satisfaction he hadn't in years. Though the sexual magnetism between them was undeniable, she was his brother's wife. He and Trey still had their issues, but it was never supposed to come to this as some sort of oneupmanship or conquest over something that was Trey's.

"I think this was a mistake," Clyde muttered, still tasting Ivana on his lips.

Ivana lay her head back on the pillow. "Maybe you should have thought about that before now."

"Yeah, maybe I should have." He lowered his eyes upon her. "Look, it's not you, Ivana. You were great—"

"We were both a little tipsy, and things just happened," she said, her legs still splayed invitingly. "Don't beat yourself up about it."

"I'm not," he insisted. *I betrayed Trey and there's no getting around it. We both did.* "But it can't happen again."

Ivana sat up. "Do you want me to go?"

Clyde eyed her naked body, feeling a fresh surge of arousal. Part of him wanted nothing more than to make love to her again and again after that. The other part knew it couldn't happen. It would only aggravate an already regrettable situation.

"Maybe you should, for both our sakes."

"Fine," she hissed, sliding out of Clyde's powerful arms and off the bed in one motion.

"Wait," Clyde stopped her with the deep sound of his voice. He got up and approached without touching. "We can't ever tell Trey what happened tonight."

Ivana's eyes flickered. "Do you think I would?"

Maybe if you wanted to stick it in his face and make him hurt the way he hurt you. "No, I don't," he told her. "Just want to make sure we're on the same page with this. No one needs to get hurt by this—especially Trey."

"Since when have you given a damn about Trey's feelings?" Ivana's voice thickened. "Was it before or after you screwed his wife?"

Clyde wrestled with that thought, blaming himself for being put in an unenviable position.

"Guess I deserved that," he said in a low tone. "I've always cared about my brother, believe it or not. This was never about him."

"Uh, excuse me, but I think we both know it was *only* about Trey to one degree or another." Ivana covered her breasts. "He's caused us both pain and we've had to deal with it in our own ways. Maybe this was the inevitable result."

Clyde could not dismiss that assumption altogether. He had always been in Trey's shadow, even going to prison for him. Even now, he still saw himself as trying to pull even with his brother, while knowing they remained miles apart on so many levels. Could it be that sleeping with Trey's wife had been a way to beat Trey at his own game, by doing something highly personal that he apparently wasn't able to accomplish himself much of late?

It made Clyde feel no better about what happened. "Trying to psychoanalyze it makes no difference now. It's over and done with. Let's just leave it at that."

"Whatever you say." Ivana sneered at him. "I'm sure when Trey gets back we can all just go about our lives pretending everything is normal, but knowing otherwise."

Clyde gazed at her nice ass through the chemise as she left the room. He wasn't sure what normal was. Or if his life would ever be normal. Maybe it wasn't meant to be. Not when tempta- tion was staring him in the face, making him do something he hadn't fought hard enough to reject. He wasn't sure what would happen next. Only what wouldn't. He would make sure of that.

Ivana stepped out in the hall, fuming. Clyde had taken her to bed, and now he wanted to push her out of it and his life, as if nothing had happened. To hell with him. In spite of feeling this way, she half expected that he might come after her and at least offer comfort in his powerful arms, if not much more. But it wasn't the case. Like Trey, he had apparently become set on his position and nothing she could do would change it.

At this point, Ivana doubted she wanted to change anything. She certainly had no interest in leaving Trey to become involved with Clyde in a serious relationship. And go where?

Do what? He struck her as a man who wouldn't know what to do with a real woman outside the bedroom when push came to shove.

But it was in the bedroom—his bed—where Ivana felt confused. Was it unbridled lust that drew her into sleeping with Trey's brother, leaving her wanting more? Genuine feelings for Clyde? Or just a way to make Trey pay for what he'd done to her?

In her own room, Ivana somehow felt even lonelier. Would that change when Trey returned? Or put an even greater divide between them, now that his brother had taken her to new sexual heights and left his mark on her, whether she liked it or not?

She shed a few tears, though not sure for whom—her, Trey, or Clyde.

Willie parked his car outside the gated entry to the property owned by Trey Lancaster. He had followed Clyde there from the tavern, keeping a safe distance. He wasn't prepared to mix it up again with Clyde. Not just yet.

I'll bide my time and make sure I do it right. The bastard can live like a king in his brother's mansion, but I'll bring them both down to size and get the last laugh.

Willie took a swig of the bottled beer in his hand. He was high on meth, and the beer added to it. He had once wanted to rob Trey Lancaster of many of his valuable possessions, but Clyde had interfered, forcing Willie to abort the plan. Maybe he could still go after the man. Surely Trey had accumulated even more valuable things after all these years. Things that Willie believed could support the lifestyle he'd long envisioned for himself.

He contemplated having a closer look at the house without being seen. *Maybe I can climb the fence and sneak a peek. If there are guard dogs, I'll get my ass out of there in a hurry.*

Willie drank more beer before getting out of the car. He went around to the side of fence, awash in shadows, and managed to climb over. The grass was damp, causing his shoes to make a sloshing sound with each step. He moved more slowly to lessen the noise announcing his presence. No sign of dogs. He breathed a sigh of relief.

Passing through some tall rosebushes, Willie got near the house. An impressive house it was, at that. He imagined replacing his digs for a place like this. Maybe some day. There was a light on in an upstairs bedroom. With his one good eye, Willie spied through open blinds an attractive, scantily-clad woman standing near the window. He suspected it was the wife of Clyde's million-aire brother. He'd heard that she was a former model and could envision that. She seemed to be looking out. At him.

Instinctively, he ducked behind some shrubs, fearful he'd been spotted. Soon, it became clear that the lady was not aware of his presence, seemingly caught in a trance while holding a drink.

Bet you're lookin' to get some, ain't you, baby?

The mere thought gnawed at Willie's libido. He regained control of his mind, realizing that to get to her, he'd likely have to go through the Lancaster brothers. Or at least one of them.

Another time.

He heard a sound, and realized that the front door was opening. Panicking, Willie decided he'd better get the hell out of there before getting caught. The last thing he wanted was to come face-to-face with his arch-nemesis right now. Or be arrested for trespassing and maybe be connected to the vandalism at the car dealership.

Willie hustled out the way he came, nearly tripping, before reaching the fence and climbing back over. Sure he was being followed, he got in his car and sped off without looking back.

Next time he came there, Willie fully intended to take what he wanted. And that included the fine-looking woman he'd laid eyes on.

Clyde stepped outside, thinking he heard something. He had been unable to go to sleep, and came downstairs for some water. He followed what sounded like hurried steps toward the front gate, then heard a car drive off before seeing who was driving it.

Had an intruder been on the property? Or was he imagining the whole thing—including what seemed like shoe impressions in the wet grass—simply as a way to take his mind off what happened between him and Ivana tonight?

On the way back to the house, Clyde spotted what looked like a raccoon racing across the wet grass. *Maybe that was my intruder?* he thought.

Or maybe not. He would speak to Trey about improving his security around the perimeter of the property.

When Clyde reached the house, he saw Ivana's light turn off. It made him think of the time they spent in his bed. Mistake or not, it was something that he would carry with him for the rest of his life, as Clyde knew she would.

It was still a stupid thing to let happen—to lose control as he had. He only wondered what the consequences would be for all parties concerned. He hoped to hell he never had to find out.

Chapter Twenty

Trey's plane arrived two hours late. He collected his car from the short-term parking and headed home, ringing Ivana during the drive. The fact that she answered caught him by surprise, considering yesterday.

"Why didn't you pick up?" he asked gently. "I must have called half a dozen times."

"I'm sorry, Trey," she said levelly. "I wasn't really in the mood to talk."

Are you ever? "The trip went well, thank you."

"Let's not fight, Trey."

"Who's fighting?" And who usually seemed to almost look forward to it?

"I'm going to take a bath. I'll see you when you get home."

Don't sound so enthusiastic. "Yeah, all right."

Trey decided maybe it was time he stopped feeling sorry for himself and do something about it. He made a detour to a florist and bought a dozen long-stemmed red and yellow roses. *Hope she likes them. It's a start anyway.*

When he got home, Trey spotted Clyde's car in the driveway. It looked like it had been freshly washed, cleaning away whatever the rain left and would likely leave again, if the forecast was accurate. It pleased Trey to know that his kid brother took care of what had to be his prized possession at the moment. He was happy to give him ownership of it, and hoped it was just a stepping stone for Clyde to bigger and better things.

"You must be hungry," Francine told him the moment Trey walked into the kitchen.

He had eaten something on the plane, but responded, "Always."

She smiled. "Good, then I'll whip you up a real treat."

"Sounds great."

Trey left her in search of his wife and brother. Instead he found Emily, busy tidying as usual.

"How was your trip?" she asked, noting the flowers.

"Eventful." He studied her. "Everything okay around here?"

Emily grinned. "It is now."

Trey blushed, wishing everyone in the household felt the same. "I think you've earned a little something extra in your paycheck."

"You don't have to do that."

"I want to. After all, it's only money and I've got plenty to go around." He didn't bother asking her where Ivana was, assuming she was still taking a long bath, whereas Clyde could be anywhere in the spacious house.

Upstairs, Trey found Ivana in her huge bathroom, in the Jacuzzi. She was surrounded by bubbles and looking sexy as hell.

"Hi," he said.

"Hi."

"These are for you." Trey held out the roses, knowing she wasn't exactly in a position to do anything with them.

Ivana reacted. "Thank you. They're lovely."

"Not half as lovely as you," he expressed sincerely. In fact, she seemed to have an added glow about her this morning.

She put a smile on her face. "That's sweet, but I'm not sure I deserve those."

"I'm sure you do. And a hell of a lot more from your husband."

"Oh, Trey, don't—"

His eyes grew with befuddlement. "Don't what? Don't tell my wife how I really feel? Or don't feel that way because you don't?"

Ivana ran a soapy hand across one breast. "I didn't mean that . . . any of it."

"So what did you mean?" Maybe he should just leave it alone. But he couldn't. If they were at a standstill in this relationship, might as well get it out in the open.

Ivana cast her eyes upon his warily. "I only meant that it may take a lot more from both of us to get back to where we were," she said. "But I'm willing to try . . ."

Trey took that as meaning she was at least willing to shoulder some responsibility for where things stood between them. "I'm happy to hear that."

"I know you are."

"Why don't I go put these in a vase?"

"That would be nice, thank you."

She smiled, and he returned it, believing that maybe they were starting to work their way back, slowly but surely, giving him hope for the future.

"You're back," commented Clyde without looking as Trey walked into his room. He'd already heard Trey talking with Ivana, and Ivana trying to dodge her husband and his romantic overtures.

"Yeah, with another trip to put behind me," Trey said. "Wish you could've been there. We could have played the slot machines."

"Not much of a gambler," Clyde said, wishing he were anywhere but there at the moment.

"Neither am I, unless it's a sure bet."

What was these days? Clyde mused. Maybe stupidity, for some people.

Trey spotted the duffel bag on the floor half stuffed with clothes. He looked up at Clyde. "What's this?"

"I'm moving out," Clyde said tonelessly, and resumed his packing, avoiding meeting Trey's gaze.

"Moving out? Where?"

"I don't know. I'll find something."

"But why?" Trey probed.

"Why not?"

"You have a home here."

Clyde faced him. "No, I don't. This is your home. It's time I found one of my own."

Trey frowned thoughtfully. "What's going on, Clyde?"

I slept with your wife and can't stay here feeling guilty as hell about it and not knowing who to blame or how to face you. "Nothing's going on," he tried to assert. "It's just time for me to go."

"But why so suddenly?" Trey peered at him. "Did something happen yesterday while I was gone?"

Clyde stiffened and contemplated coming clean, but couldn't do it, even if a side of him wanted Trey to experience just a little of what it felt like to come in second. This time with his own wife.

"No, nothing happened," he said with a straight face. "I did some soul-searching and came to this decision."

Trey scratched his cheek. "I don't suppose I could talk you out of it?"

"Don't waste your breath." Clyde grabbed more clothes to stuff in the bag.

"Did you talk to Ivana about it?" Trey persisted. "If not, maybe she can—"

"There's nothing she can say to make me change my mind," Clyde said snappily. Or do, for that matter. The more distance he put between them, the better for everyone.

Trey sighed. "Well, if you need anything. . . ."

"I'll let you know." Clyde zipped the bag and flung the strap over his broad shoulder. Now for another dagger to throw at his brother. He turned to Trey. "By the way, I also quit my job."

Trey's eyes bulged. "You what?"

This was harder than Clyde intended, but it needed to be said. "I'm through with the car-sales business. I tried, but it's not for me."

Trey's jaw clenched. "I won't try again to talk you into staying. It's your decision. If you should change your mind, there will always be an opening for you . . . and a place to stay."

"Yeah, I appreciate that." Clyde nearly backed down then and there to say he would at least stay on the job 'til something better came along. But what would that accomplish, other than to delay the inevitable? "I won't be coming back. It's time I found my own way and place in the free world."

"How are you for money?"

Nearly broke, Clyde thought, *if the truth be told.* But he didn't want his brother's charity to bail him out. Or the guilt of taking more from Trey than he already had—including his wife, albeit for one night.

"I'll survive," he said, leaving it at that.

"You sure about that?" Trey gave him a doubtful look.

Clyde's brow furrowed in response to what he perceived as Trey staring down at him as the rich brother. "Yeah, I'm sure. Say good-bye to Ivana for me."

Trey did not respond as Clyde walked by him, resisting the urge to look back.

Trey had known this day would come sooner or later. He just hadn't expected it to be today. It pained him to see Clyde turning his back on not only free room and board, but a great job with benefits he wouldn't find anywhere else. But what could Trey do if Clyde had made up his mind? He couldn't force him to stay. Or find words that hadn't already been said.

Still wondering if there was anything he could have done differently in appealing to Clyde, Trey found Ivana poolside, working on her tan and a martini.

"Clyde's moved out," he informed her.

Ivana looked surprised, but seemed to recover. "I guess he got tired of living under his big brother's roof."

"Did something happen yesterday that made him want to leave?" Trey regarded her with an accusing eye. He couldn't help but think that Clyde's rather abrupt departure had to have been triggered by more than just a need to strike out on his own.

"Such as?" Ivana questioned him uneasily.

"You tell me? Maybe you bitched at him one time too many and he'd had about all he could take."

"So now you're blaming me for your brother deciding it was time to get on with his life without you looking over his shoulder?" Ivana huffed. "Maybe you need to look in the mirror before suggesting I had anything to do with Clyde leaving."

Trey honestly didn't know what to believe. He had overreacted in pointing the finger at Ivana and regretted it. She and Clyde had actually gotten along well lately, and he saw no reason to believe Ivana had anything to do with his brother's abrupt departure. Trey blamed himself as much as anyone for Clyde deciding he wanted to get away from his world.

Maybe I put too much pressure on him too soon, and he couldn't handle it.

"Anyway, it's over and done with," Trey said glumly.

"Clyde's not dead, for heaven's sake!" Ivana voiced evenly. "He's entitled to make his own choices on where to live."

"And I guess work." Trey sighed. "Clyde also turned in his resignation from the dealership."

Ivana sipped her drink coolly, but he could tell she was shocked. "Maybe he has something else lined up," she tossed out.

"Yeah, right—like collecting unemployment." Trey's jaw jutted. "I really don't know how the hell he's going to survive since his stubborn pride won't let me help him."

"As I've understood it, Clyde survived whatever way he could for much of his adult life without your help."

"And look where it got him." Trey thought about Clyde's prison stint. Might he be headed down that road again? And what, if anything, could Trey do about it at this point?

"Your brother served his time," Ivana pointed out. "Don't continue to use that against him. Maybe you should just leave Clyde alone for a while."

"You're right," Trey said resignedly. "He wants his space, he's got it." *I have to spend more time working on my own life instead of my brother's. Starting with saving my marriage.* "Maybe we can go out to dinner tonight, just the two of us. What do you think?"

He expected her to come up with any excuse as to why they couldn't, bracing himself.

"I'd like that." She looked up at him warmly.

"How does seven sound?" Trey asked.

"Seven works for me," she said sweetly.

"Good."

Feeling encouraged, he bent down and gave her a kiss on the lips and had it returned. Suddenly Trey began to view Clyde's leaving as not necessarily a bad thing. Perhaps having the house all to themselves again was just what they needed to put things back on track. *I'll do what I have to in proving my love for her. I couldn't stand the thought of losing Ivana to another man.*

Trey didn't delude himself into thinking for one moment that Ivana was not still a great catch for any man out there. Quite the contrary, she was the very best. Even if he sometimes took her for granted and had done something stupid, his heart was still in the right place.

He hoped the same could be said for Ivana's at the end of the day.

Chapter Twenty-one

The motel was a far cry from the multimillion-dollar home Clyde had begun to get used to. He questioned the wisdom of his decision to move out two weeks ago. Maybe he should have simply tried to coexist in a house where he had to see Ivana every day, and wanted but didn't dare have her. He certainly could have stayed on the job with the generous salary Trey was paying him.

But it all got to be too much. Trying to dance around Ivana every time she got near him without tipping their hand to Trey was something Clyde didn't have the stomach for. His brother didn't deserve that, regardless of Trey's often overbearing style and penchant for always trying to lead rather than follow.

This was precisely why Clyde had turned his back on the job. He didn't need to constantly be led by the hand of his big brother, knowing that Trey would forever be in the driver's seat. Clyde would rather scrap for pennies than be at Trey's beck and call.

Feeling hunger pains, Clyde grabbed his keys and headed out the door for a nearby McDonald's. He hopped into his car, the one thing given to him by Trey that Clyde kept.

Getting rid of the wheels would've been crazy. I need transportation to find employment and eat—even if both figure to be a struggle for the time being.

Clyde drove off, fearing that his dream of being self-employed and successful suddenly seemed further away than ever.

Trey looked up at the One Stop Motel in a seedy part of town and cringed at the thought that Clyde had chosen such a place to stay over his comfortable house. Was it really pride that had driven him out? Or something else?

Trey had tracked his brother down, wanting to make one last-ditch effort to at least give him enough money for a decent place to live. *If that doesn't work, I won't feel guilty for not trying to do right by him.* He hated the thought of Clyde drifting back into a life of crime and waywardness. Not after all the progress he'd made in trying to get his life together since being released. *I owe him this much, whether he chooses to accept or not.*

Trey's thoughts drifted to Ivana. Things had been better between them of late, if not still strained. It was as if Ivana was elsewhere, even when they were together. All he could think of was that she was still grappling with the miscarriage and wanting to blame it on his affair with Helene, even when they both knew that wasn't the case.

I was a damned fool. Now I want to try and make it up to Ivana, if she'll let me.

Trey felt that they seemed to be headed in the right direction. He didn't press her to have sex, though he longed to be inside Ivana's warm body with her wanting him there just as badly. Rushing her could jeopardize the gains they had made and put them back to square one.

I can wait as long as she needs me to. So long as she is still committed to the relationship and willing to meet me halfway.

Trey also wanted to be there for his brother, though something told him that Ivana would prefer he left well enough alone. In this case, he had to use his own judgment and deal with the potential fallout.

He knocked on the door. It was quiet inside, but Trey knew Clyde was there, spotting his car in the lot.

Another knock, then the door opened.

"You look like hell," Trey said truthfully, noting he was unshaven while wearing wrinkled clothing. "And smell like it, too."

"No kidding," Clyde offered sarcastically. "Guess I'm used to that."

"You don't have to be."

Clyde looked at him. "How'd you find me?"

"I have my ways." Trey met his gaze. "Can I come in?"

"Do I have a choice?"

Trey felt there were always choices, but in this instance didn't want to risk being turned away. "Not really," he said.

Clyde turned around and went back inside, leaving the door open. Trey took that as his invitation to enter.

"Can I get you a beer?" Clyde asked. "It's about all I've got to offer."

Trey glanced around at the small, cramped room and saw the mini-refrigerator. "Yeah, give me a beer."

Clyde got out two cans out and tossed one to Trey. "So what are you doing here? Or did you come to gawk at how the other half lives when not holing up in your grand palace?"

"You know that's not true."

Clyde shrugged. "If you say so."

Trey drank the beer. "Always so distrusting of me, Clyde. What did I ever do to make you feel I think I'm better than you?"

"How about everything you've done your whole life," Clyde answered coldly.

"Being successful isn't a crime." Trey regretted the insinuation right away.

"Yeah, guess that's what separates us—you're the good guy, I'm the bad."

"I didn't say that."

"You didn't have to. I've known since we were kids that you were always going to walk the straight and narrow, while I was more likely to stray whenever the opportunity was there."

Trey tasted the beer thoughtfully. He wanted to say it was all about right and wrong paths, but refrained from preaching what Clyde already knew. Or should have.

"I'm anything but perfect, Clyde. I've made my fair share of mistakes over the years, so I certainly can't judge you."

Clyde gave him an uncomfortable look. "Are you ever going to tell me why you're here? Or should I guess?"

"I wanted to check on you," responded Trey. "Is that so wrong?"

Clyde softened his rigid face. "No. As you can see, I'm making due the best I can—which hasn't been very good."

"So I take it there have been no job prospects?"

"Nothing serious. Not many people are keen on hiring ex-cons with bad tempers."

One person is. "Why don't you come back to work for me?"

"I don't need your pity," Clyde said.

"I'm not here out of pity, Clyde. I'm here out of love. You're my brother. There's no need for you to live in squalor to prove a point."

"What point?"

"That you don't need anyone but yourself—certainly not me."

Clyde took a swig of beer. "Guess I've always been bullheaded when it comes to that."

"Mama certainly wouldn't argue the point if she were still alive," Trey said.

Clyde grinned. "Yeah, I guess not."

"Why did you move out?" Trey gave him a straight look. "Was it something I did or said? Or didn't I do enough to help you?"

"No. Wasn't any of that." Clyde turned away.

"Did Ivana say something to set you off? I know that you two haven't always gotten along, and she can be very opinionated at times as part of her nature."

"Ivana never said or did a thing," Clyde insisted. "Like I told you, it was all about me just wanting to do my own thing—even if it got me nowhere. At least I'd know I wasn't being propped up by my older brother."

"You were never being propped up by me, Clyde," Trey said. "You were earning your keep in more ways than one. You brought fun into our household again and fresh ideas at work. Come back to both."

Trey hadn't planned to make such an offer, certainly not without talking it over with Ivana at home and his team at work first, but it seemed like the right thing to do. He would deal with the consequences later.

Clyde stared at the offer. "I can't," he said after a moment or two. "I'm not going to intrude on your life again. I don't belong there. It's better this way for all of us."

"Is *this* what you call better?" Trey took a sweeping glance and back.

"I call it my own thing," Clyde said proudly.

Trey sucked in a deep breath. *This obviously isn't working. Maybe I need to try a different angle.*

"Let's talk about your 'thing,' Clyde. You've alluded to ideas about what you want to do with your life. So tell me what it is."

Clyde sat down on an old sofa and drank more beer, caught in thought. "All right, there is something on my mind."

"I'm listening."

"I'd like to open up a jazz supper club," Clyde admitted.

Trey cocked a brow. "You mean like the Violet Supper Club?"

"Yeah, only I'd replace the piano music with some real jazz—a singer."

Trey was surprised. He tried to picture Clyde running a jazz club. Crazy as it seemed, he could actually imagine such. Obviously, Clyde felt he could do it. Maybe he was right if given half a chance.

"So why not go for it?"

Clyde chuckled. "Yeah, right. Look around you. Does it look like I can afford to buy a jazz club?"

Trey thought about his friend Blake planning to retire and closing his supper club. What if they took it off his hands?

"Why don't we buy one together?"

"Together?" Clyde's head snapped back .

"Yeah, why not?" Trey asked. "I'm always looking for a good investment. Also happen to know a club that's about to shut down and its owner. I can buy half the club as a silent partner and lend you the money for the other half. It would be yours to run as you please. If you make it work, then the money should come in, and my investment would pay off nicely."

"You would do that?"

Trey smiled. "Why not? If it's something you think you'd be good at, I want to help you bring it to fruition." If it bombed, he could use it as a tax write-off and maybe coax Clyde into coming back to work for him. "So what do you say?"

Clyde's sipped more beer while chewing on the notion. "We would be partners, fifty-fifty?"

"Yes, you can even take fifty-one percent, if it makes you feel better," Trey offered to sweeten the pot. "I just want us to do this as brothers."

Clyde's eyes connected with Trey's. "Then I'm in."

Trey grinned. "Great. I'll have my lawyer draw up the papers, so we can keep it all nice and legal. I think this can work, Clyde, and in the process, we can keep a local landmark from going under."

"I'll drink to that."

Trey raised his beer and drank some satisfyingly. Maybe there was hope yet for them being brothers again in all the ways that counted most.

Clyde heard Trey's car drive away. He hadn't known what to expect when his brother showed up at the door. His first instinct was to be suspicious and turn his back on what he saw as the high and mighty coming to rescue the down and out. A fleeting thought was that Ivana had told Trey about their one-night stand, and he had come there hell-bent on a confrontation, but then came the partnership offer. Though this caught him off guard, Clyde couldn't help but be interested, all things considered. He had to swallow his pride and look beyond the fact that Trey would still be in the driver's seat like before. Clyde thought of a promise made to Raymond to go into business together when he got out. This seemed to be a first step toward keeping that promise.

Clyde stepped outside for some fresh air, something he never got enough of after being denied it for years. He was still a tad leery about this new arrangement with Trey. After all, it meant Clyde would likely be seeing more of his brother than he cared to. This meant having more opportunities to run into Ivana. What if she tried to seduce him again? Or had it been the other way around? Did they really want to play with fire and end up getting badly burned, along with Trey?

Overall, Clyde believed it was worth the risk. This club could finally be his ticket to a good life on his own terms.

Maybe his luck was finally about to take a turn for the better. He'd learned, though, to never take anything—or anyone—for granted.

Chapter Twenty-two

"I can't believe you're giving your brother a supper club— just like that." Ivana's eyes locked on Trey across the dining room table.

"I'm not giving him a club," he said defensively. "We're going into business together. I'm loaning Clyde half the cost, and he'll pay me back when the profits begin to come in."

She peered at her husband with a healthy dose of skepticism. "What if there are no profits?"

"Are you kidding me?" Trey dabbed a napkin on his mouth. "People love jazz in this town. Turning Blake's club into a jazz showcase is a brilliant idea. I only wish I'd thought of it myself."

Ivana forked a piece of her fruit salad. She supposed that it could be a profitable venture at some point down the line. Not that they needed more money. She didn't necessarily want to give it away either to someone who hadn't truly earned it.

Am I jealous of Clyde? Or jealous that he's developing a life without me being a direct part of it?

"I suppose you want him to move back into the house?" Ivana asked, wondering if that was a bad or good idea. The thought of being able to slip into Clyde's bed again and make love caused a warm sensation between her legs, even if she wished that hadn't been the case. Ivana managed to suppress this urge. She needed to steer as far away from him as possible and hope Trey never found out what they had done. "I don't think that would be a good idea."

Trey cut calmly into a roundhouse steak. "Actually, Clyde's planning to get his own place."

"Well, good for him," she voiced. "I'm sure Clyde is grateful to have a rich brother to dig him out of any hole he crawls in."

Trey frowned. "Why don't you cut him some slack? He's out of your hair, so what do you care if I help him to get and stay on his feet? After all, that was the grand plan when Clyde got out of prison, was it not?"

"It was *your* grand plan!" Ivana made clear. "I only went along with it to try and keep the peace. I've stated all along that your brother could be trouble waiting to happen."

Trey gave her a look of suspicion. "Do you know something that I don't?"

Me and my big mouth. I hate when he looks at me like he knows I'm hiding something.

She swallowed the guilt in her throat and prayed that he couldn't read her mind "No," she said convincingly. "I just want you to do a reality check. Clyde's agenda is not necessarily the same as yours. Who knows what type of people he'll invite or attract to the club? Are you sure you want to be a part of something that just might blow up in your face?"

"He's my brother. Clyde deserves a shot at achieving something he can proud of—and me too, frankly." Trey lifted his glass of water. "I could see it in Clyde's eyes: he's really latched onto an idea that I believe he's totally committed to and has no desire to see fail."

"If you say so."

"Let's not fight about this."

Ivana recognized that she was coming across as a spoiled and unreasonable bitch. Obviously blood was thicker than water in this instance. It did her no good to try and get Trey to side with her against his brother. It was in her best interests to not make waves. Clyde was not her lover or husband. They both agreed it was best to end things where they ended.

I'm not in love with Clyde, not matter how great we were together in bed, Ivana thought.

She loved Trey, realizing that now more than ever, even if taking a wrong turn with the worst possible person. Would that come back to haunt her?

"I hope you get the club, and it's a big success," Ivana said in an about-face

"Do you?"

"I don't mean to be a bitch sometimes," she said, trying to take the high road. "Clyde is your brother and does need to do something with his life to keep from falling back into the cracks. If this is the answer, I won't try to mess it up for him or you."

"Thank you," Trey told her, offering a smile.

Ivana tasted wine while wondering if Clyde's continued presence in their lives was bound to cause more trouble that either of them needed.

"So it's really gonna happen?" Raymond asked incredulously.

"Yeah, count on it," Clyde assured him over the phone, knowing his time behind bars was drawing to an end. He was short on specifics, not wanting to get Raymond's hopes up too much, just in case things fell through. "With any luck, I'll have something solid on the table by the time you get out." At least that was the plan. But plans did not always work out. For all he knew Trey might change his mind and decide to keep the supper club for himself.

"Glad to hear it. I'm looking forward to doing somethin' real with my life that don't include being on the wrong side of the law."

"You and me too," Clyde said.

"Who would've thought the financing for our dream would come from your brother, of all people—a dude you once despised almost as much as that Willie dude."

"I think it was more the other way around." Or so Clyde had come to believe over the years as a reason why he never got along with Trey. Maybe it was just that sibling rivalry thing. Or firstborn versus second born.

"Guess he's developed a soft spot for you as his next of kin."

"Maybe we have for each other," conceded Clyde, knowing Trey was the only brother he was ever going to have, like it or not. It was time that they stopped behaving as though enemies, even if often over the years it felt like they were. Right now that seemed like ancient history, as for once he and Trey had a common goal that could only bring them closer together.

"Are you bopping anyone yet, man?" Raymond's voice cracked. "And don't tell me you're still saving yourself for that special lady."

Clyde thought about Ivana and how well he'd gotten to know her intimately one special night.

He could still smell her sweet body and taste her orgasm. Yet Clyde wished to hell he had stayed away from her, in spite of Ivana making him feel like a man again.

"I had a little something," he said unenthusiastically. "No big deal." Not anymore.

"That bad, huh?"

I only wish it were. Just the opposite. "Yeah, man, that bad."

"Well, maybe the next one will be better," suggested Raymond.

"Maybe."

"And if you happen to run into someone right for me—nice on the eyes, big tits, bigger ass, full lips made for kissing mine—put in a good word for me, will ya?" Clyde grinned. "I'll do that." A knock on the door startled him. "I've got to run. See you soon."

"Yeah, later." Clyde set the cell phone down and went to the door. He imagined, for some reason, Willie Munroe on the other side with a gun, ready to blow his head off the moment he opened the door.

Get a grip! He's got no idea where I'm staying. Not to mention he probably learned his lesson after our last meeting. Nevertheless, Clyde was leery.

"Who's there?"

"It's Ivana . . ."

It took every bit of courage and several martinis for Ivana to show up at Clyde's motel room, having gotten the location from Trey's appointment book.

"What are you doing here, Ivana?" Clyde looked her up and down.

"I came to talk." She noted he was shirtless and looking as hot as ever.

"Not a good idea."

"Probably not," she conceded, "but I'm here."

"You've been drinking," Clyde spoke in an accusing tone.

"So maybe I have," Ivana hissed. "That never seemed to be a problem for you before."

"My mistake." He stared at her. "Does Trey know you're here?"

"He thinks I went to see a movie."

"Did you tell him anything?" Clyde asked uncomfortably.

"What do you think?" She gave him a moment to consider it. "Why would I do that and ruin both our lives? Besides we agreed not to."

Clyde sighed. "Yeah, we did."

Ivana looked up at his eyes impatiently as they stood at his door. "Well, can I come inside?"

He hesitated. "What if Trey followed you?"

"He didn't," she stated emphatically.

After a moment, Clyde stepped aside. She brushed against him when passing by, causing her body to react. She waited 'til he shut the door before moseying over to him.

"So I understand congratulations are in order?"

"You mean the club?"

"Yes, Trey told me all about your partnership."

"It was his idea," Clyde said uneasily.

"You don't have to convince me," Ivana told him. "Trey's always coming up with something."

"We'll be in this together." Clyde gazed down at her. "But I'll be running the club without Trey looking over my shoulder or pulling rank."

She wondered if Trey could truly have that type of willpower to back off and allow Clyde to run the show. "I'm sure you will, and you'll be very successful."

Feeling tipsy, all Ivana could think of in that moment was being kissed by him passionately, the way he had that night. She wondered if the same thing was going through his head.

"You shouldn't have come here," Clyde reiterated, but still remained close to her.

Her eyes lifted to his. "There's a lot of things we shouldn't do, but we do them anyway."

"This can't happen again," he told her succinctly, taking a step backward.

Caught in a fog of alcohol and lustful thoughts, Ivana ignored him and her better judgment, wanting to give in to her sexual impulses that he had ignited. She moved right up to him so she could breathe in his manly scent, feel his warm breath on her cheek.

"Why can't it?" she asked boldly. "I know you want me."

Clyde's face creased. "No, I don't want you and you don't want me! Not really. We can't do this anymore, only to end up hurting Trey."

Ivana's mouth became a straight line. "He can't possibly hurt as much as he hurt me."

"Oh, I think he can hurt a hell of a lot more—especially if you keep this up."

"Keep what up?" she demanded.

"Throwing yourself at men."

She felt irritation at the insult. "How dare you. I've only cheated on Trey with one man—you!"

"And we *both* have to live with that," Clyde said flatly. "Let's not make things any worse."

"Why not? Trey never has to find out." Ivana tiptoed and put her arms around his neck, forcing his face down to kiss her. She knew this was wrong and hated herself for succumbing to this sexual magnetism between them, yet couldn't help but want him again.

Clyde pried their lips apart. "Stop it, Ivana!" he said with a snap. "Go home to your husband and leave me alone. Don't mess things up for either of us. Please—"

Ivana was stung by the snub and ashamed for ever having come there. She fixed him with narrowed eyes. "I think it's a little late for that, wouldn't you say?"

He took a breath. "So why make it worse?"

She stepped closer. "Because I can't stop thinking about you—us . . . what we did—"

"Can't you see, there isn't any *us*," he stated unequivocally. "And there never has been. We had a moment . . . now it's passed and we have to get on with our lives. Don't throw yours away over one stupid mistake. I sure as hell don't intend to."

Ivana got the message loud and clear, even if it was painful to hear. He was just like so many other men—got what he wanted from a woman, then turned his attention elsewhere. What did she ever see in him in the first place? Why didn't she steer clear of the ex-con when she knew instinctively that he was very bad news?

"Go to hell!" Ivana hurled at him, turned, and got out of there as fast as she could.

Disregarding the part of him that wanted to quit while ahead, Clyde went after Ivana, not wanting things to end like that. But he stopped at the door, realizing this was precisely how things should end. If Ivana got him out of her system for good, then maybe she could refocus on Trey and making their relationship work.

If not, I'm screwed. Especially if she becomes vengeful and tells Trey about us.

Clyde did not even want to think about that and what it could mean to their future partnership. Or relationship as brothers. He hated that, to a large degree, his hopes and dreams rested on Ivana keeping her mouth shut. But he had brought this upon himself. She was simply too much to resist for someone fresh out of the pen, whose judgment was clouded by beauty and physical needs. With Ivana's reckless drinking and continuing issues with Trey and him, Clyde feared it was only a matter of time before he had to face up to one night of passion and regrets.

Ivana quietly entered Trey's room. She could see his silhouette through the darkness, lying in bed atop the jacquard quilted comforter. He was snoring lightly and wearing only boxers. Ivana stared at her husband for a moment, having mixed emotions about being there. In the end, she knew it was something she had to do.

Ivana slid the silk charmeuse wrap off her shoulders, dropping it to the floor. She was completely naked. She climbed onto the bed and moved between Trey's legs, slightly parted as though waiting for her. Opening his boxers, Ivana bent down and put his penis in her mouth. Within moments, it had gone from flaccid to fully erect. She took him to the base of her throat and felt Trey's body tense.

"Baby . . ." Trey gasped.

Ivana made a moaning sound of understanding, his erection filling her mouth. Before he could climax, she lowered herself onto Trey, feeling him impale her deeply and tightly. She began to move slowly up and down him, running her long fingernails across his chest. Ivana wanted him to feel good, even as she tried to distance herself from past sins and pleasures.

Trey gripped her breasts, putting the nipples between his fingers and caressing them expertly. Ivana quivered from the sensations, along with those from her clitoris rubbing against him. She felt herself constricting around his penis. She bent down and began to kiss him feverishly. Trey gave back as much, putting his tongue in her mouth.

Ivana pressed her thighs tightly against Trey's body, feeling her orgasm coming. Her mind meandered between Trey and Clyde, as if making love to two men at once. She ultimately settled on her husband and one true love as he gripped her buttocks, raising and lowering her onto him with a needy passion. She felt his throbbing climax and listened to Trey's quickening breath, matching her own.

Ivana allowed Trey to suck her nipples and hold her tightly as she came. The surge ripped through her body, slick with perspiration, leaving her exhausted and satiated.

"Oh . . . Trey," she murmured as his hard erection continued to fill her with wonderful sensations.

"I'm right here," he promised.

Ivana took that to heart as they clung to each other for a few moments of silent intimacy before she lifted off his body. She kissed Trey's mouth. "I'm going to my room now."

"Stay the night, Ivana. Please?" begged Trey. "I just want to keep holding you."

She thought about it, but wasn't ready. Too many issues swam through Ivana's head about love, infidelity, miscarriage, and definitely shame.

"I can't—not tonight."

"I understand." Trey kissed her hand. "Take all the time you need. I love you."

Ivana looked at him sadly. She wished she could turn back the hands of time and take away any memory of being with Clyde. Would Trey ever be able to forgive her?

"I'm sorry," she whispered and added with meaning to soften the blow, "Love you too."

Ivana moved away from Trey and off the bed. She picked up her wrap and quickly left the room. The abashment of giving herself to Clyde for all the wrong reasons settled in like a thick haze. *What have I done?*

Tears filled her eyes, and Ivana allowed them to flow down her cheeks as she reached the relative comfort of her bedroom. She had fallen into a trap of her own doing in hoping to maybe punish Trey, along with misguided lust for the wrong man. Now she felt cheap, humiliated, and bewildered. She couldn't look at Trey without seeing Clyde. And vice versa. How would she get past this, so her life with Trey would not suffer?

Chapter Twenty-three

Willie sat in a coffee shop eating blueberry pancakes and sausage links. He watched as Roselyn brought plates to another table, flirting with a man though his woman was sitting there, and began to walk toward him.

"Hi, baby." She gave him a bright smile.

"You lookin' to replace me with that asshole or what?"

Roselyn glanced over her shoulder. "You mean him?"

"Yeah, I do," Willie grumbled, feeling sorrier for himself than usual and a little jealous, even if she had given him no real reason to be.

"Get real. The man's old enough to be my daddy. Besides, you're more than enough man for me, Willie."

He blushed. "That's good to know." *I'll decide when it's time to go our separate ways.*

She flashed her teeth. "Want a second helping? It's on the house."

Willie finished off the last stack of pancakes and found his stomach still had room for more. "Yeah, why not?"

"Coming right up, along with more coffee," she told him.

"Wait," he said, grabbing her hand. "What time you gettin' off?"

"About two hours. Why?"

He eyed her breasts through a tight uniform. "Thought we could have some fun."

She giggled. "Sounds good to me. Pick me up and we can have as much fun at your place as you like."

"How about your place?" Willie gazed up sharply.

Roselyn frowned. "We've already been over this, baby. There's too much friction between you and Gail. I'd rather not deal with you two coming face-to-face and maybe to blows right now, if I can help it."

That bitch. Keeps sticking her nose where it doesn't belong. Maybe I'll break it for her trouble. Or worse.

"Yeah, well, whatever," he muttered. "Wouldn't want to come between you and her."

Roselyn smiled. "Thanks for understanding and being so sweet about it." She leaned down and kissed him on the mouth. "Let me go place your order. You'll get dessert tonight." She winked at him.

"Can hardly wait." Willie envisioned getting her naked and having his way.

Ten minutes later, Willie was enjoying more pancakes when Luther joined him.

"Got your message," he said, sitting on the opposite side of the booth.

"Hungry?" Willie asked. "I can get my lady to fix you up."

Luther grinned. "Sure, why don't you."

First things first. "I need you to do something for me, man."

"Yeah, what's that?" Luther grabbed an empty cup on the table and turned it over in preparation for coffee.

Willie leaned forward and said in a conspiratorial undertone, "I need a piece, man."

Luther's eyes expanded. "What happened to the one you had?"

"I tossed it. Too hot to handle." Willie didn't mention that he'd used the gun in a solo store robbery and didn't want it traced back to him.

"You got the money for it?"

"I'm workin' on it," Willie said, and thought about his sex date with Roselyn tonight. He'd sweet-talk her into giving him what he needed in hard cash.

A crease dented Luther's forehead. "I'll need a few bills."

"Don't worry about it. Just line up the piece and you'll get your money."

Luther paused. "All right. I'll see what I can do."

Willie flashed a half smile. "Good."

"So what you got goin' on?" Luther asked curiously.

Willie pondered that. He planned to use the gun to go after Clyde when the time was right. But no need to let Luther in on the details just yet, particularly since Willie was short on particulars while long on intent.

"Always pays to be prepared . . . just in case."

"For what?"

Willie tasted cold coffee. "You never know when a war might break out. If it does, I want to be sure I get the first shot." And the last.

Luther leaned forward. "Are we talkin' about going after Clyde Lancaster . . . and maybe his rich-ass brother?"

Willie paused and said noncommittally, "Let me put it to you this way: I always pay my debts. And I also like to see to it that I collect what's owed me with interest—no matter what it takes."

He spotted Roselyn and signaled her to come over.

***

Trey arranged a meeting with Blake Lewis at the Violet Supper Club, hoping to be able to entice him into an earlier retirement. The club was the ideal place to take over, with the least amount of cash influx needed for renovations. But Trey had already lined up some other properties to look at should this one fall through. He really wanted to give Clyde this opportunity to make something of his life, along with allowing them another chance to work together as business partners and brothers.

"Thanks for meeting with us, Blake." Trey shook his hand, followed by Clyde.

"I have to admit, your offer was intriguing and more than generous," Blake said. "Let's sit down."

Trey watched Clyde take a seat on the other side of Blake. Though seeming composed, he imagined his little brother had butterflies, in taking maybe the biggest step in his life on the right side of the law. Trey was only too happy to guide him through the process.

"We think we can carry on your legacy with this place and make you a generous offer to sell it," Trey told Blake, while holding a glass of Pinot Noir.

He cast his eyes on Trey. "I'm listening . . ."

At the last moment Trey decided to defer this part to Clyde, since he would be running the club, wanting him to feel like the front man. "Why don't you tell Blake your plans for the club, Clyde?"

Clyde straightened his shoulders and took a breath. "I'd like to add a regular jazz singer to the mix," he explained, "while maintaining the piano music and fine food. Maybe have the singer sing a blend of standards, Latin, and even some jazz-pop. We could probably also fill more seats if we had a ladies' night and even a special night for the men."

Trey wondered if Clyde had laid it on a bit thick, putting off Blake and his more old-fashioned views on what a supper club should be. Maybe Blake might think he'd be better off closing the place lock, stock, and barrel, and preserving his memory—and everyone else's.

Blake gave Clyde a thoughtful look before putting a broad grin on his face. "I think I like your brother, Trey. He has some interesting ideas on what to do with the club. It needs the passion of some younger people to better reflect today's clientele. I believe that we can do some business, and I can live to see what I started succeed with a new generation."

Clyde gleamed, as did Trey, who was impressed with his brother's concise and well-thought-out presentation.

Half an hour later the three men shook hands on an agreement. It was Trey's suggestion that the new club be called, appropriately, Clyde's Jazz Club. Trey wanted his brother to really feel it was Clyde's place to run, with Trey putting up the capital while staying in the background. He was beginning to feel more and more like this venture would pay off handsomely.

Clyde could hardly believe what had once seemed like little more than a pipe dream had suddenly turned into reality. He felt as if this was the break he'd waited for all his life. Now that it was on the verge of happening, he had to do all he could to make sure the faith Trey placed in him was not mislaid. Or that he didn't allow anyone else to stand in the way of what Clyde saw as the opportunity of a lifetime for someone whose life had seemed to go downhill far more often than up.

That included Ivana. Clyde was leery of her, given the way he'd rejected her latest advances. Would she try and ruin him in Trey's eyes? Or recognize things for how they were and should be between them, with Trey being the wild card? He could only hope she did right by his brother and committed herself to making their marriage work.

Clyde finished off the rest of his drink in solitude before catching up with Trey, who had stepped away to call his wife to share the news.

Chapter Twenty-four

"What's up, man?" Clyde smiled as he stood outside the prison gates and watched his ex–cell mate, Raymond Gunfrey, emerge a free man.

Raymond, six foot five, bald, and built like a freight train, had a wide grin on his face. "Hey, dude." The two embraced and then exchanged a sturdy handshake. "Thought this day would never come."

"Tell me about it," Clyde said.

Raymond took one look back at the prison. "If I never see that place again, I'll be one damned happy man."

"You won't—not if I have any say in it." Clyde had taken it upon himself to steer Raymond clear of the types of bad choices that led to his incarceration.

Raymond scratched his pate. "We'll try to keep each other on the right side of the law."

Clyde patted him on the shoulder. "Let's get out of here."

"Any place in particular?"

"Yeah, my place."

"Cool." They walked to Clyde's car. "This yours?"

Clyde nodded, almost embarrassed. "A gift from my brother."

Raymond gazed at the BMW approvingly. "Nice. Good thing you've got someone with deep pockets lookin' out for you."

"Yeah, I guess."

Clyde didn't always agree with that, but now it seemed like it was a very good thing that Trey was in his corner when the chips were down. He doubted that Trey would be as agreeable about his renewed association with Raymond. Clyde could almost hear Trey's lecture about bad influences. He'd heard it all before. Only he didn't consider Raymond to be a bad influence. Just the opposite. He was someone who had been there and understood what it was like to do time and try and regroup in the outside world.

I'll just have to deal with it when Trey gives me his two cents and more.

"This is it," Clyde said of the spacious loft apartment over the club that he'd inherited from the previous owner when he moved in three weeks ago. It had restored white oak hardwood flooring, exposed beams and rafters, and an open floor plan. Clyde had purchased a few retro furnishings to spruce up the place, and still had a ways to go before considering it truly his own. "Make yourself at home," he told Raymond.

"This could take some gettin' used to after a six-by-nine cell," Raymond said. "But I'll try . . . at least 'til I get my own crib."

"Stay as long as you like," offered Clyde. "You can bunk over there." He pointed to a futon against the far wall.

"Thanks." Raymond tossed his bag on it. "Can hardly wait to get my first night's sleep in the free world."

"Definitely makes a difference."

"Yeah."

"Why don't we go grab some chow," suggested Clyde, certain that Raymond was ready for some real food.

"You took the words right out of my mouth," laughed Raymond.

Fifteen minutes later, they were seated at a table with barbecued ribs, salad, and biscuits. Clyde watched with amusement as his friend ate like it was his first meal. Or last.

"Don't let me stop you," he said, chuckling.

Self-consciously, Raymond seemed to force himself to hold back from enjoying the meal. "Guess I've forgotten what it was like to eat somethin' that wasn't crap."

"I hear you," Clyde remarked, and thought of the pure ecstasy he'd experienced when, fresh out of the pen, he'd first tasted Francine's cooking. Raymond drank beer to down the food and wiped his mouth, studying Clyde. "So what's this big plan of yours for us? Or are we not there yet?"

"You're sitting in it," Clyde responded after a moment.

Raymond reacted. "You mean this club?"

Clyde grinned. "I own the place—at least half of it. Bought it last month with my brother. Still in the process of making a few changes, but for now it's business as usual."

Raymond scanned the surroundings and gazed at him in shock. "This is for real?"

Clyde laughed. "Would I lie? I'm turning it into a jazz supper club—Clyde's Jazz Club, as a matter of fact—a classy, elegant establishment that'll be *the* place to be in Paradise Bay."

Raymond shook his head in utter amazement. "*You* runnin' a stylish supper club? Who woulda thought?"

"No, man, *us* running one," Clyde told him. "Just as we planned."

"Tell me more . . ."

Clyde tasted his beer. "I'll be handling the day to day operations, with Trey doing his thing behind the scenes. I figured you could be in charge of security—you know, make sure things stay orderly and trouble free. You can also have a stake in the club, so it becomes more than just a job to you."

Raymond's face lit. "Yeah, that could work."

"We'll make it work."

Raymond bit into a biscuit. "I gotta say, when you get somethin' in your head, you really stick with it."

"Just trying to make a good life for myself," Clyde said, realizing that this opportunity had sort of fallen into his lap, and he was taking full advantage and thinking positive. "I want you to have that good life too."

"We're definitely on the same page there," Raymond agreed. He stuck his hand out for a shake. Clyde took it. "Thanks, Clyde, for not forgetting about me."

"That wasn't going to happen," Clyde assured him.

Raymond met his eyes. "I won't let you down, man."

"I know you won't." *Have to make sure I don't let myself down, or Trey,* Clyde thought, aware that there were always potential pitfalls along the road.

"You did what?" Trey flashed Clyde an incredulous look, turning from the steering wheel.

Clyde had expected this negative reaction to the news that he had hired Raymond and offered to sell him a stake in the club. *So just be cool and don't backpedal.*

"We talked about getting together and making something of our lives while in prison," he explained. "I'm just following through on that."

"You don't make deals with ex-cons," snapped Trey.

"I'm an ex-con," Clyde reminded him. "And you put your trust in me."

"But you're my brother, for crying out loud."

"Yeah, and he was like a brother to me while I was in a bad place. If Raymond hadn't been a steadying influence and had my back, I might never have made it out alive."

Trey's hard stare seemed to soften. "So maybe you do owe the man something. Does that mean he's entitled to a piece of the club?"

"It won't come from your half," Clyde promised him. "I'm only keeping my word. Besides, Raymond deserves a break, just like I do. He'll earn whatever he puts into the club."

"I doubt that," said Trey. "Hiring an ex-con to be in charge of security is like hiring a bank robber to run your savings and loan."

Clyde bristled at the suggestion. "It's not like that. Raymond used to have his own security firm before he ran into bad times. He's the right man for the job!"

"If you say so. I just hope you know what you're doing and who you're dealing with."

"I do," Clyde maintained and looked out the passenger-side window. He knew he could count on Raymond through thick and thin. He wasn't sure if the same thing could be said of Trey. Especially if Ivana ever decided to spill her guts.

Ivana went for her monthly visit to the hair-dresser. She actually welcomed the chance to spend a few hours away from home, which she associated with so many things, good and bad. On the good side, the situation was relatively calm between her and Trey. They had resumed a sexual relationship and even spent the whole night together a few times as she eased her way back into their sharing the same bedroom permanently.

On the bad side, she still felt terribly guilty for cheating on Trey with his brother, even if part of Ivana believed the experience had brought her out of her shell and made her reassess what she truly wanted out of life. And whom.

"You're doing good, girlfriend," Jacinta said over her. "It won't be too much longer."

"Just make sure you don't ruin my hair," Ivana half teased her. She was giving tree braids a try, believing they would look nice on her.

"Not a chance! My business depends too much on pleasing rich folks like you to misstep."

Ivana smiled. "I figured that."

"How did things go—or not—with your brother-in-law?" Jacinta asked.

You would remember that. "Excuse me?" Ivana played dumb.

"I seem to recall that you had a thing for the man. Did you ever act on it?"

At first, Ivana wanted to deny any such thing. But she needed to get this off her chest and not with a therapist, who would likely only end up reporting it to her husband. "Yes, something happened—" she hummed.

"Oh, really?" Jacinta's voice rose.

Ivana swallowed. "It wasn't planned."

"No one's pointing any fingers at you. You're human—so is he."

We'd both been through a long dry spell, Ivana thought, seeking to justify their actions to herself. It was almost inevitable that this would draw them together sexually. Even if it also tore them apart.

"Well, how was he?" Jacinta asked. "Details, please . . . I know I'm shameful in asking, but my own sex life is a big bore, so it's nice to live vicariously through others."

"He was wonderful," Ivana admitted. "The man definitely knew what he was doing, and did it all." The memory caused a prickle between her legs and she fought to resist such feelings further.

"I'm jealous," said Jacinta. "I can barely keep up with one man and you have *two* brothers competing for your affections."

"It's not like that," Ivana stressed, feeling the guilt come back in droves. "It was just a onetime thing with the brother. I still love my husband . . . and want our marriage to work."

"I'm happy to hear you say that, girl. No reason to see it go down the drain for all the wrong reasons. You got the brotherly sexual attraction thing over with and can now get on with your life and make the *real* relationship work."

I want that to happen more than anything, Ivana thought. Maybe she and Trey really could go back to when there was no one else coming between them. Yes, there was hope for that.

Trey shook hands with Clyde's ex–cell mate and imagined that by the size of him, he might be better served as a bouncer at the club than head of security, though he doubted Clyde would concur.

"Clyde's been telling me a lot about his rich big brother," Raymond said as the three men huddled near the kitchen in Trey's loft, holding beers.

Wish I could say the same. "Just don't hold any of it against me." Trey forced a smile.

Raymond grinned. "Wouldn't think of it. I know you've got Clyde's back like I do."

"Yeah, I guess that is what's most important," conceded Trey. "So I understand that you have a background in security?" *How did you ever end up on the other side of the law*?

Raymond nodded. "Did a stint in the Persian Gulf for the army, and then opened up my own private security firm. It paid the bills—least for a while, before things went south on me. . . ."

"I see."

"No, you probably don't see," Raymond said. "I made some bad investments, followed by poor choices, and paid the piper for it. I doubt you could relate."

"Don't be so sure about that." Trey gazed at Clyde and wondered how much he had divulged to Raymond about his infidelity and the problems it caused in his marriage. "We all do things we regret. Hope you make the most of your second chance."

Raymond gave a half smile. "I intend to."

"I plan to put ads in the paper and maybe on the Internet for a new bartender and jazz singer," Clyde broke in. "Maybe we'll get lucky and put the right pieces in place from the start."

"Good idea," Trey said, wanting to support him in every way. "The sooner we have the team ready to go, the sooner we can concentrate on making Clyde's Jazz Club the hottest place in town."

"I'll work on that right away." Clyde looked at Raymond. "We'll also have to assess what's needed in the security area. That's your baby."

Raymond nodded. "I'll take good care of it." He raised his bottle. "Here's to Clyde's Jazz Club and new beginnings."

Clyde lifted his beer in toast, and Trey did the same thing, happy to see that Clyde was taking charge and committed to making this work, as was he. Apparently Raymond would have a positive effect on his brother, which should be enough to keep both of them out of trouble.

Chapter Twenty-five

Clyde walked up to the bar, watching Albert put some clean glasses on a shelf behind it.

"Looks like you haven't lost your touch," Clyde said.

Albert turned, a crinkling smile appearing on his face. "I can still run rings around the young people in this line of work if I want to."

"I don't doubt that for a minute." Clyde had come to the bar with exactly that in mind. He thought briefly about Albert's niece before turning his attention back to the man himself. "How about I buy you a drink?"

Albert's thick brows lifted. "How about I buy you one?"

"You're on."

Albert filled two glasses with malt liquor and passed one to Clyde. "How are you getting along these days?"

Clyde tasted the suds. "Pretty good."

"Nice to hear." Albert gazed at him with narrowed eyes. "You haven't run into Willie Munroe again, have you?"

"No."

"Knock on wood." Albert hit the counter twice with his fist. "Maybe the man has finally gotten off the vengeance-is-mine bit and will leave you alone to live your life."

"I'm counting on it." But taking nothing for granted, Clyde thought wisely.

"So what's up?"

Clyde smiled. "Well, I've gone into business."

"Oh, yeah? What kind of business?"

"My brother and I bought a supper club."

Albert's eyes widened. "That wouldn't be the Violet Supper Club, would it?"

Clyde nodded with surprise. "That's the one."

"I heard the owner was shutting down. Didn't know he'd put the place on the market."

"He hadn't planned on it—at least not so soon. But Trey and I convinced him to do so."

Albert smiled. "I'm happy for you, Clyde. Sounds like a great opportunity. And the club is in a nice location, so you should have no trouble picking right up where Blake Lewis left off."

"I think you're right." Clyde paused. "Especially if I had one of the best in the business to oversee the bartending, alcoholic beverages, and whatnot."

"You offering me a job?" Albert asked.

"I can't think of a better person I'd want to work with—one who understands me, sometimes better than I understand myself."

"I'm flattered, man, but I've been here a long time. It's not that easy to just uproot from a job that's given me some sense of security."

"But you'll have more security and more money if you come to work at Clyde's Jazz Club."

Albert laughed. "Clyde's Jazz Club, huh? It's got a nice ring to it."

Clyde agreed. "You'll be doing me a favor if you at least seriously consider the offer. I don't have much experience running a club, and my brother will mainly be a silent partner. I could really use your help. Maybe it's time for you to say good-bye to the tavern and hello to the newest, best jazz club in town."

Albert stared at the notion. "Maybe you're right. I'll definitely give it some strong consideration."

"I have another situation I could use your help with." Clyde hoped this could lead to someone more reliable to fill the post than advertising for it.

"What's that?"

"I'm looking for a good jazz singer to work the club full-time. Male or female, doesn't matter, so long as the person has the pipes and experience to satisfy the audience and keep them coming back. Since you've been around, I thought maybe you know some people in the business who could—"

"My niece is a jazz singer," Albert interrupted. "I think you met her once."

"Stefani?"

"Yep, that's her. Sings like Sarah Vaughan and Ella Fitzgerald combined, with a little bit of Nancy Wilson thrown in for a little soul. Been at it since she was lead singer in the junior choir."

Clyde could picture the beautiful woman he'd met briefly as a jazz vocalist. "She's living in Seattle, right?"

Albert nodded. "She's there for now, but I know Stefani is looking for that kind of work at the right place and would almost certainly want to come down and audition for the job."

"I'd love to hear her sing," Clyde said. It would be nice to see her again, too.

"Then I'll make it happen." Albert put the glass to his mouth. "It could make for a perfect union."

Clyde thought about that. He definitely wouldn't mind hooking up with someone like Stefani. But would she ever want to be with someone like him with the baggage he carried? For now, he'd just settle for seeing if she could really carry a tune and if she was willing to work full-time in Paradise Bay.

"That union would be even better if I got your niece *and* you as part of the bargain in coming to work for me," Clyde said, hoping to twist his arm.

Albert chuckled. "Well, let's take one step at a time and see how it works out. I'll get on the phone with Stefani and I'm sure you'll be hearing from her."

"I'll look forward to it."

Clyde drank the malt liquor and contemplated the recent events in his life that had practically changed it overnight. He didn't want to screw things up for anyone, least of all himself. The responsibility he'd been given was like a godsend. It was up to him to make this opportunity count as if it was his last, which Clyde believed could very well be the case.

Chapter Twenty-six

Stefani McNeal stood in front of the class of eighth-graders going through the motions as a substitute teacher. She knew that most children viewed subs like they were invisible, leaving them to do as they pleased. She would have none of that. Even if this was only a part-time gig for her to make use of a degree in elementary education, Stefani took it seriously.

"Okay, settle down," she said. "Let's go over our assignment for today."

Two students were goofing off, ignoring her to see how far they could get. When she approached, they stopped and glared up at Stefani like she was interrupting something that was none of her concern.

"Is there a problem?" she asked the bushy-haired male named Adam.

"You tell me," he muttered.

Stefani eyed him sharply. "Okay, I will. I think you expected another pushover sub. Well, you're dead wrong about that. I'm an army brat, which means my dad made a career fighting wars for this country. He taught me how to fight my own battles, if I need to. Now, do you really want to test me, or can we try and get through today's class without any trouble?"

He sat, mute, lowering his head. Same thing for the boy he was misbehaving with.

"That's better," Stefani said. She walked back to the front of the room with a faint smile on her face. The truth was, though her father was tough as nails, he was a softie when it came to her, up until the day he died three years ago. Her mother had since remarried, and Stefani considered herself fortunate that she had a stepfather who she actually liked.

Too bad she couldn't say the same for her last boyfriend. She had kicked him to the curb two months ago after learning he was seeing two other women at the same time, and had the audacity to actually want them to live together as one big, happy family.

Thanks, but no thanks, she'd thought, and moved on. There had been no one since, but Stefani remained optimistic there was someone special in her future.

After class, Stefani drove to her apartment. She passed by the Space Needle and marveled at other attractions in Seattle, where she had lived for only two years after relocating from the Midwest. She passed the Green Room, where she had performed a few times as a solo jazz artist.

Stefani's first love had always been music. Her mother had been a jazz musician, performing with some of the greatest classical jazz singers. Stefani had inherited her talent, influenced as well by the likes of Sarah Vaughan, Louis Armstrong, Billie Holiday, Frank Sinatra, Nina Simone, and others who had left their mark on the genre.

While her long-term goal was to record music, Stefani was happy just performing when and where she could right now, and teaching to pay the bills.

She pulled into the parking lot, squeezing her Subaru into the thin parking space assigned to her unit. After checking her mail, she waved to some neighbors in the complex of mostly young professionals, before heading up to her third-story unit.

Stefani had barely tossed her handbag on the leather sectional and kicked off her sandals when her cell phone rang.

It was her Uncle Albert calling. Stefani had become closer to her father's brother since moving to the Pacific Northwest. She had even been to Paradise Bay to visit him a few times, along with friends she had met who were into the jazz scene.

"Hi, Uncle Albert," she said cheerfully.

"How are thing's going up there, Stefani?" he asked.

"Good. Just trying to keep those kids in line, perform, and enjoy the sunshine."

"So how would you like to do those same things here in Paradise Bay?"

Stefani smiled. He had been trying to get her to move there since she broke up with her boyfriend, suggesting that the landscape was perfect for a talented twenty-something to find employment opportunities and a love life. She hadn't been convinced on either score, though finding it pleasant enough there.

"Maybe someday," she told him politely. "Right now, I think I'm better off in Seattle."

"Well, maybe I can sweeten the pot," Albert said. "A friend of mine is opening a jazz club here. He's looking for a full-time jazz singer. I told him about you and that you might be interested."

Stefani switched the phone to her other ear, piqued. Admittedly, she had longed for the opportunity to get a more permanent gig as a performer. But with the stiff competition in Seattle, and fewer spots available for newer artists to perform, this had become more of a dream than reality. Maybe if she were in a smaller, slightly out of the way, yet still exciting city such as Paradise Bay, it could give her a venue to prove herself for future possibilities.

"Tell me more."

"The place is called Clyde's Jazz Club. It's in a great part of town and figures to attract a lot of attention for an up and coming jazz artist like yourself."

Flattery just may get you everywhere, Uncle.

Stefani thought about the club's name. "That wouldn't happen to be the same Clyde I met at the tavern a few weeks ago?"

"That's the one. I'm surprised you remember him."

How could she forget? The man was superfine, fit, and had a certain amount of coolness about him. But that didn't mean she wanted him as her employer.

"So he's looking for a singer, huh?"

"Yeah, and I'm sure that you're the right person for the job. All you have to do is show up and prove me right."

Stefani wasn't sure she was truly ready to relocate to Paradise Bay. But it did seem like a golden opportunity, so long as Clyde didn't expect her to come dirt cheap. Not to say that she couldn't find substitute teaching jobs in Paradise Bay to supplement her singing income. Still, to move had to be worth her while.

Guess I won't know 'til I check it out.

"When can you set me up for an audition?"

"You can set it up yourself. I have his number right here."

Stefani punched it into her cell phone.

"I'll give him a ring," she promised.

"I know you will." Albert cleared his throat. "By the way, Clyde offered me a job, too. I think I'm gonna take it. So maybe we can both take a step forward and see where it all leads."

Stefani was surprised someone had been able to coax her uncle into giving up his longtime job at the tavern. Clyde obviously had made him an offer he couldn't refuse. She wondered what other tricks the man had up his sleeve.

Clyde was still trying to find his way with the club he'd inherited and the responsibilities it entailed. He had kept most of the staff, who wanted to be in on the new club with its exciting possibilities. Trey had stayed mostly in the background as promised, but Clyde had called on his businessman brother for advice and stability in keeping things running smoothly, and Trey had responded with anything Clyde needed to get off to a running start.

With the pieces beginning to fall into place, Clyde got more good news when Albert took the job offer and his niece phoned. Clyde had tried to be all businesslike in talking with her, but found himself enjoying the conversation as if they were setting up a date rather than audition.

"Heard you were looking for a jazz singer?" Stefani said.

"Heard you were a jazz singer," Clyde countered amusingly.

Stefani chuckled. "Cute. I think I can bring it home."

"Only one way to find out."

"I'm up for the challenge. Just tell me when and where."

"How about this weekend, say Saturday?" Clyde asked. The club was still open for business and it would be a good opportunity to see how she performed before an audience.

She paused. "Sure. I think I can take the train down."

Clyde grinned. "Didn't know people still took the train these days."

Stefani laughed. "Where have you been? With the gas prices these days, it's the only way to travel from state to state and enjoy the view at the same time."

It hit home right then for Clyde that his time behind bars had robbed him of life's simple pleasures, making him want to make up for lost time in every way. He imagined he would enjoy a train ride with someone as attractive and intriguing as Stefani. Maybe someday.

"Guess I'll have to take your word for that," he said.

"Well, I'm always as good as my word," she joked. "So I'll see you on Saturday."

"I look forward to it."

Clyde had meant every word of that, and now, three days later, he got to see the lady again in person as he stood toe to toe with Stefani at the club.

"Nice to see you again," she said, poised and looking great in a striped boat neck top, tight pants, and leather boots.

"You too," Clyde said, and shook her extended hand, finding it warm and inviting. He introduced her to Raymond and the club's piano man, Winston Everly.

"Hi." She smiled at them.

Raymond gave her a hug, as though old friends. "Clyde says you're from Seattle."

Stefani nodded. "Have you been there?"

"Yeah, a time or two. Great city."

"I'd say you're just what this places needs," Winston said, touching his glasses.

Stefani grinned at the forty-something, thin pianist. "Maybe you'd better wait 'til you hear me."

"So why wait?" Clyde drew her attention back to him, feeling a little left out, while admittedly eager to hear her sing. "Let's see what you can do."

"I'm ready," Stefani boldly declared.

"You pick the number and I can play it," Winston said confidently.

Within moments, Stefani was standing on a small platform beside him, and began singing the Gershwin tune "They Can't Take That Away From Me."

Clyde and Raymond took a seat up front and listened as Stefani began to belt out the song as though written specifically for her.

"Man, she's got it going on," Raymond stated admiringly.

"Yeah, she does." Clyde felt a chill listening to her voice. More importantly, he could see that all eyes in the club were glued on her, equally riveted by Stefani the lady. She was definitely the real deal, and he had better not let her get away. He didn't intend to.

"You're hired."

"Just like that?" Stefani gazed across the table at Clyde. He had invited her to dinner at the club to discuss her employment future.

Clyde grinned. "Yeah, I can't think of any better way to say it."

She flashed pearly white teeth. "Neither can I." Before she got too carried away at the notion of being the featured singer at a jazz club, Stefani came back down to earth for a few practical matters. "What type of pay are we talking about?"

Clyde stared at the question. "Honestly, I don't have any experience in this type of thing. Why don't you tell me what sounds fair to you and we'll go from there?"

She laughed. "Okay, let me think about it." Stefani threw a number at him, believing it probably wouldn't fly. But since she would be giving up her teaching gig and singing in Seattle to relocate, it didn't sound unreasonable to her.

"Sounds fine to me," Clyde said without prelude.

"Really?"

"Yes. If it's not enough?"

"It is," Stefani said. She didn't want to get greedy.

"Then are we in business?" he asked in a serious tone.

Stefani beamed. "Yes, I'd say you have yourself a singer."

"Great! So when can you start?"

Stefani considered the question. "Well, I'll need time to get things together since this is something I obviously hadn't planned on."

Clyde gave an understanding nod. "If you need any help with moving or anything, let me know."

She lifted a brow whimsically. "Are you always this generous and accommodating?"

"Not always. Guess I'm just eager to get my new jazz singer set up in town so she can woo my customers with some great tunes the way she wooed me."

Stefani blushed. She found herself looking forward to it as well, viewing this as a great opportunity. Being employed by such a handsome, sweet man didn't hurt things either. But what made him tick beyond the very likable facade? Maybe she'd find out sometime.

"So how long have you known my uncle?"

Clyde sliced into a honey-glazed pork chop. "We go back a few years."

"I see." She scooped up some diced carrots. "He thinks highly of you."

"Works both ways," Clyde stated. "Albert's a good man."

"I agree, though I've only really gotten to spend time with my uncle recently." Stefani noticed there was no ring on Clyde's finger. Not married. Good to know. But did he have a girlfriend?

Am I really ready to jump back into a relationship with the first good-looking man to intrigue me since breaking up with my boyfriend? Was Clyde even boyfriend material?

Clyde thought back to the first time he saw Stefani. She was even more gorgeous now, if that was possible. Did one of those friends she had in town include a boyfriend? Or was he waiting for her in Seattle? Any man in his right man would never let her get away, even as a career move. *I know I wouldn't if she were my girlfriend.*

He looked across the table at her, finding himself intrigued beyond her gifted voice. "Tell me a little something about yourself, Stefani, other than singing."

"Well, I'm twenty-five, a substitute teacher, love to jog, and read women's fiction."

Sounds like the perfect combination. "Single?" *Hope the question doesn't make her uncomfortable.*

Stefani angled a thin brow. "Yes," she told him candidly. "I broke up with my boyfriend a while ago. Just didn't work out."

"Too bad." Actually, Clyde considered that a good thing.

"How about you?"

"Single too," he answered coolly, leaving it at that for now.

"Guess we're in the same boat then," she said.

"Let's just hope the waters remain calm. Would not want to run into any sharks."

Stefani laughed. "Neither would I."

Clyde thought of Ivana and their brief tête-à-tête. It hardly qualified as dating. Then there was the reality that he'd been out of the dating scene for several years for reasons beyond his control. Would Stefani hold that against him?

"What made you want to start a jazz club?" she asked over her goblet of wine.

"Good question," conceded Clyde. "The short answer is, the opportunity presented itself and I took it."

"And the long answer?" She grinned. "Or is that best for another time?"

He flashed a half smile. "Another time," he said simply, and wondered if the time would ever come where he would feel comfortable divulging some of his dark secrets.

"Well, I'd say it was a good move. Jazz is hot right now, and having a club in a good location like this can keep it that way."

"I couldn't agree more." Clyde tasted his wine, eyeing his lovely new singer. Things were definitely starting to look up with each passing moment.

Chapter Twenty-seven

"This is my brother, Trey," Clyde introduced Stefani.

"Nice to meet you, Trey."

Trey offered a smile. "You too." He could see now why Clyde seemed so smitten with the young woman who he couldn't seem to stop talking about since she auditioned for him a week ago. Maybe his baby brother had finally found someone he could go after romantically, if Trey read the vibes correctly. "I hear that you have an amazing voice that's packing them in."

Stefani blushed. "Not sure I'm packing them in just yet. But so far the reviews have been mostly positive."

That was an understatement, Trey thought. Seemed like she had the golden touch when it came to singing jazz from everything he'd heard, which was plenty. Add to that the complete physical package one could envision of a stunning, shapely, sultry crooner, and it was obvious that Clyde had a winner in his jazz vocalist in more ways than one.

"Why don't you bring Stefani over for dinner tomorrow night?" Trey suggested. "I'm sure Ivana would love to meet her. Maybe they can even become friends."

Clyde hesitated. "Sounds good, but I'm sure Stefani has other plans."

Trey gazed at her, unwilling to give up so easily. "You'd be doing me a favor if you could come." He didn't want to pressure her, yet hoped she would feel at ease with him and Ivana, as an employee of the club in which he was half owner.

"I'd love to come." She looked up at Clyde tentatively. "If that's all right with you."

"Why wouldn't it be?" he said hastily and faced Trey. "We'll be there."

"Marvelous." Trey smiled, though he sensed his brother's uneasiness for some reason. He assumed it had to do with fear of failure where it concerned a potential relationship, something Trey had never known Clyde to have with anyone. Maybe Stefani could provide the type of stability he needed in balancing his personal and professional life.

Clyde forced a grin at Trey, and then Stefani, as they stood in the club. He was nervous about having dinner at Trey's place for a damned good reason. He doubted Ivana would want to see him, and figured she probably wouldn't be too crazy about meeting Stefani and becoming her friend. But he couldn't exactly tell that to Trey. Not without admitting he had a one-night stand with Ivana and that she'd wanted it to go further. The fact that he passed on her offer wouldn't win him many brownie points with Trey, considering that he'd already slept with his brother's wife.

Clyde bit his tongue. He had no choice but to go along with the program and hope Ivana didn't do anything crazy, ruining things for both of them. Aside from damaging his relationship with Trey, the last thing Clyde wanted was to blow what had the potential to be something special with Stefani.

"Your brother seems nice," Stefani said after Trey left.

"Don't let that smooth voice and calm demeanor fool you," Clyde told her.

She frowned. "You mean he's not so nice?"

Clyde chuckled. "Just playing with you. Trey is a great guy and the best brother one could have. Without him, I wouldn't be where I am today."

"Then I guess we're both in his debt, as I'm here as a result."

He smiled. "Good point. I'll have to thank Trey later for that."

"Are you sure you're okay with having me as your unofficial date for dinner with Trey and his wife?"

"I'm more than okay with it," Clyde assured her. "And, if it's all right with you, I'd like to make that an official date."

Stefani showed her teeth. "I think I can handle that."

Clyde grinned while wondering if Ivana would be half as gracious.

"I invited Clyde and Stefani over for dinner tomorrow," Trey told Ivana that night.

"You might have told me beforehand," she complained.

"Come on, it's no big deal. Stefani's the new singer at the club, so I thought it would be good if you got to know her."

"Why on earth would I want to get to know her?" Ivana's lower lip hung open. "We have absolutely nothing in common."

"How do you know that? You might have a lot in common."

She doubted that. "Such as?"

"Well, Stefani's beautiful, for one, just like you; and Clyde is into her, even if he hasn't come right out and said they're dating."

Ivana bristled at the thought. So Clyde had found someone else to share his bed with. Was she better at pleasing him?

Why should I be jealous? We're so over and done with. He can bed whoever he wants. Can't he?

"Good for him," she said, trying to keep her voice blasé.

"I think its damned good for him," Trey said. "To tell you the truth, I'm flabbergasted that he's gone this long without any action that I'm aware of. Not that he'd share his sex-life details with me. We never really got that deep about it when we were younger. Why start now?"

Maybe because you'd hate your brother if he told you where he'd gotten some action, Ivana thought. *And your wife, too.*

"Some things are better left unsaid," she told him.

"Well, actions speak louder than words," Trey stated thoughtfully. "For Clyde's sake, I hope Stefani is the real deal, and that he recognizes it before someone else snatches her."

You mean like you? Ivana grew angry at the thought of Trey lusting after this singer the way he did Helene. She could imagine him trying to pull one over on her again, while coming out on top where it concerned his brother. *Don't even think about it.* Ivana would sooner leave Trey—if not kill him—than be humiliated again by his wandering eye and overactive libido.

***

"You didn't tell me your brother was rich," Stefani said, marveling at the size of the house before her.

Clyde downplayed it. "I don't really like to talk about much. It's no big deal."

"I agree," she said. "Just surprised, that's all."

Now Clyde felt he was being overly defensive for some reason, as if he were competing with his brother. Maybe he was, in many respects. "Trey's always been the go-getter in the family. It's paid off for him. I'm only trying to hang in there without being left too far behind."

Stefani grinned. "Do I detect a little brotherly competition?"

"Maybe a little," Clyde conceded. "Comes with the territory. Trey is a tough act to follow, though. He's motivated me to at least go after my dreams and let the rest take care of itself."

"Sounds like Trey has your best interests at heart."

"That hasn't always been the case, but I think you're right." Clyde thought back to protecting Trey's interests when Willie wanted them for himself, and the price he had paid. So maybe they were even now. For the moment, Clyde only wanted to get through this night without any major fireworks or embarrassment. "Ready to go in?" he asked his date.

Stefani smiled with a nod. "Yes, it should be fun."

Clyde held his breath on that one.

"Ivana, this is Stefani McNeal," Trey introduced. "The jazz vocalist Clyde hired to sing at the club."

Ivana surveyed her. *She's lovely, just as Trey indicated, with a nice body to match.* Feeling a tad envious, Ivana couldn't help but wonder how she measured up to Stefani in Clyde's eyes, not to mention Trey's.

"Thanks for having me," Stefani said.

"Thanks for coming," Ivana responded nicely to keep up appearances. She met Clyde's face with a hard gaze and he averted his eyes.

"You have a beautiful home, Ivana," Stefani told her.

"It's taken a lot of hard work, but we're happy with it." Ivana glanced at Trey.

"Yes, we are," he agreed. "But in the end, it's just bricks, wood, plaster, and a lot of expensive things to fill it. What's really important is that guests are as comfortable here as we are."

"That's a great attitude to have," Stefani said with a smile, eyeing Clyde.

"My brother has always had a great attitude about all the important things," Clyde indicated.

Ivana begged to differ. Trey hadn't considered his marriage important enough to keep from falling into the arms of another woman. Not that Ivana was faultless, having done the same thing when at her weakest moment, only to find that Clyde had cast her aside and put his focus on the attractive singer.

Now Ivana was left to deal with the betrayal of both brothers, coupled with her own betrayal. She could only hope to make the best of her messed-up life, if it was possible.

So far, so good, Clyde thought, having Ivana and Stefani under one roof without Ivana getting crazy on him. *Let's hope it stays that way.* He had mixed feelings in returning to the house. It was there that Trey had put him up after being released, giving him a chance to get back on his feet. Clyde couldn't thank him enough for that. But it was also where he had crossed the line, regretting it more than he could express. There was no turning back the clock, though. The damage had been done, and it was best to move on, which he was trying hard to do.

He wasn't convinced Ivana felt the same way, as she'd given him the evil eye ever since they'd arrived. Had Trey noticed? Stefani?

"If everyone's ready, then the food is served," Francine said, entering the living room.

"Let's eat!" Trey voiced, leading the way. He put an arm around Clyde's shoulder. "Hope you brought your appetite with you, little brother."

"Always," Clyde said, smiling thinly. He glanced at the women taking up the rear. Stefani grinned at him, looking as lovely as ever. Ivana was unreadable, but she seemed to be adjusting to the idea that what they had was over and that even friendship was probably a bad idea at this point. Maybe now she would give her relationship with Trey a real chance to succeed, just as Clyde was interested in seeing if anything good could come out of his attraction to Stefani, which seemed very mutual.

"Did you have to stick it in my face?" Ivana asked Clyde bluntly. She had followed him into the huge downstairs bathroom while Trey showed off his vast collection of jazz CDs to Stefani.

"What the hell are you talking about?"

"You know damned well," she retorted. "Bringing another woman to my house to show off."

"Wasn't my idea to come here," he told her. "And even then, why would I want to stick anything in your face?"

Ivana wickedly cast her eyes down below his waist. "You tell me. You seemed to do a pretty good job of it before."

"Give it a rest, Ivana." A vein bulged in Clyde's temple. "What happened between us is over and done with. Let's not go there and stir up a hornet's nest."

Ivana sneered. "So is she *really* all that?"

"We're not dating, if that's what you're asking. Not yet, anyway. But Stefani is all that when it comes to singing."

Ivana gave him a dismissive look. If they weren't dating, it was only a matter of time before he got into Stefani's panties. She supposed it would have happened sooner or later that he'd find someone safe to be with. Didn't mean Ivana had to pretend there weren't still mixed emotions where it concerned Clyde and their hot night of passion. Even if her heart belonged to Trey.

"Go back to your singer," she told Clyde through puckered lips. "Hope you don't break her heart. You Lancaster brothers seem to be very good at that."

"Maybe you should look in the mirror at your own faults, Ivana, before jumping on us," he suggested. "We all step off the wagon at some time or another in our lives. When it happens, you have to deal with it and not drown in the muddy water."

"Spare me the philosophy crap, Clyde. It's not you." Ivana peered at him. "Or are you becoming your brother without even realizing it, Mr. Jazz Club Co-owner?"

Clyde bristled. "I think you know the answer to that."

"Question is, do you?—considering you've been *everywhere* he has and more."

He jutted his chin, but offered no response as they joined Trey and Stefani. Ivana wondered if she should have kept her mouth shut and not been so brutal, since what they had was over and done with. Or had he got everything he deserved?

"Thought we'd head out now," Clyde told Stefani.

Trey frowned. "But you practically just got here, and the night's still young."

"Actually, we were thinking about catching a late movie," Clyde said, gazing at Stefani.

She offered a brief smile. "I'm always up for a good movie."

It was obvious to Ivana that he was lying through his teeth in a bid to get away from them—or her. Maybe it was a wise decision, all things considered, for having him there only made her feel guiltier.

"Well, the movie's on us," Trey said, putting an arm around Ivana. "Clyde probably told you that we own a few movie theaters in town."

Stefani was taken aback. "No, he didn't."

"I didn't want to overwhelm you with the fact that my brother practically owns half the city," Clyde joked.

Stefani gave a little laugh. "Well, I suppose it could be a bit daunting, but fun to know."

"It's not a big deal," Trey said, downplaying. "I just want you to enjoy the movie. And throw in some popcorn and a drink as our treat."

"You're very kind, but—"

"Don't argue with him," Ivana cut in. "When Trey wants something, he usually doesn't take no for an answer."

"Well, in that case, guess I won't say no," Stefani said with an uneasy grin.

Ivana looked up at Trey, imagining he was pleased that she put him on a pedestal. She had a feeling Clyde had mixed emotions on the issue. For her part, Ivana had grown tired of fighting with the two brothers. She just wasn't sure how to resolve the issue that was threatening to tear them apart.

"What was all that about anyway?" Stefani asked Clyde during the drive.

He feigned ignorance, angling his eyes at her. "I don't follow you."

"I didn't realize we had talked about seeing a movie."

How can I explain without divulging things I shouldn't? Clyde looked back at the road over the steering wheel. "Guess I just felt a bit stuffy in there. And with Trey seemingly ready to invite us to stay the night, I had to think of some way for us to leave."

Stefani chuckled. "So it's a brother thing, huh?"

"Yeah, something like that," Clyde said. Along with a sister-in-law thing. He wanted to kick himself for allowing Ivana to get under his skin. And to think he believed she might have been starting to come around. Instead, it was the same old bitter and jealous woman who seemed determined to stir up the pot and make him sweat.

"Are we still on for a movie?" Stefani regarded his profile. "Or was that simply to get out of there?"

"Unless you have something better in mind?" Clyde turned to her, hoping that was the case.

"We could go to your place instead," Stefani suggested.

Clyde, who had been a perfect gentleman around Stefani, felt his libido go up a couple of notches. Only yesterday Raymond had moved out, finding a place not far from the club. Maybe things were happening as meant to be. One could only hope.

"Sure, we can go to my place," he said. "As long as you don't expect a replica of my brother's grand estate."

"No expectations," she promised. "Let's just play it by ear."

"Okay by me." Clyde imagined nibbling on her ear, then the other, and much more thereafter. The notion agreed with him wholeheartedly.

Chapter Twenty-eight

The moment they stepped inside the loft, Clyde and Stefani were all over one another. They ripped off each other's clothes and barely made their way to Clyde's platform bed. It was Stefani who pushed Clyde onto the matelasse coverlet, admiring his six-pack abs and tightly muscled physique. Her eyes lowered to his magnificent, full erection and she felt a tremor at the thought of it being in her.

She bent down and kissed his penis, licking the shaft once, teasingly, and feeling Clyde shudder, before trailing hot kisses along his stomach and up his chest. When Stefani's mouth arrived at Clyde's handsome face and waiting lips, she went for them with the passion of a woman who somehow felt as though she'd met her match in Clyde Lancaster. She didn't know who he'd been with before her, or what issues there may have been, but in Stefani's mind it was ancient history, just as her own intimate past. She wanted only to focus on the here and now, and sensed Clyde felt very much the same way.

As though they were longtime companions, Clyde and Stefani began to make love zestfully and tirelessly, exploring each other's bodies, inhaling scents, and leaving no stone unturned.

"You feel wonderful inside me," Stefani murmured in Clyde's ear as she absorbed his measured, mighty thrusts, wanting him to go deeper and deeper. She nibbled at his earlobe and ran her hands over and across his shaven head, wanting to enjoy every bit of him.

"I'm loving being in you," Clyde spoke in a throaty voice as Stefani wrapped her legs high across his back, holding him tightly while they went at each other with utter abandon.

Clyde pulled Stefani atop him and they continued to have hot sex without missing a beat. He held her thin waist and arched his back to meet her time and again as she rode him lustfully. Soon, they were on their sides, kissing, licking, tickling, touching, and caressing, before changing positions and starting all over again as though neither could get enough of the other.

By the time they shared an explosive climax, their bodies were wet with lust and spent energy. Clyde put his tongue in Stefani's mouth, enchanted by her taste, before sucking her lips and thrusting himself into her during one final burst of dizzying heights. He slumped beside

Stefani while catching his breath and trying to come to terms with what just happened. It was unreal, yet the most real thing he may have ever experienced.

"Did I just dream that?" he asked with a low laugh

Stefani hummed and ran a finger down his chest enticingly. "If you did, then we were both in dreamland."

"Then don't ever wake me up. Unless, of course, I'm opening my eyes to you."

She flushed. "Guess we make a pretty good team, huh?"

"More than pretty good," Clyde said. "How about a *great* team!"

Stefani raised her chin. "Do you think it's a good idea to mix pleasure with business?"

He didn't have to think about it very long. "Yeah, in this case, it's very good."

"I was thinking the same thing."

"The club can have you as one hell of a jazz singer," Clyde said. "But you're all mine as a beautiful, vivacious, sexy-as-hell woman I want to be with."

"And you're mine as a gorgeous, sexy man who definitely knows how to mesmerize this lady."

It made Clyde think about being with Ivana, and how they had charmed each other. But that was different. He didn't experience the highs with her that he had with Stefani and was still feeling right now. If this wasn't love, it was damned close.

I'd better not go there right now. No need to spoil things by scaring the lady to death for something she may not be ready to hear.

At the same time, Clyde felt that if they were going to go somewhere with this, he should be up front about an important part of his past. If she couldn't handle it, he needed to know now.

"I have to tell you something," he spoke softly in her ear.

"Please don't tell me you have a wife and three children somewhere," Stefani joked humorlessly.

"No, nothing like that." Clyde drew in a deep breath. "I spent some time in prison."

Stefani raised her eyes at him. "Really?"

"Yeah. I got into a fight with a friend and, well, things got out of hand."

She was aghast. "Did you kill him?"

"No, but I hurt him pretty bad."

"So what made you get into this fight with a friend?" she asked curiously.

Clyde pondered the question. He didn't want to involve his brother in this discussion. Or even think about the secret he carried about Trey in that regard.

"It was something stupid," he said regretfully. "We had a disagreement and came to blows. He got the worst of it and I ended up in prison. I wish it hadn't happened, but it was a time in my life when I was too immature and hung out with the wrong people." One person, in particular.

"It's all right," Stefani told him. "Life can sometimes be a lesson to us all. I'm sure that part of your life is behind you."

"It is," Clyde promised, hoping to hell it didn't come back to haunt him again. "I just wanted you to know before Albert mentioned it."

"Uncle Albert likes you, Clyde. I doubt he'd ever hold past sins against you."

Clyde mused. *I hold them against myself, but that's another story.* "That's good to know."

She tilted her chin and went for his mouth. "I'm a big girl. I make my own choices in men based on chemistry, intelligence, good looks, and what my instincts tell me. And I choose you."

Clyde grinned, feeling warm all over. "That means more than you know. I choose you too."

He kissed her, and it turned into more passionate kisses. They made love again, slow and sensually, then fast and furious, before Clyde reflected on the start of what promised to be a lasting, satisfying relationship, minus the drama and second thoughts of his brief involvement with Ivana.

Chapter Twenty-nine

Luther handed Willie a brown paper bag. "Check it out, man. I think this is what you wanted."

Willie opened a bag as they stood in an alley. He pulled out a Ruger P345 automatic pistol and liked the way it felt in his hand. "Yeah, this'll work just fine. Where'd you get it?"

"Friend of a friend," said Luther. "Been stripped, so it's cool."

Willie took solace in that. "How much?"

Luther told him. "You're getting your money's worth."

"I know that."

Willie got out the hundred-dollar bills that Roselyn had taken from an advance on her credit card, and handed them over, aware that Luther was only acting as a middleman here and, as such, Willie didn't want to take a chance in screwing someone else over.

"So you gonna rob a bank now, or what?"

Willie smiled, tucking the pistol in his pants. Not that he hadn't considered it, but he had other plans for the gun. "Naw, man. I'll leave the bank robbin' to the pros. Like I told you before, I just want to have an insurance policy, in case somethin' goes down."

Luther looked at him suspiciously. "You still plan on gunning for Clyde?"

"What if I am?" Willie asked tersely.

"I'm with you, man. But he ain't worth spending the rest of your life in prison. Everyone knows what he done to you. Including the cops. You think if he's offed they won't come lookin' for your ass?"

Willie's nostrils flared. The thought of rotting away in some cold cell with cockroaches at his feet didn't exactly sit well with him. Neither did letting bygones be bygones where it concerned his ex–best friend, Clyde. If Clyde could survive years behind bars it couldn't have been too bad.

Don't mean I want to follow his footsteps. Or watch him live the good life while mine continues to suck.

"I got a score to settle with Clyde," Willie said without apology. Maybe more than one. "There's other ways to get it done than taking a life." He could think of few things that would be just as satisfying.

"I agree," Luther said, sounding relieved. "He's got a weakness just like everyone else. Once you find it, you'll know what to do."

Willie grinned mischievously. "Yeah, like Samson. Only I know it ain't shavin' his head."

Both men laughed, but inside Willie was anything but jovial. Clyde Lancaster had gotten the upper hand on him one time too many. He planned to change that in a way he wouldn't soon forget.

Willie lay beside Roselyn in her bed, smoking a joint. It was a sweet aftermath to going at it for a good hour or more. The woman was insatiable. He wasn't complaining, though, as Willie gave as much as he received. And maybe a little bit extra. More importantly, she gave him money when he needed it, which was often. Seemed like a fair exchange to him.

Roselyn took the joint from Willie and inhaled deeply, then gave him a toothy smile. "That's so nice," she hummed.

"You like it?" He smiled, amused.

"Not as good as sex, but yes, it's good."

Willie grabbed the joint and sucked on it, already feeling his libido and erection returning.

"Will you take me to the grand opening of that jazz club Saturday night?" asked Roselyn.

Willie's left brow shot up. "What jazz club?"

"The one over on Broadway. Used to be the Violet Supper Club. Now it's called Clyde's Jazz Club. Think I heard that these two brothers bought the place and it will feature a jazz singer. I just love listening to that kind of music."

Willie barely even paid attention to her as his mind was still caught on the jazz club owned by *two* brothers. *Clyde's Jazz Club?*

He knew instinctively who the brothers were and which one had financed the buyout. It irked Willie that Clyde had gone over to the other side, deciding it was better to take his brother's money than resent it like before.

Maybe I'll take some of it too. And this time I won't let him or anyone else stop me.

"Well, how about it, honey?" Roselyn entreated. "It would be fun."

"Yeah, let's go. Maybe we'll even run into this Clyde dude himself."

Willie sucked on the joint and felt it taking effect. So too was the anger boiling over in him like water in a kettle in seeing his old friend leading the good life as if he had a right to. *You'll get yours and so will your rich-ass brother*.

Roselyn took the joint from him. "Think I'm in the mood for something else now."

Willie felt an adrenaline rush. "Yeah, me too."

"So let's do something about it."

"Whatever you say, baby."

Willie climbed on top of her and started to have sex, while thinking about raining hard on Clyde's parade so he never knew what hit him. 'Til it was too late.

Chapter Thirty

Clyde was admittedly nervous for the official grand opening of the club. It was the first time in his life that he was actually pretty much solely responsible for something other than himself. He wanted this to be big in Paradise Bay and something that even Trey would have to approve of.

"Chill out, man," Raymond told him, straightening Clyde's burgundy silk tie. "Nothing's going to go wrong."

"Wish I could be so sure," Clyde said, fearing that bad things seemed to follow him around like a shadow.

"Look at it this way: we both just spent time in hell. How much worse can it get than that?"

Clyde nodded thoughtfully. "Good point."

"Damned good one." Raymond tucked the tie into Clyde's charcoal suit. "I'd say you're all set now for your grand opening."

Clyde favored his friend in a pinstriped suit. "I think we both are."

Raymond buttoned his coat. "Hey, anything beats prison denims."

"Amen to that."

A little later Clyde was talking with Albert, confirming that the bar was well stocked and ready.

"The folks can order anything they want and we've got it," Albert said.

"That's what I like to hear."

"We aim to please—you and everyone else."

"I appreciate your joining me over here," Clyde told him sincerely. Not to mention introducing him to his niece.

Albert's eyes crinkled. "You kidding? And miss out on a chance to move up a bit in the world? My pleasure, Clyde."

"About Stefani . . ." Clyde hesitated, not wanting to say the wrong thing. "I don't know how much you—"

"I know you two have become an item and I'm cool with it." Albert patted him on the shoulder. "She's a wonderful niece and I know you won't hurt her and have to answer to me."

Clyde grinned. "Wouldn't think of it."

"Then I hope things work out for you."

They were already working out better than he could have expected as far as Clyde was concerned. Stefani had given him a whole new reason to live; one he didn't intend to turn his back on. He was happy to have Albert's blessing to take this wherever it was meant to go.

"Well, time to get the show on the road," he said, taking a breath.

"I'm with you all the way," Albert told him genially.

Trey took his seat beside Ivana for opening night of what he suspected would be a very successful venture he and Clyde had embarked on. After a hard life, Clyde deserved to find some success and happiness. Maybe even love in his life. Clyde had indicated to Trey that Stefani might be the one.

Trey hoped that was the case, as the two of them seemed to belong together and Stefani was definitely a calming influence on his brother's life. It was rather ironic to Trey that, while things seemed to be coming up roses for Clyde, he was still trying to get his own life together. On the surface, Trey and Ivana were still one of the most envied couples in Paradise Bay. But behind closed doors, they were anything but the ideal couple.

Trey was still trying to make amends to his wife for past sins. Though continuing to sleep in separate rooms, they had managed to find more time for each other, including in bed. Trey sensed that Ivana was still holding back on him, unable or unwilling to give her all to him intimately or emotionally. He would take each day as a step forward, slowly but surely, determined to win Ivana back in full, loving her that much and never wishing to have a life without.

Trey ordered cocktails, with an eye on not allowing Ivana to overdo it. The last thing either of them needed was for her to go off the deep end and ruin the grand opening, while setting things back in their progress as a couple.

"You look beautiful tonight," Trey told Ivana, and she watched his eyes admiring the designer crimson halter dress she wore.

"Thank you." Ivana gave him an appropriate, sweet smile. She didn't necessarily feel beautiful, but it was nice to hear the words from him. At least if he focused on her, Trey's eyes wouldn't wander to Helene DeCroch, whom Ivana had spotted there with her husband. Or Stefani, who Trey seemed as attracted to as Clyde. *Or am I just imagining all this and getting worked up over nothing?*

Perhaps Trey now really did only have eyes for the woman he was married to. Ivana wasn't sure she could say the same as Clyde approached their table, looking resplendent and at peace with himself.

"How's everyone doing?" he asked, avoiding her gaze.

"We're fine," Trey said.

"Good." Clyde scratched his cheek. "If you need anything—"

"We'll be sure to holler," Ivana said with a catch to her voice, while wondering if he truly meant *anything*. Including anyone.

He met her eyes briefly. "You do that."

"Go run your club," Trey said affectionately. "We've got things covered here."

"All right." Clyde nodded, patting him on the shoulder.

Ivana watched him walk away, seemingly content with his life these days. She only wished hers was as satisfying. Maybe in time it could be again. Or would there always be obstacles to finding true happiness with her husband again?

She sipped her drink and gave Trey another smile as he studied her as if to see if she was going to lose it. Ivana had no intention of making a fool of herself in public. She'd done that enough in private to last a lifetime. All she wanted now was a little peace and stability, even if both stood on shaky ground at the moment.

"It's time," Clyde told Stefani after Winston had warmed up the full house with his terrific piano playing.

"I'm all set," she assured him.

Clyde surveyed her stunning almond strapless crinkle gown. Her hair was pinned up and her mouth shone with mocha ice lip gloss. He wanted very much to taste those lips, but kissed her cheek instead so as not to mess up her makeup.

"You are totally hot tonight," he uttered.

She flashed him an admiring smile. "You too."

"Maybe we can do something about that later. What do you think?"

"I'm counting on it," she said teasingly.

Clyde met her eyes hungrily. "So am I. Every moment I'm with you, I don't want to be anywhere else."

Stefani squeezed his hand. "You certainly know how to make a woman feel special."

He thought momentarily about Ivana. "That's because you are special."

She lit up. "Thank you."

"No, thank you," he said honestly. "Knock 'em dead out there."

"I'll do my best."

A few minutes later, Clyde was transfixed as Stefani stood before her audience and the club was completely silent. She glanced at Winston and nodded, signaling the time to begin playing. She began belting out, "I'll Be Seeing You." This was followed shortly after by, "I Thought About You."

Clyde joined everyone in applauding. It was clear that Stefani had the crowd in the palm of her hand. She would do wonders to draw people in and keep others coming back. More importantly, Stefani was there for him at a time in his life that Clyde needed her. He didn't take that for granted, or what they could do for each other in offering comfort and romance.

"She's really good," Roselyn said.

Willie studied the singer, having seen her cozying up to Clyde before she went on. *Bet he's banging her. Bastard. Something I wouldn't mind doing if I had the chance.*

"I've heard better," he grumbled and sipped the cocktail that had him feeling a bit courageous in combination with the joint he had smoked before coming to the club.

"Where?" she challenged him. "Certainly not in Paradise Bay."

"Yeah, whatever."

Roselyn turned to him. "What's got you in such a crappy mood? I thought you wanted to come?"

Why would I be happy to be in a place owned by my sworn and bitter enemy? "I'm cool," he told her. "Enjoy the show."

Willie felt antsy just sitting there. He got up.

"Where are you going?" Roselyn asked.

"To take a leak. Be back in a minute."

After separating from her, Willie took another look at the sexy singer before heading in the direction where he saw Clyde going. It was time he told him what he really thought of his ex-homie and this club Clyde was using to hide from his past.

"Glad you could make it," Clyde whispered to Grant and Helene DeCroch. He made it his business to circulate amongst those who came, knowing it was a smart thing to do as an up-and-coming businessman. Even if there was some history between Trey and Helene that had indirectly led to Clyde getting it on with Ivana.

"We wouldn't have missed the grand opening for the world," Helene said agreeably. "Thank you for inviting us."

"My pleasure," he said, knowing that it was more Trey's doing than his.

"That singer is magnificent," Grant said. "Where did you find her?"

"I'll never tell," Clyde quipped, sensing that Grant's interest was more than passing.

"Well, if you're ever foolhardy enough to let her go, she's got a place at one of my hotels."

"I'll keep that in mind, but I don't expect Ms. McNeal to be vacating the premises anytime soon."

Grant grinned. "I would have been surprised if you'd said otherwise."

Clyde grinned back. *So would I.* He expected Stefani to be an important part of this club and his life for some time to come. He could even imagine them one day tying the knot and bringing a new generation of Lancasters into the world. The thought made Clyde consider that Trey had lost out on the chance to become a father. Whether another opportunity would come along for Trey and Ivana was anyone's guess.

One of the security staff interrupted Clyde's train of thought. "We've got someone trying to stir up trouble," he whispered. "Apparently this dude is asking to see you and refuses to take no for an answer."

Clyde raised a brow. "Where is he?"

"Over there."

Clyde looked toward an area near the entrance and saw Willie Munroe glaring at him, while being restrained by Raymond and another staffer.

How the hell did he get in here? And what does he want with me? As if I don't know.

Clyde took a breath and walked away smoothly so as not to attract attention to himself and away from Stefani.

"What seems to be the problem?" Clyde asked as though confronting a total stranger rather than someone he had a history with that he would just as soon forget.

"This dude looks like he's got a death wish," growled Raymond, gripping Willie firmly.

"Tell your brute to get his paws off me, man." Willie shot Clyde a wicked gaze.

"Not a chance, asshole," Raymond voiced.

The last thing Clyde wanted was to make a scene. Maybe if he spoke to Willie man-to-man, he would go away quietly.

Maybe.

Clyde made eye contact with Raymond. "Let him go."

He did so reluctantly, but stayed within arm's reach.

"What do you want, Willie?" Clyde asked tartly.

Willie stood mute with his mouth open in a sneer.

Raymond's eyes widened. "You know this punk?"

"We go back a few years," Clyde reluctantly admitted. That still was no reason for him to show his face there after Clyde had made it perfectly clear the last time they met that he didn't want to see Willie again. Now he had to deal with it. "All right, Willie, you've got my attention. Say what you have to and get the hell out of my club!"

Willie glared. "Okay, I will," he snapped. "You and me, we ain't through yet. Playing Mr. Big Shot in this club ain't gonna change nothing. It's because of you I'm only seein' out of one eye. That's something I got to carry the rest of my life. If you think—"

"I think you need to get a life!" Clyde cut him off, having listened to enough. "Grow the hell up, Willie. We both know you should have spent time in prison too, but your ass was let off the hook. Now do us both a favor and leave me alone. I don't want to see your face anymore!"

"What about what I want?" Willie spat, his mouth turned down menacingly.

"You won't find it here," Clyde insisted. "Whatever went down between us ended a long time ago. That's where it stays!"

"Don't bet on that!" Willie sputtered and lunged toward Clyde, but he was intercepted by the bigger Raymond.

"Get him out of here," Clyde said simply and walked away without looking back.

"It'll be my pleasure, man."

Raymond, with the help of another burly member of the security staff, roughly ushered Willie out the door.

Clyde felt a tap on his shoulder a couple of minutes later. It was Raymond. "Got that problem taken care of."

"Good." Clyde could feel his heart pounding, riled up after being confronted by Willie and staring their sordid history squarely in the face.

"I take it that asshole is the same Willie responsible for your time in the pen?"

"Yeah, that was him. A bad dream that doesn't seem to want to go away."

"The worst kind." Raymond scratched his chin. "Look, this is your night. Don't let the dude spoil it. If he shows up again, I'll take care of it."

"I don't need you to fight my battles," Clyde said toughly, though appreciating his support.

"I know you don't. But I owe you. We have to stick together, man. Can't let some jerk holding a grudge bring you down."

"I don't intend to ever allow that to happen," Clyde assured him. Not when he suddenly had so much more at stake than just his personal welfare. Only he feared that Willie Munroe was hell-bent on doing whatever he could to create havoc in his life.

I'll stay on guard and deal with whatever comes my way. So long as Stefani doesn't get hurt, or anyone else I'm close to.

Clyde managed to catch Stefani's last song before the break, which got her a standing ovation. He found himself clapping too for this very talented woman who helped him forget about the darkness and hone in on the ray of light who suddenly made his life worth living.

Chapter Thirty-one

"How about a trip to Fiji or the Bahamas?" Stella suggested.

Trey looked up at her across his desk. "You think Ivana would like that as an anniversary present?"

"What woman wouldn't want to escape to a tropical paradise?"

Trey liked the idea of it. He had to believe that spending some time on a beautiful, secluded island far away from home might be just what they needed to not only spice up their sex life, but continue the process of rebuilding their relationship. The fact that their anniversary was still a month away meant he had time for Ivana to get used to the idea.

"You could also consider taking Ivana on a cruise," Stella offered. "There are some fantastic ones at this time of year, so long as she's not prone to getting seasick."

They had never gone on a cruise before. As far as Trey knew, Ivana had no problems with the water and getting seasick, having done a few modeling gigs out at sea. Perhaps a cruise could work as well.

"Those are all great suggestions," he said. "I know Ivana's always loved Hawaii. We went there the second year of our marriage. I know there are some Hawaiian cruises. Maybe we can take one and get double the pleasure."

"Now you're getting innovative, Trey." Stella smiled at him. "Women love when their men take the initiative and do something really special."

"I'll make a note of that." Trey imagined that with things going well with Clyde and his new lady, his brother might also benefit from a romantic getaway, something the old Clyde was too busy getting into trouble to ever consider. Wedding bells might not be that far off either, mused Trey. And children thereafter.

Trey considered that he and Ivana might try again to have a child. Whatever issues they had, he knew they would be great parents and brought a lot to the table in terms of passing on a legacy. Even adoption wasn't out of the question. He wanted only to make Ivana happy and complete, whatever it took.

He turned his attention back to business and directed Stella to carry on with her thoughts before he had intruded in seeking a woman's perspective on the perfect anniversary gift.

Clyde had his arm around Stefani as they sat in a movie theater, courtesy of Trey. The movie premiere, a thriller, was only so-so. He was far more interested in the woman beside him, who, in a short time, had become his best friend and lover, along with the star attraction at Clyde's Jazz Club. He couldn't have imagined a few short months ago that he would get out of prison and turn his life around to this degree.

I just pray I don't wake up and find this whole thing has been a dream. Someone else's dream.

Stefani grabbed a handful of popcorn and put some in Clyde's mouth. She giggled as he chewed it and then kissed her. She looked super-sexy to him, even in a dark theater. He imagined peeling off her clothes and taking her right then and there. That was how much he had come to desire the woman, her scent, taste, feel—everything.

As far as Clyde was concerned, there was no limit to how far this relationship could go. He wouldn't have it any other way. He sensed Stefani felt the same way, and that was enough for him to continue to do what he needed to make this work in every way.

"Can't get into the movie either?" Clyde asked as they continued to smooch.

Stefani smiled. "Not really. Maybe we should cut this short and find something more entertaining to do with ourselves."

"I'm with you there." He could think of a few ways that might entertain him. Or should he say *them*.

They left the theater, hand in hand, and ended up going to a museum of natural history. This was followed by a Chinese restaurant, before going back to Clyde's loft, where they made love for hours on end and never seemed to tire of satisfying one another.

The next day, Clyde invited Stefani to move into the loft, feeling he wanted to go to sleep at night and wake up every morning with her in his arms. She readily agreed, and he couldn't have been happier. He saw no downside of living with someone he couldn't seem to get enough of. He looked forward to sharing his space, while not crowding Stefani or taking away her freedom.

Though he had yet to say the words, there was little doubt in Clyde's mind that he had fallen in love with Stefani McNeal. And something told him that he and Stefani were very much on the same wavelength. In spite of this, Clyde treaded carefully, unwilling to jump the gun in moving too soon in what was uncharted territory for him.

Also standing in the way of his joy was the belief that Willie continued to lurk out there, looking for some sort of warped revenge. In the process, Clyde didn't doubt the crazed man might try to go after Stefani in spite of being warned to stay away. Until he could be certain that Stefani would be safe from harm, Clyde felt it best to take a wait-and-see approach while being guardedly optimistic as to what the future held.

Ivana was drunk, and she didn't deny it to herself or the housekeeper, Emily, who had made a habit of sticking her nose where it wasn't wanted. At least not by Ivana. Fact was, the latest bout of drinking allowed her to forget everything not right about her life. She was a total screwup as a wife, potential mother, and ex-model who had always been a little insecure about her looks, even when others felt she was beautiful and perfectly proportioned. What did Trey see in her, anyway? Would he still feel the same if he knew her deepest secret?

None of it mattered, she told herself, sipping on another martini, the alcohol coursing down her throat and making her mellow. All she wanted to do now was sleep. Or was that too much to ask when she could barely make it to the stairwell without falling flat on her face?

Ivana suddenly threw the wineglass against the wall and watched it shatter. Emily came out of a room.

"I'll clean that up," she said.

"Forget the damned glass," Ivana slurred. "I don't need your pity."

"I just want to help."

"If I needed your help, I would ask for it," Ivana said, trying to maintain her balance while feeling woozy.

"Do you want me to call Trey?" Emily voiced with concern.

"No, I don't want you to call Trey," Ivana said in a mimicking voice. "Just leave me alone."

Ivana reached the stairs and somehow, some way, managed to reach the second floor and stumble to her room, unsure what to do next.

Trey was already on his way home when he got the call from Emily to say that Ivana was inebriated and, as she put it, "out of control." He wondered what it was this time that had made her get wasted. Not that she needed a reason these days. Seemed like alcohol had become her best friend, and it was high time he did something about it, before she hurt herself. Not to mention destroy any chance they had to get their marriage where it should be and keep it there.

So much for talking about anniversary plans this evening, Trey thought, knowing Ivana likely wouldn't remember in the morning.

When he entered the house, Emily was there to greet him.

"Where is she?" he asked succinctly.

"In her room. I didn't dare go in there and have her bite my head off."

"I understand," Trey said. "Your housekeeping duties don't include dealing with my wife's alcohol problems."

Emily filled him in on Ivana's temper tantrum and other behavior while under the influence.

Trey heard all he needed to. He mounted the stairs for his confrontation with Ivana, wishing it hadn't come to this, knowing he should have done something a long time ago.

He opened the door to the room they once shared and found Ivana passed out on the bed. But not before she had done a number on the bedroom, tossing items on the floor haphazardly as if searching for something she never found. Trey scooped her up into his arms and carried to the shower. She never woke up along the way, which pretty much put things in their proper perspective as far as he was concerned.

Continuing to hold her firmly, Trey cut on the cold water, bracing himself as it sprayed onto both of them. Ivana jumped when the water splashed into her face and over her body. Her eyes opened.

"What are you doing?" she screamed. "Let me go!"

"Not yet," said Trey. "I want to make sure you're at least halfway sober to hear what I have to say."

Ivana fought to be released but Trey was too determined, ignoring her wailing and flailing. Finally when he felt his mission had been accomplished, he carried her back to the bedroom and tossed her onto the bed, soaked, as was he.

She glared. "Have you lost your mind? What the hell was that about?"

"It's about you and your drinking," he retorted. "It's gone too damned far this time."

Ivana looked around the room she had trashed. "I'll clean it up—or get Emily to do it."

"Forget about the damned room."

She ignored this. "That bitch—she called you, didn't she? I want her fired!"

"This isn't about Emily," Trey said. "And she's not going anywhere. But you are."

Worriment crossed Ivana's face. "What's that supposed to mean?"

"It's means this has gone on long enough. You're an alcoholic and it's time we did something about it." He paused, peering at her, wishing it hadn't come down to this, but it had. "I want you to check yourself into a substance-abuse treatment center."

"I'm not checking myself into any damned treatment center," Ivana argued, "and I'm not an alcoholic."

"You are and you will," insisted Trey. "This isn't up for debate."

She flashed him an icy look. "Who made you my master?"

"I'm not your master. I'm your husband and I love you too much to let you kill yourself."

"That won't happen."

"Damned right it won't," Trey told her. "Not if I have anything to do with it."

"You can't make me go somewhere I don't want to go," Ivana said hotly.

"Maybe not, but if you refuse . . ."

"Then what?" she challenged him.

Trey considered his next words carefully, knowing this could be a turning point in their relationship one way or the other. In the end, he had to take a stand that was in her best interests and his. "If you turn your back on getting professional help, then this marriage is over!"

Ivana swallowed nervously, "You don't mean that?"

"Yes, I do," he assured her painfully. "The choice is up to you."

She got to her feet and met his gaze. "I can stop drinking, I swear, if you'll help me. But here at home."

Trey stood flat-footed as she wrapped her wet arms around his waist, laying her head on his chest. For an instant, he nearly succumbed to Ivana's attempt to get him to back down and put his trust in her to do what she clearly was incapable of doing on her own. And he surely was not qualified to rid her body of the alcohol craving, even if he was with twenty-four/seven.

He pulled Ivana away and peered into her eyes. "The only way to get this under control is at a treatment center," he told her. "I want the lady I married back, sober. It's our only chance to make our marriage work for the long term. If you do this, you'll prove to me that you're as committed to that as I am. I'll make some calls and find the right place for you."

Trey kissed the top of her head. "Better get out of those wet clothes before you catch a cold. I'll do the same." He paused. "I love you."

He left the room on that note, hopeful that she would do the right thing, and that they could successfully move on to the next chapter of their lives.

Chapter Thirty-two

Trey sat with Helene in a small café, drinking coffee and sharing in friendship the latest turn of events in his marriage. He welcomed the opportunity to discuss Ivana's drinking problem with an outside person who had proven to him that she could be both objective and understanding.

"I had to twist Ivana's arm, so to speak," Trey finished his monologue, "but she's agreed to seek treatment."

"I recommend you try the Sea and Shore Retreat," said Helene. "It's a posh detox center in nearby Garden Hills. My brother spent time there to treat his alcohol addiction. He came out a different man."

"I want the same Ivana to come out—that is, the one I married who enjoyed a drink every now and then, but never used it as a crutch."

"We all have our crutches, Trey. Alcohol is one of the easiest to lean on. I can only imagine how difficult it must have been to lose the child you both wanted. I don't blame you for that, but some women are never the same thereafter."

Trey gazed at her over his mug. "You're saying Ivana may never be able to shake that, even if she's no longer alcohol dependent?"

"Not at all," Helene told him. "She won't forget, but doesn't mean she can't keep put it behind her. She's still a young and generally healthy woman, from what you tell me. There's no reason why you can't take another crack at having a child."

"I'd like that," Trey said. "Once this ordeal is over, Ivana and I can talk about trying again."

"Grant and I may be headed in that direction too."

"Oh, really?" Trey's head lifted. Somehow he hadn't thought Grant DeCroch would be interested in having any more children, seeing that he already had two adult ones from a previous marriage.

"We're exploring the possibility," Helene stated. "If it's to happen at all, we'd want it before Grant reaches the point where he feels he'd be too old to appreciate being a father again."

"Thankfully I've got a lot of years left on me to take up that role," Trey said dreamily. "But first things first. We have to get Ivana sober and take it from there."

"I really hope it works out for both of you. It's obvious how you feel about Ivana, and I'm sure her feelings are just as strong for you. Every marriage hits a few snags, mine included. That's what love is all about—being able to forgive each other and remember what brought you together in the first place."

"I agree." Trey sat down his coffee and smiled. "We'll be all right. I'll give this Sea and Shore Retreat a ring and go from there."

He wanted Ivana to have the very best in treatment and comforts during her stay. But he also wanted it to be as short as possible so they could take the next steps in their marriage and future.

Ivana sat on the indoor chaise lounge, a martini in hand to calm her nerves. She was expecting Trey at any moment, having already phoned to tell her about a rehab center that he'd made arrangements for her to check into. The thought of being put away in such a place frightened her. But not as much as dealing with guilt of betrayal that threatened to engulf her. She couldn't hold it in any longer, even though confessing what she'd done might well destroy any chance of her and Trey making a clean slate after she completed her rehab.

I don't want there to be any more secrets between us, she thought, her lips quivering while sipping the drink. *Please don't hate me, Trey. I couldn't live with that, not after everything else we've been through.*

"Ivana . . ."

She looked up at the sound of Trey's voice. "Didn't hear you come in."

His expression was one of disappointment. "Couldn't you lay off the booze? Or did you feel the need to get soused one more time before you get treatment?"

Ivana sat the glass down, resisting the urge for one more taste. "I'm sorry."

"So am I, but we'll deal with it."

"I don't know how to say this. . . ." she spoke uneasily, feeling the courage beginning to wane.

"You don't have to say anything," Trey told her gently. "There will be plenty of time to talk later. Let's just get your things and—"

"I slept with your brother—"

Trey's face contorted. "What did you just say?"

The words even sounded foreign to Ivana. Her eyes watered. She could read the anguish in his face, which made this all the more difficult. But it was too late to turn back now, as she needed to own up to this.

"Clyde and I had sex," she reiterated, her voice cracking.

"When was this?" Trey asked quizzically. "You hardly ever leave this house, and he's hardly ever here."

"When you were in Vegas," Ivana explained nervously. "It only happened once. We'd both been drinking and, I don't know, things just went too far—"

"Too far!" Trey snapped. "You're telling me that you had sex with my own brother and try to justify it by saying that things just went too damned far?"

Ivana stood up on gimpy legs, reaching out to him. "I never meant to hurt you, Trey. Or maybe I did. I hated you for what you did to our marriage. Clyde was everything you weren't, and he wanted me. I was lonely; so was he. I know that's no excuse, but you insisted on bringing him into our home—"

"And that's how you pay me back—by taking Clyde to bed?"

"It wasn't like that. And I didn't take him to bed. We took each other to bed," she needed to make clear. Ivana touched Trey's face. "I still love you. I understand that now. I've always known it in my heart. Can't we please just forget this ever happened?"

His jaw clenched, Trey pushed her hand away. "How could you do this? he asked in a disbelieving tone.

"I didn't plan it," she responded contritely, knowing how hollow it sounded. "Neither of us did."

"I gave you everything, including my love and this is what I get in return—bedding my brother behind my back?" Trey's face contorted. "You disgust me!"

Ivana watched as Trey began to leave. "Where are you going?" she asked, though suspecting it was after his brother.

"To kick Clyde's ass, if you must know!" he confirmed. "He's as much to blame for this as you, and I won't let him get away with it."

Ivana ran after her husband, but he was too quick and determined to do bodily damage to his brother. Would he actually kill Clyde once he got his hands on him? Or would Clyde kill him instead?

She found herself praying like never before, while second-guessing herself for telling Trey the truth about her and Clyde.

I only wanted to do what was right. Now it all seems so horribly wrong.

Ivana hoped she could somehow avert disaster. She went back inside and grabbed her cell phone. Calling Clyde was the last thing Ivana wanted to do, and felt she was the probably the last person he wanted to hear from. But what other choice was there with so much at stake?

She got his voice mail and imagined he was probably preoccupied with the apparent love of his life. The last thing Ivana wanted at this point was to come between Clyde and Stefani. She hoped when all was said and done they could get past this, difficult as it may be. Ivana wanted more than anything to somehow salvage her own relationship; for both her and Trey to learn from their mistakes and errant judgment.

But was it too late now for any of that?

She left Clyde an urgent message, and could only hope he got it in time to at least prepare himself for coming face-to-face with a very hurt and vengeful-minded Trey.

Trey was livid, while finding it hard to wrap his mind around what Ivana had told him. He wanted to believe this was some kind of cruel nightmare that he would wake up from and realize none of it was true. But that wouldn't be the case. His wife and brother had done the unthinkable—engaged in sexual relations with each other. This trumped anything Trey had done to either of them, even if it didn't excuse his affair with Helene. He would never have slept with Clyde's woman, whether married to her or not.

So why did he have to pick Ivana, my wife, to do his thing with? And why the hell did she let him?

He'd given his brother everything, and Clyde had taken away the most important thing in the world to him: his wife's fidelity. Trey gripped the steering wheel so tightly that his knuckles ached. All he could think of right now was letting his fists pound Clyde's face 'til it hurt like hell, the way Trey was hurting. He had no illusions that his brother would take it like a man, given Clyde's fierce pride and own temper. Nor was Trey sure he could take him in a fair fight, since Clyde was a bigger man and battle tested. But he sure as hell would try and make his brother very sorry for his act of betrayal. And what it would cost him.

As for Ivana, Trey didn't even want to think about what this sorry revelation might mean to their marriage. Or her rehab, which for the moment was no longer his primary concern. Right now, he couldn't even bear to look at Ivana, much less think about her getting sober and resurrecting their marriage. Trey wondered if this was something that could ever be forgivable. Or was it too much to overcome, effectively ending their life together as husband and wife?

Trey's thoughts returned to the other half of his utter disappointment. Did Clyde really think he could have a piece of Ivana and then wipe the slate clean by turning his attention to Stefani?

Think again.

Chapter Thirty-three

Clyde had just finished shooting hoops with Raymond, and dropped by the club a few hours prior to opening. He wanted to admire in solitude the place that was half his and helped turn his life around. It was still hard to believe that the club bore his name and gave him something to be proud of.

He was sure his mother was checking him out from heaven and applauding for turning things around in his life. Clyde doubted he would ever be able to take Trey's place as the all American success story in her eyes. He had no problem with that. All he'd wanted was to leave his own mark and make his life count for something other than bad choices.

Clyde was confident he'd made good choices with the club and Stefani. He heard a sound from behind and turned around. It was Trey.

"Hey," Clyde said. He noted that Trey's countenance was rigid. "What's up?"

Without warning or time to react, Clyde was hit in the face by Trey's fist, causing him to stagger but remain on his feet.

Clyde, feeling the sting in his jaw, peered at his brother. "What the hell did you do that for?"

"You backstabbing bastard," hissed Trey, hitting him again, this time in the mouth.

Clyde tasted blood as he bit back the pain. "I don't know what I did." He had a pretty good idea upon reflection, hoping it was something else.

"I'm talking about you sleeping with my wife!"

Damn. She actually told him? "It's not what you think," Clyde voiced tonelessly, wishing that were the case, but knowing otherwise.

"Like hell it isn't!" Trey roared. "At least be a man about it and admit that you had your way with Ivana!" When Clyde hesitated, Trey hit him again with a solid punch to the head, knocking him to the plush maroon carpeting. "Get up, asshole, so I can finish what *you* started!"

Clyde dragged himself up, feeling sick to his stomach that Trey knew what he never wanted him to. How could he make things right? Or were they way past that?

"It was never about you," he told Trey. "Or Ivana. I just got caught up in a moment. It could've been with anyone."

Trey rejected this with a firm gaze. "But it wasn't with just anyone, dammit. It was with my wife! How could you do something so self-centered? I let you into my home when you had nowhere else to go. I trusted you to respect me. I bent over backward to do right by you. And this is how you respond—by stabbing me in the back and twisting the knife every which way, so the pain was beyond compare?"

"You have every right to be pissed," said Clyde, knowing he would have been equally upset had the tables been turned. "I never meant to hurt you, Trey. If I could do it all over. . . ."

"That's just it—you can't. The damage done is irreversible. The trust has been broken into a million pieces. I wish now that your ass had rotted in prison. That's where you belong. Once a common hood, always one."

Clyde's nostrils ballooned. He had this coming, but he still resented the statement. Especially since it was because he'd tried to protect Trey from Willie's crazy and dangerous scheme that his ass had ended up in prison in the first place.

You've got me all wrong. I'm not the man I used to be. And never will be again.

Trey took another swing at Clyde.

This time he blocked the blow with a powerful forearm. "I'm not going to fight you, Trey."

"Why the hell not? Isn't that what you do best?"

Trey threw more punches, which Clyde easily deflected or dodged. His lashes descended over a baleful stare, and he remembered when his fists had ended up getting him sent to prison. And for what? A brother who hated him now more than ever. Maybe he should have just allowed things to happen as Willie had wanted, and let the chips fall where they may. Then Trey would have had to fend for himself and likely come out on the losing end.

In spite of feeling his temper rise, Clyde refused to be baited into fighting Trey. The worst thing that could come out of this was to physically injure his brother on top of the mental wounds he'd already inflicted upon Trey.

"Not anymore," Clyde responded tartly, lowering his eyes. "Not where it concerns you."

"Well, maybe you'd better get back into it," Trey said hotly. "Because I'm not through with you. Not by a long shot."

He took another wild swing, and Clyde ducked and came up behind Trey, getting him into a neck lock.

"Enough!" Clyde said commandingly. "This is getting us nowhere. I screwed up big-time and have to live with it for the rest of my life. Don't let this take us down too."

Trey tried to wrestle himself free but was being held too tightly. "I think it's way too late to be thinking about brotherly affection. You took 'us' down when you decided to have sex with my wife. I propped your ass up out of love when you were down and damned near out and you just threw it all away."

Clyde gulped, not liking the sound of that. He released Trey, while keeping his guard up. "So what are you saying?"

Trey turned around and knitted his eyebrows. "I'll make it very clear for you. I'm saying I'm cutting off all funding for this place and incidental expenses. You and I are through, you understand me? If you want this club to remain open, you'll do it without my money or support. I don't give a damn what happens to it—or you—from this point on."

"You don't mean that," Clyde said, searching his brother's face.

"I mean every damned last word," Trey maintained. "I never want to see your sorry ass again. And stay the hell away from my wife—or the next time . . . Well, I won't go there, but don't test me."

On that note, Trey stormed out the door.

Clyde wiped blood from the corner of his lip, shaken that one mistake was about to cost him everything. And, once again, he had no one to blame but himself.

Now what I am going to do? Have my dreams suddenly gone up in smoke?

He got out his cell phone, intending to call Stefani, though unsure what to say. Clyde noted he had a message. The caller ID indicated that Ivana Lancaster had left it.

Clyde had expected Stefani to think he was the world's biggest jerk, incredibly selfish, and unworthy of her affections, much less love, when he fessed up about his brief, ill-advised involvement with Ivana. He'd waited for the ax to drop.

Instead, Stefani took him to bed and showed him the type of support and affection he probably didn't deserve, but was very grateful for nevertheless.

"You should have told me," she said after they had made love hot and heavy and were still clinging together in the afterglow.

"It wasn't something I was proud of or wanted to share with the first real woman to come into my life," Clyde said honestly. "I should have stayed the hell away from Ivana, and she should have stayed away from me. But we let misplaced feelings cause a moment of irresponsible weakness. I ended things after that and tried to forget it ever happened. I never wanted Trey to find out—or you . . ."

"Maybe it was best to get it out in the open," Stefani said understandingly. "Holding that in would have only put more stress and strain in your life, especially where it concerned your relationship with Trey and Ivana."

"It doesn't exactly feel like this will make my life easier," Clyde muttered, though suspecting deep down she was right. Living with a secret had cost him once dearly; doing so again had been even more costly, for it had taken away his brother. And maybe everything else he had going for him. Except for Stefani.

If he didn't know it before, Clyde certainly knew it now. He cared for her more than he ever had any other woman. He held Stefani a little tighter and met her eyes. "Thanks for standing by me."

Stefani held his gaze. "Did you think I wouldn't?"

"Not many women would have."

"I'm not most women."

He half-grinned. "I can see that, and I love you for it."

Stefani's cheeks rose. "You do?"

"Yeah." His voice deepened. "I'm in love with you, Stefani. This probably isn't the best time to say it, but—"

"It's the perfect time to say it," she broke in. "Especially since I feel the same way."

"Really?" Clyde somehow doubted the words, even if it was everything he could possibly have hoped for from her.

"Yes, I love you, Clyde Lancaster," Stefani affirmed. "I would've told you sooner, but I wanted to hear it from you first. Whatever you did in the past has no bearing on the future, unless we allow it to."

I only wish I could believe that, he thought. His past mistakes had come at a high price. Could they really be so easily pushed aside? Or would they continue to catch up with him in ways he couldn't foresee?

Clyde smiled tearfully at Stefani. "Have I ever told you that you're the best woman in the world?"

She grinned. "No, but I don't mind hearing you say it."

"Then I will every day, baby."

Clyde tilted his head and kissed her. Stefani took the kiss and returned it with equal ardor. They made love again, and Clyde relished being inside her, finding it a comfortable place to be, unlike the rest of his world that was threatening to crumble around him if Trey remained steadfast in his promise to destroy the life Clyde had successfully built for himself.

Chapter Thirty-four

Willie got high in his apartment. He'd had to kiss Roselyn's ass to keep her from breaking things off. Ever since he was kicked out of Clyde's Jazz Club a week and a half ago, things had been strained between him and Roselyn. No doubt her meddlesome roommate, Gail, had been playing with Roselyn's head, trying to poison her against him. *That bitch needs to be put in her place. Someday I'll do just that.*

Right now he had to placate Roselyn and make her feel special. No one walked out on him until he was good and ready for it to happen. He saw no reason to throw away a good thing. At least not until a better one came along.

Willie smoked the meth, his thoughts turning to his arch-nemesis, Clyde Lancaster. It was his fault for the strain between him and Roselyn. *That asshole is the cause of all my problems. He took half my sight. Now he's trying to take away my manhood.*

Willie wasn't about to let that happen. Clyde needed to pay for the troubles he'd caused him. And so did Clyde's brother. If it hadn't been for Clyde trying to protect Trey's property, Willie was certain things would've turned out differently for him. For one, he could have sold whatever he swiped from Trey's place and made a lot of money. And, just for the hell of it, he would have smashed Trey's face in had he been stupid enough to get in his way.

I would've shared some of the stash with Clyde if he'd stayed out of the way. But he suddenly decided he didn't hate his brother as much as he'd said when it came right down to it.

To hell with both of them, Willie thought. They needed to be brought down a few pegs from their lofty position.

It was time he did just that. Clyde couldn't be protected forever by that brute at the club. Neither could his brother, who seemed to think he owned Paradise Bay and everyone in it.

The bastard doesn't own me and never will.

Not like he owns Clyde and that fine woman Trey married.

Willie inhaled the meth, closing his eyes while feeding on the sensation. He opened them and studied the gun beside him in the couch. He grabbed it and aimed, pretending to shoot Clyde right between the eyes.

Chapter Thirty-five

After driving around in circles, Trey found himself in his own driveway. He really didn't know what the hell to say to Ivana, still stung by her revelation of having a one-night fling with Clyde. Trey wanted to hate her the way he did Clyde for betraying him in the worst way possible. But he couldn't. Not when Ivana was the love of his life and someone he couldn't ever imagine living without.

I still love her, no matter what she's done. I think she still loves me, in spite of what happened between her and Clyde.

Trey blamed himself for destroying the sanctity of their marriage by straying. He had opened the door for Ivana to seek the attention of another man after she'd lost her trust in him, and thereby her desire to be loyal to him intimately.

I don't want to lose the best thing to ever happen to me. I just can't. We'll find a way together to get past the indiscretions and distrust.

Trey headed toward the house, so intense in thought that he never even noticed Ivana's car wasn't there.

Inside the house, he expected to find his wife frazzled, not particularly eager to see him after the way he'd handled things. Or unsure if he would still want her. But Ivana was nowhere to be found. Trey considered that she may have gone ahead without him and checked herself into rehab, perhaps believing that was more preferable than having to face him again.

But he found Ivana's bag still in her room. Where the hell was she?

Trey looked out the window and noticed that her car was gone. Damn. Considering her fragile state of mind and having had at least one drink and likely more, panic set in.

He found Emily in the great room, watering plants with headphones on, no doubt listening to the classical music she loved.

When Trey got her attention, Emily removed the headphones. She could see the concern etched in his face. "What's wrong?"

"Where's Ivana?"

Emily flashed a blank stare. "I don't know. I didn't see her leave."

"Her car's not in the driveway," Trey said, ill at ease. "I'm going after her. Please call me if Ivana comes back."

Emily's forehead crinkled. "Tell me what happened, Trey."

"We had a fight," he responded, leaving it at that. "And I have to find her, let Ivana know that it's not the end of the world. Or at least our world."

"I'm sure everything will be fine," Emily said. "She probably just needed to clear her head."

Trey doubted it was that simple. He feared that Ivana, despondent and probably inebriated, might do something crazy. If anything happened to her, he'd never forgive himself.

"Search the house and see if she left a note or anything," Trey instructed Emily, not wanting to waste precious time doing so himself. "Oh, and ring the detox center, just in case Ivana decides to check herself in."

He ran out the door, hopped in his car and sped off, praying that Ivana hadn't wrapped her car around a tree.

Or worse.

Ivana tried to stay focused on the road through tear-filled eyes and a mind gripped by guilt and misgivings. She could no longer stay in that house where she was apparently no longer wanted. Trey made it perfectly clear how he felt about her. It seemed as though he was the only one capable of making mistakes in their marriage. She was somehow held to a higher standard than Trey held himself.

It wasn't fair. She had frailties just like anyone else. Getting involved with Clyde was probably the biggest mistake of her life and one she would forever regret. But she couldn't undo the damage.

I'm sorry, Trey. Even sorrier that it was Clyde. I doubt you'll ever forgive me, because I'll probably never forgive myself.

Ivana wiped away tears, not sure where she was headed, knowing only that she wanted to go somewhere far away from the life she knew. She just wanted to feel loved and protected. And not consumed with things that no longer mattered.

She prayed that Trey and Clyde had not killed each other. Clyde had not responded to her message, leaving Ivana to wonder. Maybe in the end they realized they were brothers and needed each other more than not.

Leaving me out in the cold as the scarlet wife.

It was a tag Ivana could not live with. She took a deep breath and pondered what else might be out there for her, believing that she no longer had a home or husband to go back to.

Chapter Thirty-six

After searching high and low for Ivana without success for more than an hour, Trey was consumed with fear for her safety. He'd tried her cell phone, but she wouldn't pick up. Or couldn't.

He phoned a friend who worked for the Paradise Bay Police Department. Trey knew that it took more than a couple of hours of a person's absence for one to be declared missing. But he was desperate, and his friend, Eric Cordell, owed him a favor after Trey had given him a great deal on a car for his college-bound daughter.

"This is Detective Cordell."

"Hello, Eric. It's Trey Lancaster."

"Hey, Trey. Calling to offer me another bargain, this time for my youngest daughter?"

"Not exactly." Trey composed himself. "My wife's missing. . . ."

"Really? Missing, like how?"

"I think she might have run away," Trey gulped sadly.

"Oh, yeah? Tell me what happened."

Trey told only what he felt was necessary to get him to look into her disappearance.

Five minutes later, Cordell said, "I'll see if we can locate your wife's car. I'll also check to see if she's taken a plane, train, or bus out of town."

Would Ivana have gone that far to leave the city? And go where—to London, to be with her friend, Naki?

Trey realized the detective was bending the rules on his behalf. "Thanks, Eric. I really appreciate this."

"No problem. I'll let you know as soon as we have something. And I wouldn't worry too much, though I know that's easier said than done. Chances are Ivana will show up safe and sound. And then you can deal with the issues between you."

"I hope so," Trey said, though less than convinced. Ivana was in a particularly vulnerable state right now, meaning he wouldn't feel comfortable 'til his wife was home where she belonged. Then they could indeed work out their issues faceto-face.

The last person Clyde expected to show up at his door was Trey. His brother looked worn down and Clyde's first thought was that Trey was there to punch his lights out again.

"Ivana's gone," Trey said glumly.

Clyde glanced at Stefani, who had opened the door and reluctantly allowed Trey to enter. "What do you mean, gone?"

"She left the house after I came to see you. No note, no nothing. I'm afraid Ivana could be hurt somewhere . . . or otherwise unable to contact me."

"You have any idea where she might have gone?" Clyde asked, somewhat shocked that Ivana had apparently left Trey high and dry. On the other hand, he had seen this building for some time. Only Trey seemed to be clueless for the most part. Clyde hated that his actions had only deepened the division between Trey and Ivana, leading to her driving off and his estrangement with his brother. Pushing aside their differences, Clyde felt for Trey, realizing it couldn't have been easy for him to swallow his pride and reach out after their last meeting.

"Could be anywhere," Trey replied forlornly. "She doesn't have a whole lot of friends in Paradise Bay, and no other family."

Clyde looked down at him sympathetically. "I'll do whatever I can to help." He glanced at Stefani. "We both will."

Stefani reiterated that. "I can call my uncle, and he can call whoever he knows to help look for Ivana."

"We'll find her," Clyde said definitively and thought about Ivana's warning left on his voice mail, which he'd listened to too late to prepare himself for Trey's wrath.

Clyde was more than a little concerned, knowing Ivana was prone to alcohol abuse and probably under the influence wherever she was. That could spell trouble, if she ran into it. He suspected Trey was aware of this as well, seeing that that man had lived with Ivana 'til now. But Clyde didn't want to let on his fears in this regard, only making matters worse as his brother went in search of a runaway wife.

Trey gave him a hopeful look. "I'm counting on that."

Clyde grabbed his keys, deciding that Trey was probably too shaken to be driving. "We'll backtrack from your place and see where it leads us." He faced Stefani. "Will you be all right?"

"I'll be fine," she told him, squeezing his hand. "Just go and bring Ivana home."

"That's the plan," he said and kissed her on the mouth.

What Clyde didn't know was what to expect when he came face-to-face with Ivana again. Would that prompt more fireworks and her leaving Trey again? Would it stir up more anger in Trey so he wanted to use his fists once more to blow off steam?

It was a bridge Clyde was more than willing to cross when he got to it. For now, he had to put his brother first and do whatever needed to be done to try to make things right between them. As well as with Ivana.

There was eerie silence in the car as Clyde drove. Trey glanced at him and tried to find words, but decided it was best to leave him to his own thoughts. Though the animosity Trey felt toward his brother was still strong, that had to take a backseat to the moment at hand. Ivana was missing, and nothing else mattered to him other than locating her safe and sound.

Trey looked out the side window, wondering if Ivana would be home when they got there, which would be the best-case scenario. Or had at least phoned to say she was all right. He was angry that Ivana had scared him like this, apparently without considering what her disappearing act might be doing to him.

Why would you leave me just hanging like this, not knowing if you were dead or alive? Didn't I earn that right as your husband?

Or had he given up such rights after his own affair that had hurt Ivana so deeply? Not to mention his overreaction to her news of sleeping with Clyde.

Trey faced his brother, who was focused intently on the road as if it would lead to somewhere satisfying for them. He saw the slight swelling on the side of Clyde's face where he'd hit him. Trey wished he had gone about it differently, but wouldn't back away from what he'd done. He imagined had the shoe been on other foot and he had bedded Stefani, Clyde would have been royally pissed too and taken it out on him in a similar manner.

But no amount of fighting, threats, or disappointment could take away from the fact that they were brothers for life. Their mother had seen to that. Whatever their differences, they would always have to deal with them, like it or not.

Clyde looked at him as though reading Trey's mind. "Guess things were bound to blow up between us sooner or later."

"And whose fault is that?" Trey argued.

Clyde hesitated. "Mine, all right? Seems like every time something good happens, I find a way to mess it up."

Trey did not argue against the conclusion, though he was hardly without a few faults of his own and things he regretted. "The important thing right now is to find Ivana," he said evenly. "We can deal with us later."

"Yeah," Clyde muttered, as if bracing himself.

Dealing with pent-up anger was what Clyde was afraid of as he pulled onto Trey's street. He was tired of rehashing all the squabbles that seemed to mark much of his relationship with Trey. He just wanted it to be over and get on with what was left of his world. That included Stefani, who saw only the good in him, unlike Trey, who could only see his faults.

No matter how things ended up with Ivana, Clyde suspected Trey would never let what happened between him and her rest and, as a result, would make Clyde's life miserable in any and every way he could. Meaning Trey could well wrestle control of the club from him out of spite, leaving Clyde without a visible means for support. Or much of a future to look forward to.

I'll just have to let it play out and see what happens and hope I'm not left in a dammed canoe without a paddle.

They arrived at the house, and were greeted by Emily and Francine.

"Any word yet?" Trey asked anxiously.

"She hasn't called," Emily said sadly. "But we do have something."

Francine produced a piece of stationery. "Found this in Ivana's room. It was balled up in the waste-basket. Apparently she had changed her mind about leaving it for you—" Trey took the note. It was scribbled in Ivana's poor handwriting. Clyde leaned over Trey's shoulder. "What does it say?" Trey swallowed and read out loud:

> *Trey,*
> *I'm sorry I disgust you so much. Maybe now you know just a little bit how I felt when it was you who did something really stupid. Not that it excuses in any way what I did, because it doesn't. I was just hoping that maybe we could put all our cards on the table and come out of it with a stronger marriage.*
> *Guess I was wrong. So was Clyde. But something tells me that if you two didn't kill each other, you've found a way to forgive him. Or come to terms with it.*
> *So why not your wife?*
> *I need to get away, Trey. I need to think about everything that's happened in our marriage, just as I'm sure you do. Don't bother looking for me, which you probably won't, since you'll be glad to get rid of me once and for all, if I read you correctly.*
> *I just need to be alone for a while.*
> *Ivana*

Trey's eyes welled with tears, and he didn't give a damn who saw them. He folded the letter and put it in his pocket. Gazing at Clyde made him feel even worse that he had essentially abandoned Ivana in her greatest hour of need.

I'm sorry, baby. About everything.

"I have to go after my wife," Trey said, eyeing Clyde without prologue.

"I know," he told him. "We both need to bring her home." Trey nodded, feeling some solace in having Clyde there and on the same wavelength as him. "Keep trying to reach Ivana on her cell phone," Trey directed Francine and Emily.

"We will," Emily assured him.

"And check the TV for any reports of accidents." Trey prayed Ivana hadn't gone off the road, inebriated and hurt.

"You might also call the hospitals to see if Ivana has been admitted or treated for anything," added Clyde.

"Okay, we'll get right on it," Francine said.

Trey wasted no further time before heading out with Clyde, knowing that every second counted if Ivana was in some sort of trouble.

Or headed in that direction.

Chapter Thirty-seven

Ivana grew tired of driving and seemingly going nowhere. The tears had her face feeling dry and the emotional turmoil turned her stomach into knots. She craved some alcohol to at least give her a little buzz to get through whatever the rest of the day had in store for her.

She wondered if Trey had even bothered to look for her. Or was he too caught up in his disappointment and hatred to give a damn about his wife and what she may have been going through?

Maybe she didn't deserve his pity or concern. She'd made her own bed and now was left to wallow in it.

Ivana spotted a place called the Westside Tavern. *Why not?* she thought, even if it looked like a dump and not normally a bar she would be caught dead in. She was past the point of self-respect.

I just need a drink. Or two.

She pulled her Jaguar into a thin slot. After applying some lip gloss and patting her hair, she headed inside, wearing the stiletto boots she had only purchased the day before, never expecting to break them in like this.

The tavern looked pretty much as Ivana expected: old, small, nondescript with a mildew odor in the air. It was empty except for a young couple kissing at a table with a half-empty pitcher of beer, and an older, bearded man at the bar drinking what looked to Ivana to be hard liquor.

She parked herself at a table and waited for someone to take her order.

They went to every place Trey could think of Ivana might have gone, but there was still no sign of her or her car.

"Maybe she checked into a hotel to stay the night and get her head together," suggested Clyde.

Trey rubbed his chin. "According to my friend with the police department, Ivana hasn't used any of her credit cards."

"What about cash?"

"She never carries much money afraid of being mugged."

"Have you checked with her hair stylist?" Clyde asked.

Trey's right brow elevated. "No, why?"

"Ivana mentioned once that she and the woman were tight. Maybe she went to her."

Ivana had gone through at least a dozen hair stylists, as far as Trey knew, and never seemed to be that satisfied with any of them. "Did Ivana happen to mention the name of this hairdresser?"

"I wish she had," Clyde responded bleakly.

Trey didn't even want to think about when Ivana and Clyde might have talked about her hair stylist. Right now, he would take any clues that might point to Ivana's whereabouts. As it was, Trey had never accompanied her to get hair done, and now regretted not taking a more active interest in even the small things in her life. He prayed the opportunity came to change that

Trey called Emily. If anyone knew who the hairdresser was, it would be her, since Ivana often told the housekeeper where she could be reached.

When Emily picked up, he cut right to the chase. "I need to know the name of the salon where Ivana gets her hair done."

"It's called Bordeau's Palace," she said immediately. "I recommended the place to Ivana, since I go there myself. The owner and Ivana's hair stylist is Jacinta Bordeau. I have her number and address right here."

Trey took down the information. "Thanks, Emily. I'll be in touch."

"You want to head over there?" Clyde asked Trey.

"Yeah, I think so. If Ivana went to the salon, I'd rather not tip our hand by calling, only to have her go elsewhere, just to get away from me."

Clyde rubbed his nose. "She doesn't hate you, Trey, if that's what you're thinking."

Trey shot him a look. "How would you know? Or does banging my wife one night qualify you as a shrink?"

Clyde turned away. "No, it doesn't," he conceded. "I'm just telling you what I think, for what it's worth. No matter what I did with Ivana, I believe she loves you, man. You hurt her, she hurt you; but at the end of the day, you were always the one Ivana wanted—and stayed with. Forget about me. Give her a chance and give yourself one to work things out."

Trey wanted to strike out at him verbally for inserting himself so deeply into their problems, but thought better. He knew that Clyde was only trying to help in his own way. Even if in some respects it was too little, too late. But maybe there was still hope that if he could get his wife back, he could repair the broken connection with her and Clyde too.

***

Trey and Clyde entered the premises and were greeted immediately by a woman who introduced herself as Jacinta Bordeau.

"Emily called and told me you were looking for Ivana," she said.

Trey's mouth tightened, though he couldn't fault Emily for phoning her. "Yes, we were hoping she had contacted you. Or might have come here."

Jacinta studied him. "You must be Trey? Ivana talks about you nonstop." She turned to Clyde. "And you've got to be his brother?"

Clyde cleared his throat uneasily. "Yeah."

"I could tell. You two look alike."

"That's what they tell me."

Trey had often been told the same thing, but he wasn't much in the mood for brotherly love or closeness in appearances. "About Ivana," he said hastily.

"Haven't seen her since she had her hair done last month," Jacinta stated. "But we did talk on the phone, oh, I'd say about a week or so ago. Nothing but small talk."

Trey was disappointed, expecting more. "My wife's going through some stuff right now. Do you have any idea where she might go to chill for a while?"

Jacinta thought about it. "We talked about going bar-hopping, but never did it. I think she was friendly with a couple of my other customers. I can make some phone calls."

"That's a good idea."

"No problem." She looked from one man to the next thoughtfully. "I really like Ivana and don't want anything bad to happen to her. I'm happy to do whatever I can to help."

"Thank you," Trey told her. His wife had more people who cared about her than she may have realized. Starting with him. And he supposed even Clyde cared in his own way.

In the car, Clyde got Trey's attention. "I think we should check all the bars in town."

Trey looked at him sideways. "You think my wife is a drunk?"

"I think she has a problem with alcohol," he responded diplomatically. "Probably not my place to say."

"It's mine," Trey admitted. "Ivana has been abusing alcohol for a while now. Guess I just didn't want to face up to it." He sighed. "She was supposed to check into a detox center this afternoon. Somehow it all fell apart and now heaven knows what will happen."

"Ivana called me once to pick her up at a bar after she'd had too much to drink," Clyde told him. "Apparently the bartender refused to serve her anymore."

"And you didn't bother to mention this to me?" Trey asked, upset.

Clyde's chin lowered. "She asked me not to."

Trey sucked in a deep breath. He hated that Ivana had felt more comfortable confiding in his brother than him. Maybe if he had made himself more accessible things might have been different. Of more concern to Trey at the moment was finding his wife before the drinking led her down a dangerous path.

He could only hope they would get a second chance to make up for everything that went wrong in their lives.

"Whatever it takes, I need to let Ivana know she doesn't have to go through this alone," Trey said determinedly. "If what I did or didn't do caused her to be harmed in any way—"

"Let's not go there," stressed Clyde. "There's no indication anything has happened to Ivana. If she's still in town, we'll get to her and bring home."

Trey found he almost believed his brother, who was proving coolheaded under fire. But Trey wouldn't get his hopes up only to have them dashed. Not when he knew Ivana was out there somewhere, frustrated and vulnerable, with any potential predator ready to take full advantage of her.

Chapter Thirty-eight

Well, look who's here. Willie spotted her the minute he walked into the tavern. *If it ain't Mrs. Trey Lancaster, all by herself.* He recalled that he'd watched her undress in front of her bedroom window when he'd slipped onto the Lancaster estate. She'd turned him on like crazy. Just as the lady was doing now, looking lost and as if she'd found the one place she wanted to be.

As good-looking and sexy as Willie thought Ivana Lancaster was, he was much more interested in the fact that she was someone he could use to hurt his former friend turned enemy, Clyde, along with that sorry excuse for a brother of his.

It occurred to Willie that Trey, or even Clyde, could have gone to take a leak and might be back any minute now. But that thought passed when he saw no signs of anyone joining the lady.

Guess my lucky day has finally arrived. And I sure as hell ain't gonna blow it.

He pulled out his cell phone and called Roselyn, but got her voice mail. Normally that pissed him off, but in this case he'd rather leave a message than hear her whining about their suddenly broken date. "It's me. Hey, look, something came up and I ain't gonna be able to get away for a while. You should check out the movie without me. Later."

For an instant, Willie had second thoughts about ditching Roselyn and possibly losing her forever. It was a chance he was willing to take, especially when the golden opportunity had arisen to settle some scores.

He made his way to the table. Ivana seemed deep in thought. Or maybe it was more like half dozing.

"You look like you could use some company." Willie gave her the best smile he could manage.

Ivana looked up through bloodshot eyes and a faint smile crossed her glossy lips.

Willie took that as a yes and sat down beside her. He noted the nearly empty glass on the table and wondered how many she had already put away. "Can I buy the lady another drink?"

Her eyes grew hungrily. She batted her lashes. "Sure, why not?"

Willie grinned and signaled a waitress. He studied Ivana and decided that she enjoyed the buzz of alcohol about as much as he did getting high. But what they mainly had in common was the man who was her brother-in-law and his arch-enemy.

"My name's Willie," he told her sweetly.

"Ivana."

"Nice to meet you, Ivana." He stuck out a hand and waited for her to shake it. Her hand was damp and soft with long mauve-colored fingernails perfectly manicured.

Yeah, very nice. I'd love to feel those hands on every part of my body and put my own hands and fingers all over and inside of her.

Maybe he would do just that when all was said and done and the scores were settled.

Ivana's eyes were sore from crying. She stared vacantly across the table at the man who bought her a drink. He was solidly built with dreadlocks and a goatee. She noted that there seemed to be something wrong with his right eye. Or was she just imagining that after a few drinks? Her first thought had been to tell him where to go, that she wasn't interested in company—certainly not his. But he seemed nice enough, and since she'd lost the man she loved, what harm was there in a little attention from someone else?

"So are you from around here?" she asked.

"Yeah, you could say that," he responded coolly. "I'm guessing you're way outside your comfort zone. Am I right?"

Ivana gazed at him over the rim of her glass. "I think I'm pretty comfortable right where I am."

Willie laughed. "I can see that. I think we're gonna get along just fine."

"Maybe so, maybe no," she teased, flashing her teeth.

Ivana tasted the drink. The more she looked at Willie, the more familiar he seemed. Did it have anything to do with being tipsy? Or was he someone she'd met, but couldn't quite put a finger on?

She supposed it didn't really matter. As long as he was buying, she was happy to have him as a new friend.

Clyde and Trey must have gone to ten or more watering holes and there was still no sign of Ivana or any indication that she had been there.

Trey was growing frustrated. And desperate. "Maybe we're looking for her in all wrong places?" He considered that Ivana might have gone to the DeCroch Hotel bar, far enough away from the crowd but in a more appropriate setting than the dives they had looked at. This seemed unlikely, though, as Ivana would probably not want to risk running into Helene and feeling her own humiliation all over again.

So where the hell was she?

"There's still probably at least half-a-dozen more bars in the city," Clyde told him from the passenger seat. "She could be at any one of them."

"Or none of them," muttered Trey.

"I say we stay on this track—unless you've got a better idea?"

That was Trey's whole problem: he had no better ideas. It was as though Ivana had disappeared off the face of the earth. She could be anywhere—in Paradise Bay or long gone from the city where they lived. There was no guidebook for tracking down a missing wife after an argument about her sleeping with his brother.

If Trey could do it over, he would have tried to see things from Ivana's perspective. Maybe even Clyde's. Instead, he'd handled it like the typical jealous macho male, right down to attacking Clyde.

I can't change what happened, but I can make damned sure it doesn't happen again. If only I could find Ivana safe and sound.

Trey turned the corner. "Why don't we just keep looking and hope for the best."

Clyde's cell phone rang.

"It's Albert," he said, answering it. "Hey." A moment later, he turned on the speaker.

"Stefani told me about your little problem. I think I may have solved it—or at least can give you some sort of direction."

"Go ahead, Albert," directed Clyde.

"I just got a call from a guy who used to work for me over at the Westside Tavern. Name's Zack. He says someone fitting Ivana's description left the place a little while ago with a man."

"What man?" Trey asked, his heart skipping a beat.

"That's all I got," Albert said apologetically. "I can call back and—"

"Don't bother," Trey said. "We're not far from there."

"I hope it was Ivana and you can track her down," Albert said.

Clyde hung up and faced Trey. "What do you think?"

"I think we need to check it out for ourselves and go from there," he said.

Trey hated the thought of false hope leading to a dead end. He couldn't imagine that Ivana would have willingly gone off with a stranger to who-knew-where. On the other hand, if she had been at this tavern and inebriated, any kind of reckless behavior was possible.

An unsettling feeling in the pit of Trey's stomach told him that some asshole had exploited his wife's susceptible state of mind to try and take advantage of her. And Ivana might be in no position to resist.

When they arrived at the tavern, a police cruiser was outside. Trey and Clyde walked to an officer who was standing beside a ginger Jaguar.

Trey identified himself. "That looks like my wife's car."

The burly officer studied the vehicle. "We got a call to be on the lookout for a car with that license-plate number. Is your wife Ivana Lancaster?"

"Yes." Trey checked the car and saw that it was locked, but there was no sign of Ivana. He turned to the officer. "Have you been inside the place?"

"Just got here. If she's in there . . ."

"The bartender said that she left the bar with someone," Clyde said.

"And we need to find her before they get very far," Trey said with desperation.

"Are you saying your wife was abducted?" the officer asked.

"She might have been." Even if she left of her own free will, Trey was certain Ivana was too out of it to think clearly. Or be able to break away from someone determined to have his way and possibly want to get rid of her afterward.

"I'll need to phone this in." The officer rubbed his nose. "Then we'll try to get to the bottom of it."

"You're wasting precious time," Trey's voice boomed. "My wife could be with a psychopath."

Clyde stepped between the two men. "Let the man do his job, so we can get on with this."

Trey took a breath, not wanting to make things any worse than they already were. "Fine."

The officer looked from one to the other. "Be right back."

Not wanting to wait a moment longer, Trey headed into the tavern, hoping to find answers. Clyde followed.

Inside, they went up to the bar where the thirty-something, tall bartender was putting liquor bottles on a shelf.

"You must be Zack," Clyde said.

"Yeah, that's me. Who are you?"

"I'm a friend of Albert's. This is my brother, Trey. We're looking for his wife, Ivana. You told Alb—"

"Right," Zack cut him off. "I think I did see your wife in here, based on how Albert described her. She had a couple of drinks and then a man joined her. I don't think she knew him, but I can't say for sure."

Trey suddenly had a dark vision of Ivana, in a drunken stupor, being beaten and raped by the man. He couldn't bear the thought of that happening, and both of them having to live with that on top of everything else.

"What did the man look like?" he asked restlessly.

Zack rubbed his chin. "Let's see . . . he was on the husky side, had dreadlocks . . . probably his early thirties . . ."

"Willie—" Clyde blurted out, feeling his pulse race upon hearing the description.

"Who?" Trey asked edgily.

"Sounds a lot like Willie Munroe."

Trey locked eyes with him. "You're telling me that the man you beat up now has *my* wife?"

Clyde slumped onto a bar stool. He understood the implications of his words. The last thing he wanted to do was scare the hell out of Trey unnecessarily. And he wasn't positive it was Willie who Ivana left with. But since he knew Willie liked to hang out at taverns, along with his fixation on revenge against Clyde—and Ivana caught in a helpless situation—it all made sense.

Or did it?

"It's a good possibility," Clyde hated to say. He looked at the bartender. "Could the man only see out of one eye?"

"I couldn't tell you about that one way or the other," the bartender stated. "Sorry."

So was Clyde. He was sorry that he hadn't finished the job on Willie when he had the chance. Especially now, since it seemed likely that Willie had Ivana and knew exactly who she was in using to exact his revenge.

Trey recalled some commotion at the jazz club not long ago where security had escorted out a man—a man who was rumored to be an ex-associate of Clyde's. Trey never brought it up to him, figuring the problem had been resolved. For whatever reason, it hadn't clicked that this person was Clyde's ex-best friend turned arch-nemesis, Willie Munroe.

Had Willie come to the club looking for revenge? Had he been intending to go after Ivana all along? Trey believed it all fit, and was totally unnerved at the thought.

"So what are we waiting for?" he demanded, unwilling to allow the slow moving police procedure to run its course. Not when every second that bastard was with his wife was one second too many. "Let's go after him."

"Yeah, let's," Clyde said and stood up.

Trey handed the bartender his card. "If Ivana should come back here—"

"I'll give you a call," Zack finished.

Outside, Trey and Clyde ran into the officer. "I take it your wife wasn't in there?" he asked Trey.

"You take it right," he answered, deciding this wasn't the time to engage in a long, drawn-out question-andanswer session with the cop. "We have to run."

"And where can I reach you in case I need to?" the officer asked suspiciously.

Trey met his gaze. "Just call Detective Eric Cordell of Criminal Investigations. He'll tell you anything you want to know."

Chapter Thirty-nine

Ivana was feeling sick to her stomach after she'd had too much to drink. When Willie offered to walk her to her car, she agreed. It caught her totally by surprise when he grabbed her arm and forced her into another car. Ivana tried fighting him, but was too weak and disoriented under the influence of alcohol and his raw determination.

Now she found herself in the passenger seat next to a madman—unlike the sweet and charming man he'd pretended to be—who was holding the steering wheel with one hand and a gun in the other. It was pointed at her.

Ivana wondered if he planned to rape and then kill her. She could imagine him dumping her body in a marsh on the outskirts of the city, leaving her to die a slow death or to be eaten by wild animals. Either scenario was too scary to think about.

She couldn't just sit back and allow it to happen. But what could she do? He had all the power, and she had none. Trey had no idea where she was. And he could probably care less for all she knew.

Ivana looked at Willie, who had given her no indication where they were going or why he had taken her.

After recovering somewhat from the shock of it all, Ivana finally got up the courage to say something. "Why are you doing this?"

Maybe he recognized her as the wife of a local millionaire businessman and kidnapped her. Do kidnappings really happen by coincidence? Did he plan to collect a hefty ransom? Would Trey even be willing to pay one cent to get her released?

Maybe he'll think he's better off getting rid of me and saving himself the cost of alimony and a property settlement.

I can't think that. No matter what, I know Trey would help me out of this mess if he could.

"My husband has money, if that's what you want." Ivana told her abductor. "He'll give you what you want. Please, don't hurt me." *Any more than you already have by taking me against my will and proving yourself to be an asshole of the worst kind.*

Willie looked at Ivana with a crooked grin, but remained mute.

Ivana wanted to knock that stupid, eerie smile off his face—as though he had conjured up something particularly devious in his plans for her—but she didn't dare try. Not when he had a gun and seemed more than willing to pull the trigger if she gave him the slightest reason.

"Just tell me what you want!" she demanded. *Do I really want to know?*

Willie stared at her. "I want Clyde, for starters," he said tersely.

"Clyde?" Ivana was taken aback. What did he have to do with this?

"Yeah, your bastard brother-in-law."

"Why do you want him?"

Willie paused thoughtfully. "The asshole blinded me in one eye and stabbed me in the back at the same time."

Ivana's mind raced, clouded by the alcohol, as she considered the problem with his eye that she'd noticed earlier. When her thoughts became clearer, the image of Clyde nearly beating a man to death and spending years in prison as a result finally registered.

Willie Munroe. She remembered where she'd seen him—or a much younger version of him. There was a picture of him and Clyde when they were in high school in one of Clyde's photo albums. A photo taken long before friends had turned into bitter enemies.

Ivana swallowed the bile in her throat. If nothing else, she knew that Clyde had regretted what happened with Willie every day since and had tried to make up for it in his own way.

But apparently that wasn't enough for Willie. Not nearly.

"If you think using me will get you Clyde, forget it," she told him. "We have our own issues. He certainly won't give a damn what happens to me."

"Is that right?" Willie asked coldly.

"Trust me on that." Ivana mused about her one-night stand with Clyde and her spilling the beans to Trey, giving his brother a reason to hate her just as much as she imagined Trey did.

Willie gave Ivana the once-over. He tried to envision what issues there were between the attractive lady and Clyde. Maybe the dude had banged his brother's wife once or twice. Or had tried to. He wouldn't put anything past a man who'd spent years in the pen and needed to get his rocks off with anyone who happened to be around. And, if Willie read her right, Ivana might not have been an unwilling target.

But that didn't mean Clyde would turn his back on his damn brother when push came to shove, including trying to rescue Trey's lovely wife. Willie suspected that Clyde would do just about anything to save the bitch.

He was counting on it.

"Let's just see how little your bro-in-law cares about what happens to you," Willie told his frightened captive.

It was time to settle things between them once and for all.

"We know all about Willie Munroe," Detective Cordell told Trey over the phone.

"Meaning what?" Trey had elected to fill the detective in on their suspicions, not wanting to wait 'til there was proof that Willie was behind Ivana's disappearance.

"Meaning the man's been in and out of trouble all his life. He and a buddy of his are under investigation right now for several armed robberies."

Trey thought about the vandalism of his car dealership. So far, the case had gone nowhere. Was Willie behind it after all? If so, had Clyde known about it and chosen to keep it to himself?

"Well, I think you may need to add kidnapping and assault," Trey strongly suggested. He could only hope Willie wouldn't do anything worse to Ivana, though his track record of violence suggested otherwise.

"Maybe. But as far as we know no crime's been committed involving Ivana," Cordell pointed out. "You said yourself, and the bartender confirmed, that your wife apparently left the bar of her own free will. There's no proof that she was kidnapped, much less assaulted."

Trey's nostrils ballooned. "Dammit, Eric, we're talking about my wife here! There's no way she would have left her car at some bar and gone off with Willie—unless he forced her do it."

Would she? Even if it were to get back at him or if she suddenly saw herself as worthless, Trey was sure Ivana had more self-respect than that. He doubted the same could be said for Willie Munroe.

"You said that Munroe and your brother have some history," Cordell said. "Care to elaborate?"

Trey looked over at Clyde, who was driving and dutifully doing his brotherly part to try and rescue Ivana from harm's way. Though Trey hated having to dig up the past, he didn't feel he had any choice. They needed to have the police on their side now and not after all was said and done.

"Willie Munroe has held a grudge against Clyde ever since they got into a fight nearly a decade ago."

Clyde flinched and looked at Trey, who met his gaze unapologetically.

"Is that right?" hummed Cordell. "Tell me more . . ."

Clyde listened as his life was being probed and dissected. He didn't blame Trey for laying all his cards out on the table to try and get Ivana back safe and sound. Clyde would have done the same had it been Stefani in harm's way.

Only his brother didn't know the full story. Maybe it was time he did.

Five minutes later, Trey was off the phone. "So what are the cops going to do?" Clyde asked skeptically.

"Eric says they have a make on Munroe's car and know where's he's staying," Trey answered. "They're supposed to send a squad car over there to see if he's keeping Ivana against her will."

"You don't sound very optimistic."

Trey eyed him. "The police have a way of dragging their feet," he said wearily. "The truth is, with no witnesses or proof of a crime, Eric can only do so much at this point. Meaning we're pretty much left on our own to track Ivana and that asshole who took her down."

Clyde shared his sentiments. "To hell with the cops. We'll be at Willie's apartment in no time flat."

"Then what?" Trey asked. "What if he's armed, since we're not? I sure as hell don't want to be at a disadvantage or allow that animal to harm one hair on Ivana's head or body."

Clyde would not put it past Willie to have a piece—or more than one—and a willingness to use it if he had to. Being a crazed and revenge-minded drug addict only made matters worse.

I won't tell Trey how concerned I am about that.

"We'll just deal with things when we get there and trust that two of us will have the advantage over one man," Clyde said, assuming Willie had taken Ivana by himself.

"He can't possibly think he'll get away with this," Trey voiced tensely.

"Willie thinks he can get away with anything," Clyde offered. "He definitely thought that ten years ago."

Trey tilted his head. "What are you talking about?"

Clyde kept his eyes on the road before saying tonelessly, "I'm talking about the night I was arrested," he uttered painfully. "Willie had gotten high and set his sights on looting your house and taking you down if you got in his way. I tried to reason with him, but there was no reasoning with the man." He sighed, realizing how hard it was to divulge the truth even after all these years, going against the side of him that had wanted to bury it forever. "I hated you for everything you had that I didn't. But you were still my brother. I couldn't let Willie take away what you'd worked so hard for. We got into a fight when Willie tried to go through me. I took my fair share from him and gave back more. I think you know the rest of the story."

Trey's eyes bulged in disbelief. "You're telling me that you damn near killed the man and went to prison *just* to protect my property?"

Clyde hated to admit it, but the cat was out of the bag. "Yeah, that's what I'm saying."

"I didn't need my little brother to protect me from the big bad wolf!" Trey told him flatly.

Clyde wasn't so sure about that, but went along with it. "I know it was dumb, stupid, whatever you want to call it. Guess at the time I thought I was doing the right thing. It just got out of hand." He chewed on his lower lip and looked at Trey with some relief. "So now you know the secret I've been carrying with me all these years."

"Why didn't you just come clean back then?" Trey asked. "None of what happened as a result was necessary."

Clyde shrugged. "Guess I was just trying to be a man and be responsible for what I did," he said. "Or maybe I figured it wouldn't matter to you one way or the other, given the bad blood between us."

"It was never so bad that I'd want you to go to prison for something that obviously had extenuating circumstances," Trey insisted. "Mama went to her grave thinking you simply did a hotheaded thing, damn the consequences."

"Hey, I screwed up," Clyde conceded, wishing he hadn't let his mother down, or Trey. "I wanted to tell you many times, but pride got in the way. I was an angry person back then. Angry that you seemed to get all the breaks. Angry that I paid the price for standing in Willie's way, while he got away with it scot-free. Angry that it seemed like me against the world and there was nothing I could do but suck it all up. I didn't want to hear you preaching to me about what I should and shouldn't have done, making me feel even worse." He drew in a deep breath. "I know now that I went about it the wrong way. I'm sorry, man. I never wanted this to come full circle, with Willie still carrying the vendetta all these years later, affecting you and Ivana."

"I'm sorry too," Trey said emotionally. "You put yourself out there for me, and deserved a hell of a lot more than you got in return. I just wish we had communicated more back then. Maybe a lot of things could have turned out differently all the way around."

Clyde agreed, but couldn't bring himself to say it. "Or maybe it would've turned out exactly the same—me getting in over my head and you having to deal with the mess I left behind."

Trey could hardly believe what Clyde had just divulged to him. Everything he thought he knew about his brother's reckless behavior and selfishness had been wrong. It made Trey feel guilty that he hadn't seen what had been staring him in the face all along. Clyde had loved him even when he thought the love wasn't being returned, which only widened the divide between them.

Trey could sense that Clyde was still bitter after all these years—and understandably so, under the circumstances. He had gone to prison as the black sheep of the family while Trey had ridden the white horse to success and fortune. Now he realized there was much more gray area between them than on the surface. Neither was perfect or guiltless when it came to making poor or life-altering choices.

In many ways we would always be in competition, Trey thought, even if on a subconscious level. He supposed a part of him had always suspected Clyde had taken one on the chin for him. Perhaps this was why he had tried to make things right when Clyde was released from prison. Only it seemed to have backfired, leaving them both shattered and uncertain of where to go from here.

I have to try and patch things up between us, even if the issues run deep and the waters remain murky at best.

But first, I need to do right by my wife, and that's no easy task, especially since I don't even know for sure where the hell she is. Or what condition she's in mentally and physically.

Trey remained resolute not to lose Ivana, not if he were given another opportunity to make their lives count for something other than mistrust, betrayal, and regrets.

He looked at Clyde. "Whatever has happened between us, let's just focus on finding Ivana right now. After that, we can figure out where we are and hopefully resolve our differences and get back to being real brothers just like Mama wanted."

"Yeah, that sounds good to me," Clyde said.

Trey felt that was at least a start on the long road to recovery.

Having a chance to put the past behind them was more than Clyde could have expected at this point as they neared Willie's apartment complex. Only hours ago he thought he'd lost Trey for good, along with a big part of himself, while bearing much of the burden for that. Now they had a window of opportunity to patch things up. Maybe they could still have the type of rock-solid relationship between brothers that he'd always dreamed of, but never believed was possible. Trey seemed more than willing to meet him halfway now that the cards were all out on the table.

Clyde knew that any such possibility of a happy ending hung in the balance, so long as Ivana remained missing and presumably in grave danger at the vengeful hands of Willie Munroe.

Chapter Forty

Stefani pressed the bell at the gate, and was allowed onto the Lancaster estate. It was the first time she had gone to Trey and Ivana's beautiful home alone; the house where Clyde had his surprising tryst with Ivana, resulting in an understandable falling-out between the brothers.

Truthfully, Stefani wasn't quite sure what she was doing there. Or if she would be welcomed were Ivana home instead of apparently off with another man. Stefani's uncle seemed uncertain if Ivana had been abducted, or went willingly with the man from the tavern.

I'm not here to pass judgment or condemn anything Ivana has done, even if I would've taken a different direction had I been in her position in life.

Stefani feared for Clyde's safety, not wanting to see past mistakes come back to haunt him today. If this Willie was as frightening and vindictive as Clyde indicated, then he couldn't be taken lightly.

They could be entering a tinderbox, ready to ignite. The last thing she wanted was to see Clyde caught in the line of fire, jeopardizing their future that suddenly seemed so promising if not for this situation.

Stefani drove up to the house. She had no idea if he and Trey would ever resolve their differences, but was somehow guardedly optimistic that were they to get through this latest crisis, it was entirely possible.

She wanted to find some way to lend her support beyond spiritually, figuring it was better to reach out and see where it got her than to just wait around going crazy with worry.

So I'm here. What do I do now? Guess I won't know 'til I go inside.

Stefani knocked on the door, actually hoping she would come face-to-face with Ivana, ending the suspense of her disappearance. Instead, it was the housekeeper, Emily, who answered.

"Nice to see you again," she said.

"You too." Stefani forced a smile.

"If you're looking for Clyde—"

"I'm not," Stefani clarified politely. "I know he's with Trey, looking for Ivana. I just wanted to come by to see if there was anything I could do to help."

"How nice of you," Emily said, inviting her in. "There's not much either of us can do for now but wait and see."

Stefani frowned. *I was afraid she'd say that.* "I guess we can always pray that everything works out." Hope she doesn't have anything against the power of prayer.

"That we can do," Emily agreed. "Would you like some coffee, tea, lemonade, Coke, or—"

"Coffee sounds good."

"Okay, then I'll have a cup too."

Stefani followed her toward the kitchen. "Where's Francine?" She hoped it wasn't a dumb question, considering that neither employee lived at the house and, as such, probably came and left at different hours of the day.

"Oh, she's spending time with her daughter who's visiting. I told Francine that it wasn't necessary for us both to be here right now taking up space, even though there's a lot of it."

Stefani watched as Emily got two ceramic mugs out of the cupboard. "Has Ivana ever just gone off like this before?" she asked curiously.

Emily looked up. "Not really. She and Trey have had their spats—some more serious than others—but this time I guess it sent her right over the edge."

Stefani tried to put herself in Ivana's shoes in getting something that weighty off her chest, only to have Trey turn on her, even if it was a natural reaction under the circumstances.

"Sorry to hear that."

Emily shrugged. "It happens. I'm sure once Ivana is back home and into rehab, she and Trey can get some counseling and they'll be just fine."

Stefani wondered if it could ever be that simple. Was counseling truly the cure-all for troubled marriages? Or any relationship?

They sat in the breakfast nook, and Stefani found herself briefly admiring the yellow floral wallpaper before meeting Emily's eyes.

"I heard that you and Clyde are becoming pretty close."

Stefani colored. "Yes, we are."

Emily beamed. "I'm happy for you. From what I've heard, Clyde's had a hard life and it's time he got a second chance to get it right."

Stefani wondered if she knew about Clyde's one-night stand with Ivana. If so, maybe Emily understood that things happened sometimes, but shouldn't ruin one's life forever. Including Ivana's.

"I agree. Clyde's a good man and he's really trying hard to make everything in his life work."

"Well, with a good woman in his life, I'm sure it can happen." Emily said.

Stefani felt the same way. The good woman in her was perfectly happy doing right by her man and being supportive when he needed her to be. Now was such a time.

Ivana's cell phone rang. She reached into her purse, only to have Willie poke her hard in the shoulder with the barrel of his gun, causing her to wince.

"Let it ring!" he commanded in a sharp tone. "No reason to spoil the fun before it begins."

Ivana choked back tears, removing her hand from the purse. Earlier, she'd turned the phone off, not wishing to talk to anyone. Certainly not Trey, who had turned his back on her when confronted with something he couldn't handle. But she had turned the phone back on while at the tavern.

Now he won't allow me to answer it. Could Trey be trying to reach me? Had he somehow been tipped off that I'd been taken against my will by this monster?

Or was that only wishful thinking when she and Trey were currently so at odds?

Ivana glanced at her captor, who kept the gun aimed at her while driving. Would he actually shoot her if she tried to jump out of the moving car? Did she dare try, risking serious injury if he didn't kill her first?

She speculated about where he might be taking her. Maybe out in the woods to rape and brutalize her in other ways. The thought gave her the chills.

I can't let that happen. But how can I prevent it?

"If you just let me call my husband, he'll give you—" she started to say out of desperation.

"Your husband," Willie snickered. "He's owes me plenty— just like Clyde. They're both gonna pay for gettin' in my way. But not 'til you and me get to know each other better . . ."

Ivana gulped as he ran the cold steel of the gun across her cheek and then chest. He was confirming her worst fears, leaving her helpless and starting to feel hopeless.

Willie drove toward his apartment complex and spotted a police cruiser parked not far from his door, lights flashing. It gave him a bit of a start, even though being high had made it easier to digest.

Were they looking for him? Or her?

Looks like I ain't gonna have some fun with Clyde's sister-in-law after all. Not here, any-way.

Peering at his imagined sex slave, Willie saw that she too noticed the police car. "Don't get any ideas," he told her, pointing the gun at her side. "They can't help you."

"Please don't hurt me," she whined.

"How about *pretty* please, sweet lady?" He chucked wickedly and drove away, hoping not to attract any attention.

Chapter Forty-one

Clyde turned into the apartment complex. He thought about his imminent confrontation with Willie. It was inevitable that they would have to settle this one way or the other. Clyde didn't want Trey and Ivana dragged into it. But that was exactly what had happened, and now he had to deal with it and hope they all came out of this thing in one piece.

"You ready?" Clyde looked across the seat at Trey.

"Yes." Trey took a breath. "Let's go see if the son of a bitch brought my wife here."

They left the car and looked across the lot for any sign of the vehicle Willie drove. Detective Cordell had provided the make. There was no evidence that it was there.

"Maybe he took her somewhere else," Trey speculated. "Or he's driving another car."

"Or maybe he parked in back." Clyde scanned the surroundings. "I say we check his place out."

"Yeah, let's."

At the door where Clyde once confronted Willie, there was no indication that anyone was home. Clyde rang the bell and knocked hard on the door. There was no response.

"Damn," he cursed under his breath, wondering if they were inside, with Willie forcing Ivana to remain silent.

Trey banged on the door, then kicked it. "Where the hell are they?"

"Maybe we should take a look inside," Clyde said, aware of the implications.

Trey's mouth hung open. "What are you suggesting?"

Clyde met his eyes. "I think you know."

"Breaking and entering wasn't part of the bargain."

"Neither was kidnapping, and who knows what the hell else your wife is being put through. For all we know, Ivana's in there, bound and gagged, maybe even drugged. There's only one way to find out for sure . . ."

"You're right," Trey relented. "Whatever it takes." He held Clyde's gaze. "So how do we do this?"

"I've got it covered." Clyde studied the door lock, which was cheap by most standards. He'd learned a bit about picking locks back in the day, and more while incarcerated, never expecting to be put to the test again. He removed a pen top from his pocket and put it in the lock, jimmying it.

After a moment or two, the door opened.

Clyde and Trey went inside, their guard up. The pungent scent of marijuana filled the air like poison. The place was dark and gloomy. Drug paraphernalia and remnants of meth and marijuana were spread out on a living-room table.

"Ivana," Trey called out. "Are you in here, baby?"

There was no response. He tried again and got the same result.

They went from one untidy room to the next, but saw neither Ivana nor Willie.

"Maybe they were here and left," Clyde suggested, though doubting it. He strongly suspected that Willie had anticipated this and was one step ahead of them.

"The bastard took her somewhere else," Trey said dolefully. "But where?"

They were standing in a bedroom. The bed was unmade and clothes were strewn about. Clyde thought about Willie's partner in crime in the dealership break-in. He wouldn't put it past Willie to have recruited him for his latest act of crime, if in fact Ivana wasn't with Willie voluntarily, which didn't seem too likely at this point.

Clyde spotted an answering machine on the dresser that blinked with messages. He pushed the button.

"Hi, Willie. I've been trying to reach you. I'm disappointed that we can't go out tonight. But that's just how I am. If you change you mind, I'll be home."

Clyde looked at the caller ID. It showed the message was from a Roselyn Pesquera. He recalled seeing her name on a piece of mail on the kitchen table.

"Let me check something," he told Trey, and went to look at the envelope. It had Roselyn's return address on it. Willie was apparently involved with this woman. She obviously had no idea what she was getting herself into. Or did she know exactly who she was dealing with, even to the point of helping him commit a crime?

Trey followed Clyde into the kitchen. "What's up?"

Clyde explained his thoughts. "It may be a long shot, but Willie could have taken Ivana to his girlfriend's place. Or, if not, she might know something . . ."

Trey sighed. "Right now, I'm willing to try anything that could help us find Ivana."

Clyde concurred, understanding that Willie might hold the key to any chance he had to make things right with Trey and Ivana.

"I keep trying Ivana's cell phone, but there's no answer," Stefani told Clyde over the phone as she drove, feeling frustrated.

"Well, keep trying," he said. "Maybe we'll get lucky and she'll pick up and tell us where she is."

"Where are you now?"

"We're on our way to see a woman named Roselyn Pesquera. She may be able to help."

Stefani didn't ask how. She knew that he and Trey were pulling out all the stops to try and find Ivana. But they weren't detectives, and Stefani did not want to see either hurt.

"Please be careful, Clyde. If anything were to happen—"

"I'll be fine," he promised. "Right now, we need to worry more about Ivana. Willie knows we're onto his ass, and he's probably running scared, which makes him even more threatening."

"What are the police doing?"

"Not enough," Clyde grumbled. "We heard they stopped by Willie's apartment and found nothing suspicious, so they left. Guess they're waiting for Willie to confess or a body to show up before doing what they should be. By then it could be too late, so we're taking matters into our own hands."

Stefani gazed out over the steering wheel. She knew the police were usually more reactive than proactive, but the fact that they were on the case at all suggested it would be resolved sooner than later.

Would Ivana be able to escape her ordeal by then, relatively unscathed?

"I'm on my way to the club," Stefani spoke into the speakerphone, not particularly in the mood to perform. "If you want, I can go home and—"

"That's not necessary," Clyde broke in. "There's nothing you can do there. Trey and I want it to be business as usual, at least 'til this is settled. I'll get there when I can. Meanwhile Albert and Raymond will handle things."

"All right."

"Gotta go, baby."

"Love you," she reaffirmed.

"Love you too," he said, warming her heart.

Stefani neared the club. She was proud of Clyde that he'd apparently been able to bury the hatchet with Trey while they went after a common enemy. In the end, they seemed to remember that they were brothers first and foremost. And on a mission that neither could afford to see fail.

It didn't go unnoticed by Trey that he'd heard Clyde say the word *love* to Stefani. He had assumed they were getting pretty close, but now it was clear that they were developing a deeply emotional commitment as well as an intimate one.

It was what Trey used to have with Ivana. He prayed they could get a second chance to rediscover the early part of their marriage and what it meant to be a husband and wife who loved each other more than life itself.

If I can get you back, baby, I swear I'll never let you down again.

"You all right?" Clyde asked.

"Ask me that when we find Ivana." Trey took a breath. "I think this whole ordeal has made me appreciate everything I had and nearly threw away."

"I know what you mean," he muttered.

"Once I have Ivana back and she's sober again, if she'll have me, I think I'd like to renew our wedding vows."

Clyde gave a thoughtful smile. "That's a great idea. I hope it works out."

"Thanks." Trey believed he meant it, even after what happened between him and Ivana.

"Looks like you and Stefani have found something special."

"Yeah, we have," Clyde admitted. "She makes me whole, and I feel like I deserve someone who's got my back, along with the right combo of brains, beauty, and talent."

"You do deserve it, Clyde," Trey said sincerely, forgetting for the moment that it was his own mistakes that often stood in the way before now. Maybe that would all change for good.

Clyde blinked. "I think we both do, big brother."

Clyde and Trey stood outside the ranch-style house. There was no visible sign of Willie's car. Instead, there was a Honda Accord parked in the driveway.

Clyde rang the bell. A pretty woman opened the door.

"Are you Roselyn?"

Her eyes darted suspiciously. "No, I'm not. Who's asking?"

"I'm Clyde and this is my brother, Trey."

"So you're friends of Roselyn?"

"Yes, something like that," he said smoothly. "Who are you?"

"Gail. I'm Roselyn's housemate."

"Is Willie here?" Trey asked straightforwardly.

"No, he isn't." She tensed. "What's this all about?"

"It's about life and death and wasting too much damned time trying to explain it!" Trey blared.

Gail's face contorted with confusion, and she looked at Clyde.

He sighed, realizing he needed to keep his cool. After all, it was his idea that Willie might have come here with Ivana. Maybe it wasn't such a good idea.

"We believe that Willie Munroe kidnapped Trey's wife," he told her candidly.

"What?" Gail's eyes widened.

Clyde gave her an abbreviated version of the story. "Willie was seen leaving a tavern with her, and Ivana's car was still in the lot. They weren't at his place, so we thought maybe Willie had brought Ivana here against her will. She won't answer her cell phone."

Gail's nose crumpled. "That no-good bastard. I knew he was trouble from the moment I laid eyes on him. I told Roselyn to stay away from him, but she wouldn't listen." She clasped her hands. "Willie wouldn't dare show his ass here with another woman, voluntarily or otherwise. If Roselyn wouldn't kill him, I would."

"I take it Roselyn isn't home, then?" Trey asked evenly.

Gail shook her head. "She was supposed to go to see a movie with Willie tonight. When he canceled abruptly, she decided to go to that new jazz club alone. And I'm going to join her later."

Clyde flashed a faint smile that business was still booming in spite of everything else, before getting back to the seriousness of the matter at hand. "If you hear from Willie, could you let us know?"

"I'd be glad to." She took Trey's card. "Hope you find your wife before that Willie does something crazy."

Clyde had an uneasy feeling in his stomach, knowing firsthand just how unstable Willie was, and what that meant for Ivana's chances to come away from this unharmed.

Chapter Forty-two

"I've got your sister-in-law," Willie said over the phone. He looked at Ivana and made sure she understood the gun pointing in her direction would be used if she did anything stupid.

"If you do anything to hurt her—" Clyde warned.

Willie grunted. "You'll what, bitch? You already took your best shot."

"You only think I did," Clyde said tartly. "Believe me, it can get much worse for you. Let her go, Willie, and we can forget this ever happened."

Yeah, right, Willie thought. *The minute I release her, he'll come after me. Probably joined by his brother. And even the cops to haul my ass off to jail. Or shoot to kill and call it justified.*

"I don't think so, homie. You ain't gonna forget this any more than I can forget what you done to my eye."

"That's between you and me," Clyde told him.

"It was never between you and me!" barked Willie. "It was between me and that high-and-mighty brother of yours. You stuck your nose where you shouldn'ta. Now you're gonna be sorry you ever did."

"Let Ivana go and I'll take her place," Clyde offered.

Willie sniffled, feeling the meth residue in his nasal cavity. "Yeah, you'd like that, wouldn't you? To be a hero in your brother's eyes. Well, it ain't gonna happen—not this time."

"I'm no hero," Clyde told him. "Certainly not to Trey. I just want the lady released so you and me can settle this any way you like."

"What I want is to see you *and* your brother dead," Willie hissed bluntly. "And maybe his pretty and drunk wife too."

"You son of a bitch," Trey blasted into the speaker. "If you hurt her in any way, I swear I'll kill you."

"Yeah, you really got me shakin' in my shoes," Willie scoffed. "I figured Clyde was there with his big brother to hold his hand. Or is it the other way around?"

"The police know about this," Clyde said. "No matter how you slice it, Willie, you're screwed. If you let Ivana go now, we can call it a big misunderstanding and you won't have to spend the next twenty years in prison. Trust me when I say it's not a place you want to be."

Willie considered his words. He wasn't interested in doing hard time. He had seen what it
had done to others, even though Clyde seemed
to have survived well enough.

*Even with two good eyes it would be hard to
watch my back in the pen. And with only one, it
would be damned near impossible.*

He fixed his good eye on Ivana's frightened
face. Maybe he should cut his losses and set her
free. No, it was too late for that. It had gone too
far, but not nearly far enough.

Whatever happened, happened.

If he went down, Willie wanted to make damned
sure Clyde and company went down with him. He
ran the gun barrel slowly across Ivana's cheek and
saw her flinch, making him grin.

"No deal," he said into the phone. "But I've got
one for you."

Clyde sucked in a ragged breath. "I'm listening."

I'll bet you are. Willie collected his thoughts,
fuzzy as they were, deciding upon the perfect
way to settle the scores built up over the years.

"If you wanna see the bitch alive again, you
and your brother come alone where I tell you."

"How do we know she's alive right now—and
not hurt?" Clyde asked.

Willie peered at the nice-looking wife. "You don't, asshole."

"We'll meet you anywhere, anytime, Willie—after we know Ivana's alive and well. Put her on the phone!"

Willie wanted them to suffer a bit longer, not knowing for sure if he had taken her out, as he had suffered for so many years. But the end would be just as sweet either way.

He cast a menacing stare at Ivana. "Looks like someone has somethin' to say to you. Watch what you say, bitch, otherwise it might be the last words to come out of your mouth."

Ivana sat next to Willie in the car, parked on a dark street just a short distance from Clyde's Jazz Club. It might as well have been on the other side of the world, for there were no other people in sight she could scream to help her. And if there had been, it would only have given him an excuse to shoot her in the face, ending whatever life she had left to look forward to.

She watched Willie press the speaker button on his cell phone and then point it at her. He'd already warned Ivana that if she tried anything like cutting him down or getting out of the car, he wouldn't hesitate to gun her down.

"She can hear you," he grunted.

"Ivana?" It was Trey.

"Trey—" Ivana never thought she would be so happy to hear his voice, even under trying circumstances.

"Has he hurt you?"

Ivana looked at Willie. He glared back. In fact, aside from pushing her into the car and poking her once or twice with the gun to get his kicks, she had not been hurt physically. But how long would that last, considering that she was being held against her will by a madman who also seemed desperate enough in his desire for revenge against Trey and Clyde?

"No, I'm fine," she said after taking a calming breath. "Just scared to death."

"Don't be, baby," Trey said. "We'll get through this together."

"Do you really mean that?" Her voice rang with doubt.

"Every last word of it," he promised. "You just stay strong."

Ivana's face lit up at the prospect that she might make it out of this alive and Trey would be there for her in spite of everything. *Maybe I'm hoping for the impossible, but I want us to work out, no matter what happened before or what challenges may lie ahead.*

"That's enough!" Willie yelled. "Okay, so now you know she's alive and I've got her. The rest is up to you—"

"You've got our attention," Clyde stated tersely. "Where do you want us to go?"

Willie grinned thoughtfully. "Let's see . . . How 'bout your precious club," he said. "The place where you had your goons throw me out on my flabby ass."

"Why don't we meet somewhere more private?" Clyde asked uncomfortably.

"Because I say we don't!" retorted Willie. "You got half an hour to come—both of you. And no cops either, otherwise the Missus here will be the first to take a bullet . . . messing up real bad that pretty face of hers. Oh, and if you call the club and one of your brutes tries to stop me from comin' in or sends other people out, I'll take my hostage somewhere else and you'll never see her again, 'cept on a slab."

Ivana felt her heart beating wildly. She wondered what devious plan he had in mind, and if there was any way out of this alive for any of them. The last thing she wanted was to die without being able to hold Trey in her arms one more time and tell how much she loved him. Would she ever get that chance?

Chapter Forty-three

Stefani sat in her dressing room practicing her songs for the night. She wasn't exactly in a singing mood—not while Clyde was out there making himself a target for a man who wanted him dead. She had no doubt that was what Willie Munroe had in mind at the end of the day. He wanted to get back at Clyde for getting in his way so many years ago, costing him in more ways than one. Ivana was obviously just a pawn in his plans, but Stefani was pretty sure he was capable of hurting her. This meant everyone associated would be hurt, including herself.

I have to think positive that everything will work out. Clyde has come too far along with Trey, only to have the likes of Willie Munroe destroy their lives out of a sick need for revenge.

Stefani thought about calling Clyde again. She didn't want to become more of an irritant than anything, which he didn't need right now. She was certain that if something came up, he or Trey would let her know.

"How are we doing in here, sweetheart?" Albert leaned his head in the doorway.

Stefani's eyes twinkled at her uncle. "Just getting ready to go out there and do my thing."

"I know you are, and the folks out there are ready for you."

She stood, drawing in a deep breath and convincing herself that everything would be fine. "Then I guess I can't disappoint them, can I?"

Albert wrapped his arms around her. "Look, I know that you're worried about Clyde, Trey, and Ivana. We all are. But worrying only gives you wrinkles and doesn't change the facts any. Willie Munroe has been like smoldering dynamite for a long time now, ready to explode. He's looking for some attention, and he got it. In the end, he'll only end up imploding on his own hatred; then Clyde can be free of him once and for all."

"You really think so?" Stefani gazed up at her uncle.

"I know so. It was only a matter of time before this day came. Now that it has, Clyde will deal with it, along with Trey and the authorities. Willie doesn't have a chance in hell to beat the strength in numbers." Albert kissed the top of her head. "Now go out there and make Clyde and your uncle proud. Give the people their money's worth."

Stefani flashed a smile at him, feeling better about things. She followed Albert out in anticipation of wooing the audience.

She saw Raymond in the hallway.

"Looking as gorgeous as ever," he said. "If Clyde ever loses his mind and says bye-bye, I'm available."

Stefani smiled, aware that his flirtation was innocent. The last she'd heard, Raymond was seeing someone. Nevertheless, she told him, "I'll keep that in mind."

A grin creased his cheeks. "Now I can die a happy man."

She waved him off, amused. "Just make sure it's not for another fifty years or so."

His cell phone rang. "Excuse me."

"Knock yourself out," she said. "I've got a show to perform."

Stefani watched as Raymond waved and walked away from her. She couldn't help but think it was nice that Clyde and he had formed a friendship under adverse circumstances that had sustained itself to the benefit of both.

She stepped on stage and conferred with Winston on the song selections.

"Excellent choices, as usual," he said. "Let's do it."

"Let's." Stefani moistened her lips and put on a cheery face while still having a sense of dread that something was wrong. Or not quite right.

"We've got a problem," Clyde told Raymond over the phone, with Trey listening in. They were both stunned at Willie's demand of where to go in order to save Ivana. The jazz club had been the last place Clyde would have figured him to hold Ivana hostage. And apparently everyone else inside, including Stefani and Raymond.

This left them little choice other than to comply with his demands. Or else risk him killing Ivana and possibly Stefani.

"What's the problem?" asked Raymond.

"Willie Munroe," Clyde replied stiffly. "He's got Ivana and he's bringing her to the club."

"I'll send some of the guys out and—"

"No!" Clyde's voice raised an octave. "Let him through. Willie demanded that Trey and I meet him there. The man has gone off the deep end and no doubt has a gun. I don't want anyone hurt, least of all Ivana or Stefani."

"So what do you want me to do?"

Clyde thought about this long and hard. He and Trey had discussed the situation and decided not to bring the police in just yet. It wasn't worth riling Willie and provoking into attacking Ivana or someone else. They suspected Willie must have been holding Ivana somewhere close to the club when he called, meaning that if they had a mass exodus, he'd see it and might do something crazy.

"I—we—want you to quietly get as many people as you can to exit through the back door."

"What do I tell them without creating a panic situation?" Ramond asked.

Clyde looked to Trey, who answered, "Tell them that it's just a precautionary evacuation while the place is checked for excessive levels of carbon monoxide in the air—and that it shouldn't take long and no one should be concerned."

"If you think that'll work," Raymond said.

"It has to," stated Trey.

"We'll be there in a few minutes," Clyde said. "Just try to keep things as normal as possible inside. Don't have anyone attempt to confront Willie—you know what he looks like. We don't need any heroes, especially not dead ones."

"Got it," Raymond responded. "We'll do it your way—or Trey's—and hope we all live to get a good night's sleep afterward."

Clyde echoed those feelings and hung up. He looked at Trey, who had to be stressed out hearing Ivana's voice and knowing he was still powerless to take her from Willie right then and there. But at least they had a lead on where he was taking her.

Clyde knew that his onetime friend was gunning for him and as many others as he could take with him, starting with Trey. He wasn't about to let that happen. Not if he could help it. And what if he couldn't?

I can't think that way. It would only be playing into Willie's bloody hands and put us all in even more jeopardy.

Trey hadn't been comfortable with Willie's crazy demands. But what choice did he really have but to comply? He didn't quite know what they were in for, dealing with someone who wanted to see him and Clyde both dead. Doing as Willie had instructed could amount to suicide, while rejecting it could cost Ivana her life. Or make her wish she were dead.

I can't lose Ivana now. Not when we have the chance to right the ship before it sinks.

He turned to Clyde behind the wheel, impressed that he had handled this so calmly while surely feeling the heat of the moment. Trey was seeing a whole new side to his brother and wished he had seen it earlier in their lives. The important thing now was that they were doing this together and trying to avert a disaster that put Ivana and Stefani in the line of fire.

Clyde eyed him askew. "If you're having second thoughts about contacting the police—maybe your friend on the force— it's not too late to get them in on this."

Trey gritted his teeth. As much as he wanted to call Eric and request that they do it by the book, he feared it could leave Ivana seriously injured or dead. This would devastate Trey, for he couldn't imagine living without her. Especially if she were taken from him by senseless violence at the hands of someone who should have been locked up years ago, instead of Clyde.

"No police," Trey said categorically. "We'll do it his way and hope to God we don't live to regret it."

Willie held Ivana's arm in a viselike grip as they approached the club. "Don't be stupid, bitch," he warned. "I've still got the gun in my jacket and you'll be the first one I use it on if you try and get away."

"I won't," Ivana said weakly. "I'm too tired and sore to run. Besides, I doubt I'd get very far before you shot me.

"At least we understand each other." Willie felt a sense of power and retribution at once. He could almost taste the blood he wanted spilled from Clyde, Trey, and anyone else he could take down.

They went up to the door where a brawny bouncer looked them over. "You got some IDs?"

Willie froze for a moment. Taking out his wallet would leave him vulnerable to attack and might allow Ivana to flee. Think.

"Do you really think we're underage?" he questioned.

The bouncer gave them the once-over and backed off. "Naw, I guess not. Enjoy your evening."

Willie grinned. "We plan to."

Ivana noticed that the bouncer did not make eye contact with her, though she was trying to get his attention without Willie being the wiser. She suspected that, against Willie's orders, Clyde had phoned the club to announce their arrival and the circumstances surrounding it. What Ivana didn't know was how they planned to handle it. Was someone prepared to intervene on her behalf? Or had they been told not to make any moves that might endanger her life or any other lives? Given the type of person they were dealing with, Ivana feared that no one could prevent Willie from carrying out his sick act of vengeance.

She didn't want to die. Or see Trey, Clyde or anyone else hurt in the process of trying to save her. Especially when Ivana knew her husband and brother-in-law were walking into a deadly trap that they may not be able to escape any more than her.

Ivana blamed herself for the predicament she and everyone else were in. *I should never have gone to that tavern for all the wrong reasons.* Had Willie followed her there? Planned the whole thing? And she'd fallen for it, caught up in her bitterness, self-pity, and effects of too much alcohol in her system.

Willie was still clutching her arm as they walked through the club. The crowd was sparse, but there were still enough people to make a bloodbath should he start firing the gun in his pocket. Ivana cringed at the thought while looking for a way out of this nightmare without ending up in a coffin six feet under.

Stefani's voice was velvety strong as she piped out a stirring rendition of Antonio Carlos Jobim's romantic jazzy tune, "Wave."

She watched her audience get to their feet in applause as she hit just the right note to finish the song.

Stefani nodded with a big smile in appreciation for the support. *I really am on my way,* she thought. *This club has been the perfect venue for displaying and honing my talents.*

Not to mention finding the love of an incredible man. No small feat after her less-than-successful previous relationship that nearly turned her off men for good.

Gazing back at those in attendance, Stefani took note that it had dwindled by about one-third since she took the stage. She might have thought they were turned off by her, had she not seen Raymond and some others from the security team whispering to patrons, who then followed them toward the normally off-limits, employee-only area of the club.

It was obvious something serious was going on that they were being careful to keep under wraps. Stefani considered putting a stop to the string of standards, but since her break was just two songs away, she decided to stick with it unless told otherwise.

She mused about Clyde and Trey, sensing that progress had been made in their efforts to locate Ivana. But how much? And were they out of danger? Or running into it?

Stefani swallowed and glanced at Winston for coordination on the next song.

Trey and Clyde waded through patrons who were milling around outside the back of the club, assuring them that soon everything would be fine and drinks would be on the house. Clyde felt the rapid beat of his heart and knew there were no guarantees this would end like a fairy tale. Willie was a ticking time bomb just waiting to go off. And he had Ivana and everyone else inside, including Stefani, to blow up with him.

While wanting to take me out—and Trey—if given the chance.

Clyde hoped that wasn't the case. He counted on the element of surprise and quickness to thwart Willie's murderous plans. At the door, he glanced at Trey and could see the doubt in his face as to whether they were going about things the right way.

"We can do this, Trey," Clyde tried to assure him, if not himself.

Trey flashed a wary look. "Guess we really don't have much of a choice at this point but to go after the man threatening Ivana," he said soberly. "I'm ready."

"Then let's take down the son of a bitch!" Clyde's said.

They went inside and were immediately met by Raymond.

"Are they here?" Trey asked anxiously.

"Yeah, they're here." Raymond towered over him. "Munroe's got Ivana near the stage at an angle so he can see who's coming and going. Ivana doesn't seem to be hurt."

"I want to keep it that way."

"I hear you, man." Raymond faced Clyde. "So what's the plan?"

"There is no plan," he admitted truthfully. "We play it by ear and hope to hell Willie gets too caught up in himself to be able to carry out whatever he has planned before we can stop it."

Raymond produced a piece. "You may need this."

Clyde eyed the Glock. He had handled a gun before, but wasn't particularly comfortable using one in this situation, even if justifiable. The last thing he wanted was to shoot someone—even Willie—and maybe end up back in prison himself. But he owed Trey and wanted to do right by rescuing Ivana from a man who took her to get back at him.

Clyde was surprised when Trey grabbed the gun instead, doubting his straitlaced brother had ever used one before. But he knew that people found courage under adversity. Still, Clyde was concerned. He didn't even want to think about Trey doing time for firing an unlicensed weapon.

Clyde peered at his brother. "Maybe I should take the gun—"

"I can handle it," insisted Trey. "I'll only use if I absolutely have to."

Clyde nodded. He preferred getting physical with Willie if he got the chance, but only if he could keep Ivana uninjured at the same time.

"Whatever happens, I've got your backs," Raymond told them both.

Clyde eyed his friend and Trey directly. "Let's end this now."

They went to confront Willie.

Chapter Forty-four

Ivana tried to will herself to stay calm. She knew Trey and Clyde were coming, just as Willie had demanded. But what then? She certainly didn't want to see Willie kill Clyde and Trey, like he planned. And probably her too.

What can I do to stop him without making things worse for everyone?

She winced from the pain of Willie gripping her arm tightly as they stood amid others who were apparently clueless to the danger while they watched the performance.

Ivana gazed up at Stefani. She was singing beautifully, but seemed tense, as if she knew something was amiss.

If we all survive the night, Ivana thought, *I hope Stefani and Clyde keep their relationship going, since they both seem right for each other.*

As for her marriage, Ivana wanted nothing more than to have the opportunity to try to make it work again once she got herself cleaned up. She and Trey had been through so much. It couldn't end for them. Not this way.

Or could it? She knew there were no guarantees this would end without tragedy. "My feet are starting to hurt standing here," she told Willie, if only for a reaction.

"That's too damned bad," he said gruffly. "Guess you shouldn't have worn them high heels. Now be cool. Shouldn't be much longer now."

That was what Ivana hoped and feared most.

Willie felt on edge, as if everyone in the club knew exactly who he and his pretty captive were, but were trying to pretend otherwise. Well, soon it wouldn't matter. The moment he laid his eyes on Clyde and his made-of-money brother, the shooting gallery would begin—starting with Ivana Lancaster.

"So something's come up, huh," the voice said snidely, catching Willie's attention.

He turned to his right and came face-to-face with Roselyn. She wore a venomous scowl and had one hand planted firmly on her hip.

"What the hell are you doing here?" was all Willie could think to say.

"I should be asking you the same thing." She glared at Ivana. "Who is this?"

Ivana regarded the woman, and was about to speak, when Willie squeezed her arm tighter and gave her a warning look.

"She's nobody," he spat tersely.

Roselyn narrowed her gaze at him. "Well, if that's true, then why are you holding her like she's your girl—instead of me?"

"It's not what you think," Willie said, trying to clear his head of the meth, while glad it was there to calm him somewhat.

"Sure looks like it!" she huffed. "If you wanted to cancel our movie date because you were taking *her* to the club, you should've been man enough to admit it, Willie. Then I wouldn't feel like such a damned fool!"

Willie hated that she was at the club to witness this, but would not back down from his master plan. "Look, baby, I can explain—but later . . ." He used his free hand to reach out and touch Roselyn's face, while maintaining a viselike grip on Ivana.

Roselyn backed away from him like he was the devil himself. "Don't touch me, you bastard! I can see that you've got your hands full. I don't need this crap."

Neither do I. Willie shot her a wicked look, done with his nice-guy bit. "Get the hell outta here—now!"

Roselyn's nostrils flared defiantly. "Why should I? So you can get it on with her?"

"So you don't end up gettin' hurt," he told her flatly. "Just go, for your own good."

Roselyn held his hard stare, then averted her eyes, planting them sharply on Ivana. "You can have him. He ain't worth my time—not anymore!" She stormed off.

"Your girlfriend?" Ivana asked wryly. "Or should I say *ex*-girlfriend?"

"Shut the hell up, you stupid bitch!" Willie rounded on her, suddenly feeling as though the situation were getting away from him.

Not if he could help it.

Stefani was singing "Harlem Nocturne" when she spotted Ivana with a man who was holding her arm. Willie Munroe, no doubt. Clyde's worst nightmare. How did they get into the club without being stopped by security?

She noticed that Willie had one hand in his pocket, as though he were holding a gun. Ivana looked nervous, but seemed to be keeping it together under the circumstances. Stefani doubted she'd be able to keep herself together if she had a bitter, dangerous man at her side.

She'd watched as another woman went up to them and began talking to Willie as if she knew him. Willie seemed to be seeking to pacify her before turning angry. The woman walked away, vexed.

Then Stefani saw Clyde and Trey. They were approaching Willie and Ivana from opposite sides; with Raymond and others from the club behind them, including her Uncle Albert.

Stefani swallowed, wanting to stop singing at that moment, but fearful of tipping Willie off if she did and possibly causing him to go ballistic. So she tried to keep her voice steady while staying on note with Winston at the piano, even as Stefani made eye contact with Clyde, who seemed to tell her that everything would be all right.

Stefani only wished she could be as certain.

"Willie," Clyde approached him cautiously, softly telling others to back away.

Willie shifted in Clyde's direction and quickly pulled out the gun, putting it to Ivana's head. "What took you so damn long to get here?"

"I got here soon as I could."

Willie chuckled snidely. "I was startin' to think you'd chickened out, worried about savin' your own sorry ass."

"I think you know me better than that," Clyde said unperturbedly. "I'm here now, Willie. Let her go."

"You think I was born yesterday or somethin'?" he muttered. "It ain't gonna be that simple."

"It can be," Clyde insisted. "I'm the one you want pay back against, right?"

Willie kept the gun pinned to Ivana's temple. He damned sure did want payback, but against more than just Clyde. He turned his head and saw Trey—the other object of his revenge—approaching from another angle. "So now the rich big brother has come in on his white horse to save his woman."

"Yeah, man, all I want is to save my wife," Trey said somberly. "If you want me, here I am."

"Please, Willie," Ivana said tearfully. "You don't have to do this."

"She's right, Willie," Clyde echoed. "Lay down the gun and no one gets hurt. You can walk away and it'll be over."

"It'll never be over, man—not 'til one of us is dead," Willie sputtered. "Along with a few others thrown in because I say so. " He rubbed the barrel of the gun against Ivana's cheek.

"Just stop it, Willie," he heard Roselyn's raised voice. She came out of the gathering. "I don't know why you're doing this, but you can't go around shooting people no matter what the reason is. This isn't you—"

"Think again, baby." Willie curled his lip. If she only knew what he was capable of outside the bedroom and whispering in her ear. It was probably better she didn't know. Except for the fact that there was no way out of this for him, other than to follow through with his plans.

Clyde had to pay for what he did. And so did his brother. And the wife. Even the singer who Willie believed Clyde was banging, though she had stopped singing while remaining on stage.

They all had to die.

Then he'd kill himself and be done with it once and for all.

Something told Ivana that Willie would actually follow through on his threat to kill her, Trey, and Clyde. As she would likely be the first to go before Trey or Clyde could intervene, it was up to her to at least try and throw Willie off balance. Then hope for the best.

I have to muster up the courage to try to prevent a massacre.

When she felt his gun hand grow unsteady, Ivana knew it was now or never.

She chose now.

Allowing herself only a breath to maintain bravery, Ivana clamped her hands around Willie's wrist and thrust the gun up in the air. Simultaneously she drove the heel of her stiletto into his ankle as hard as she possibly could.

Willie yelled in pain even as the gun discharged. But he managed to recover enough to bring it back down. Ivana swiftly dug her teeth into his wrist, drawing blood and causing him to howl in more discomfort.

His face contorted with fury, Willie backhanded Ivana, sending her sprawling to the floor. He pointed the gun at her and Ivana said her prayers, fearing he would shoot and kill her.

But then she saw a fast-moving Clyde lunge at him. Willie was able to turn the gun toward Clyde and pull the trigger, hitting him.

Trey watched in horror as his brother went down. Willie then fired two more shots indiscriminately, apparently not caring who he hit at this point. Trey felt it was up to him to stop this psychopath before anyone else was hurt. Willie made it easier by pointing his gun directly at Trey. Only he had already aimed the gun in his hand at Willie's chest and pulled the trigger first. Willie crashed to the floor facedown as panic erupted in the club with people screaming and running for cover.

Trey rushed over to Ivana even as Raymond climbed atop Willie, who had been attempting to get to his feet, and held him at bay.

"Are you all right?" Trey asked affectionately.

"Yes," she sobbed, wiping blood that was trickling from her left nostril. "I am now. But maybe Clyde isn't."

Trey shifted his eyes to his brother, who was being tended to by Stefani. Clyde looked at him and gave a thumbs-up to indicate he would live.

"He's going to make it," Trey said. "It's over."

"Is it really?" Ivana clung to him, as if never wanting to let go. All the anger and self-pity seemed to be gone.

"Yes," he promised. "Willie Munroe is never going to hurt you again."

"I'm sorry, Trey," Ivana said tearfully. "About everything."

"So am I." Trey put the blame for most of their troubles squarely on his own shoulders. Now it was up to him to make things right. "We'll work everything out. I love you, baby, and don't ever want to lose you."

"I love you too," she said. " More than ever."

Trey embraced Ivana and kissed her passionately. He knew how close he'd come to losing her and Clyde in one fell swoop had Willie succeeded in his master plan. It would have prevented Trey from being able to make amends with Ivana and bury the hatchet with Clyde once and for all.

Right now, Trey only wanted to breathe a sigh of relief that Ivana had survived the ordeal to see another day, and they could now try to make their lives count again as something special.

He felt Ivana tense in his arms. "What is it?"

"Someone else was shot," she said.

Trey had noted that people were scrambling this way and that, trying to come to terms with what had happened. He followed Ivana's gaze to a group huddled around in a circle. They walked toward it and made an opening.

Trey saw a thirty-something woman lying there with blood coming from a head wound. "Does anyone know who she is?" he asked.

"I do," Ivana responded bleakly. "From what I gathered in a heated conversation she had with Willie, they were dating—"

Chapter Forty-five

Stefani rode in the ambulance with Clyde as he was rushed to the emergency room. He had been shot in the shoulder, and was drifting in and out of consciousness. She couldn't stop crying over the thought that Clyde could have been killed, and the sheer joy that he would survive.

"I love you," she sobbed.

Clyde smiled at her through the oxygen mask on his face. "Is that a promise?"

"Yes, definitely!"

"Good." He closed his eyes, but still had a grin on his face.

Stefani held his hand throughout, not wanting to leave Clyde's side 'til he had made a full recovery. The entire horror show they had all been forced to witness replayed in her mind like a nightmare.

Thank God, Ivana escaped with only a few bruises during her abduction and confrontation with Willie.

Trey, who was a hero right alongside Clyde, had been unharmed.

Unfortunately, the same could not be said for Roselyn Pesquera, the woman said to have been involved with Willie Munroe. She was struck by a single bullet from his gun to her head and had died at the scene. Another innocent bystander was nicked on the arm.

Stefani thought about the man who had brought about this night of terror. Trey had shot him in the stomach in what was clearly a case of self-defense and preventing Willie from killing others. The last she'd heard, Willie Munroe was also being rushed to the emergency room, his fate unknown.

He deserves to die for all the hatred and vindictiveness he carried, Stefani mused, looking at Clyde's handsome face and realizing how easily he could have been gone from her life forever.

Stefani backed off from her death wish for Willie. She didn't want to see Trey have to carry the burden of killing a man, even one as vile as Willie Munroe. She hoped the man made a full recovery so he could stand trial for murdering his girlfriend and the attempted murder of Clyde, and spend the rest of his miserable life behind bars where people like him belonged.

Stefani lit up when she saw Clyde open his eyes again and smile at her, as if to say, *Everything's going to be okay with us. Just a little bump in the road that we'll step over to continue to build on what we already have.*

She couldn't agree more.

Though Ivana had insisted she was fine—other than being shaken up and scared out of her wits—Trey made her go to the hospital to be checked out anyway. She hated doctors and all their poking and prodding, but in this case wanted to give Trey peace of mind, if not herself as well. She was just happy to be alive after what that awful man put her through. Trey had shot Willie before he could shoot her or himself, risking his own life. That spoke volumes to her, for Trey had selflessly come to her rescue in spite of everything that had gone wrong in their lives.

He still loves me even when I tried to do everything I could to push him away. How could I have been so foolish to jeopardize that?

Ivana felt tears burn her cheeks. She would get off the booze dependency, realizing that alcohol and self-pity had nearly ruined everything and everyone she cared about.

"I've made such a mess of things," she told Trey in the examination room. "Can you ever forgive me?"

"We both made mistakes," Trey uttered. "We have to forgive each other and try to put it all behind us now."

Ivana saw the sincerity in his eyes. "I want that," she promised. "I never stopped loving you, Trey. I just forgot how much."

He kissed her. "Then let's build on that, because I never stopped loving you for one moment. We can spend the rest of our lives making up for lost time."

Ivana liked the sound of a renewed commitment to each other. "It works for me."

Trey's eyes watered and he grinned. "I'm glad."

"But right now, I want you to go check on your brother," she said adamantly, knowing he was just down the hall. "Clyde needs you more than I do at the moment."

"Thank you," Trey told her. "For everything." He kissed her cheek. "I'll be back in no time flat."

Ivana's lips curved upward faintly. "I won't be going anywhere—at least not 'til the doctor gives me a clean bill of health."

Ivana watched Trey walk away and thought about Clyde. Like Trey, he had risked his life to save hers, proving there was a lot more substance to the man than she had wanted to believe. She could never thank him enough for what he did for her. But she would try, while hoping that they too would be able to put the past where it belonged and work at being normal in-laws again.

Clyde was a bit groggy as he opened his eyes to find Trey at his bedside. His shoulder was bandaged and there was some pain, but it wasn't unbearable. He thought briefly about the events that led to this moment and how much his past had shaped the circumstances. Maybe the future could bring about more positive results.

"Guess you can't keep a good man down," he joked through a dry mouth.

"Not if he happens to be a Lancaster," Trey said with a weary smile. "It may be a while before I can whip your ass on the basketball court, but other than that, you'll live to see another day. Make that many, many more days."

"I'm counting on it." Clyde adjusted his body slightly. "How's Ivana?" He knew she'd been through hell in her ordeal with Willie. But her actions had prevented him from doing more harm to her and others.

"Oh, she's a lot tougher than probably both of us put together once her instincts kick in," said Trey.

Clyde grinned. "I wouldn't doubt it—not after the way she manhandled Willie."

Trey laughed. "Yeah, she hit the guy where it hurt, that's for sure."

"What about you and Ivana?" Clyde asked on a serious note. He'd hate to think that after all they had been though their relationship was still on shaky ground.

"Things are looking up for us, as a matter of fact—thanks to my little brother," he said confidently. "You took a bullet that could have had either of our names on it, Clyde, and I'll be forever indebted."

"Wasn't anything you wouldn't have done had the tables been turned." Clyde cringed at the thought of Willie putting his grubby hands on Stefani, and remembered it was Trey who had shot the son of a bitch. It occurred to Clyde that he had no idea whether his ex-pal was alive or dead. He looked at Trey. "What about Willie?"

Trey frowned. "He's going to pull through. The bullet lodged in a soft spot in his big belly while doing little internal damage, but I bet it still hurts like hell."

"Good," Clyde said with satisfaction. "I want Willie to live a long time to see what it's like to spend a good chunk of his miserable life in the pen."

Trey's face darkened. "Unfortunately, a woman who had made the mistake of dating Willie was shot and killed by him at the club."

Clyde felt a lump in his throat. "Roselyn—"

Trey nodded sadly. "Yeah."

Clyde recalled the message she had left on Willie's answering machine. The lady deserved much better than she got. "Sorry to hear that," he said.

"Just one of those things. Maybe something good can come out of her death, such as getting Willie off the streets so no one else will ever be the victim of his out-of-control rage."

Clyde agreed, but wished he had been able to get his hands on Willie after Ivana caused the gun to misfire, thereby saving a life. He realized that beating himself up about it wasn't going to bring the lady back. It was Willie's fault alone that he ended up killing someone, which was his plan all along. Except he had gunned down the wrong person—someone who actually gave a damn about the man—and would have to live with it for the rest of his days.

"Well, look who's awake—"

Clyde shifted his gaze to Stefani entering the room. She flashed a brave smile on an otherwise strained face. "You never looked more beautiful than now, baby."

Stefani's eyes watered while her smile widened. "You'd say anything, just to get a reaction."

"Guilty as charged, but still true nonetheless." He looked at Trey for some support. "Trey, back me up, big brother. Tell her. . . ."

Trey smiled broadly. "I couldn't agree more, Stefani. You're hot and there's no getting around it."

She shook her head playfully. "How sweet to hear from you both. Nice to know you brothers are on the same page for once."

Clyde liked the sound of that and hoped it was true. He met her pretty eyes. "I never wanted to confront Willie Munroe again . . . not if it meant losing you—"

"You did what you had to do out of love for Trey and Ivana," she told him approvingly. "And you're never going to lose me, mister, so you might as well get used to having me around for a very, very long time."

Clyde grinned. He was happy to know Stefani was there for the long run, especially since he was too. No one else had ever made him feel this way before and he counted his blessings.

"Wouldn't have it any other way," he assured her.

Stefani bent down and kissed him tenderly. Clyde bit his tongue when she leaned into his surgically repaired shoulder, but knew it never hurt as good as her touch.

In the hospital corridor, Trey saw Detective Eric Cordell waiting for him. He had expected to be questioned by the police for his part in shooting Willie.

"How's your brother?" Cordell asked.

Trey regarded the fifty-something detective. "He's on the mend."

"Good. So is Munroe."

A flash of sorrow hit. "Too bad the same can't be said for Roselyn Pesquera."

Cordell scratched his pate. "Yeah, it is. Looks like you and your brother may have prevented a lot more people from dying at the club."

"We only did what any owners would to protect their property and its patrons." Trey replied.

"Not to mention save your wife."

"That too," Trey admitted. "Ivana was just an innocent pawn in Willie's sick game."

Cordell sighed. "Why don't you go through it again, Trey, how you came to shoot Willie Munroe—just for the record."

Trey thought about his words carefully. The last thing he needed was for this to turn into a case of attempted murder or some other ridiculous charges against him.

"After Willie shot Clyde and started shooting wildly, he turned the gun my way. I shot him in self-defense with a pistol that's registered to the club's security, defending my wife and everyone else present."

Cordell nodded. "Okay, your story seems to be backed up by everyone I've spoken to."

"Anything else?" Trey held his breath.

Cordell eyed him. "Just one more thing. Next time you and your brother want to play detectives, save that for those of us who earn a living doing it. I wouldn't want to have to take my car business elsewhere because my favorite dealer got himself foolishly killed."

Trey smiled and shook the detective's hand. "Thanks, I'll keep that in mind. Now, if we're done here, I think my wife is waiting for me."

"Go then." Cordell paused. "Keep an eye on her."

"I intend to." Trey was thoughtful in that regard, wanting only to be there for Ivana from this point on through thick and thin while smoothing out the wrinkles in their marriage.

Chapter Forty-six

On a sunny afternoon, Trey visited the Sea and Shore Retreat detox center. It had been a month since the confrontation with Willie Munroe and its aftermath. Two days later, Ivana had checked herself into the center, with Trey's full support, to overcome her alcohol dependency. Trey had kept in contact with Ivana as much as the rules would allow, but was perfectly willing to let the treatment run its course, knowing that a completely sober Ivana could only lead to a stronger marriage as the end result.

Trey missed the love of his life terribly and tried to compensate for her absence by pouring himself into work and helping Clyde make the jazz club as profitable as possible. His brother had recovered from the gunshot injury sustained in the battle to bring down Willie and resumed running the club successfully and enjoying his burgeoning romance with Stefani. Trey was happy for his brother and how far he'd come.

They had made their peace with the past and moved on in getting to know each other better as men and siblings.

Trey entered the courtyard. It was filled with common purple lilacs and multicolored hydrangeas with the Pacific Ocean as its backdrop. He followed a curving stone walkway onto a freshly cut lawn, making his way down a hill and past a bubbling fountain 'til he came to a creek. Ivana stood there with her back to him. She was staring at a flock of seabirds that had just taken flight.

Trey almost hated to disturb her intense admiration of nature doing its thing. Worse would have been to turn away from the best thing to ever happen to him.

"Ivana . . ." he uttered in a tentative voice.

She turned his way, the sun shining on her beautiful complexion, surrounded by glimmering Senegalese twists like a halo.

Ivana's cheeks rose into a beautiful smile. "Trey."

He smiled back and gave her a kiss on the cheek, followed by a long hug. "It's good to see you, darling."

"Good to see you too."

Trey studied her. Ivana was wearing a pink puff sleeve cardigan, sable twill slacks, and flats. She looked like she had lost some weight, but was still in great, practically-model shape.

"How are they treating you?"

"Well," she said. "The counseling has been great and the staff really seems to give a damn instead of simply going through the motions."

"That's nice to know." He'd certainly paid them enough to take good care of his wife and turn her away from the alcohol.

Ivana gazed at him. "Have you come to take me home?"

Trey was afraid she might ask him that and hated to have to let her down.

"Not yet," he uttered relucatantly. "They seem to think that, although you've come a long way, you need to spend just a little more time here before you're ready to get back to the outside world."

Ivana wrinkled her nose. "How much longer before I can get to see my house again?"

"Soon, I promise," was the best Trey could say and hoped it would suffice. "And then we'll make our marriage everything it should be."

"I can't wait," she told him.

"Neither can I," he said, eager to make up for lost time and their missed moments of happiness as husband and wife.

Ivana studied Trey's handsome face, appreciating it more than ever. She realized he wasn't the enemy—not any longer—and only wanted to be with him again as his wife in every way to resume their real life and show Trey how much she had changed. She understood it would take time before they could learn to fully trust one another, but there was all the time in the world to make that happen as long as both their hearts were into it.

"There's something else I think we may need to work on," Trey told her.

"What's that?" she asked, willing to do anything for him.

"Making a more concerted effort to add to our family."

Ivana's heart skipped a beat at the prospect. "Do you mean it?"

"Yes. Whatever it takes, I want us to try again. I think it would be good for both of us and not simply just a way to make up for the child we lost. I see this as helping us grow as husband and wife by bringing a little one into the world that we will cherish in every way possible. If it doesn't happen naturally, we could explore other avenues such as adoption."

"Thank you, Trey," Ivana uttered tearfully and gave him a big hug. A child was the one thing missing in her life to make it whole and she wanted that more than anything. If it was God's will, she would get pregnant and have a beautiful, healthy son or daughter. If not, she would definitely be open to adopting a child they could love as their own.

"I want you to be happy, Ivana," Trey told her affectionately. "You deserve to experience the joys of motherhood. I think I can be a good father, too."

"I know you can be the best father," she voiced emphatically, envisioning them as parents and the wonderful life they could provide for a child or children.

Trey met her eyes. "I've got one more surprise for you."

Ivana's mind raced, wondering what it might be. "What?"

"Just a little something to look forward to when you get out of here."

Ivana honed in as he removed a ticket from behind his back. She saw that it was for a Hawaiian cruise, something she'd always wanted to go on. She looked up at Trey, knowing they had missed celebrating their anniversary. "Are we really going?"

He laughed. "Of course we are. Much better to be late than never, don't you think?"

Ivana blinked back tears. "Oh, yes! You know I do." She raised up on her toes and wrapped her arms around his neck. "You've made me so happy."

"That works both ways." Trey put his arms around her waist. "Thanks for coming into my life and sticking with me in spite of my many flaws. We have the rest of our lives to kiss and make up for everything that's gone wrong."

"Promise?" Ivana gave him a doubtful stare.

"With every fiber in me."

She held his cheeks and brought their mouths together, feeling optimistic. "I love you."

"I love you back, baby."

Trey gave her a mouthwatering kiss and Ivana felt herself melting into his arms while counting the days 'til she was released so they could put their strong love and plans for a family and travel into practice.

Chapter Forty-seven

Ivana sat alongside Trey at the club as Stefani sang, "Someone to Watch Over Me" melodiously. She peeked at Clyde across the table, who seemed transfixed on his woman. Ivana had made her peace with him, managing to put behind their onetime sexual escapade that had once threatened to destroy everything dear to both of them. She was pleased Trey and Clyde had come to terms with their differences and secrets that had been exposed and were brothers again, minus the baggage.

Ivana gazed at her husband lovingly. Ever since she'd gotten sober a few months ago, they had been virtually inseparable. She and Trey had just returned from a two-week Hawaiian cruise and were already booked for another one. Having renewed their wedding vows, they were trying to have a child and were totally committed to making the marriage work for a lifetime.

Trey caught her eyes and smiled. They were holding hands and enjoying the show, but more keen on finding new reasons to love each other.

I'm so glad we got through the bad times without totally losing our way.

Ivana gave Trey a toothy smile and leaned over to kiss him. Though only a quick kiss, it resonated throughout her whole body, something she had begun to expect again from any affection between them. Ivana could never tire of Trey's love or returning it with every cell in her.

Trey loved kissing Ivana, having never forgotten how it was at the beginning of their marriage when they kissed all the time. Now he had his wife back and didn't intend to ever come close to losing her again. Not when they had so much life left to live together and many great plans in what to do with it. He hoped their second try at having a child would result in a healthy girl or boy being born to dote over and watch grow up. But, for now, Trey was content to give Ivana all the attention she deserved with a promise to himself that she would always come first, no matter what business interests he had on the table.

He looked at Clyde, who couldn't seem to take his eyes off the club's star attraction and the clear love of his life. Trey was happy for them both and equally happy to know that Willie Munroe was out of Clyde's life for good, allowing him to close the book on that dark chapter of his life, which—unbeknownst to Trey at the time—had played a big role in the distance between him and his brother. But that was history, as far as he was concerned. They had a real opportunity now to let bygones be bygones and find true success as brothers and business partners. That was all Trey could ask for, in addition to Ivana's love and trust, neither of which he would ever again take for granted.

Stefani was looking directly at Clyde as she belted out the classy romantic song. He was all smiles and felt warmth inside that only she could make him feel. Their relationship had moved to a new level these past few months and Clyde couldn't be happier. She had given him more than he could have thought possible and he tried to thank her for that each and every day.

He gazed at his brother and sister-in-law. They were caught up in each other as much as the stirring music. It was almost hard for Clyde to believe that they were the same couple who had taken him in when he was released from prison, but were seemingly worlds apart from each other.

Clyde was pulling for them every step of the way, just as he knew they were pulling for him in wanting the best for each other and their future. He felt relieved of the burden he'd carried for so many years in trying to protect Trey and no longer carried the bad blood that had marked much of their lives as brothers.

Clyde refocused his attention on his girlfriend. He couldn't help but smile as the lyrics registered with him, coming from the woman who had changed his life for the better in so many ways. There was no one he could imagine wanting to watch over him more than Stefani.

She wrapped up the number to a round of sustained applause. He knew this was her last song of the evening and, as such, his cue to share the stage with Stefani.

Trey's curious gaze rested on Clyde as he stood.

"Going somewhere, little brother?" he asked.

Clyde grinned slyly. "Only for a minute. There's something important I have to do."

Making his way onto the stage, Clyde walked up to Stefani, surprising her. He kissed her lips gently and put his muscular arm around her, trying not to show a major case of nerves for what he had in mind.

"What are you doing?" Stefani whispered.

"You'll see," Clyde told her, being deliberately cryptic.

Facing the audience, he thought briefly back to when Willie went berserk there and how it could have put the club in the toilet. Instead, most patrons saw it as an isolated incident and continued to show up in a full house to enjoy great food, music, and atmosphere.

"I think everyone should give Stefani another round of applause for a fantastic show she put on this evening," he declared.

The audience reacted accordingly.

When the noise died down, Clyde said evenly, "Oh, there's just one more thing—" He faced Stefani and looked very serious as he took her hand. Abruptly, Clyde dropped to one knee, removing a diamond ring from his pocket in the same motion. "Will you marry me, Stefani? Please say yes and make me the happiest man on the planet."

With the crowd prodding her, Stefani's face glowed. "Yes, Clyde Lancaster, I'll marry you any time, any place!" she promised merrily.

Clyde was elated as he placed the ring on her finger. It was a perfect fit. "I love you, Stefani."

"Then get up and prove it," she quipped, helping him to his feet. Her lips parted and waited for his.

Clyde did not disappoint, embracing Stefani and tilting her, kissing her passionately to the audience's delight and cheers.

When he pulled back, a dazed Stefani said with humor, "Well, I guess that's proof enough for now. Oh, and by the way, I love you too."

Once again the patrons cheered, led by Trey and Ivana. Clyde smiled at them lovingly while taking his fiancée's words to heart, knowing this was what life was truly all about. He just wished his mother was still alive to witness him becoming a man she could be proud of. Something told Clyde that she knew and would be with him in spirit 'til the day he died.

Clyde invited Trey and Ivana on stage. He kissed Ivana lightly on the cheek and then gave his brother a big hug.

"Looks like I'm finally following in your footsteps," Clyde told Trey, without whose support he would never have gotten this far.

"I'm delighted to know that."

"It won't seem real unless I know you'll be my best man."

Shock registered on Trey's face. "I just assumed that Raymond would—"

"You assumed wrong," Clyde said. "He'll definitely be part of the wedding party, but you're my one and only brother."

"That I am." Trey grinned. "I'd be honored to be your best man."

"I was hoping you'd say that." Clyde couldn't have been more pleased as all of his dreams were suddenly coming true, beginning with the love of family and the woman he couldn't live without. He put his arm around Stefani's shoulders. "Let's go home and start planning that wedding."

"I'm all for that," she crooned and looked out at the audience. "Oh, by the way, you're all invited to the wedding."

Everyone cheered, including Clyde, who could not wait 'til Stefani became his gorgeous, sexy bride in what he imagined would be the social event of the year in Paradise Bay. Beyond that, Clyde hoped in the not-too-distant future to start a family so he could pass along his hopes and dreams while avoiding the mistakes he had made that could have resulted in a very different ending.

ORDER FORM
URBAN BOOKS, LLC
97 N18th Street
Wyandanch, NY 11798

FICTION ARCHER

**Archer, Devon Vaughn.
Secrets of Paradise
Bay**

R4001027916

NWEST